Roc's Steadfast Heart

Sweet McKenna Book Nine

Christine Young

ISBN: 978-1-62420-809-6

Credits
Cover Artist: Design by Ms G
Editor: Sherry Derr-Wille

Chapter One

Modern day
Scottish Highlands

"Come back. Sit for me. I'm almost finished," Rafe Frasier called to Dallas, a soft chuckle hiding the frustration he felt.

He understood Dallas felt some of the same annoyance. The irritation wasn't because she was tired of posing for the painting he was working on, but it was because of their bizarre relationship. As much as they liked each other, the association was going nowhere.

Wearing a robe of pink satin belted at the waist, Dallas looked over her shoulder at him, her lips thinning to a small pout Rafe recognized. She huffed for a moment, "I'm tired. Can we put this off until tomorrow?"

Her long copper colored hair flamed as the strands picked up the dying rays of the sun filtering with soft golden tones in through the window. There were so many different shades coloring the silken strands, he always believed her hair to be the color of a sunset. Her lips were almost the same color as her nipples, with just a tinge pinker to them. Her eyes the color of blue-buttons, focused on him, pleading for him to relent. He had the devil's own time forcing his way on her. For some reason he couldn't comprehend, this time he felt an urgency to complete this painting. He would have to insist on more time tonight.

"Ten more minutes."

Holding up both hands then wiggling his fingers, Rafe bartered for more time knowing full well that ten minutes could turn into sixty once she returned to her pose.

This respite was meant as a short break, not a cessation of the session. She promised him she would stay until he finished this last sketch of her. He was farther than that. Rafe was poised to begin adding the oil colors to the drawing.

The scrunched-up face told him what she thought of his proposition. Her tiny chin pointed into the air a notch higher than it had been the previous second. "A glass of beer, after that I'll stay as long as you need me. I'm trying to understand your impatience. Why are you in such a rush?"

With that comment Rafe understood he had won her over. She too had trouble telling him no. He nodded. "That's fair. I'll bring up two glasses. You relax in the over-stuffed chair while I'm gone." Rafe headed out the door, hoping she meant what she said. Sometimes Dallas was so flighty, she didn't remember her promises after he made the concessions.

Before he could get past the door to the third-floor studio, she walked beside him, linking her arm in his. She moved closer, her soft scent of citrus flowers teasing his nostrils. "I want to get out of this stuffy room for a minute. I'll walk down the stairs with you. Been sitting so long..."

"Your restless tonight?" he asked accepting the fact Dallas would do as she pleased. "I'm surprised you were able to sit for me at all."

She turned so she could place her hand on his chest. Her smile showed beautiful, even white teeth. She spent three years after she turned ten wearing braces. "Very restless. I feel as if someone or something is calling to me. Don't understand that feeling. It's too bad you aren't the man seeking me out."

She leaned into him, her head resting on his shoulder. He placed his hand on her cheek. He wished for that too.

He felt the softness of her breasts pushing against his chest. Once they thought they would suit each other. He'd always been drawn to her. After their first experimental kisses, Dallas pushed her hair from her face to stare at him with those beautiful blue eyes of her then said, "Rafe, there is no spark. I don't feel anything when you kiss me. Shouldn't there be something more?"

The unfortunate truth of the matter was that he didn't feel the spark either. Ever since that day, they'd been friends, good friends. She told him everything as if he was her beloved older brother. He spoke of all his fears along with his dreams. She was as a sister to him. Dallas was a remarkable model. He'd painted her several times. This was the first time she wore nothing at all. The sight of her naked, day after day, stole his breath yet he felt no quickening. The sight of her wearing nothing at all didn't cause an erection. In every way except sexual, they were perfect for each other.

Her happiness meant everything to him. Dallas was a remarkable photographer. The woman sported a natural eye for what would be the best picture. "Tomorrow, you should go into the hills. Spend the day taking pictures. If you like, I'll go with you. We could go together, take a basket lunch, maybe even a bottle of wine. Some of that merlot you like. It will be good for both of us to get away from my studio. What do you think?"

Even though he offered, Rafe wasn't certain it was a good idea. They both needed to stretch their wings, find a partner for life. As it was now, they spent too much time in each other's company.

Her trilling laughter left him feeling amused. Dallas was going to refuse his offer. "You don't have to go with me. I'm not a little girl who needs to have her big brother take her places." She pushed away from him, a smile on her lips. "I'm independent, a modern woman."

Big brother...little sister...he supposed that was the best and only way to describe their unique connection.

"I'd like to go with you. Enjoy spending time together," he said as they strode down the steps. "You're more fun to be with than most of the females of my acquaintance. You haven't mentioned Seth Peters in a long time. You stop seeing the man? In my estimation he isn't good enough for you." He lifted an eyebrow in speculation before he spoke again. "No spark?"

"Not even a *wee* bit of heat."

Still arm in arm, they walked into the kitchen. He pulled out a chair at the table for her before ambling to the refrigerator. When she sat, she pulled the lapels of the robe closer. Deep inside he chuckled at her modesty. He just spent several days looking at her buck naked. After they finished the beer, she would uncover herself, pose in the nude. What was between them was simply platonic.

"Only saw him once. Seth is an animal. I can't be with a man who doesn't understand the meaning of the word no." She crossed her legs, the pink of her robe slipped down the side exposing her slightly tanned skin.

"Oh? He took what you didn't want to give."

Beneath his breath, Rafe cursed. His fists tightened with the need to protect Dallas. She wasn't his to protect.

This was her time to smile, "No, after the man tried to kiss me then groped my breast, I pepper sprayed him. His eyes must have been red for at least a week. I didn't stick around to see."

He set a glass of Guinness in front of her. "Still your favorite beer?"

Dallas lifted her shoulders, unfettered breasts swaying beneath the robe she wore. Her nipples poked against the fabric, tightening with the slight friction her movements caused. Despite the fact there was no electricity between them, he loved to look at her breasts. They were lush, very full. The round globes could probably invite any man who wasn't a saint to want to taste. He read the invitation loud and clear. He wasn't going to take when he couldn't give back the feelings she needed. He could never give her love. She deserved a man who would love her not just care for her. Hell, he didn't even lust after her. That would be an emotion he could understand.

Her hips were wide. Her stomach rounded. If any female possessed an hour glass figure, Dallas did. It was nearly perfect...no, her figure was the perfect hourglass. All her womanly curves were generous. Rubenesque always came to mind when he looked at her. Dallas hated her body. Was always dieting to make herself smaller. Even when she lost weight the roundness would not go away. She would never have one of those concave bellies that women nowadays wanted. Her breast would never be less than generous mounds a man could lose himself between.

"I like Guinness. Can't say favorite... What about you? Are you still seeing...?" She drummed her fingernails on the wood table where they sat her expression pensive. "Can't seem to remember the girl's name. She's pretty but an airhead. Doesn't have a brain. If she does, she chooses not to use it."

"Shelly Grant? Is that the name you were looking for? You're

4

right, as for brains she is lacking." Watching her, he leaned back, stretching his long legs his hands clasped together on his lean, washboard abs. "No, no spark with her either," he told her before she could ask the question. "Don't know if I'll ever find the woman I'm looking for. As of now, don't believe that special female exists for me."

The sigh parting the softness of her lips seemed to surprise her. "What are we? Too picky for our own good? What is it that we're looking for? Does love exist in this modern world?"

"Don't know about picky. Thought you were the one for me. Still believe you are. Nonetheless, there is no denying the fact there is something wrong between us, something illusive that is keeping us apart. Until I figure out the missing component, we can't be together as lovers. Won't take your innocence." Rafe held up his hands to keep Dallas from commenting. "You would have told me if you found that special guy. If you gave away your virginity. When that happens, know I won't be seeing you every day."

"You think so?"

"Know so."

To Rafe's ears she sounded hopeful. Hell, he was always hopeful where it concerned Dallas. Undying love wasn't there for them. Since they were kids in grade school, they'd been attracted to each other. In high school, he dated her a few times. He took her to a concert in London when they were in college together. It seemed the harder he tried to find that elusive thread that would bind them together through eternity the more convinced he became the thin filament didn't exist at least where the two of them were concerned.

"I do."

He punched his fist into the palm of his hand. Damn, he wanted to find his mate, to go through all eternity with her. If he didn't find his mate in this lifetime, what then? Were the rumors true? Would he forever be kept from her?

There were too many days to count where Rafe wondered if he would ever find his eternal love. He would never hold his woman in his arms or show her his cat. Sometimes he wondered if that happened to him before...in another life. If somehow, the heart of his soul illuded him.

How did one go backward in time so he could fix the problem? If he understood the complexities of time travel, he would do whatever was necessary to secure his woman. In this there were no guarantees.

With absentminded thoughts ruffling in his head, Rafe cracked the knuckles on both hands. The act seemed to relieve tension while he watched the woman who should be his but wasn't sip her beer. He never told Dallas about his clan, Clan Chattan. She didn't know he could change his form to a black panther. It was something a man didn't show just any woman. Even though in his mind, Dallas wasn't just any woman. He could never let himself be so vulnerable. Only for his mate could he risk so much.

Sometimes at night, desperate fears filled him. He tried to see backward in time. Never was he ever able to do so. Conversations with his parents didn't help. What could they do? They could not scavenge a mate up for him. All they ever said was to be patient. In time, he would find the woman meant for him.

With a wistful gush of air, she finished the glass of beer. "Shall we go upstairs? I'd like to get home tonight before...well...I suppose it will be dark. You're going to want to work until you can't stand up any longer."

Dallas stood, hugging the robe closer, outlining her breasts along with her hips.

Damn, but he wished there was something tangible between them. There just wasn't. When he looked at Dallas, he saw a beautiful woman with generous curves. That was all. "All right. I'll walk you home when I'm done. Don't want you walking the streets by yourself in the middle of the night."

"I appreciate that. Though I'm certain I can get home by myself. As we both know, nothing much ever happens in Carnoch. I do have my pepper spray. Refilled the cannister after the last incident."

"Of course, you can. The fact that remains is that I'm not going to allow you to go by yourself." He headed up the steps behind her, staring at the delicious butt she presented to him...eye candy. She was that. She checked off all the boxes he had for a partner. All the boxes expect the ones that counted the most.

Love. Sparks. Flames. Sexual need.

They stepped into his studio. The lighting needed to be just right. What he never told her was that the rest of the sessions would have to be at dusk so he could get the light with exact precision the way he wanted it. Just as the sun shone through the window now. Rafe needed to see the golden tones light up her hair.

When she stood by the couch, her small hands on the belt, she appeared reluctant to remove the garment. He watched the rise and fall of her breasts beneath the silk cloth. Too many seconds passed while he felt the upsurge of guilt for keeping her, for even suggesting the nude painting. He'd wanted to paint her naked, needed to capture her spirit on canvas. Rafe didn't understand the reasons why but the need wrestled within him. Sometimes the thoughts kept him awake at night. Resting would not be possible until he put her form on the canvas.

The robe slipped to the floor. Nodding her head in the direction of the table, her long copper hair spilled across her breasts hiding them only to reveal them a second later. She arranged herself on the markings put there so they would remember where she was to place herself. While he studied her, he stepped back. A flash, a fleeting glimpse of something so close yet so far away swamped him, almost sent him to his knees. In the ensuing moments, it was as if he was seeing her for the first time. He blinked, focusing in on her. Whatever he thought he saw or felt vanished.

His Dallas was a beautiful woman. She should be his. Would never be for him. Leaning over, he placed the long tendrils of hair so they covered her in just the right way. When the back of his hand brushed a hard tip of her breast, he should have felt lust surge within all his masculine parts. To his immense disappointment, Rafe felt nothing but a tiny sensation that didn't reach his loins. The feeling was in his heart.

Loss.

Pain.

She should have reacted to his touch against her nipple. Dallas didn't. She never noticed.

"What is it?" she asked looking at him as if she could see all the way through him to his soul. "You look, you look as if you saw your death...or someone's...mine? You're creeping me out. Don't look at me that way."

Rubbing his hand on the back of his neck thinking he needed to control his wayward thoughts better, he told her, his voice taking on a husky tenor. "Nothing...nothing at all for you to concern yourself with. What I...my imagination...that's all. I thought I saw you in a different way. I didn't."

God, she was beautiful. Why wasn't Dallas his mate? Over the years he asked himself that same question so many times he couldn't count them all on both hands. "Let's get on with the business at hand." The sooner he finished this painting the better for both of them.

He stepped back, picked up the paintbrush along with the oils he laid out for this particular moment.

"You don't look as if this is nothing." She sounded hurt that he wouldn't confide. If there was anyone he could burden with his thoughts, that person was Dallas. With this he couldn't. Simply because he didn't understand.

She stiffened.

"Relax, sweetheart."

Rafe didn't like the way his voice sounded just then. She'd done nothing wrong. He was treating her as if his changing mood was her fault.

The room heated to an inferno. Sweat beaded along his collar. He opened a window. Evening sounds made their way into the small upstairs studio room. A small drop of perspiration slid between her breasts leaving a trail behind. In the distance a car backfired. People chatted as they walked along the sidewalk in front of the house. Everything seemed normal, except in his studio. To his fine-tuned cat senses, there was something different here. He felt the changing of the universe.

Dallas' lashes drooped. He shouldn't push so hard. She needed a break, to rest. They'd just returned from the kitchen. The need to remove her from the studio catapulted through him. He didn't understand. He wasn't one to ignore the sixth sense that was always an integral part of his life.

"We need to stop for the night," he gritted out as he saw the rise of exhaustion fill her blue eyes.

She wouldn't even take money for modeling. He promised that no one would see the painting except him. That was a lie. The commission he was promised was in the thousands for this painting. What he would do is be certain her face would never be recognized. What he didn't know was if he could part with it when he finished.

"If we work for another half hour, you will be that much closer to finishing. I'm not too tired. The beer made me drowsy. That's all. Do as much as we can, please, Rafe."

Rafe knew he could finish this without her. Didn't want to. The sketch was finished. He put a lot of color on the canvas tonight. The final painting was so close to completion. If he tried to finish without her though, the painting might not be as authentic...as pure.

"Another half-hour," he agreed, half-reluctant, half-pleased. "No more. Don't want to wear you out." He dipped into the copper color he mixed for her hair adding some of the tints of the sunset. That was what the color of her hair reminded him of...the setting sun...maybe the dawn of a new day. Rafe loved her hair more than her lush curves.

Maybe not.

The ensuing time passed faster than he could imagine. When he stepped back to look, he felt the warmth of a smile grow within. This was the best painting he'd ever done. Deep in his heart, he understood it wasn't his skill that made the painting so good. His model was the reason. She was beautiful. To his delight, he caught the essence of her.

"We're finished for tonight. There will be some extra touches to be made at another time. Need to step away for a day or two."

"Ah..." She stretched out her arms, lengthening her muscles, shoulders, back, triceps. Easing muscles that had been in one position too long, she moved her legs, testing them on the floor before she stood. "I'm stiff as a fire poker," she mumbled. She stumbled when she tried to stand.

He was beside her, holding onto her arms. She leaned against him, her curves pushing against him. This was his Dallas, so trusting. Good God, she was naked. He was holding her. He didn't have one carnal thought in his head except for the fact there were none.

Letting her support herself on his body, he bent over to pick up her robe. He wrapped it around her. "Go get dressed then I'll take you home."

Brushing back hair from her face, she nodded. Stiff movements hindering her steps, she walked to the small dressing room in the corner of the studio. She didn't bother to draw the curtain. What would be the point? As if she was now in a rush to get home, she slipped into a pair of cutoff shorts and a tank top. Her bra and panties she stuffed into a bag she brought with her. Rafe had to laugh at the fact she was going *sans* underwear. It was just like his Dallas. She hated constricting bras. Didn't realize she disliked wearing panties too.

Dallas finger-combed her hair, pulling it back into a ponytail. With her hands, she scrubbed her face then shook her head as if she tried to wake up. The hour was almost midnight. This wasn't the first time tonight he was besieged with a strange sense of *deja vous*. When he looked out the window, it was almost as if he saw Dallas standing on the sidewalk. The hazy woman he saw for an instant wasn't Dallas though she could be her twin. Who was the lady?

"Can we walk? I need to stretch out some more, loosen up my stiff muscles. If I don't, I'll never get to sleep tonight."

"Whatever you would like." Hand on her elbow, he ushered her to the door. "Did you bring a coat?" Rafe asked as he stared at her long, naked legs. They were tanned. When she posed for him, he noticed the tan lines marking her skimpy, thong bikini. When she sunbathed, she didn't wear much. In order not to have tan lines, she untied the top when she was lying on her front, then pulled down the tiny shoulder straps when she was on her back. The lavish curves of her breasts were outlined in tiny white triangles.

He didn't like to think of other men seeing so much of her. Whenever his thoughts veered in that direction, he always made a point to remind himself he wasn't her mate. Would never be her husband or lover. Jealousy would never be tolerated.

All his thoughts and feelings conflicted with each other. She pulled a lightweight sweater from her bag to put around her shoulders tying the sleeves so the they knotted over her breasts.

"What have you got in there?" Rafe took the satchel from her as if he meant to search through to see the contents. "Enough items to live through the week?" he asked laughing as she scrunched up her face to show him what she thought of his question.

"Just what every girl needs in an emergency. That's all. Nothing exceptional. Never go without the essentials."

She smiled at him as she took the bag back into her possession then slipped the long strap over her shoulder. Not waiting for him, she walked.

Once he caught up to her again, he wrapped his arm around her shoulder pulling her close. By her ear he whispered, "I always wanted to know what a lady would need in an emergency. What's essential?"

"Did you now?" She laughed seeming lighthearted for the first time today. "Does that mean you are going to search my bag? Ruffle thought it to embarrass me?"

"Tell me," Rafe coaxed sensing her playful mood and hoping to exterminate the tension. "What do you have in there."

"If you think about it, you might be able to guess as to a few things. You do know me so well."

"Yes...well..." Rafe could make a few stabs in the dark. He did know her well. Probably better than anyone except her mother and father, no, better than them. "I would say you've a change of clothes...even two different outfits...underwear...maybe a bikini, one of those skimpy ones you so like to wear."

"True, obvious guess though. What else?" She winked at him, understanding he could relate the entire contents of the huge bag she always carried with her even though he'd never seen the inside of her bag.

"You could take the suspense out of this and give me a list."

He ran his hand along her arm then back to her shoulder. She fit against him with perfection. He let out a long breath of air understanding that no matter how much he wanted things to be different between them, they were not. He could muddle this over in his brain again and again until exhaustion overcame him. Nothing would change. It was past time to put an end to his musings about the possibility of Dallas becoming someone special to him. Well, she was special, just not in that way.

"Where would be the fun in that? Try again."

She poked him in the chest. It was a playful poke, not in the least suggestive. The gesture was something a sister would give her brother. No matter, Rafe could never think of her as his sister.

He caught her finger then enclosed her hand within in his. She was meant for someone else. That fact had been apparent from the first time they thought to kiss. Jealousy flooded him at the notion of some other man possessing her. He could no longer hold onto her. Letting her go was a deed he would have to undertake.

"Let me see," he paused while he began to think, tapping a finger against his chin and hoping not to embarrass her.

She'd come to him once in tears, the pain of her periods so intense she could only curl into a tiny ball on his bed. At that time, he comforted her the best he could all the while believing if her relationship with her mother was at it should be, Dallas should discuss this with her mom. He gave her some pain medicine. When she could talk, she told him about her cramps. He took her to the doctor, waited for her in the waiting room. He'd know she had taken birth control pills since she was sixteen to regulate her periods.

She giggled appearing pleased with herself. "It can't be that hard. You do know more about me than anyone else on planet earth."

"No, I just didn't want to cause any embarrassment. I'm certain you have birth control pills in the bag."

"Yes, two months' worth. I'm not embarrassed. A lot of women have to do the same even though they aren't sexually active."

"You could be though."

He didn't want to fish for information. Rafe wasn't certain why he suddenly needed to know if she had a significant man in her life. Earlier she told him Seth was not appreciated, her words, "He's an animal." Could there be someone else, a man she didn't wish to speak of around him? Most of the time with him, Dallas was an open book.

"Yes....I could be." Dallas lifted her eyebrows at him, questioning his integrity he didn't doubt. "Do you carry condoms with you?" she asked prying into his life with the question.

Just as he pried into hers. "No... If I ever meet someone, I would like to be intimate with, I would."

"You should. As a just in case. That's why I keep a box of condoms with me in my bag. You're not implying to me that you're a virgin? If you are, I won't believe you." She let out a puffy breath of air stopping to turn in his arms. Her hands rested on his chest. "I want to be prepared in case..." She sifted in a deep breath of oxygen. "In case the right man ever comes along. I'm beginning to think there is no one out there for me."

"Geez, Dallas, I've those thoughts all the time too. Since the right person isn't you, I doubt if there ever will be a perfect woman for me. Not that she has to be perfect...without flaws. Hell!" He was managing to confuse himself.

"I understand what you're trying to say, Rafe. I just wish I understood what went wrong between us. I can tell you anything. Speak of whatever pops into my head without one concern you'll gossip. Sometimes I feel that I've known you forever. You even took me to the doctor."

"I don't like you carrying condoms."

What the hell was the matter with him? She was right on all counts.

"You don't want me to have safe sex?" she asked, her eyes open wide, walking away from him, her back stiff, shoulders squared as if she tolerated him, nothing else. He was pretty certain her chin would have risen at least an inch.

The closeness between them evaporated with her questioning. If he could, he would get that lightheartedness back.

He couldn't. At least not tonight.

"Here we are." They stood in front of the door to her apartment. "Can I come in?" Rafe wasn't at all certain why he asked. He did know he wanted to retrieve something of what was lost during that last conversation. The only way to succeed would be to spend more time. It was late.

Dallas was shaking her head, her lips turned down in a small pout of displeasure. "I don't see why you would want to. Go home, finish up the painting or don't. Tomorrow I'll go up into the hills. I'll take so many pictures it will take us hours to look at all of them. After that if you need me to pose for you again, I will."

"Sorry I upset you. Didn't mean to," Rafe mumbled in a whisper that he hoped she didn't hear. Looking up, he brushed hair from her eyes. "Don't like to say things...well, we both understand with time there will be someone else in our lives. We're going to have to get used to that notion. Damn, the thought of you with another man eats at the very heart of my soul."

"It's the same for me when I think about you with some unnamed woman. What are we to do with each other? This can't go on. I should move to another town."

Rafe wiped a tear from beneath her beautiful blue eyes. "Don't cry. Don't move either. I don't know what we are to do. For me there isn't anyone except you."

"There's no spark."

"The connection isn't there."

Opening the door, he waited for her to set her things down. With a tentative smile on her face, she closed the door leaving him standing alone on the porch staring off into the distance at nothing.

With slow measured steps, as if he was going to his execution, Rafe walked home. He didn't understand the feeling, but he felt certain he was about to lose Dallas to a man. Even more prevalent in his thoughts was that after tonight she would be gone from his life.

His gut twisted. The pain sent him to his knees.

~ * ~

When the misty fog covering the ground cleared to brilliant sunshine, Dallas felt as if she was seeing a new world. The spring scented air swept around her. Long grass waved with startling rhythm coupled with the soft breeze blowing down from the craigs. Perhaps she was seeing this world in a new light. She'd driven to a spot about thirty miles from Coronach, traveling toward Inverness. She knew of this beautiful place. Had always hoped to stop here. Until today, she never made the time. The pictures would be amazing. Rafe would tell her which ones should be enhanced with colors. Which ones to mount then take to the art gallery in Inverness. She had scheduled an exhibition of her photographs for July. It was almost time to prepare all the photos.

Today, she wore a tight-fitting dress. The baby blue fabric molded with love to all her curves, showing off all her best assets. Rafe didn't like the dress. Told her she was encouraging every male who saw her to touch those assets. If not touch to stare. Didn't matter if she encouraged. No one would dare. She always kept her distance from leering-eyed men. She did keep her pepper spray handy.

Too bad, Rafe!

She meant to wear the dress whenever she wished. Her high heels were in her bag. For the photo shoot she wore a pair of jogging shoes. If she had to walk down paths for the pictures, the aerobic shoes would suit her feet better than the heels. Afterward, she planned to dine at this bistro in the city she heard about from a few of her friends, hence the reasons for the heels strategically placed in the satchel. Even Rafe said the cuisine was good. He took his last date there.

Date.

They weren't suited. Dallas didn't have to remind herself. She knew all too well the truth. The two of them would never have that flicker they were both looking for. Though she would be satisfied without the energy, the excitement, or the flames between them, Rafe would not. He was holding out for the best possible woman. So far, she never felt that electricity with anyone. She supposed she should hold out also. Dallas could count the number of men she dated on one hand. She was stuck on three. None of them excited her, left her breathless with longing. None of them generated the desire to have sex. They were dull, witless, fools.

"Wow!" Dallas whistled through her teeth after she rounded the corner of the path to get a full-on view of the water pouring over the cliff. This waterfall was filled to the brim with liquid. It was close to April. The runoff from the mountain snows and glaciers was filling the rivers as well as all the waterfalls. The roar was impressive tumbling through her ears. Time seemed to stand still while she gazed in awe at one of the most spectacular sites she'd ever seen. Her pictures would be amazing.

Today, there were two tourists who were taking pictures. At least she thought that's what they were. Seemed they were also planning on photographing the landscape. The time was too early for the tourist season to be at its height. She would have never stayed here if there had been crowds. She detested crowds. Hated waiting for them to clear the view so people wouldn't be in the picture. Disliked using photoshop to rid herself of the landmarks that weren't natural.

Hands on her back, she stretched to get rid of the kinks.

Dallas set up her tripod working on all the setting to get the effect she looked for. When she checked each photo, most were magnificent. She sent the ones she didn't like into the trash. After she finished, she pulled out her laptop. With the card from her camera, she put them in a folder on her desktop. Pleased with the morning's work, she inhaled a deep breath of the surrounding fresh air. This was paradise to her.

The day was turning out to be better than she expected. There was more than enough time to drive into Inverness to eat before returning home if that's what she decided to do. Curious as to its destination as well as feeling pulled by some unseen force, Dallas decided to investigate a trail that seemed to wander beneath the waterfall. She put her tripod in her car, looped her bag over her shoulder then started walking enjoying the warmth of the sun's rays as they beat down on her face.

"Beautiful day," Dallas said as she passed the older couple who were shooting selfies. She loved to see loving couples who were in their sixties and even seventies. The thought she might never find someone to love her left a cold shiver trembling down her spine.

"Yes, love...you all alone? You need to find yourself someone who will love keeping you company," the woman spoke to her as she walked past.

"Alone, going to see what's on the other side of the waterfall. Don't suppose there is someone there for me."

"Your camera...we saw you shooting pictures. Are you a professional?" the older lady asked, curiosity in her voice.

Dallas reached into her bag then pulled out her cellphone. "If I see something that warrants a better pic, I'll grab my camera from my bag. Yes, I am a photographer. I've an exhibit of my pictures coming up this summer. It will be in Inverness the end of July. You could come."

"Oh, if we would still be here this summer, we would attend. I love to support talented artists," the man spoke for the first time.

"Thanks." She sifted in her bag for a few seconds before pulling out her card. "Here, take this. If you're interested in some of my photographs you can go online to see them. They can be ordered then shipped." Dallas didn't know if the couple were just being polite. Nonetheless, it never hurt her to hand out a card. She'd made multiple sales as well as fans by doing so.

"Have fun and don't get lost. The highlands can be frightening if one doesn't know their way."

The woman waved at her as she backed down the path. She waved back, smiling, hoping she appeared cheerful despite the sudden feelings of loss as she left the two people behind.

No, she wasn't going to get lost on this path. The trail was well marked even though it wound around the falls. She hummed then cringed at the off-key noise. While she possessed a few talents, carrying a tune was not one of them. Rafe never failed to tease her about her lack of musicality. This coming from a man whose deep base voice never failed to thrill her when she heard him sing.

At the bottom of the falls, she looked up, shielding her eyes with her hand. Mist splayed out from all the rocks the tumbling water bounced off. The sun shining behind the misting, she saw the face and form of a man seeming to float in the haze. He was tall, his hair a burnished blond. Dressed in a kilt. Impossible. As if her thoughts were true, he vanished. She was left with the rainbows that crowded the water filled air.

With the palm of her hand, Dallas tapped her head. My imagination is conjuring men...in the mist of waterfalls. I didn't eat anything strange today. Haven't had anything to drink since the one beer last night. I don't think I'm obsessed with men. No, silly, you're only obsessed with finding the right man.

Trying to shake the discordant feelings, she snapped pictures with her phone then strode farther down the trail. A sudden shifting of the ground caught her off guard. Flinging her arms out, she braced herself against a sky-high boulder. The cold rock pressed against her cheek. That was different. Dallas hesitated to use the word peculiar or bizarre. Perhaps a minor earthquake was what caused her to step off balance. She gulped a gallon of oxygen. For the longest time she clung to the boulder, adrenalin racing through her. Once she felt steady again, she continued. She reached what could be described as a turning point. On one side, the terrain was flat, on the other side the land gave way to a steep slope. In either case her footpath stopped. She would have to turn around, go back to the beginning. Maybe she could find another trail to follow.

This time when she looked up beams of sunlight imprisoned that same man. His smile was wide, laughing. His eyes danced with something he must think amusing. He seemed to stare at her, holding her enthralled. Her heart skipped then stuttered. When his eyes focused on her, it seemed to Dallas he summoned her. He asked her to join him. Now, her heart stilled while she remained captivated with the very essence of this man. The breath she inhaled caught in the back of her throat, staying there until she choked. Tremors ceased her. Her body shook so hard she felt the sensations to the tips of her toes.

Captivated, she followed the laughing man, one hesitant foot in front of the other. She didn't understand the reason. It seemed he reeled her into some unknown place. Somewhere in the back of her mind, she understood this was not her usual behavior. While she continued walking the ground shook. Trembled. Undulated. She slipped, her feet skidding out from beneath her. Her arms whirled while she tried with no success to maintain her balance. Tumbling to her rear, she sat on the soft grass, sliding, falling until she was brought to an abrupt halt at the bottom of the incline. Air rushed from her lungs as she rolled to her belly, hitting the earth hard. She took another tumble coming to rest with an abrupt stop.

With her legs spread in front of her, her body framing dress hiked nearly to her hips, she leaned on her elbows in order to better survey the scene in front of her. Some point during her fall, the wind was knocked from her lungs. With pain she inhaled slow, desperate breaths of much needed air. Her eyes couldn't focus. Beneath her the earth still whirled. She saw herself or someone who looked much like her, running through this same field with a huge black panther beside her. Dallas tried to shake the nonsense from her head. This time when she sensed a presence and looked upward, she didn't see the man of her imagination. What she saw was real as well as frightening.

"Well, lookee what we have here, Scratch. An itsy-bittsy *lassie* just ripe to be tried out. See those huge titties."

"Ripe titties."

"She just sitting on the grass legs spread waitin' for us to be good to her. Should we show her what we got? She could ride us or we could rock her. Wha da ya think?"

"I get her first, Geordie," Scratch said as he slipped a hand beneath the waistband of his britches to fondle himself. "I'm the oldest."

"You no be makin' sense. I saw her first. So, she be mine first." Geordie walked toward her, his eyes glimmering with the need to possess.

Damn!

Dallas crab walked backward. Her body quivering. She couldn't imagine any of this. "No! No, I'm not going to let you touch me!"

Her hands searched the small pocket in her bag for the pepper spray she always kept there. She prayed the cannister would work. She did have if refilled. She bought the spray mostly with the hope of keeping dogs away from her on her daily jog. She used it on Seth. Refilled the cannister. Praying what little wind there was wouldn't send the pepper her way, she pulled it out. Her arm extended, she cried out, "Stop!"

Scratch roared his laughter. Hooted. Again, he pulled up his shirt to scratch his belly then lower. His grin turned to a smirk. "Stop? What kind of weapon you think you got there, my *wee lassie*? Whatever that thing is, it isn't going to keep me from what I want." He leered at her stepping forward again. "I want you, *wee lassie*. I'm going to have you. After that I plan on sharing you with Geordie here. The two of us share all our women." He cocked his thumb toward the other man.

With great effort, Dallas pushed off the ground. She stood in front of the two men clutching the small cannister. Even she didn't think this would keep the men away from her. She needed divine intervention. Still, she brazened her way. "It's pepper spray. If you take one more step, I'll use it."

Dallas was standing, her arm outstretched, shaking as she looked from one man to the other. Her heart pounded with fear. She ran her tongue across her bottom lip while she searched her surroundings for someone who might help. Divine intervention was a myth.

Scratch stepped forward. "Just want a *wee* bit of lovin.' That's not too much to ask for, now, is it? I wouldn't ask if you weren't so pretty. Your titties so big. Goin' to suck on each one."

At his words, she cringed. Gulped more air. He needed to take one more step before she could use her small weapon. She wanted a direct line to his eyes. In her wildest imagination, she never thought to be in a position such as this one. Her gaze darted from one man to the other. If they attacked her together, she didn't stand a chance.

Keep your cool. Breathe. Don't show fear.

The look on Scratch's face changed to something more feral. His lips were pulled back from his teeth in an untamed smile. His eyes came together in a fierce scowl. When he leapt at her, Dallas discharged the spray. His screech of agony didn't give her pleasure only relief. With no hesitation, she turned her attention to the other man, Geordie.

Holding the spray at arm's length, she cried out. "Don't come one step closer! If you do, I'll give you the same dose your friend just got."

She was backing away, taking slow steps trying to keep her attention on the men as well as her footing. If she went down, her fate was sealed. This man would be on top of her in a second.

"That wasn't too smart of you. What did you do to him? I'm going to..." He started forward, his fists clenched at his sides. His eyes were wild.

The applause from behind her caught her attention. She twirled to see. *Not three men.* She heard the soothing timber of his voice.

"If I were you, I'd do what the lady says. Seems to me at this moment, this *wee lassie* has the upper hand."

The voice behind her was deep and husky, holding the hint of amusement. Nonetheless, his meaning was clear.

Her divine intervention? She looked skyward to say a silent prayer. Though her family were devout Catholics, she'd never taken to the church.

Trembling, afraid to ask, she blurted the words as if she expected an answer. This new man might want the same things these two thugs did, "Who are you?" the words spoken, her voice trailing off. Dallas understood there wasn't enough pepper spray in the tiny cannister to take care of three men.

"Roc." Geordie was holding up his hands then looking at his friend who was reeling on the ground, "This isn't any of your affair. This *lassie* needs to be taught a lesson. She can't go around hurting men." He snapped his fingers. "Just like that...as if we are naught more but twigs. When we're done with her, we'll share her with you. Certain there is enough of the lady to go around. Just look at those bubbies of hers. Those wide hips. Her legs. There's so much..."

Dallas tried to slouch, to cover herself, mortified by the man's words. While she'd never heard breasts referred to as bubbies, it was obvious what the man stared at while he fondled himself.

"Why not?"

Roc had his hands on his narrow hips. To Dallas he sounded outraged at the notion of sharing.

"You meant to hurt her...or did I read the scenario wrong? Is she willing for you and Scratch to manhandle her? Did she tell you to stop?"

"You want her for yourself," Scratch cried out.

"Seems that way."

Roc turned his attention to her, his heated insolent gaze roaming the length of her body. "Get up and stand behind me. You and I are getting out of here."

The command in his voice was not to be disobeyed.

Confused. She didn't know what to think. His actions seemed at odds with his words. When she hesitated, her rescuer spoke again but didn't make eye contact. With a lift to his broad shoulders, he went on to say, "You can choose between them or me. Do it now," he spoke with a strange calm, with such composure she knew she would obey. "If you choose Scratch and Geordie, I'll ride out of here and never look back. The decision is up to you."

He waited two seconds. His following roar surprised her.

Nonetheless it broke the frozen spell she'd fallen under. "Do it now!"

"Well...when you put it that way. Don't have to be so..."

She didn't know how to finish that sentence. Picking up the bag that had fallen from her shoulders, she scrambled to his side then stood behind him cowering. Her body seemed to vibrate with the rush of adrenalin coursing through her.

"You'll regret helping her," Geordie threatened, shaking his fist at both of them. He pointed a scrawny finger their way. "I'll have my revenge on you then I'll take her. Won't be any sharin' this time."

"Who's going to make me regret helping out a *wee lass* who's in distress? Not you."

He looked at her, a genuine smile on his handsome features. "Can you ride?"

She shook her head wishing she could answer in the affirmative as well as wishing she knew what was going through his head. "Never been on a horse in my life." She wanted to yell at him that her car was just up that hill. For some reason Dallas couldn't fathom, she kept silent.

His encouraging smile turned to a sudden frown, his eyebrows drawing together in concentration. "We'll have to improvise in that case."

This was the same man who she saw in the mist as well as the sunbeams. "Roc? Your name is Roc?" If she could figure out was going on inside his brain, she felt certain she would fare better.

"Stand behind me." He motioned to where he wanted her. "Right there. Don't move a muscle."

What would he do if she twitched the wrong way? He was not like any man she'd ever met. Wobbling, her knees weak, she managed to put herself where he showed her. She wrapped her arms around herself, warding off the strange chill that seemed to float around her. Except for the pistol he held in his hand, she wondered why these two men didn't attack him. The gun looked old. Did it work? All they did was threaten. Roc didn't seem phased at all by the two of them. He was outnumbered. The man didn't seem to care one way or the other.

"You two start walking, keep walking. Don't stop until I can no longer see you." He continued with the gun pointed at them, "Who will get it first? Geordie or Scratch. Hmm...either way the world will be better off."

Geordie turned, his hands in the air as if they would stop the bullet. "Now *dinna* go gettin' impatient. We're going."

Dallas held her breath while the men walked away.

When they were out of sight, he took her hand and tugged. "Let's go!"

Dallas found herself without a single word or thought. Beside him as well as blindly, she stumbled trying to keep pace with his long strides. He didn't slow to help her. She sensed his urgency. While she didn't want to find herself in this position with a man she didn't know, this man was far better than the other possibility. At least he was clean and he didn't smell of stale tobacco and sour whiskey. Her stomach churned.

When they stopped in front of a horse, she assumed it was his horse. With her hands on her hips and with as much conviction as her frightened self could muster, she said, "Couldn't you just walk me to my car?"

Dallas understood this would be wishful thinking. The man didn't seem to be open to suggestions or negotiation.

"Car? No time." He lifted a burnished, dark blond eyebrow skyward then ignored her questions. "I'll help you up."

Before she could utter another word and voice the protest, his large hands wrapped around her waist. The first second after the contact she felt airborne, flying upward. It wasn't a sensation she cared to duplicate. Her breath caught then she found herself astride his horse. Against her legs her dress rose to above midthigh.

The horse shifted position. Terrified, she grabbed on to the animal's neck while she tried to tug the fabric of her tight-fitting dress to cover herself. The horse whinnied its objection. "I c-can't..."

She'd never sat a horse before. Her terror rose to form a lump in her throat that seemed to block further speech. Despite her efforts to the contrary, her dress rose even higher to her upper thighs. She heard a small rip and realized the pressure of her parted legs created a slit on one side, baring her on her right side to her hip. There was naught to do about that except try to ignore it. She looked down at him, the steel grey of his eyes darkening as he stared at her legs.

"You can ride. We need to leave before Scratch can see again. I'm getting on behind you. Hold still."

"T-trust m-me he won't see well for at least twenty-four hours. That stuff is potent. Supposed to keep a bear at bay for that long. That man was not a bear."

Her voice lost all its intended force when she saw his hands on the saddle horn in front of her. Damn, she was riding away with a man she didn't know. She could not stay here as he pointed out. In the process risking a second encounter with Geordie and Scratch.

"Good." He vaulted on behind her. His hands once more touched her waist. "Steady there. I'll no' let you fall."

He won't let me fall... Who's going to keep him from falling?

That thought was no consolation and held no merit when the horse started to move. The sensation of heat vanished when he took up the reins. The animal picked up speed. She tried to sit up straight so she wouldn't find herself pressed against him. For the next minutes, nothing surrounding her registered except the man behind her, the breadth of him. The heat he generated. Every time she started to relax; she stiffened as the movement of the horse sent her against his chest. She found herself cradled between his massive thighs. His arms brushed hers. She clung to his enormous forearms. Unable to watch the forest rush past her, she closed her eyes.

"You *dinna* need be afraid of me." His voice whispered across her neck then her cheek. Heat infiltrated her body. To her dismay, she found her nipples hardening, parts of her tingling she'd never thought about before. *Sparks?*

"I—I'm not a-afraid. I'm t-terrified. More scared of the horse than you, if you must know the truth." She ran her tongue across her parched lips. "C-can't you just take me back to my car?"

He didn't answer her for the longest time. Startling her, using his soft husky voice with no amusement in the tone, he asked, "What's a car?"

Disconcerted, she whirled, her amazement obvious if he watched her. The motion upset his horse who reared his head back then sidestepped a couple of times. "Easy, *laddie*," he whispered soothing words to the animal, stroking the horse's neck with practiced skill. Seemed he knew how to calm the beast. While she watched his eyes, he spoke to the horse as if the beast understood him. "This little filly in front of me surprises me too, *laddie*. She keeps takin' me off guard. In time, we're sure to get used to her." Then, to her, once more bending close to her ear to whisper, "Don't move so fast. Moonstar isn't used to *lasses*. He wants you to like him but you keep surprising him. That confuses him so much that he doesn't know what to do."

She felt the stubble from his chin caress her cheek. "Oh!" she cried out once again surprised by him.

She felt the heat from his words. The sensation swept through her as she was doused in flames from the simple contact.

"Easy..." he spoke again. "Don't be frightened. For Moonstar's sake, don't move fast again. He's not used to riding double. Don't usually share him."

Riding double? Was that euphemism for something else?

"Wh-where are you taking me?"

She tried not to stutter. Seemed to fail. While she was both terrified as well as curious, curiosity seemed to reign prevalent. Dallas didn't understand why she was beginning to trust this man. "I," she gulped air, "don't ride. Don't know how to ride. Don't wish to be up here, so far from the good earth."

"That's obvious. Perhaps an understatement." He chuckled, his voice slightly gruff yet whiskey smooth. "As to your other question, I'm taking you to safety. Ye *cannae* stay where those men can find you. They meant you harm."

Yes, she knew. They would have forced her if Roc didn't come along. "That's also an understatement. What are your intentions? I..." She lost the stutter. He could be wanting the same as those men. It was replaced with indignation as well as annoyance. He saved her. She should be grateful for his interference even when she thought she had all under control. Under control only if there was enough pepper spray in the cannister to do in the second man. "I repeat, where are you taking me?"

"Carnoch, eventually."

"I was planning on going to Inverness for dinner. Thought I might stay the night. So, I would guess you are going the wrong direction. Though I cannot go anywhere without my car."

If she expected him to take her to her car, she was beating herself up over something that wasn't going to happen.

"Too far to go before the sun drops behind the craigs. You wouldn't make it there for dinner or to stay the night. I will feed you tonight. We can talk more about tomorrow. I can't take you to Inverness yet. Just came from there. Nonetheless, in a week or so...may be a month I need to return. You can go with me then if that's to your liking."

Dallas felt as if she was talking to someone who existed in a different dimension or century. He didn't dress the same way. She'd not noticed before. "Of course, there's time. It would only take a couple of hours to..." The distinct feeling her words went in one of his ears then out the other met with direct conflict. They were talking on two different levels.

"You *dinna* listen to me. Things will go along more smoothly if you begin to do so. From here the trip will take all day. As I just told you I don't have the time." He talked with little inflection as if he spoke to a small child he found lacking.

"Then where..." She supposed she would have to concede to his ways.

He interrupted her train of thought. "Tonight, our accommodations will be a cave I know very well. It's stocked with all kinds of delicacies."

The thoughtful then the ensuing question caught her off guard. "Do you always dress so provocatively?"

Dallas looked down at the expanse of leg she showed. "This isn't..." She looked up, caught the amusement in his eyes as well as the darkening of the color to deep pewter. "My dress ripped." Now she was angry at what he was saying but not accusing. Men! "Are you implying my attire was somehow the reason why those men wished to attack me? That's just stupid!"

She sounded too prim and proper for her ears. No, she wasn't prim or proper. What she was, was indignant that the man dare reply in that manner. Her short shorts as well as her bikini were more provocative.

"Maybe somewhat stimulating. Though that doesn't give a man the right. I find your attire very fetching. I can see every curve you possess. I find that I enjoy looking at you." Once again, there was a hint of amusement in his voice.

He set his hand on her bare leg. Heat seared her, touched that part of her his whispered words tinged a few minutes ago. *Sparks?* "If a woman doesn't want unwanted attention, she would be well advised not to show so much of herself. Whether I agree or not matters little. What I state is a fact."

Dallas tried to pull her skirt down. Sitting astride this huge animal made the task impossible. "I don't want to stay in a cave. I didn't dress to go riding. If you didn't come along and hoist me up here, I wouldn't be showing so much of my legs. Though I've...well...my short shorts show a bit more," as she confessed, she felt heat rise to her face. Why was she telling him this?

No, not when a quick trip to Inverness would get her a nice four-star hotel.

"Short shorts?"

"Yes." Her chin rose to prove her point as well as show him she didn't care for his words of warning.

"Suit yourself. That's where I'm headed though. You are coming with me...unless..."

He didn't act like he was about to give her a choice. She knew from the first command, there were no choices in her future. "Do you wish for me to set you down. You will have to take your chances with Scratch and Geordie."

At this point they were headed away from the falls, away from Inverness, away from her car. They'd been riding at least twenty minutes, perhaps more. The setting sun was in front of them. Yes, by the slant of the sun, they were traveling west not east. It seemed she was going to stay the night in a cave with this man. Maybe a name would help her adjust to losing her ability to choose. "What do you call yourself? You said your name was Roc?"

He barked with a sharp bout of laughter. "If it's a full name you're looking for my name is Cameron Petroc Frasier. Most call me Cameron. A few tend to use Roc." He paused for a few seconds. "You? Do you have a name?"

She sifted in a hard breath of air. Frasier? She didn't know any Frasiers by that name in this area except Rafe. Was he related to Rafe? If so, maybe that little fact would help her get what she needed. "I'm Dallas Elaine Shaw."

"Lainie," he murmured, his voice wafted over her name, his hand around her waist tightened. "I like that name, Lanie. What kind of name is Dallas?"

Her middle name tumbling from his lips felt like a soft caress filled with warmth. Leaning into him, she sighed as if he stroked her. For all practical purposes, she felt as if he had done so. She wondered when she could tell Rafe about this man who seemed to steal her senses.

"Roc?"

He shortened his middle name to something more palatable than Petroc.

"Yes?"

His hand rose on her ribcage then settled on the curve of her hip.

She felt the caress to the tips of her toes. Didn't understand why but she wanted him to do that again. She wasn't about to ask. "Don't you need to use both hands?" While she appreciated the way his hands felt on her, she would feel safer if he kept both hands on the reins.

A small chortle proceeded his next words. "You wish for me to touch you with both my hands? I can be accommodating if that's what you wish."

The amusement in his voice didn't go unnoticed. She stiffened pushing her back against his chest. "No! I want you to use both hands to steer your horse."

"Moonstar," he corrected. "I'm disappointed. Thought you wished for me to caress your beautiful curves. All you need do is ask. I'd be happy to oblige."

"No, I don't want you touch me at all."

Her voice was too indignant when all she wished for was to feel more of the heat he generated.

"As you wish." His hands fell away from her but he didn't pick up the reins. "Don't need to use two hands or even one. Can guide my horse with my knees."

~ * ~

When Dallas didn't show up the next day as she told Rafe she would, Rafe drove to the falls. He discovered her abandoned car. While her tripod was inside the trunk, her camera equipment along with her big bag she always carried were gone.

He tried not to panic. When he saw her next, she would be able to explain. Over then over again he told himself she was fine. *Nothing happened.* Dallas would turn up soon. She must have met a friend here. Why she didn't text him though was beyond his wildest imagination. She always apprised him of her plans if she was going to deviate. She always knew he would worry.

Along the way to Inverness, he stopped at stores as well as eateries to inquire if anyone saw her. No one could report seeing a young lady of her description. Later that night when he climbed the steps to her studio apartment, he searched his head for anything she might have told him that would give him a clue as to her whereabouts.

I should move to another town.

At the time she spoke those words, Rafe hadn't believed her, couldn't believe she would do something so foolish. Especially without speaking more plainly. No, she didn't move. Her home was not up for sale. Her car was now in his driveway. In the studio, he stared out the window, his heart in his throat.

She was gone from his life, at least for the time being. *Until he could find her.* He would too. He would never give up his search for Dallas. It would not be so easy to disappear. If necessary, he would hire a private detective. She was not skilled in vanishing. She would leave traces of her passing. Dallas would use her credit card. She would withdraw money from her bank. She could not remain missing for long. Rafe was certain she wasn't attempting to hide from anyone.

After he uncovered the oil painting of her, her body seemed to fade, change in subtle ways. His imagination worked overtime. For the longest time he stared at the painting, remembering her.

No, she wasn't gone. Dallas would come back to him. Yesterday was not the last time he would see her.

He prayed.

Dallas, where are you. I'll miss you. You cannot be hurt or in need of help. I will come to you.

As the days passed, Rafe became more desolate. His best friend in the entire world went missing. There was nothing he could do about finding her. At least not any more than he already was.

Every time he passed a woman with copper colored hair, he stared. Now, he painted furiously. Sketched her from memory. Water colors, acrylics, charcoal, were all different medias he used to portray her. His walls were wallpapered with paintings of her.

At times he thought himself a bit crazed. Many times, he found himself staring out the window into the setting sun or the dawning sun. He ate little and slept less.

His friends stopped coming by to see him.

He was disheartened. Rafe visited a therapist. After a session when the doctor hypnotized him, the man pronounced him sane. Rafe supposed that was a relief even though the doctor's words didn't bring Dallas back to him.

After several months, Rafe began to recover. The process was slow. He still spent most of his time in the third-floor room, drawing and painting Dallas. She was all that was on his mind. The detectives he hired turned up nothing. It seemed she vanished leaving no trace of her behind.

His mother came to see him. Told him he looked terrible and smelled even worse. He knew her words for truth. Supposed a bath would be in order along with a shave. He didn't like how the unkept beard aged him. He didn't like the fact no one wanted to see him. Rafe understood he needed to snap out of the depression where he floundered.

By the time he finished bathing and dressing, he felt better.

Stepping out of his home, he strode along the bustling city streets of Carnoch. The wind seemed to blow in from the sea. The air felt clean and crisp. He felt rejuvenated. The sky was a brilliant blue with few clouds. A weight seemed to be lifted from his shoulders.

For the first time in months, he felt as if he had something to live for. When he caught his first glimpse of her, his heart stopped for a moment. She turned down a street filled with people, tourists...so many tourists. The woman disappeared. Rafe ran after her, calling out her name, waving his arms to get her attention.

Dallas, his whispered word echoed in his head. The woman couldn't be his Dallas. If she was here in town, she would have come to see him. She would not walk from him. Dallas would have sensed his presence then turned to look at him.

This woman sure as hell looked like Dallas. Who the devil was she? An unknown twin?

Rafe decided he was going to find out.

Chapter Two

Highlands 1756

At the entrance to the cave, Roc helped her from Moonstar. Her inside thighs protested when they touched earth. She caught herself from collapsing by grabbing the stirrups. The horse wasn't pleased. He reared and sidestepped dragging her with him as he tried to get away. She cried out.

"The devil!" Roc roared. "What's wrong with you?"

"Nothing. Everything."

Dallas cringed, wishing she could stand. When she let go of the stirrup, she crumpled to the mossy ground. Her body ached. Her head spun while the earth seemed to rise up to meet her. With a halted breath of air, she realized how far over her head she was at the moment. This wasn't her fault. Riding for two hours had its downfall. She looked at him, moisture in her eyes. Damn, but she didn't want to cry in front of this man. Unbidden tears slipped from her eyes.

"Foolish woman! Why didn't you tell me you couldn't stand up?"

He stood beside her now. She thought he would shake her or berate her even more. "You have to learn..." He rubbed the back of his neck as if seeking patience with her. "You need to learn to tell me how you are feeling. I cannot guess."

Dallas caught the words she wanted to toss back to him and stopped them before she could make him angrier. With meekness she never before felt, she said every abbreviated word echoing the intense pain that throbbed through her. "I didn't have any idea I could not stand. This riding thing is new to me. As soon as I stretch out the kinks, I'll be fine. Don't worry your pretty little head about me."

"You think so?" This time she didn't hear amusement when he

voiced the words. "You won't be fine in a second or two."

"Yes. I know so!" Were the only words she could say without the drums in her head beating harder. "Oh!" She found herself tossed against his hard chest. Unable to do anything else lest she fall again, Dallas clung.

He scooped her into his arms before striding inside the cave. Hanging on to him, she wound her arms around him. She was afraid she'd be claustrophobic inside the place as she pictured a deep dark cavern with stalagmites and stalactites jutting from the floor and ceiling, maybe some ancient drawings decorating the walls. This wasn't how she pictured her evening. She was supposed to be in Inverness, at a plush restaurant enjoying herself while she ate delicious food.

After he stopped juggling her in his arms, she was treated to a small cavern. Closing her eyes for the time it took her to count to ten, she set her head against the hollow of his shoulder. He was forever surprising her. "I could have walked if you would have given me a minute."

He ignored her comment. "Don't move." He set her on a pallet. Striding to a far wall, he rummaged through a nearby trunk. After coming up with a fur, he shook it out then handed it to her. "Wrap this around you or sit on it or leave it on the floor. Wait for me to come back here. I'm going to take care of Moonstar then I'll see to you."

See to me?

Those words sounded ominous. She didn't need seeing to and she'd be damned if she was going to stay put. When she tried to stand, it appeared she would be staying put at least for the short term since she couldn't rise. Her legs would not cooperate.

Dallas groaned. After that, she folded the fur into a pillow then placed it behind her head. Before he returned, she realized she wasn't going to do anything but follow his orders. As she stretched out on the pallet, she let out a soft whoosh of air. This was a different world. Everything she was feeling as well as seeing was all new to her. While she appreciated this man's confidence, she balked at his need to give orders he expected her to follow. He was arrogant in a titillating sort of way. As long as he allowed her to express her feelings, she could handle his masculine bravado. He was handsome, too much so. Dallas found she might even enjoy a good argument with him. She also didn't want to admit, even to herself, she might hope to have reason to use the condoms in her bag.

When she woke it was to the wonderful scent of fresh brewed coffee and perhaps beans. There were several lit torches giving light to the small cavern. She wasn't fond of beans. Nevertheless, her stomach growled telling her the cuisine was palatable and she needed to eat her fill. The last food she ingested was oatmeal more than several hours ago. She sat up, pushing hair from her face.

"Welcome back to the land of the living. You've slept for a while." His grin charmed all her female sensibilities. She couldn't help but smile back. "Are you hungry? There is plenty of food but not a lot of variety."

"How long did I sleep?"

"Only an hour."

Dallas pushed away from the pallet, tugging at more lose tendrils of hair from her face. She must be a mess. The pony tail holder was slipped from her hair. Finger combing the best she could, she secured her hair on top of her head. She was hungry.

"I like it better down." His voice was once again husky, smooth. "The color becomes you."

Dallas shivered at the way the sound made her feel. The vibrations weren't cold shivers but filled with warmth. They traveled the length of her spine. Created tingles inside. Was this the spark she and Rafe talked about? If it was, she could get used to feeling the sensations.

"That's what Rafe always said about my hair. He always told me the color of my hair reminded him of sunsets all filled with varying shades of red and gold."

"Rafe?" His question had the hint of annoyance written in the sound. "Who is this Rafe? Should I be worried he'll come charging in here to rescue you?"

"A friend."

She didn't understand his scowl of displeasure. Men and women had friends. Friends that were platonic. She lifted her shoulders accepting the cup of coffee he handed to her. Bending close she inhaled the tantalizing aroma of fresh brewed coffee. "Not that it's any of your business. The man is just a friend. He's been my buddy for years, since we first met in grade school. He's like the brother I never had."

"You're right. Grade school? You went to grade school?" Now he didn't sound sincere. "Who this man is as well as what he is to you is not my concern. I was curious. Nonetheless, I want to make it my business."

Was that all he intended to say on the matter? You're right. Though so far, his concession that at least her words made sense was music to her ears. "I am right. Thank you for acknowledging that little fact. Didn't believe you would do that."

He grunted then continued to stir the beans. "If you can walk now, come get a plate. You can dish up your food." He held out a plate as if he meant to challenge her.

His affront to her abilities irked her. "I can walk. Been doing so since before I turned one." She pushed off the pallet then fell back. Struggling, changing her position, she tried again. Now she was on all fours, trying to push herself up. Her lips thinned. Perspiration dripped down the bridge of her nose. She was more determined than ever to succeed. Success was not happening.

"As soon as you're ready to confess you might need help, I'll bring you dinner. Like I said, you need to tell me what you feel. Honesty is important."

He was hunkered down watching the little scene she was making. He held two plates heaped with food.

Foolish woman, was an apt description this time. He wasn't sending out accusations. The lopsided smile he sent her way gave rise to more temper. She tried again. Sitting back on the pallet, she blew upward to dislodge another strand of hair from her face.

"This time you are right. I don't like to be waited on but I suppose you will have to bring me dinner."

"Glad you see reason. If I'm unable to walk, I wouldn't mind if you brought me my food."

His grin sent another cascade of warmth through her. He could smile at her any time.

After he reached her, he sat down beside her on the pallet. "Thank you."

She bent her head, unwilling to meet his smiling eyes. He was staring at her as if he wanted to devour her. She'd never been looked at like that before.

"You don't do humble well." He scooped up a spoonful of beans before chewing. "I do, however, enjoy your spirit. The feistiness is quite refreshing in a woman. Don't appreciate women who pander to everything a man says."

"Don't suppose you do humble either," Dallas shot back at him thinking he was anything except humble. He would always be the one in charge.

Barked laughter caught her attention. "Men aren't supposed to act humble or contrite. The man has the last say. Always will. Must consider other options though."

"Generalizations," she told him, smiling now unable to resist the lure he cast around her. She waved her spoon around in the air. "You cannot make assumptions such as that. It's not right for you to not except women's rights. Where I come from a man doesn't always get the last word."

"Women's rights? Interesting concept. In your mind what are they? I'd know more clearly what we are talking about. What's got that bee in your bonnet." He stared at her as if she broached a topic he had not thought of before.

"Equality, of course. Women are equal to men. They should be given the same opportunities as well as the same considerations."

She wondered at the lopsided smile she was coming to adore. Not for one second anything she said could be construed as amusing. As he chewed on his beans it seemed to Dallas he was also chewing on her words, running them around in his head as if he'd never heard anything like that before.

"In many ways women have more opportunities than men." He held up his hands as if he knew she was going to argue. "They can never be equal in everything." He paused for a second watching her. What he didn't know was that she wanted to hear more of what he had to say. She wasn't going to interrupt. "Men are stronger, more powerful. You could not have won the contest of strength between Geordie and Scratch. Yet when it comes to the need of a delicate hand, a woman is better. Man or woman, they have different abilities so cannot be equal."

Though she didn't want to admit he was right, she would have to do so. "True. Geordie could have held on to me, done what he wanted then given me to his friend." Unable to help herself she snorted with the disgust she felt at the thought of either man touching her. "Though, I do think I had enough pepper spray for both of them."

"A man needs to protect his woman or a woman he comes upon unexpectedly."

"I don't want to be protected or coddled." She pointed to him with her spoon. "You have no obligations to me. We don't even know each other. No need to protect me."

"Today you did," his words were simply to the point. "Are you finished eating?"

Her plate was empty. She nodded and handed it to him. Taking several seconds to mull over his words while sipping her coffee, she watched him walk from the cave. A few minutes later he returned with the clean dishes. He put them in what appeared to be a storage bin.

"Do you stay here often? The place almost appears to be a home away from home."

There were all kinds of things stored. Blankets, food, coffee, even a bottle of wine she saw when he lifted the box to put away the dishes.

"Should we try and walk?"

He held out his hand to her. This time he would help her stand so she wouldn't make such a fool of herself. She imagined he could have done that the last time. It seemed Roc wanted to make a point. Wanted for her to understand how much she needed him.

"Yes."

She needed to stretch her legs. When the palm of her hand connected with his, she emitted a startled little gasp. When her eyes met his, she saw the tender amusement in his steel blue gaze.

Dallas stood, wavering while she tried to get her balance. He wrapped an arm around her, escorting her around the perimeter of the cavern. With each step she grew steadier until she was walking on her own.

He stood in front of her; his arms crossed in front of him. "Don't overdo the exercise. Your muscles will rebel if you do. Tomorrow, we have an even longer ride ahead of us."

"Rebellious muscles," she mused with a slight chuckle. "We wouldn't want that now would we?"

"Tell me something about you. You're different from any woman I've ever met. You say things that I've never heard of before. The pepper spray... Your clothes are different."

"What do you want to know? You haven't asked a question. Ask me something and I'll explain what I understand to be true."

She thought his confusion both adoring as well as strange. All men should have heard about women's rights as well as their bid for equality. Not so much by his words but by his lack of words, did she think he was both curious as well as confused.

"Tell me about the pepper spray."

"All right. Someone, an inventor, I suppose must have had the brilliant idea to give a woman something she could hold in her hand that would help protect herself against a man who meant harm. I'm certain that inventor must have been a woman."

"So, there is pepper in that little cannister. You're right, a woman wouldn't need strength to use it against a man. I've never thought about having pepper sprayed into my face, my eyes. Though my mother one time put too much pepper in the venison stew. One taste sent both my father as well as myself rushing to the pitcher of water on the table."

"Yes." She didn't know what else to tell him, almost laughing at his distress. She shut down her amusement. "What else would you like to know?"

Roc moved to the pallet and was now rummaging through her bag. She cringed knowing he would find things that might embarrass her. He would find things about her she might not want him to know. When she lunged to make a bid at wresting the bag from him, he was quicker, holding the satchel high in the air away from her reaching fingers. "I want to see what you carry with you. It will tell me something about you. When I find something that piques my curiosity, I will ask questions. You will explain."

Explain? He should understand everything he would find. There should be no explanations necessary. "It's not polite to go through a woman's bag."

Her hands were clasped in front of her. She never cared if Rafe looked in her bag. She knew Rafe, trusted him. Rafe knew everything about her. This man knew nothing.

"Why not?" He pulled out the cannister of pepper spray then set it aside as if he knew all that needed to be known about it or all that he wished to understand. Next, he pulled out the spandex jogging pants that were her change of clothing for the next day. For his perusal, he held them high in the air staring at her then back to the leggings.

"Well...well..."

His disapproval was obvious and very clear in the way he stared at her. He wouldn't know she wore them...foolish woman...what else could he possibly assume? She didn't know what to say. Words seemed to leave her brain when she looked at the man. "What is in my bag is private. Not for your eyes. I don't wish to share. I don't know you."

Dallas didn't understand the apprehension nagging at her.

"I'd like to know if I have to sleep with one eye open tonight. Do you be havin' another type of weapon in here? Something besides your spray of pepper?"

"Oh..." She was taken aback by that thought. Her body shook with the idea. "I won't carry weapons; knives, guns or anything except my pepper spray. I don't like violence."

He pulled out the jogging bra, held it up with a raised eyebrow. "This and this?" he pointed to the leggings then waved the bra in the air to emphasize his point. "These two items are supposed to be clothing?" His brow rose in speculation. "I *dinna* see how they would do anything except expose you...every curve. Do you enjoy flaunting yourself?"

He was right. That wisdom didn't change anything as far as she was concerned. "My change of clothing for tomorrow," she told him sticking her chin in the air, her fingers woven together. After all, he should recognize those items as common fashion pieces. All women wore them at some time or another. "They are more comfortable than jeans. I like comfort."

"You wear this?" This time there was shock in his voice, quite a lot actually. "I'd like to see you in these but I doubt if I'd want another man to have the same view. Will you model them for me? Now? Tomorrow when you can walk better?"

Now he was reaching. Dallas didn't know whether she should be offended or pleased at his comment. "What does that mean?"

Deep in her chest her heart throbbed beating hard against her ribs. Even clasped together, her hands were shaking.

His words were slow as well as seemingly to the point. He didn't blink or waver in his confession. "If you were mine, I would forbid you to wear these except when you were with me. Where I alone could appreciate the view. These articles are not appropriate for random men to see."

"Oh..."

Dallas asked the question. His answer didn't help her indecision. The idea he thought he could forbid anything didn't sit right with her. On the other hand, she liked the rest of what he told her. He tossed the clothing aside. She watched him reach one more time into the bag.

"What's this?" He pulled out a small container. Held it up to the light from one of the lanterns, turning it one way then the other. He'd opened it and was perusing the contents. His brows drew together.

In anticipation of his comment or question, she held her breath. Men would know what it was unless they'd been sheltered away from people their entire life. Dallas wished to snatch it away from him. While she could talk about this in front of Rafe, she couldn't speak of the reasons why she carried the pills. He would never give up the question. From what she'd learned so far about Roc, he would pursue the topic until he learned everything. She would have to tell him. "My birth control pills."

"Birth control? As in...keeping from having a child?"

"Yes!" She did try to snatch it from him. He was faster, holding the container from her reach. She stumbled into him before she gained control of herself. "You've no right. Don't pass judgment on something you know nothing about!" She was furious with him, with his arrogant assumptions.

"Perhaps not. I find this confusing. How does it work? I don't believe I like this either. I should toss it into the fire."

"No!" She reached out for the container. Roc held it away from her. "You can't. I need them."

Of course, he wouldn't. No domineering arrogant man who wanted to control everything concerning a woman's reproductive rights would like the thought of the woman controlling her destiny where it concerned child birth. She tried for the honest truth. "Those pills will keep me from conceiving a child."

"You are a prostitute. I could make you my mistress. That would be safer than giving yourself to multiple men." His voice turned harsh when he spoke of her seeing other men intimately.

"What?" This conversation was going nowhere. "Never! I'm not...not a prostitute. I won't ever be a man's mistress. So, get that idea out of your male brain. They are meant to help me with my periods. When I have my monthly flow, it is too heavy. At that time, for days I'm in pain from cramps. The pills ease that. I don't sleep around," she finished lamely realizing they were getting off to a very rocky start.

She was rambling. He was listening attentively. Her heart raced.

After closing the lid then running his hand around the container, he set it in her bag. He didn't give up the bag though. He delved for some other items. "You speak plainly for a woman. I'm not used to that. Most young women don't know anything about conception, blush when their monthly is brought up. Not you. Why is that?"

Was that an accusation of some kind. He brought out her cell phone. "My phone."

She didn't have an answer for his comments because he didn't make sense.

"Phone? I'm afraid to ask what it does." After he turned it over in his hands, rubbed it in different ways, the screen still dark, he handed it to her. "How does it work. It should be clear to you I've no idea."

She thought she should call Rafe. He could rescue her. Dallas wouldn't be able to give him her location. *Some cave between Carnoch and Inverness.* She lifted her shoulders in silent resignation. "No bars," she murmured. "I use it to call people who are my friends. If you were my friend, I would call you. You can't open it up because you don't have a password which she put into the phone before handing it over to him. "See..."

He jumped when the flash of light went off, his eyes wide with curiosity. "How does it work."

"It doesn't right now, at least the phone part doesn't," she said watching frown lines form on his forehead. "If you come here, I'll take a picture of us. No, I'll come to you." She scooted so they sat side by side. After she held the phone in the air, she pointed it toward them. "Smile." Once more, the flash went off, lighting up the cave.

He took it from her. "What did it do?"

He was turning it over in hands. His eyes wide with curiosity. Now that she opened the screen all her apps were staring at them.

"Let me show you." When she found the picture of them, she handed the phone showing the picture of them to him.

With the widest eyes she'd ever seen, he stared at the photo. He looked as if he wanted to say something to her. Instead, he handed the phone back without a comment.

"You act as if you..."

"I'm going for a brisk walk. Need to check out the area. With hope, Geordie and Scratch will stay away. Cannot see them walking this far."

He seemed to be mumbling to himself. His strides taking him away from her were long and powerful.

With her mouth open she watched his stiff, unyielding back as he walked from the cave. Dallas spent the ensuing time trying to weave the threads of everything said and done into a realistic picture. She didn't like the results the conversation intimated. Pouring herself another cup of coffee, she wandered to the mouth of the cave to stare into the darkness. It was night, the darkness all consuming, the stars bright against the velvet backdrop of the night sky. She wondered where he went...if he was safe. The only light came from a half-moon that was ghosted by clouds. She realized Rafe would be worried when she didn't return tomorrow. He would believe she was ghosting him. Ghosting... She wasn't. Telling him that, would be impossible. She didn't think she would see Rafe again. Not unless she could find her way back to the falls.

As it stood now, she wouldn't be returning to Carnoch, at least not the Carnoch she knew. She no longer thought she existed in twenty twenty-four. She wondered what year this was. As Dallas mulled over the changing expressions on his face, asking Roc didn't seem prudent. Roc seemed confounded by all he found in her bag. He had not perused her camera yet, nor the condoms which would also lead him to believe she was a woman of loose moral values. Before she found the portal that sent her here, she meant to take as many pictures of this man as she had time for. Damn, but he was a man, a real man. She had no illusions about him. She wanted to remember him for the rest of her life.

His woman.

If she were his woman, he would forbid her to wear her leggings. While the man was eye candy to her, she would never fall for a male who would forbid her to do anything, especially dictate what she wore. He didn't understand equality. In whatever century this was, he wouldn't be able to change his way of thinking so it would conform with hers. She would never go backward.

She sent a quick look at the moon then strode inside. This was as good as any time to get herself more comfortable. She needed to rid herself of her bra. The underwire was uncomfortable and cutting into her skin. The metal clasps in the back bit into her too. She heaved a huge breath of air before letting the oxygen filter with ease from her lungs. He would come back sooner than later. She best rid herself of the unwanted clothing before she saw his handsomeness again. Before she gave into these strange feelings.

Sitting on the pallet, she reached behind her for the zipper. Usually doing so was easy. This time her muscles seemed to say no, cramping whenever she assumed a position that would ease the zipper down. Imagined the discomfort as well as fatigue was generated from the ride on his horse this afternoon. She tugged on the fabric of the dress trying for a better location. As she slipped the metal fastener down her back, it caught. If anything would go wrong now, it would.

"Curse it!"

She tried again, pulled the tab back up then sent it down only to have it get caught on the fabric again. She couldn't seem to remove the material from the zipper. Frantic, she tugged on the clasp. There was no give.

Frustrated to no end she hung her head, breathed in deep again then again. Breathed in then out. Sucked air. She rearranged her body, contorting herself so she was coming at the zipper from a different angle. It wouldn't budge.

"Damn!"

She held several curse words behind her lips. Letting them out would make her feel better.

"Would you like help disrobing? I'd be happy to oblige. Did I read this wrong too?" His booted feet seemed to thunder on the uneven ground in the cave.

At the sound of his deep voice, she whirled, her arms akimbo at her sides. A broken sound split from her vocal cords. Dallas felt both indignant along with furious that he would always assume the worst about her. "I'm not disrobing!" she cried out in a feeble attempt to convince what he saw wasn't what was happening.

Roc stepped closer, his hands resting on his hips. His smile was wide. "Oh? Looks like it to me. What, pray tell, do you call what you are doing? Nonetheless you look quite charming wiggling your body this way then that way. I'm intrigued. Would like nothing more than to help."

"Getting more comfortable. I'm trying to rid myself from some uncomfortable pieces of underwear so I can feel more at ease."

"Naked, I hope." He waggled his burnished eyebrows at her. Teasing, he went on to say, "I can help if you ask. Be the gentleman. Anything you desire."

She stiffened, the wind whooshing from her lungs. On the last pass of the zipper, she realized it was caught going both directions.

~ * ~

When Roc saw her wriggling, struggling with the unusual fastener on her dress, he was intrigued, nay, more than intrigued, fascinated. Lainie, she was so damn beautiful. He'd always enjoyed curvaceous women, never thought the one who tugged his heart strings with so much intensity would possess the perfect hourglass figure he always dreamed of.

Her breasts would overflow his large hands while her hips were wide. That intriguing butt of hers appeared deliciously round, ripe for fondling as well as kissing. Her stomach wasn't flat. He was certain it would be round and soft. Lainie was prickly though, bent on the strangest notions he'd ever heard pontificated. He would have to approach her with caution. He didn't want to get ahead of himself. A woman like Lainie would appreciate a slow hand. He didn't know what to think of the pills or the clothing that would show all those delightful feminine curves to anyone she walked past. If he had his way, he wished to keep the show to himself. For now, he didn't have a say in her life. He meant to change that aspect as soon as possible.

After she flashed what she called a picture of them, he had to get air. She was a witch. She did and said things that were foreign. Her English was well spoken, educated. This woman wasn't from a different country. She was Scottish to her core. So...where...who was she? He didn't want to believe she was a witch.

Now she stood, her hands loosely held at her sides, her mouth gaping open. He set his finger beneath her chin then closed her mouth, the sweet kissable mouth he longed to taste. What he wanted was to open her lips with his tongue. He wanted to taste her. Play with her. Savor every part of her. Feel her passion rise to hunger.

"Don't gape so. You might catch a fly. If you turn around, I'll see what I can do to help," he spoke with a soft burr hoping to ease the tension he witnessed while wishing he could hide the husky tenor of his voice. If she was experienced as he suspected, she would understand what the tone meant.

She did so then watched over her shoulder at him. The slip of her tongue across her lips held his attention. She cleared her voice to speak. The sound whispered to him. "The material is caught. You will have to tug the fabric out of the teeth."

"Teeth?" Roc questioned.

"That's what the sides of the zipper are called."

"Do you care if your dress rips?" he asked looking at the contraption while deciding how to best tackle the problem. "I could rip it then you would be free."

"I've only this and the leggings you disapprove of to wear. Yes, I'd prefer to keep the dress in one piece...well...wearable. If you can, that is. It's stuck pretty bad."

"With the slit up the side you will still wear this? Seems to me this dress has lost its value as a viable piece of clothing."

"Yes." She appeared more worried about what he was doing now than what was happening with the dress. "Right on both counts. I might be able to stich the rent seam."

"I don't approve of this dress either, at least not to be worn in public. When we get to Carnoch, I'll see what I can find for you to wear." When he struggled with the fabric and the... "What's this called?"

He jiggled the tongue on the zipper.

"A zipper."

Looking over her shoulder, she grinned at him.

He pulled and pushed, wiggled the material as well as tugged. "We should sit down. This isn't going to happen too fast. You must remember I'm new at this business. Never seen a zipper before. In most situations, I'm rather adept at disrobing willing women."

He thought he might be telling her too much. What he knew was that they were too far from the Kinnel Stones for her to have traveled through time in that manner. "Now, could this be considered my second rescue of the day?"

"No, given some time I would have figured out how to fix it."

"As you say." Beneath his knuckles he felt the soft texture of her skin. Realized how she shivered when he touched her. He tried to stay neutral, attempted to keep distance between his fingers and her back. He didn't want to frighten her. Though from everything she'd said coupled with the items she carried in her bag, in addition her clothing, she wouldn't tell him no if he seduced.

"Making progress?" she turned again, trying to see what he was doing.

"Done!" Roc pulled the zipper to the end revealing the long length of her back, the crevice in her butt the twin dimples on either side of her spine. He caught his breath, holding the oxygen until it burned deep in his lungs. Unable to resist, he touched her spine. "Is this the offending garment?" he asked as once more he was greeted with a piece of clothing he didn't understand. "What's its purpose?" he asked even though he had a few guesses.

He unclasped it, tugging at the hooks.

She clutched the gown to her chest. His hand dropped away understanding he needed to distance himself from her or he would do something he shouldn't. Something he might soon regret. Mistakes with this woman were not something he could afford to make.

"Thank you," she said while her eyes told him she waited for his departure.

Instead of leaving, he stretched his legs out in front of him then crossed them. He wasn't going anywhere until he was good and ready. With a great deal of intensity, he watched her. The deep blue of her eyes darkened. Her bottom lip was caught beneath her teeth as she worried the soft tissue.

Roc wondered if more curse words would erupt from her tender, kissable lips. He wanted to know her thoughts. Would give more than a penny for them. He didn't believe she would tell him much. Except to leave. The way her eyes shimmered with anger or perhaps frustration told him how desperate she was for him to walk from the cave and leave her in privacy.

"Could you go outside for a minute?" she asked, her voice thin. As her knuckles started to turn white, she was gripping the dress with so much force.

"I could." He wasn't going to unless she asked. Watching her had merits he didn't wish to give up.

Pressing her lips together, she turned then worked her dress off her shoulders. As the fabric moved down her arms, he was treated to a show of sun bronzed skin coupled with tiny lines of white, which must show the true color of her skin.

Another puzzlement for him to unravel.

Once the fabric disappeared off her arms, she tugged at the piece she wished to remove. It slipped from between her dress and her body. The garment fell to the pallet where he sat. It appeared to be fashioned to mold lovingly to her breasts. Just as he imagined. He wanted his hands to mold to her curves.

Intrigued filled with curiosity, he picked it up, held it, turned it over in his hands. When his attention returned to Lainie she was still clutching her gown to her chest.

"What is this called?"

"Can't you just leave a moment? I'd like..."

"What's this called," he repeated as he stuffed it into her bag. "I would know the term you use for it."

"Thought every male knows what it is. It's a bra," she said as she sat down in what appeared to be a huff next to him. "I'll need you to zip the dress back up."

"No...I've got something else in mind for you to wear. What's this bra do?" Even though he asked, he wanted to hear the use from Lainie. No, just one guess. He wanted to hear her tell him of its purpose.

"Supports me," she sighed sounding resigned to answering all his questions.

His hoot of laughter got him what could only be contrived as a dirty look from Lainie. "With breasts the size of yours, I can understand why they'd need to be supported. If you would tell me yes, I would enjoy supporting your beautiful breasts with my hands."

Without saying anything else, he strode to his saddlebags. He pulled out one of his shirts. "This will do for comfort. It can also be used as a nightshirt for you. You won't have to sleep in something that will keep you awake."

Roc handed the shirt to her. He didn't want to think of her tossing and turning during the night. He'd be of a mind to keep her awake himself. "Slip it over your head then you can shimmy out of your dress. I won't see anything. Promise. I won't even try to look."

A few seconds of her staring at him passed. "Thank you." She accepted the offering then proceeded to do as he suggested. When she was finished, she sat on the pallet, her bare toes wiggling in the fur throw that covered the bed.

Roc thought he would love to suck on those toes among other things. He stood, his movement abrupt. "I need another breath of cold air."

As he strode from the cave to the frigid darkness he sought, the image of her long back pounded in his head. Tomorrow, he would take her to Carnoch. He would hand her over to his mother for safe keeping. After that, he would enjoy a night free of thoughts of her. The devil, she was beautiful. He swallowed the lump forming in his throat. He'd never be free of thoughts about this woman. She came to him unexpectedly. His mate. He was certain of that fact the moment he set eyes on her.

While he leaned against the cave entrance, his body took its time to calm as he breathed in then breathed out. Breathed in again. Held the air. He did it again then again. His erection no longer pulsed against his buckskins. He caught the scent of flowers before he heard her or sensed her presence. He didn't recall that scent or what flower it might have come from.

Lainie stood close to him but not close enough to touch. When he looked to see if she was wiggling her toes, he noticed she'd put her shoes on. Beneath his shirt, her legs seemed to go on forever. "What scent do you wear?"

She cleared her throat. "Roc...oh, it's gardenia."

He didn't recognize the scent or the name. Something else unique about this woman. The devil, everything about her was different.

When he turned to look at her, her chin tilted. He didn't think there was anything she would have difficulty asking him. It was apparent that at this time there was some hesitation. Curiosity surged to the forefront of his brain.

"Can I do something for you?" he asked trying to keep his laughter in check.

Once more he had guesses as to her immediate problem. He wondered how long it would take her to tell him what she needed.

"Yes and no, well you can help me but you can't do it for me."

Her hesitant smile left an endearing scar on his heart. She had this way of saying things.

Amusement twitched his lips. "Is that a riddle I'm supposed to solve? Are you going to tell me before I perish from curiosity?"

"No...I have to pee," she blurted her thoughts. "I don't know where...to go. That's how you can help."

"Anywhere. You've got the entire forest to choose from. Just don't go far. I want to be able to hear you."

He was pleased at the contrite expression on her delicate features. The scowl she gifted him with. The widening of her eyes, all told him she understood what he spoke of.

"Hear me?" Dallas leaned forward then thought better of it. "Show me where to go. Just point. I'll figure it all out."

"Around that rock you can..."

He wasn't at all certain how delicate he needed to be. With this woman, he thought he could say most anything and his words wouldn't embarrass her. This time he was surprised to see the slight flush that encompassed her cheeks "I'll wait here. If you need help call out."

"That won't be necessary." He watched her as she walked away, her shoulders squared, her back straight. Saw her disappear behind the boulder he pointed out. Heard her curses. Bushes rustled. Rocks slid. The cry of pain shocked him. His heart leapt to his throat. He should have gone with her, stayed closer. She would never allow that. Protective thoughts bombarded him.

He ran, raced to see her on her bare butt pushing off the ground. Breathless, he blurted. "What the devil happened? You were just supposed to pee."

He stared at her. From his vantage point nothing he could see could have caused her to scream.

Silence.

"Lainie...?"

Roc reached to pick her up by her arms. The resistance to his help surprised him somewhat. He was quickly learning that surprise was part of her name. He hoped she heard the demand in his voice. "Tell me what happened?"

Her feet slid on the rocks, slipping and sliding as she tried to right herself. He held her now, her feet touching the ground. Whimpering, she bent over to pick up something that was sheer and white on the ground. She caught a sob of pain in the back of her throat. He wanted to shake her until she spoke.

"N-nothing..." she whimpered, tears in her voice.

"Why did you cry out if nothing happened?" He did give her a little shake as he turned her. "Lainie answer me!" He calmed himself. "If I'm to help, I have to know."

She set her head against his chest. "I...I hurt myself. I sat."

He felt as if she was making him pull out all her teeth even while her tears wetted his shirt. "You sat." He reserved judgement until he could look at her bottom. If she sat on something, she might have hurt herself, a sharp rock. His mind couldn't fathom anything else. "For a woman who can speak of things such as your monthly and peeing without blushing overmuch, you've grown unaccountably silent," Roc understood his voice was harsh, would scare her.

She nodded. Gulped air. "On a nettle."

He cursed then swung her into his arms. "I'm sorry for that. Did you slip? I should have been there for you."

Roc didn't want to proceed this way but he understood the irritant, knew he would have to attend to her. Her bottom would hurt for at least twenty-four hours, sting as well as itch. She would have trouble sitting in front of him on the horse tomorrow. He could spend more private time with Lainie. They could stay in the cave. He found he liked that idea. He could get to know her better before he introduced her to his family. Discover more truths about Lainie Shaw.

"It was so dark. I didn't see. I wouldn't have let you stay with me. Some things are too private to share with a stranger."

Ah, her steadfast personality was coming back. He didn't feel like a stranger. She wound her arms around his neck. Once inside he set her stomach side down on the pallet. When she turned to look at him, he pointed at her. "Don't move. Don't even flinch. I want you exactly in that position when I come back."

As if all the hounds of hell were after him, he poured heated water into a basin he scavenged from one of the trunks that lined the walls of the cave. He found a soft cloth along with a bar of soap. When he reached the pallet, he sat down beside her, pleased she was lying still. Her eyes were closed. He hoped she wasn't asleep. He had a much-needed lecture for her.

"What are you going to do?"

Her soft-spoken question surprised him. She pushed up on her arms to see him better. Her eyes were a vivid blue, her lashes dark, sultry looking. She lowered them for a moment before looking at him again.

Roc wondered if he should put this delicately or shoot for the unadulterated truth. He went for flat out truth. "Wash your butt."

He waited for a protest. What he heard was a soft groan. Interpreting the meaning of the sound impossible for him.

"You wouldn't happen to be a doctor, would you?" she asked as if that would make a difference to her. He didn't suppose it would. "I could almost tolerate the exposure if you were medical. I would know you weren't looking at me...at my butt." She closed her eyes setting her cheek on her hands. "Just do what you must."

"My brother is a doctor. Does that help? I'll be gentle. Won't look if that will make you feel better."

How the devil was he not going to look at a part of her he craved to see, to kiss, nip. He lifted the hem of the shirt he loaned her so only the globes of her delectable rounded bottom showed. The flesh was red, irritated. The rash seemed to be spreading as he watched and her bottom quivered in the most provocative way.

"No, I've never..." It seemed she didn't know how to finish the statement. Then, "How are you going to help me if you don't look?"

Damned if he knew.

It became his intention to finish the sentence for her. "Now, you can say you have done so."

Though he could only surmise the direction of her thoughts. He dipped the cloth into the water then lathered the soap. "I'm going to touch you now. This shouldn't hurt."

"All right," she acquiesced.

When the cloth caressed her, she flinched. All he wished for was to make her feel better. "Did I hurt you." The devil he didn't like this scenario. The entire process had to be a bit painful for her. He needed a gentle touch...Roc tried.

"No, I was surprised." She rested her head on her hands, closing her eyes as he continued to touch with as much gentleness as possible.

"Would you tell me if I did? If I hurt you?"

He hoped this would continue throughout their relationship. All he hoped for with anyone, new acquaintance or old was honesty. He wished for more than friendship with this woman. Damn, she was his mate. He needed everything from her.

"Yes...maybe..."

That answer told him nothing he could wrap his mind around. He continued to clean the rash, washing then rinsing, trying to make all the irritants vanish. So far in this relationship she didn't know if she could always be truthful. Her answer made him wonder about her true character. "I don't have anything to put on the rash. You are going to feel this for a day or two. You won't be able to sit with any comfort."

"I do. In my bag there is some cortisone cream. It will help the itching as well as the sting." She closed her eyes as if she didn't want to see what he was doing. "I should get it, put the lotion on myself."

"No need for that. I'll make certain all the irritation is covered."

Rummaging in her satchel he found the cream along with a box marked condoms. TROJAN Sensitivity Ultra Thin Lubricated Condoms, he read the box. He set the condoms aside for further conversation. There was more in the bag he would enjoy investigating. Now was just not that time.

"I'm going to spread the cream on now. You will feel my fingers. I'm only going to touch you where the rash is. Is that all right with you? I'm not..."

He saw her nod her head. He clamped down on his teeth as he tortured himself to keep his hands only where they belonged.

"You say your brother is a doctor? What do you do?"

"Print the news and whatever else needs printing, runoff pamphlets. See to some of the merchant ships my family owns," he said. "Not very exciting."

Her rump quivered when he stroked the cortisone cream on her bottom. He was thorough, covering all of the affected area. The bright red color receded to a sweet pink. After he finished, he sat back, loath to cover her, enjoying the intoxicating scene. Watching the play of her muscles when she moved fascinated him. With so little provocation he was rock hard...like granite.

"You should probably stay on your belly. Sitting might prove uncomfortable." He stoked the fire before making up another pallet for him to sleep on. "Can I get you anything. For the rest of the evening, I'll be pleased to tend to your needs."

The snort he heard told him she understood his meaning or guessed. "I'd like a glass of wine. Don't suppose you have any?" she questioned. "Imagine that's wistful thinking."

Much to his disappointment, she tugged his shirt down so it covered her to mid-calf. The filmy confection he found at the scene of her accident, she started to put on then had second thoughts. She put the tiny piece of clothing to the side. He supposed the article was meant to cover her bottom. It looked as if it might. "Ask and you shall receive." He carried two mugs of wine, handing her one of them. After he sat, he picked up the box of condoms rereading the inscription on the box. He pulled one package out. It was wrapped in foil. When he started to open the package, she stopped him.

"No, don't open it." Her hand rested on his forearm. She had to do some quick maneuvering to reach him before he unwrapped the package.

"Why?" Puzzled he stared at her. A slight flush to her cheeks surprised him. This was something she was embarrassed about. He liked the knowledge that she wasn't as brazen as he previously thought. This little wrapped package called TROJAN, embarrassed her.

"It won't be any good. You would have to throw it away," she mumbled showing miniscule awkwardness.

"I didn't mean that. Why do you carry condoms with you?" He wondered if discomfiture would show on her face or in the cadence of her answer.

She rolled to her side. Her breasts pushed against the fabric of the shirt she wore, the tips hard and rose colored beneath the material. Perhaps her clothing, tightly fit as it seemed to be, would have hidden her curves from him better than the white muslin his shirt was made from. He gave it to her to wear because he needed distance from her ripe body. This wasn't giving it to him.

Only because he allowed it, she took the box from him. She turned it over in her hands several times before she looked sharply at him. "What year is this?"

Ah, she made guesses too. He'd been expecting a question of this sort though. If she didn't know of the Kinnel Stones, she would be hesitant. "Why?" He didn't mean to allow her to abandon his question. It would be so easy to find himself with answers of a different sort before he got the one he sought. "Why condoms in your bag?" He would answer her question later.

"You aren't going to..."

"No, I need an answer. One that is palatable to me. Why condoms? Women don't carry prevention unless..."

He didn't know how to be direct without being rude. He didn't want to imply something about her that might be false. Roc recalled he'd already done so. All his senses told him she wasn't a prostitute.

"I know what you think. It's not true." She ran her fingers through the fur she lay on, playing with the material. "I'm not... well..." Her hesitation told him very little.

His mind transformed the picture of her fingers to her wriggling toes. "Tell me then. I'm a good listener. At least I've been told as much. What are you? Who are you?"

"For the record, let it be known that I don't wish to answer you." Resting on her elbows, she sipped her wine. "I don't know you. Don't want to tell you anything more about me. You've no right to enter into my personal life."

"I've seen your bare bottom. That should count for something, knowledge of my person since I didn't take advantage of the situation. I could have, given everything I've seen, what I know about you. My doubts about your virtue abound."

"There is that. For the record..."

"For the record," Roc agreed, grinning, abandoning the other topic while waiting with patience he didn't feel. "For the record, I would like an honest answer. Why do you carry condoms."

The ensuing silence told him she was having difficulty with the question. Perhaps it was the honesty part she didn't like. He was surprised when she answered. He thought he was going to have to pursue this from a different angle.

"Safe sex," she said with a calm in her voice he didn't believe she felt. "As a just in case it happens...if I meet the right person. I don't want to contract a disease. There are so many. Don't like doctors...shots..." Her eyes widened as she realized what she told him. "I'm not a..."

"You will like my brother. Everyone does."

"I didn't mean..."

"Let's get back on the topic I wish to know about. I take it you have not yet met the right person. Does that mean you are a virgin?"

He stretched the point, understanding he would be surprised if she answered either his statement or his question.

"What year is it?"

She was back to that. He imagined she had the right to know. Just as he wished to learn what year she traveled from. While he hoped she was a virgin, the fact didn't matter. She would be his. Roc put the box of condoms into her bag. He wasn't up to anymore revelations from her. Given enough time he would get the answers he sought. Her yawn gave him reason to believe she was ready to go to sleep.

He stood by the fire, sipping his wine watching the flames. Without turning around, he asked, "Did you come through the Kinnel Stones?"

If she didn't, she might not know what he spoke of. If she did, how did she get to the place beneath the falls where he found her. He'd never heard of anyone entering this area from another time in this part of the highlands. A vortex, he supposed. Anything was possible. It was the pagan magic of the highlands.

"I don't know anything about Kinnel Stones except an old myth that is not true."

"You should go to sleep. Tomorrow might prove to be hard on you. Don't know if your bottom will be able to take four hours bounced against the back of a horse. We might have to stay another day."

~ * ~

The chattering of her teeth was the sound that woke him. The fire burned as embers with little heat. A shrill wind whistled from outside the entrance to the cave. He heard rain pounding. There was little warmth to be had inside or outside the cave. Even if he put more wood on the fire, it would burn down before dawn.

"Are you cold?"

"What gave you that idea?" she asked with a sardonic hint to her words trying to form the words between the chatters.

That was something he enjoyed about Lainie. She saw humor where no one else would. "Come here." He wondered if she would give over to the practical side of his invitation. "We'll just share the furs coupled with our body heat. Nothing else." Though he wished for far more from her. He could bide his time until the right moment.

The silence coming from her end surprised him. From what he'd seen of her so far, he thought she would push convention to the wind. She struck him as a woman who did what she wished and hang the consequences.

"I'm not going to hurt you. Could have done that several times over by now. Seduction as well as presenting my most charming self to a young lady are not traits that are unpracticed or new to me. You'll be warmer as will I if we share the furs."

Silence still hung heavy in the cavern. He heard each breath. "All right," she murmured, her voice soft, almost husky as if she desired him. "If you promise not to..."

For her benefit, he repeated himself. "I'm too exhausted to try to seduce you. We will share warmth, that is all. We've no need of your box of condoms. I give my solemn vow. Unless of course, I'm the right man. You would have to beg."

She grunted.

He heard the rustling of the furs as she moved from under the covers along with her light footfalls while she made her way to his pallet. He lifted the fur for her to scurry beneath. She backed in, her butt against his heavy arousal. To Roc, it seemed he'd been aroused since the moment he saw her crab walking to get away from Scratch and Geordie.

Her soft sigh of pleasure didn't go unnoticed. She wiggled against him trying to get comfortable. He almost jumped out of his skin when she ran her cold feet along his legs. She tugged on his arm, wrapping it over her waist. He clamped down hard with his jaw to stop the groan from tumbling unwanted from his mouth. Roc didn't want to frighten her. He didn't want to force something she wasn't ready for. God, but he needed her.

"Are you warmer, *lass*?" he asked as his body flamed with the heat of her small lithe form so close to him. If he made it through the night without touching her further, he would feel ready for sainthood. "Though you could keep your cold feet to yourself. Don't much appreciate the ice on my legs."

Lainie answered by nodding her head, one foot still winding in and out between his legs. He allowed his fingers to go limp, hoping that sometime during the night he wouldn't explore exquisite territory. What he did while half-awake, he didn't intend to be accountable for.

He heard the soft sounds of her breathing as it slowed. In his arms, she fell asleep. It was his undoing that with his proffered invitation to this woman, sleep would be a long time coming for him. He was still wide eyed when the first rays of morning began to filter in through the opening of the cave.

What he saw next startled him. He was wide awake, realizing as dawn approached, he must have given up and fallen asleep. With his lids slitted, he watched her. She was just as intriguing this morning as she was last night. Fascinating. Couldn't comprehend what he was seeing.

Lainie was dressed in the what she called her leggings and her jogging bra. The bra pressed her beautiful breasts to near flat. He didn't like that. While he watched her, Roc was more startled by what she did than what she wore. Though he understood in a moment, his attention would find itself riveted on her butt along with the sweet outlandish curve of her wide hips. After that he wouldn't be able to keep his gaze from devouring her breasts. Those breasts of hers would overflow his hands twice. He was hungry. Famished for a taste of Lainie.

Over the cave floor she was stretched out, her arms straight, her hands on the floor while she hovered. He thought the act strange. Wondered if what she did was some religious ritual he'd never heard of before. In slow motion, she lowered herself then pushed herself up. She seemed to be watching what she called her phone.

"Five minutes," she told herself, sounding pleased.

After that she turned onto her back and began to sit up then lay down over then over again. He'd never seen anyone perform morning rituals such as the ones she was doing. He was captivated, absorbed in the give and play of her body.

She looked his way. Her lips pursed. "You're staring. Why?"

Roc didn't understand her question. "Shouldn't I be? I like what I'm watching. If you like, tell me what you've been doing." His words sounded more as a command than a request. She wasn't going to appreciate the tone. He would have to temper his words around her.

The scowl she sent his way reminded him that she would do as she pleased. "Planks, push ups and sit ups."

"Why?" He didn't wish to sound too confounded but he was. Unable to think of one sound reason for her activities, he continued to stare. "Why would you want to do something that makes you groan? Don't deny it. I heard you." He pointed his finger her way, waving it at her to make his point. "I heard the sounds of pain while you were involved in your activities." That groan of hers was different from the ones he'd hear when he made love to her.

"Need to keep all my body parts as thin as possible. Want to stay in shape." Her tone held a bit of smug when she said the words.

There wasn't anything she could do that would keep her body less than curvaceous. As to his way of thinking, her shape was perfect. "Is that what you wear when you are attempting to get smaller." The devil he didn't want her smaller. He liked her the exact way he saw her now. She was perfect.

He had no viable answer or question. Relying on the basics

always served him well. "Breakfast? How is your butt?" He grinned when he heard her gasp either from outrage or mortification, he couldn't be certain. "I'll put the coffee on. Do you need more cream? I'll be happy to apply it to your bottom."

As if to negate the thought the sudden exhalation of air was caused from mortification, Lainie snorted. "I can ride if that's what you are asking. I applied the cream this morning while you were sleeping. There is no need for you to look at me," Dallas spoke in a huff while she scowled at him.

"So you say." He pushed the covers away. While he'd slept in his buckskins, he'd left them unfastened.

Her gaze focused on the opening of his pants then his belly to move higher. Seemed to run the length of his chest back to his unfastened pants as if she wanted to see him naked there. Unwilling for her to see his growing penis, he turned from her. With a few deft moves he slipped his shirt over his head then tucked the tails into his now fastened pants. Nearly undressed he felt as if he was at a disadvantage.

Keeping his back to her, he made the coffee then heated the leftover beans. Plate in hand, he stood at the entrance to the cave staring at the pouring rain. Even though her nicely rounded bottom might be able to sit a horse for four hours, they weren't going anywhere until the rain stopped. Moonstar hated the rain. If forced outside, the big stallion would not be happy.

Chapter Three

Three days later, Lainie in front of him, they rode through the streets of Carnoch. When Roc showed her his home her stomach rolled. The two-story house he pointed to was Rafe's home in a different century. The house looked the same but different. Instead of three floors, Roc's home was two-stories. She didn't like the facts of her possible time travel piling up in front of her. She wanted to be home, in her time, not stranded in an era she didn't understand, one with no conveniences. Damn, this was no longer a possibility. It was a fact. She didn't know what to do. If she were to get home, she would have to go back to the falls. She had no viable means to do so. True, Roc told her he would take her when he had the time.

When would that be?

Yesterday, he told her this was the year seventeen fifty-six. She leapt from the twenty-first century backward to the eighteenth. *Why? Why me? Why not some other poor soul. What did I do wrong to get this sentence?*

No wonder everything was so different. Her life, what it was in the future, was beginning to fade. Everything seemed unreal even to her, the person who lived twenty-one years in a different century. He didn't understand half of what was in her bag. Her camera he marveled over. As she intended, she took close to one hundred photos of him. After she returned, she needed to remember this man who had this uncanny way of forging inroads into her heart. As the days passed, she realized she would have a difficult time leaving him. He was becoming an integral part of her emotional wellbeing. If she didn't know better, she thought she might be falling in love with the man. That box of condoms...she wished to use.

She wanted him to take her back to the falls and she didn't want him to take her back. The confusing emotions blindsided her. Sleeping in his arms those few nights felt like heaven. Having spent the ensuing days describing the last objects in her satchel to him and telling him what they were used for, she fell half in love with him. No, she fell in love with the beautiful man when she first saw him, hands on his narrow hips stopping Scratch from forcing her. His eyes fascinated her. His power thrilled her. He was all male animal. As Rafe would say, he was a man's man, whatever that meant.

And...and there was a spark. More than a spark. Electricity. Lightning.

When he touched her, there were sparks flying. No, there were flames simmering in every cell of her body. Adrenalin coupled with anticipation surged, igniting every nerve she possessed. Every night she slept beside him, warmed her feet on his legs. Roc always told her to keep her cold feet to herself. Nonetheless, he never kept her from heating her feet. There was something so very sensuous about the glide of her feet along his legs. The texture of the soft fur of hair sent her body to quivering. He held her but never touched her in the way a lover would. One time she thought he might kiss her, he tapped her on the chin then turned away from her. She didn't know what to make of that.

"You're taking me to your parents' home? Not yours? What if I tell you that I want to stay with you? Would you listen? I don't want to be beholden to your parents. I would feel like an intruder. I don't know them."

She was pulling at straws, trying to convince him she should stay at his house. He wasn't about to deviate from his plan. She knew him well enough in this short time that while he would listen to her arguments, he would never change his mind once it was made up. It seemed she would go to his parents' home.

He grunted at her last statements of cold hard facts. "Your reputation is more important to me than comfort. I won't compromise you. We are not sleeping together. I won't have my friends along with my family thinking of you as my mistress. If you lodge in my parents' home, you will be respected. In this short time together, I've come to regard you with a great deal of respect." His words stung, bit deep.

"I don't care about my reputation or respect. I care about you," she told him, her words and tone belligerent, hating the way he was deciding her life for her, giving her no viable choices.

Before she left this century, she needed to spend as much time as possible with him. Needed to remember him. He was the man she dreamed about her entire life. Lainie wanted to spend what little time she had in this century with him. "Seems I spent two nights sleeping in your arms," she snorted, her tone waspish.

At that point she quit speaking to him. She stiffened her back so she wouldn't be pressed against his hard body. Around her waist his fingers pushed as if he tried to remind her to behave herself. She wasn't having anything to do with his wishes.

More words would do her no good. His opinion was the only one that seemed to count. He was so damn frustrating she wanted to yell and scream at him. If she did, he would look at her with one curved, sardonic burnished eyebrow. He would stare at her in a condescending manner which would rip holes in her confidence. Lainie didn't think she would ever get her way with this man. He never compromised.

"That speech was verra nice. However, you understand exactly what I was saying. Whether you agree or not makes no difference in how we will proceed." He nudged the horse to a faster pace, seeming eager to get rid of her. "You will stay with my parents. They will take care of you. They will keep your reputation intact."

It appeared he was washing his hands of her. "When are you going to take me to the falls? If I can't stay with you, I need to go to my home."

She was seething. The sooner she was rid of this pompous peacock, the better.

"When I've the time."

His answer wasn't good enough for her. She wanted details so she could plan. "When? I need an answer. Maybe I can hire someone to take me there. If that is the situation, you wouldn't need to be bothered with me."

She would walk if that was the only way. She wasn't going to stay here when the only person she cared about couldn't get rid of her fast enough.

"No!" His hand around her waist tightened.

"No what!" She shouted back as him, furious as well as annoyed with his highhanded pronouncements. "You can't stop me," she said her voice calmer than a second ago. "You can tell me no but you cannot keep me from going."

"You've no coin. You cannot hire someone. I can sure as hell stop you! If I have to, I'll tie you somewhere."

"I can walk."

"You know you can't do that. It's too far." His voice calmed to a more relaxed level.

He was right about that. It would take her days to walk that far. She couldn't ride because she didn't know how and she didn't have a horse.

"Are you going to set me on their doorstep then abandon me?" Her peevish voice was back. Lainie didn't care. Roc should know how she felt.

His chuckle rumbling against her back gave her another reason to be angry. He was patronizing her. "Has definite possibilities. If I leave you on the doorstep, I won't have to put up with your nastiness."

The horse picked up its pace, knocking her back against him. She hated it when he did that. Seemed to punctuate all their arguments.

My nastiness? What about his?

As if he'd slapped her in the face, the words he spoke made a direct hit. "I'm sorry. I'm not used to having my wishes ignored. Thought...well...thought that I could... You said you were a good listener. That fact is false!" Her temper rose.

"You can't. In this situation, you know this one that concerns you, I mean to go on now as I will in the future. You will stay with mother and father. Tomorrow, Mother will take you to the dressmaker so you will have clothing befitting a young woman living in this time. I will attend with you as I know what I would like to see you wearing." He paused for a few seconds before he continued. "I listened. I am a good listener. Never told you I would agree."

She snorted something that seemed to be the only way to tell him how she felt without words. Though she couldn't stop the sentence from flowing. "I'm certain it will be something baggy that extends to my neck or beyond. Perhaps you would like to cover my face so no one will see me. They do that to women in other countries to keep them subservient to their male counterparts."

She was still feeling the sting of his words. He didn't like her leggings. Didn't like her dress or her jogging bra. Even now she wore his shirt belted and over the leggings so she would be covered more thoroughly. Tomorrow, he was going to dress her to suit his tastes...not hers.

"Yes, something like that," he told her with a grin that stole her breath as she pushed back against him, adjusting herself in the saddle.

"What will your parents think of my attire? They will question the fact I wear your shirt. I'll take it off then they can see how I came to be with you."

"I will explain your lack of proper clothing. They will understand then help me with picking out what is necessary for you. Though I don't need mother's help. You might appreciate her company."

"I've no say in anything. Where I spend the night. What clothing I will be allowed to pick out. You're a tyrant, Roc Frasier. A horrible, nauseating dictator."

He jerked, his hand clenching around her middle. When he spoke again, the words were more of the same. "Do you have coin for lodging? You do not have to stay with my parents, though I find that would be the only way you can stay out of trouble."

Stay out of trouble?

She bristled needing to retort to this bit of nonsense. "I resent that."

Lainie was certain he would have an argument for all her wishes. With this fight escalating, she thought extricating herself from his possession a grand idea. She could not do so for the very reasons he pointed out. In this century she needed him.

"We are here. I'm hopeful I don't have to warn you to behave yourself. I don't want my parents embarrassed by your pique with me. You can pretend to like me or not. Just don't do or say anything foolish."

She disliked the fact he thought she would be anything except polite with his parents. She wasn't angry at them. She was furious with him. "No, I will be sweet, syrupy sweet. Sugar will flow from my lips. On my best behavior just as you wish. I will kowtow to your every command. Get on my knees then bow down to you. You will find yourself proud of my subservience."

She was swearing mad, seeing red if the truth were to be told. Her past experiences gave her no clue how to deal with this stubborn arrogant man. He was unmovable.

"You do not have to spout sarcasm with every word you utter. I would like to see you more biddable."

Biddable...he would like... Hah!

She didn't want to argue with him. Hated the battle raging between them. He provoked her with astonishing ease when all she wanted was to live at peace with him. "Only with you when you are acting as if you can dictate the terms of my life. I've never taken orders spouted from any man."

She wasn't about to allow him to think she was good with his decisions. Her independence was important to her. Would not wallow under a man's thumb.

"I will trust your word."

He helped her down. She begrudged the fact that his hands around her waist set a fire bubbling within her blood stream. Hated the fact he could send her emotions into a tumult. No one had the right to affect her in such a manner. As if he also burned, he let her go as soon as her feet touched the ground. Good, he wanted even less to do with her than she wished to have to do with him.

"Jacob, take my horse, see to him, please."

Roc directed his comment to a man that appeared from around the house. His words were harsh. He seemed to take his anger with her out on the hired hands.

When he turned to her, his arm extended, she wasn't certain what he wanted. She didn't wish to touch him again. So affected by his closeness, she couldn't bear to touch him. She burned for him. "Roc?"

"Take my arm, sweetheart. Act as if we are friends. This morning

I thought we were. Now the light of battle shines in your eyes. You cannot have your way, Lainie. In time, you will come to accept my terms as well as understand them. Until then...behave. This world you are now a part of is not what you are used to. It would do you well to trust me. As to your going back to the falls, there would be danger in that."

"Never," she gritted out as she wound her fingers around his arm.

There was little more she could say. She would bide her time while she watched and waited.

A slight flush to her cheeks, she did what he asked. Her body heated with that small contact, her hand on his arm. This morning she had visions of them being more than friends. Once, last night, she eyed the box of condoms with longing thinking he might want to make love to her. He would be her first. When they were in bed together, he presented his back to her. Though when she woke up this morning she was in his arms, his hand cupping one of her breasts. He held her what seemed to her to be possessively.

She longed for that feeling again, that closeness that was so fleeting she now thought it must have been her imagination. Making love to anyone never appealed to her before she met this man. Now, every time she looked at him, she wanted him. She wanted to know how it would feel if she had sex with this man. Before they reached the top of the steps, the door opened.

"Cameron...who do you have with you?"

Lainie stared at him a little puzzled. He never contradicted her when she called him Roc. Of course, she never told him different when he called her Lainie instead of Dallas. He was not Cameron to her. Would never be.

"Mother, this is Lainie Shaw. I met her on the way back from Inverness. Since she was *sans* transportation, I offered to help her out. The rain storm kept us in the cave for two days. Lainie, this is my mother, Heather."

"Nice to meet you," they both said in unison.

"Come in, we've been worried about you, Cam. You've brought home a friend? Welcome, Lainie. I hope you find your stay with us relaxing." Heather linked her arm through hers. "Let's get you more comfortable."

Lainie gave his mother credit for politeness. She didn't stare at her strange attire. She didn't ask why she was brought to this home. Why she wore a man's shirt. Roc's shirt. Though she did make a veiled reference to it. "You don't need to go out of your way for me. I'm perfectly fine."

She shot Roc a scowl as she was marched into the home.

"Has my son treated you right?" Heather looked over her shoulder at Roc. "He's been a gentleman, I trust. Sometimes..." she stopped when she saw the look her son sent her.

Lainie didn't want to see the smile he would slant his mother. She wasn't about to tell him that her son was an autocrat of the worst sort. Her mother had nothing to do with her annoyance with Roc.

"He acted the perfect gentleman."

Yes, too much the gentleman for her taste. She wasn't about to tell his mother as much.

Heather patted her hand as if in disbelief. "That's good to hear. Sometimes, I've problems believing that. He has this wildness about him. Women are—"

"Mother!"

Heather stopped speaking, a wicked grin on her lovely face. "Your Lainie here, is a beautiful woman. I would hope you did not charm her too thoroughly. Come along now, I'm going to look through Harris' clothing to see if there is something we can put you in that will be more presentable than my son's shirt."

Heather was marching her up the stairs to the second floor.

Lainie looked over her shoulder to see Roc frowning at them. "You don't need..."

He didn't charm me at all. Well...until this afternoon his sweettalking was difficult to resist. That was then. Now is now. He was uncharming today.

"Of course, I do. Harris might have a skirt and a blouse you can wear. Oh my, she isn't as tall or as ..."

Heat flamed on her cheeks at Heather's sudden acknowledgement of her great size. Lainie knew what Heather was about to compare. Her breasts were over large. Not many women, even those who opted for boob jobs, had breasts as enormous. Lainie doubted if his little sister did. "I'm fine for tonight. Quite comfortable except when people stare. Your husband won't stare, will he? Roc told me he would take me to the dressmaker tomorrow for a wardrobe. I don't have any money. I wish to pay for the clothing. Can you put me to work here? I can cook as well as clean. Whatever you need done."

She didn't want to find herself owing people money, especially when she didn't plan on sticking around.

"No!" Heather sounded taken aback. Her face flushed with color. "No, to both questions. What has my son...you are not..." It seemed Heather didn't know what to say. "You will not pay us back for anything. You are our guest."

This was not going well, not well at all. "If you're implying I might be his mistress, I am not. He found me in a field of long grass. Two men were attaching me. Simply put, he saved my hide. Now, he feels that he must take care of me. Make all my decisions for me. He's a tyrant! As if I am a small child who needs guidance, he's decided to be the person to give it. I assure you I don't need taking care of. I mean nothing to the man. I will find a job in the village if you can't offer me one. I will pay for everything."

Her hands were fisted at her sides. She struggled for each breath.

"You're angry with him." Heather's laughter warmed her. "You will find that he is most imposing. Just like his father, he will command and demand until you are ready to toss him in a cold loch. It's quite easy to ignore him, at least I've no problem ignoring his father then doing exactly what I wish. You should try my tactics with my son, Lainie. Don't argue. Arguing is a waste of time," she held her by her shoulders, staring into her eyes as if that would convince her. "I see in his eyes as well as yours you are not his mistress. You are much more to him. If he hasn't told you, he should do so soon. You are a fire in his blood."

Lainie's heart warmed with Heather's words. After that she snorted. "Is that so? I shall have to try that. He is insisting I stay here with you and your husband. I wish to stay with him. I know where he lives. Perhaps I will walk there instead of back to the falls where he found me. The distance is not so far."

The shock Lainie saw on Heather's face unnerved her for a few seconds. Perhaps she spoke out of turn. This wasn't the century she was used to. Women were expected to perform in a different way. Were granted no rights whatsoever. Any independence a woman had would have to be fought for.

"You cannot!" Heather looked as well as sounded horrified by her declaration.

"That is what he told me. I would rather be his mistress than his wife. He wouldn't own me. Nevertheless, I'm not going to be here long enough to be either. Not that he has proposed either scenario. He seems eager to be rid of me. One way or the other I plan on going home. Roc can't hold me here if I don't wish to remain."

"You have to stay." Heather led her into a bed chamber but did not elaborate on why she needed to remain. "This is Harris' room. Our girl." She moved to the next chamber, the guest room."

Harris' room was a soft rose color. Everything in it was feminine, frilly and lacy. The rug on the floor was the lightest pink imaginable. Two dolls sat on the bed as if Harris refused to give them up as she aged past the time of playing with dolls.

"An unconventional name. I like it."

More unusual than her first name, Dallas. They stepped into the room where she was expected to spend the night. The room was set with yellows. It was bright as well as cheery. She liked the way the breeze from the open window delicately fluttered the curtains.

"Yes, well..." Heather searched through the armoire, pulling out one item after another. After several minutes of searching, she held up a chemise, a skirt as well as a blouse.

Lainie eyed the articles with apprehension. She didn't want to say anything negative, "They look a *wee* bit small," was her only comment.

Lainie hated being so large. She'd always wished she were petite.

"Try these on." Heather rubbed her face with her hands then gave her a quick perusal. "I hope... Oh dear, we both know they will not fit but they will have to do in a pinch. Your ankles will show. I hope Cameron will not look. I know different though. He is right about needing the dressmaker. First thing in the morning we will make the trip."

Yes, Roc would gaze his fill then berate her for wearing something so revealing. As garments went, Roc would understand this clothing concealed more than revealed if compared to the clothing that came with her.

After looking over the items Heather gave her, the only article of clothing she discarded was Roc's shirt. She chose not to try the chemise. It would not fit over her breasts. The skirt fell to just above her ankles while the shirt strained across her breasts even though she continued to wear the jogging bra that flattened her boobs. The skirt was too tight around the waist along with her rounded belly.

Lainie cocked her head to one side then lifted her shoulders in a feeble attempt to gain some comfort. "I suppose it is just as you thought. Nothing fits. Will this do? Should I stay hidden for the rest of the evening? I could remain in the room where no one will be embarrassed by my lack of clothing."

She wore skirts that didn't reach her knees. If Heather was afraid she'd be embarrassed, she could rest easy. Her string bikini covered very little of her. If this situation could be laughed at, she would.

"These will have to do until tomorrow. You have no other clothes? I only pray there will be something ready-made that will fit you." Heather was wringing her hands seeming very upset that she wasn't able to find anything appropriate for her to wear.

"I'm certain Roc has explained my situation to your husband. What now?"

She wanted to run from here. Heather was such a sweet woman. She was trying so hard, Lainie wanted to hug her. "I've a dress that has had the seam ripped. By your standards it is just as bad as the leggings. Though Roc enjoyed looking at me when I wore the dress."

She thought back on the way his gaze roamed her body. Laine thought she might have said too much.

Heather blushed at her words. "We shall go visit in the parlor. You can meet my husband, Elliott Frasier. He is much like my son, or I should say it the other way around. My son is much like my husband. I will send word that his brother, Hawk, and his wife, Maisie, should come to dinner tomorrow evening. We can hope that the dressmaker will have something already sewn that will fit you," nervously she repeated herself.

"Stubborn?" she blurted before she could stop the word. Lainie covered her mouth. "Oh, my, I promised to behave myself. Roc was afraid, with good reason, that I would stick my foot in my mouth then wouldn't be able to extricate it. I've just done so. Since I've no idea if your husband is stubborn the declaration only applies to Roc. He is infuriating at times. I've only known him for a couple of days. He has this way of pushing my buttons until I can't see straight."

"Pushing your buttons?" Heather asked before waving her hand in the air as if she dismissed the words. "Don't worry. I know exactly who my husband is. Is he stubborn? Yes. Is he arrogant? Of course he is. I still love the man to distraction. As I told you before there are ways to get around our men. I will tell you some of them."

It would be nice to learn a few ways to get around Roc's dictates. Lainie would appreciate all the help she could get. "You don't see him through rose shaded glasses then?" she asked again wishing she could keep her unruly thoughts from becoming words.

Intrigued though by thoughts of finding a means to sidestep Roc's arrogance.

"Rose shaded glasses? No, he is just a man. The man who I love with all my heart. Despite that fact, I do have a few salient thoughts of my own. We do not always agree. He can't have his way in all things." They were half way down the stairs when Heather stopped. She turned to search Lainie's eyes. A significant pause followed. "Do you love my son."

Lainie felt the lump form in her throat, felt the sting of tears rise to her eyes. Her heart squeezed tight with emotions she didn't understand. "I..." How could she love Roc? She'd only known him for a few days. She did though.

"Your eyes tell me all I wish to know on that matter. Just you wait and see. All will turn out the right way. Cameron...Roc, as you call him, will treat you right. The two of you are meant to be together. I can see it in the way he looks at you."

Giving her emotions away was not something she usually did. However, she'd never been in love before. She would be leaving him soon. Maybe not so soon.

How could I live in this century?

How could I not? I want to live wherever Roc lives.

She would be tied to him, to this era. The thought both frightened and intrigued. There were so many luxuries that were lacking. They didn't even have hot and cold running water. There was no electricity. They used chamber pots... The list could go on forever.

If I truly love him, I wouldn't miss those things. Can love do that?

When they stepped into the parlor, Roc eyed her with appreciation then a smug grin. His gaze focused first on her ankles then her bosom. She wasn't prepared for the slow creeping smile that settled on his face. His mind was too easy to read. There was nothing for it. Heat flooded her face. She ran her sweaty palms down the skirt.

"You look fetching."

Lainie didn't know what to think of his words. Were they meant to be a compliment? She didn't know. "Thank you."

She thought to curtsy. That was something she would never do in her time. She wasn't at all certain what to make of his flattery. If it was tongue-in-cheek, she would get even at another time.

"Would you like a glass of sherry?" he asked as he stepped to the sideboard. "Brandy?" He added as if he read her mind holding up the decanter. "It will warm you inside as well as out. He looked downward. "Don't know about your feet though."

Elliott hooted his laughter. Heather turned a deep shade of rose. "Cameron Petroc Frasier, what are you thinking?"

Lainie didn't care what he was thinking. She wanted what he was having. She nodded, unable to form a coherent word as he continued to look at her his eyes shimmering with heat. Her body reacted to the slow and constant perusal. Her breasts seemed to swell, an ache between her thighs was unwelcome. If she could tell him to stop looking at her without drawing attention to herself, she would.

After Lainie found a chair to sit on, he stood behind her, his hands resting on the back of the chair. The conversation revolved around his brother and sister. Upon occasion, she would feel the brush of his thumb across the back of her neck. She squirmed. With purpose, she thought he was seducing her. It would not take much. To what purpose was he making her uncomfortable in front of his parents. She could strive to guess. Dismissed that notion as too much work.

The night was going to be one of the longest of her life. Dinner followed the drinks and conversation. She was now standing with him in front of the fireplace. Her parents seemed to watch them as if in expectation. What they might expect went beyond the realm of possibilities her befuddled mind could summon.

"You will understand," he was addressing his mother, "if I would like to stay in my old room tonight. I feel Lainie has undergone more trauma than anyone need endure. First thing tomorrow, we can go to the dressmaker. When she has something appropriate to wear, I'll show her around town. Since she expressed an interest in working, she can work for me. That will keep her safe."

"You can stay here anytime you wish for as long as you wish," Elliott told his son. "I understand you prefer to keep her close. We all *ken* why."

Relief washed through her, overwhelming her. He read her mind. She understood he could not stay at his parents' home every night. Tonight...though he would be here with her. She could take heart in that fact. A heavy weight lifted off her shoulders. He wasn't abandoning her.

Thank you...

His parents retired leaving them sitting in the wing chairs in the parlor staring at the fire. Flames leapt. Strange tension hovered between them. He cleared his throat. She sighed wondering when he was going to speak.

"I'm sorry if I hurt you."

His tone was curt. He cleared his throat again. Now it seemed he waited for her to reply.

"You didn't hurt me, Roc. You devastated me," she blurted before she could find a means to curb her tongue. "I thought you couldn't get rid of me fast enough. I know I've made things hard for you. If not for me, you would have been home days ago. If not for me, you wouldn't have to spend your money on clothing I don't want or need."

He arched a brow the curve mocking. Did he mock her or himself?

"I didn't understand until I was ready to leave you here what I was doing. You don't know my parents. This was unconscionable. It's the least I could do. Nothing you've done has made my life more difficult."

"Autocratic, Roc Frasier. That's what you are."

She thought of a long list of words that would describe his behavior. As his mother told her, he wouldn't vary over his lifetime. This was who he was. At least he apologized.

"Tyrannical," he suggested, as he leaned over to smooth his knuckles down her cheek. "I would see you happy, Lainie. Don't like to know my actions have distressed you in any way. You must tell me when things are not right for you. Leaving me guessing and groping is not the way to go on together."

Go on together?

"Thought I did tell you how I felt. Wasn't that why we were arguing this afternoon? Never mind, what is done is done. I don't wish to take any steps backward. I do want to see if you will become part of my life. Wish to do this the right way."

He set his hand on the arm of her chair. His gaze bore into her as if searching her for some sign she was in agreement with him about everything. "I'll stay the night. We will see what happens after that...tomorrow. I'm not going to make a commitment. My room is next to yours." He seemed to be issuing an invitation. "If you need me..."

That was good enough for her. She smiled feeling relief at his admission wondering if that was a request for her to come to him or just a simple statement of fact that she should ignore unless there was an emergency of some sort. She would be devastated if she misread his statement. Sleeping with him was comfort to her. Except for the time she woke to find him cradling her breast in his hand, running his thumb across her nipple that was all they did, sleep.

If he would make her a priority, she would remain in this century.

She didn't believe he would make any woman feel first in his life. What she told his mother was true. If the only way she could hold onto him was to become his mistress, she would. She never cared about marriage in the sense other young women pursued the institution. Being owned by a man was not a pleasant thought. In this century it was truer than in her own. With a marriage to him, he would own her. Previous to this moment the only male she ever cared about was Rafe. They were not suited. There was no spark. At that time, she had no idea that a spark could become lightning.

Until now, she had no one else, never cared for another man.

"What did you think of my parents?" he asked as if expecting her to gush her praises. "If you haven't noticed, they are astute. They have acknowledged the fact you are not from this time period and are willing to welcome you to the family. I can tell you stories of other people who have come to us from different times. Could tell you about people we've sent to other centuries. Those stories are for a later date. To the clan's knowledge no one has entered our domain where you did."

The clan's knowledge? Lainie supposed if Heather had not asked if she loved her son, she would not be quite so welcoming. "Your mother is warm and sweet. Your father is something else entirely. He stared at me as if he thought I would flee with the silver. I didn't know what to make of him. Where I'm concerned, it's obvious he has reservations."

"It was your costume he stared at. He has no reservations or concerns about you except that you might not want to stay where you are. My father knows how important you are to me. In you, I've found something I've been looking for."

Unable to understand what he was telling her, she scowled at him, her tone annoyed. "It's not a costume. In the time where I've come from, what I had on when you met me was common attire. The leggings which you wished to cover with your baggy shirt was something all women wear. My clothing was nothing out of the ordinary."

Roc set his glass on the table between them. His smile gave her reason to falter in her disputes with him. Making her point over then over again was useless. "I will not continue that argument. We both understand what I believe. I've been honest with you. Do you think you might like to work for me. Your days would be less boring."

She fumbled with the fabric of her skirt for a few minutes. "I don't have an answer for that as yet. What would my duties be. I don't know how to set type. I'm not sure..."

She did want to spend every day with him. There might be few of them left to her.

"Would you be angry with me if I said your duties would be to look pretty behind the counter?" He held up his hands, grinning with unabashed delight. "No, don't answer. I believe you might be able to create advertisements or write out little sayings that people might enjoy. You can put together the copy before it is printed. You can design handbills that would be distributed."

"I'll have to think about it. I wouldn't do the first part you mentioned. Look pretty behind the counter. Would not like that. I'm not artistic except with my photo shoots. You've no use for those. Though if it would not get me into too much trouble, I could fashion a box camera. It was all the trend at schools about forty years ago. If you gave me a room to use that could be made completely dark, I could develop the pictures."

His bark of laughter left her discomfited. He was tapping his fingers on the crystal glass. "All that?"

"Yes," she stiffened as she watched him digest what she told him.

"We should retire for the night. I don't want you to work tomorrow though we can stop by my shop so you can look over the trappings. Don't think we should test the climate of the times with your cameras. They burn witches."

~ * ~

Roc wondered if she would sleep well. He, for one, would miss holding her in his arms throughout the night. He should have invited her to his room. If he tiptoed down the hall, he could join her in her bed.

When he woke this morning, his hand cupping one breast, he almost gave into his first impulse which was to make love to her. His heavy arousal ached. It was all he could do to get out of bed then cover her with the blankets. Even though he pretended differently, he knew she was awake. The devil bartered with his soul. From the first sight of her, he wanted to make love to her. Knew she was his mate. It was hard for him to resist her seductive charms. In time...in time she would realize she was meant to be with him. It was his experience the portals worked both for people as well as against them. This time the vortex brought his woman to him. He understood in this instance the minutes he had with her were important, he better not mess these few moments up. If he did, his life would end.

His next thought while staring at her well-shaped body was that he needed to give her some information. She was his mate. If his guess was correct, she wouldn't understand how all that worked. Lainie would never believe in shifters unless he showed her his cat.

Lainie was everything he'd ever dreamed of. Nevertheless, he couldn't show her his cat or bring up his notion that they were to be lovers through eternity. Just the concept of traveling through time was a lot for her to deal with. While his family understood the workings of the Kinnel Stones, she had no comprehension of the concept. Would not understand how easy it was to be sent to another world far different form the one they knew.

Sitting on the edge of his bed, he wondered when he decided to stay the night in his old room. He pulled off his clothes leaving them littered on the floor. Sighing, his breath heaving, he stood to rearrange the clothing he would have to wear again tomorrow on the wing chair by the fire. He stretched before rubbing the tense muscles on the back of his neck.

Naked, thinking about how sweet his life would be to have Lanie curled close beside him, he closed his eyes. He was dreaming. Running through the heather scented hills in his cat form. She watched from afar, her hands clasped tight beneath her chin. He was showing off for her. Soon, he would have to tell her things about how their lives would be intertwined. In private, he would show her his cat. So as not to terrify her, he would have to explain a few things. His Lainie would come around. She would be his.

"You sleep like the dead," her whispered words, jerked him

awake.

That fact surprised him. He'd always been a light sleeper. At first it was to keep his older brother and cousins from playing practical jokes at his expense. After that, his light sleeping was honed from outings where one had to watch his back. When his gaze fixed on her, he smiled, wishing to hold her in his arms. He didn't understand what she was doing in his room then he realized what she wanted. At first his thinking was hazy. Now, everything was clear.

Lainie sat on the side of the bed, smoothing his hair from his forehead. Her smile appeared both hesitant as well as wistful. She must not be certain that he would accept her in his bed. She was bold though coming here. He would give her credit for that. Lainie didn't fit the mold he was used to. She was so unique.

Her hair picked up the shimmering colors from what was left of the fire. The strands seemed to blaze. Reaching out he needed to test the fire. Feel the silk. She was dressed in his sister's nightgown that came to mid-calf on her. Because the nightwear was voluminous there was more than enough room for her plentiful breasts and hips and backside. Very little of her curves were revealed. He remembered what she looked like though. Recalled rubbing the salve into her rump, the way her flesh quivered with each stroke. How soft her cheeks were, how round and full. His fingers quivered for another taste of her.

"I'm naked, Lainie," he blurted out, the gruffness of his voice couldn't be disguised.

He wanted her with a necessity he never felt with another woman. If he asked her what she was doing here, she would be embarrassed. If he thought about what was said earlier in the evening, he wasn't surprised to see her. She'd wanted him to stay in his parent's home.

"I..." She ran her sweet pink tongue along her bottom lip. Her hesitation was adorable. "I...didn't know. You didn't sleep naked while we were in the cave." She sucked in a long deep breath. "I didn't know if you would want me in your bed. I missed you." She looked at the floor then back to him, a mischievous smile on her lips. "My feet are cold."

That came as no surprise. Her feet and hands were always too cold. At the cave he wore clothing, his pants unfastened when he slept though doing so was damn uncomfortable. "Now you know. What should we do about that little fact?"

"Do you want me to leave?" Her toes wiggled on the soft rug leaving an imprint where they moved.

Her hesitation unnerved him. In this she should always understand she could do as she pleased. He would never gainsay her especially when it meant sleeping with her cuddled in his arms. "No. Is the rest of you cold?" He lifted the sheets and quilts just far enough for her to scoot beneath the covers without seeing him. He didn't want to shock her. When he heard her voice, in that instant he found himself aroused. Rock hard. He didn't know if she'd ever seen a naked man, let alone one whose member was at full attention.

She faced him, her mint scented breath coupled with gardenia wafting across his chest. She set her face in the hollow of his shoulder. Her breasts pushed against him. As per her norm, she ran her cold feet along his legs, warming them at his expense. Her hands were also cold, fingers like icy talons sliding across his chest. He didn't mind. His body would warm hers.

"In the future, I'm going to insist you wear socks. Maybe even gloves when you come to my bed. Are you always this cold?"

He didn't shiver with the touch of her icy feet. The vibrations occurred because of the heat that her touch generated. He set his hand on the curve of her hip. Beneath the gown that part of her was warmer.

"I do have one pair of socks," she murmured stroking his chest, playing with the hair. "In fact, as you recall, I don't own much of anything. Most of the time I would have to wear some of yours. From what I've seen your mother wearing, those stockings wouldn't protect you from my cold feet.

"The ones that tell you which foot they are to go on?" he asked remembering taking the unique socks off her feet. She told them they were each made to accommodate the arch of one's foot, the left versus the right. Still, he rationalized why would anyone want to be told which foot the sock should be put on?

Except with her feet, Lainie never touched him before. This time was different. She appeared to be asserting herself in the best of ways.

All they ever did was sleep...except for this morning when he woke with her breast cradled in his hand.

"You can wear mine any time you wish." In truth, even if her hands and feet were frigid, he'd rather have her bare flesh caressing him than material. When her appendages finally warmed, she continued the provocative movements across his chest, venturing lower with each brazen stroke. The sensations unreal to his feeble man's brain.

"All right," she purred her acceptance.

Before they fell asleep for the night, he needed to issue an apology. "Lainie, I'm sorry you were angry today. That I was the cause of the annoyance along with the friction between us. You have to understand, I've got your best interest at heart." He did. Soon, if he had his way, she would live with him as his wife. She would agree to marry him in the way of the clan. Before that could happen, he would have to find a means to convince her to stay in this century. If he could get her pregnant with his child, that would be an underhanded way to achieve his goal. Knowing his Lainie, a pregnancy would never keep her from leaving if that was what she wished to do. He would need to follow her if possible. He would never allow a child of his own to be raised as a bastard or without a father.

"When you decided to stay the night, you were forgiven all the transgression you committed." She pushed up higher, so she rose above him. Her lips were touched with moisture. She caught the bottom one beneath her teeth as she seemed to think about how she would reply. "I didn't like being angry or annoyed or frustrated that you weren't listening to me. You didn't consider anything I said as valid or reasonable. Everything I offered, you declined. Your mother gave me helpful advice."

She set her head back on his chest. Her fingers continuing to roam across his body.

His curiosity peaked. Mothers weren't supposed to give out information about their sons. "What was that advice?"

He couldn't help the overflowing of interest. Advice from his mother to Lainie might not bode well for him. His mother knew him better than anyone. She would give her little tricks to keep him in line.

Off hand, Roc couldn't think of one that would sway him from a decision once it was made.

"That's not to be shared. Your mother would not be pleased. If I did tell you, then, the ploy would no longer work. You would build up your defenses so you could counter attack. No, you can never be told. Besides, I promised your mother. Promises must be kept." She set her lips, teeth then her tongue to his shoulder then his collar bone. She bit lightly. Her small teeth sent a spasm of lust to his groin.

He sucked air, holding as still as possible, waiting for his reaction to ebb. She was seducing him. Ah, hell, as difficult as abstaining would be, he needed to keep to his plan. "A man needs to know a woman's secrets. If you are not careful, I will uncover them."

"Not these secrets." She stopped the play of her mouth across him. "I'll never reveal them to you."

The deep breath of air he inhaled burned in his lungs when she set her hand on his belly. The skin retracted at the contact. His sex leapt again. Harder than before if that was at all possible. He swallowed hard, pushing back the need to ease himself within her warmth. He could not do so and keep his convictions as a man. Sometimes plans needed to be reevaluated...new ones formed.

"Stop, Lainie, it's time to go to sleep." His grasp on her fingers gave him momentary relief. He pulled her hand to his chest. "Keep your fingers here. No more exploring."

"All right."

In his passion dazed mind, she gave in too easily. Nonetheless, the flutter of her lashes on his skin tantalized to a point where he wanted her with quiet desperation. He closed his eyes, wishing he was sleeping. Praying she would sleep so the exquisite torture would cease. This wasn't the case. She wanted more than he could be able to give today. The devil take him, they were in his parent's home.

"I want you to make love to me," she whispered the words, the scent of mint wafting across him. "I won't get pregnant. We don't have to worry about that. Would it be so hard for you to do so? You are the only man I would give my innocence to."

His body jerked with the knowledge she could be his at this very moment. All he had to do was kiss her, charm her, touch her where he knew she would writhe with pleasure. She was willing. Begging. There was nothing wrong in that. Nothing wrong though it was not the way he intended to continue with her. If at all possible, he would stick to his plans.

"Not tonight. Not in my parent's home. Goodnight, Lainie." There was something sacrilegious about making love to a woman, even the woman who was his mate while lying in his boyhood bed in his parent's house.

Once more she pushed away from him, her eyes questioning. "You mean that. Don't you?"

With her words that were laced with pain of rejection, he almost changed his mind. He didn't want to hurt her for any reasons. There was no way he could explain to her his feelings. He didn't believe she would understand. "Yes, but not for the reasons you are thinking." He took her hand, moved it down until she closed her fingers around his erection. "Don't ever doubt that I want you, Lainie. Not here. The time isn't right." He wished to be married to her when they made love for the first time. He needed the celebration along with the claiming. He removed her fingers, setting her small hand on his chest. "Go to sleep."

"Is that your final word?" she asked though she didn't sound as disappointed as he thought she would be. Lainie sounded relieved. Even though she asked, she was uncertain, a true innocent who needed to be taken care of, not taken advantage of.

The answer didn't come to him. In time he felt her relax against him. It was just as it was the first night together. Sleep eluded him. Her breaths were soft, fluttering across his chest continuing to keep him in a state of arousal that he couldn't deny. Her heart beat steady against him.

During the long hours of the night, he knew he slept. When he woke, it was too a strident pounding on his door.

"Cameron! Cameron! Get up! Lanie is gone. You must find her."

His mother was at the door yelling and pounding to get his attention. Guilt should not swamp him. He was a grown man. Heat shouldn't rush to his face either. His mother and father must have guessed by looking at his besotted features, Lainie was his mate. There should be no surprise in that fact. He snuggled her in close, making certain she was covered in case his mother barged into the room to see for herself that she was safe as well as tucked into his bed.

"Lainie is with me," Roc called out hoping no one would push into the room.

While she wore the nightgown, sometime during the night he managed to pull it up to her waist. When the yelling woke him, he'd once more embraced her breast, his finger enjoying the satin finish of her skin. "We'll come down to breakfast if we're invited."

Roc had the horrible thought everything changed. His mother could be angry with him, for daring to sleep with her within the confines of her home. His father would lift an eyebrow then tell him he knew what he was doing. He should continue in the way he started.

"Oh, thank God," Heather said in a voice that surprised him.

It was evident she was relieved. "I was so worried. I understand she needed to speak to you about some things. Last night she was very upset about you taking over so much control. She is more independent than most females. I'll let the two of you talk. It's a good thing for the two of you to make up. Arguments between two people who love each other are never good."

Roc was stymied. Lainie moaned, her soft breath whispering across his chest then stretched pushing against him. He heard her murmured moan. "You awake?" He didn't see how she could still be sleeping after his mother's early morning call to attention. Touching her chin, he lifted her face. Beautiful blue eyes, stared back at him.

"I think so. Was that your mother? Is she angry that I'm here? Are you angry? I have no regrets. Wouldn't have been able to sleep if left alone." Her hands held the front of her gown. His fingers stilled curled around her breast. With regret, he dropped his hand from the rounded globe, smoothing his fingers along her hip as he pulled the fabric back to its place.

"No, Mother believes we are talking about the things we argued about yesterday. What did you tell her about us?"

Their conversations should be private. What they disagreed about between just the two of them.

Lainie's hair had fallen free from her braid. The long silken strands pooled around him, caressing those parts he kept from her last night. They were so soft, so cool. He picked up a strand brought it to his cheek. Rubbed... Silk.

"Everything I told you. Nothing more, nothing less. She asked me if I was in love with you. I couldn't answer."

"I see. Are you?" he purred, wishing he dared kiss her knowing he didn't see anything at all.

What he did understand was if he kissed her, they wouldn't be down for breakfast. It might be something she would regret. He needed to give her more choices. "We've got to dress. Can you get back to your room on your own?"

The moment the words left his mouth he didn't have to see the purse of her lips...the drawing together of her brows to understand she didn't like what he said...how he said the words. Laughing without making a sound, he touched the small crease in the middle of her forehead.

"I'm certain I can find my way."

She stepped from the covers, smoothing her shirt down the front of her. The hard pebbled tips of her breast pushed against the fabric. He stifled a low groan. Seemed everything she did aroused him. If they weren't married in the next day or two, he would never be able to keep his hands to himself despite his plans. "The room is the door next to yours."

She was angry with him again. He fell back on the bed, covering his eyes with his arm. Just from that small contact he responded.

"Good, I will meet you downstairs."

She stood at the closed door, staring at him. "No, I'll wait in the hallway for you. We can go down together. A united front in case they want to kick me out would be helpful to me. Although I would willingly go to your home if asked. You know I don't wish to remain here."

He shouted his laughter, pleased with her spunk in the face of the ensuing confrontation. He was afraid things would move along at a rapid pace now that they were discovered in bed together. On second consideration, his mother didn't open the door to see them cuddled next to each other. It would be inferred though. "You think you can dress faster?"

She scowled at him again.

"Wait for me. I won't take long."

Her back stiff, she exited his room. Today...today he would tell her, maybe show her some important things about himself. He guessed that something went wrong with their union the first time they met. He assumed that was now or in their future. He wasn't certain. She had to come back in time to set things right. Lainie didn't understand. If not for her relationship with him, she would have gone to a different time.

While he was terrified she would find the portal she tumbled through then return, he didn't believe it would work that way. With this situation firm in his mind, he hoped he could convince her not to try. If she did, anything could happen to change what was supposed to be. With a huge sigh, he knew first hand he would have to do better with his words. If not, she'd be asking him for safe passage to the portal that brought her to him. He didn't want that.

Roc didn't want to risk getting her pregnant before they smoothed out their difference or before they were married. Even though she told him it was impossible for her to conceive, he didn't trust her words. It seemed to him, however small, there would always be some chance. He would have to ask Hawk if he thought there might be truth in the information, she gave him. Houston too, the two doctors who were part of the Clan Chattan. Two men he could trust.

He stood beside her door, dressed, his arms crossed in front of him, waiting. His pose was nonchalant. Her humming was endearing. She carried a good tune. The song he didn't recognize. There would be so many things she didn't understand about this time but so much she knew that he would never comprehend. She spoke of transports that carried passengers in the sky. The thought terrified him. He'd rather take his chances with his feet planted on the ground.

Birth control, cameras, phones...to name only a few. She would be giving up luxuries she was used to for a life that would seem hard to her. Placed in the same circumstances, he didn't know if he would be able to do what he was asking of her. This man, Rafe, she spoke of. He might be waiting for his mate too. If Laine returned, neither his or Rafe's life would be fulfilled.

How can I ask her to give up a life of such ease? Hot and cold running water?

How can I not? Lainie is my mate. For the two of us there is no choice.

She stepped from the room she'd been given, a startled look on her precious features. "Oh! You beat me. I didn't think you would." She tossed him what could only be described as a flirty wink. Her smile ravished him.

Roc tapped her chin with a finger. "It has been my experience that men dress with more speed than women." Unable to resist, while thinking about having her once more in his bed, he touched the hair she pulled back from her head. "For one thing, I don't have to fix my hair. Nor do I have as many items to put on my body."

"You could run a comb through it from time to time," she tossed out to him with a hint of laughter. "If you let me dress in my leggings and sports bra, I would have been out here in half the time. Instead, I had to force buttons that didn't wish to fasten to do so." He looked at the gaping holes between the buttons.

Her laughter today was much more welcome than her sarcasm of yesterday. The day would have to proceed better. "I do like what I see between the...gaping holes." He held out his arm for her to take. "I shall walk you to breakfast. I hope you are hungry. Mother will expect you to eat a little bit of everything. She will be displeased if you don't do the meal justice. I would like you to eat too. Want you to keep all your delightful curves just as they are."

She punched him hard on the arm. He winced, faking the proffered pain. "What about what I want? I don't want to be fat."

"You are far from fat. I would say curvaceous. Just the way I like a woman. You need to please your man. You could never become fat. I just like it when a woman's body moves the way it is supposed to move. I want to know I'm making love to my woman, when I touch her breasts, her hips, her delicious buttocks. Don't want to have to hunt around in the dark to find the desired curves."

"You're not my..." She stopped herself at the look of his ardent disapproval. At least that was why he thought she stopped midsentence.

"Honey, you spent the night in my bed. Several nights lying next to me, sharing the heat of your delicious body. Rubbing your cold feet on my legs. I would say I've some measure of claim to you. The truth is simple. I'm yours. You are mine. There is no in between."

When she didn't respond he wasn't surprised. Despite his dislike of her need to make herself smaller, he understood her intentions. He did look forward to the challenges she presented him with. Even more he looked forward to winning. When they stepped inside the dining room, Harris as well as Hawk and Maisie were seated for breakfast.

He groaned. The inquisition would begin. He would need all his wits as well as determination to put a stop to the questions. Inquiries she wasn't ready for.

More perusal, more explanations waited for him in the disguise of breakfast with the family. He wondered when Harris had returned. It was early...no, he looked to the clock sitting on the shelf. The time was nearer to lunch than breakfast. Mother found ample time to send out invitations to meet Lainie. Everyone was present and accounted for. Roc groaned. Had never expected the entire family. He needed private time with his woman. Knew that he wasn't going to get those precious moments anytime soon.

After seating her, he made the required introductions. The silence in the dining room didn't last long. With the sudden eruption of chatter, questions were bombarded in Lainie's direction from both siblings. Her fork dropped to the floor. When her face turned ashen, he understood she would not be able to bluster her way through his rowdy but loving family. She needed immediate help from him.

Roc held up his hands in warning. His mother picked up Lainie's fork then brought her a new one. Lainie's lips were sucked together. If he guessed right, she was ready to bolt. The time for them to get on with their day was not upon them yet. They both needed to eat. They had to speak even a little bit to the clan.

"To my well-meaning family, Lainie does not need to answer any questions at the dining table. She is tired from the trip here. Exhausted by all that has happened to her over the last few days, confused as well. As you will all come to understand, while she didn't travel through the Kinnel Stones, she did voyage through time. She has told me she was born in the twenty-first century. Now, as all of you comprehend, time travel is not a universal topic, not one that can be explained with a few well-placed questions. While I have queries for my brother as well as Houston, Houston is the only one outside of the Frasiers who will learn about her travels. I'm certain Lainie will be more than willing to answer some of your inquiries at a later date even though your curiosity is not surprising. Is also expected. Please desist. For Lainie's sake."

Roc sat down pleased with his speech. He meant to protect her. During the days they spent waiting for the rain to cease, he explained about the Kinnel Stones, the family history with them. She hoped Lainie would begin to relax. She was a novelty only because she came to them from the future.

After a few seconds of silence, the chatter picked up again. The ensuing conversation turned out to be inconsequential. Nothing important but the attention of his family members was no longer centered on Lainie. Even as that was the case, she picked at her food. He needed for her to eat. When he nudged her, she sent him a scowl he was becoming quite used to seeing.

He grinned back at her, challenging. Testing her mettle.

Her eyebrows drew together forming that little crease in the middle of her forehead he was coming to adore. Roc wished he could stroke the line.

"Eat," he told her using her fork to put a bite of egg into her mouth.

With everyone staring at her, he realized she wouldn't refuse. He wouldn't mind feeding her the entire plate.

As if she guessed his intentions, she grabbed the fork. "I can feed myself."

"See that you do."

"You wished to speak with me as well as Houston. Can I ask what it concerns?" Hawk watched him as if he could render a possible stab at what was on his mind.

"Later, I'll drop by your office this afternoon after I've taken care of a few errands I need to run." He squeezed Lainie's hand, the one he took within his when he commanded her to eat. Roc knew why she scowled. It was the command in his voice. His woman didn't like being ordered as to what she should do. He imagined it had much to do with the fact he wanted her to eat and she didn't. Eating, he decided, might become a problem for them in their future. He would just have to tempt her with her favorite foods. First, he needed to learn what they were.

"Very well," Hawk said looking curious. He said nothing more on the topic.

"Mother, I'll take Lainie to the dressmakers. You needn't come." He thought the request would be appreciated. He would like to oversee her clothing. Didn't want too much of her beautiful assets to show.

"Nonsense." She pointed her spoon she'd been using to stir her tea with at him. "I promised Lainie I would go with you. She expressed an interest in having clothing that doesn't reach to her chin. Lainie told me she feels claustrophobic in clothing such as that. Since I happen to agree with her, I accepted those terms. Feel free to cry off if that is what you would wish. We are not in need of a man's opinion."

This time Roc scowled. "I will..."

Heather shook her head as if that would do any good. "You will not. Heed your mother in this. Lainie and I will attend to her clothing. Not you. You can walk with your brother to his office. That will give you time to ask the questions that seem to be on your mind."

His mother did more than give her a few pointers as to how to handle him. She took over. "Very well, I'll go to my shop. Bring her there when the two of you are finished." Roc understood he conceded them the win too soon. The look from his father confirmed that notion. He would have to learn how to not backdown when confronted with his woman. The learning might take time. Roc decided the time spent would be enjoyable.

~ * ~

"So, what was it you wished to speak with me about?" Hawk

asked as he walked with him to his office.

Roc felt some discomfort. He ran a finger around the collar of his shirt. This was Lainie's story to tell. Yet, she believed in the birth control she showed him. Expected the little pills to work. He needed to make certain something such as this was possible even though he was convinced that in time man would come up with some way to prevent conception. The devil, with time anything could be invented. Roc didn't like the fact a woman could make decisions that should be shared with her husband without a conversation. She wasn't his wife yet. Soon though.

"This is private, between you and me," Roc began. "No one else is to learn about this conversation."

"Lainie too, I presume."

"Yes." Lainie wasn't here to explain or to defend her actions. What was the world like in her time that sex would have no consequences. He supposed he didn't like that notion either. Women would sleep with men whenever they wished. While he took precautions with his mistress, he never did with the prostitutes he slept with. Prostitutes took the safeguards. Their livelihood was at stake. He hadn't slept with a prostitute for several years now. Once he took Katy as his mistress, she was his only lover. He needed to make a trip to Inverness to dismiss her. He would have to give her a nice settlement. All these years Katy listened to his problems. Comforted him when he moaned about not finding his mate. Now that he found the woman, Katy would have to be let go. Finding her a new protector should be among the first priorities on his agenda. He could never leave her to fend for herself, to go back to a brothel. He cared about her. Always had. Over the years, she'd been a good friend.

"Then..." Hawk seemed to wait with seeming patience for his thoughts to turn to words. "What is it? I won't judge."

"There you are wrong. Judging is part of the package." Roc handed him the container of pills he took from her bag, handing the object to his brother. "This. What do you think?" Roc found himself holding his breath while he waited for a comment.

Hawk turned the object he presented him with over in his hands before opening it. "I don't know what this is. I can't say anything." He continued to examine until he gave the container back to him.

Roc understood the time for a complete unveiling was at hand. "Lainie calls them birth control pills. There are thirty of them. One for each day of the month." If he didn't feel the situation to be grave, he would have laughed at the expression on his brother's face. "She takes these and..." One eyebrow lifted, making a perfect arch.

"What do you think?" Hawk shot his question back to him.

"Can they be for real. I watched her take one every morning we stayed in the cave. I would assume she took one this morning. Those little white things keep her from getting pregnant if or when she has sex. She tells me that is not the reason why she has them. I don't believe she has been with a man in the biblical sense. She had a good friend...male friend. She also implied they weren't meant for each other. Told me there was no spark. Though she didn't apprise me with the details of their relationship. Given some time as well as more trust, she might tell me." Roc put a stop to his speech when he saw his brother wanted to ask more questions.

"A pill..." he spoke with grave caution, his voice filled with both awe as well as question. "Can keep a woman from conceiving? It's hard to believe. I wish I could recreate this pill. It's deucedly hard on a woman to have a baby every year until they die in childbirth or from exhaustion. I've delivered Mrs. McCormick's tenth baby. If she had something like this, her life might not be in jeopardy with each new child. She is nearing thirty-five, it is time for her husband to take heed. I've given them..." Hawk stopped not wishing to rant to his brother. "I wonder how this works?"

"Lainie tells me she's been taking them since she turned sixteen. They regulate her monthly flows. She says they are so heavy at times and because of the severity of the cramps, she has to stay in bed for the first two days. The pills make her life much easier."

"Some women who have come to me have that same problem. It would be nice to give them something that would stop their pain. All I can give these women is a special tea that eases the pain not the symptoms. Lainie is fortunate to have something that helps control her cycles. However, if she stays here, she will use these up in what appears to be less than a month."

"Two months, she has another month's worth of pills. Do you think these will keep her from conceiving?"

"Do you have any reason to doubt her?" Hawk sounded incredulous as well as surprised by his question.

"It's just that...no. Some of what she's told me is so incredible I don't believe..." He did believe. That was the crux of the problem. "I have to trust in what she tells me. As far as I know, she has never lied to me. I don't see a reason she would fabricate stories...a tale such as this one."

"I take it Lainie Shaw is your mate. One can always tell by the way one of us looks at our woman. Your eyes tell me, she is everything to you. Does she *ken* who she is? You must tell her. I'm guessing she is already looking for a way to return to her time."

"You know? How did I give myself away?"

"It's easy to read. Mother and Father knew the moment you brought her into the house. That was why the invitation for breakfast was sent out last night. In truth it was more along the lines of a command. Though I must say even though Mother likes her, she didn't like the fact you took her to your bed, in her house."

"In my defense, I didn't intend to. Knew mother would not be pleased to find her in my bed. Last night she was afraid. Because of that Lainie came to my room. I should have expected that to happen. Should have gotten her out before Mother became alarmed. Problem was, I had a devil of a time going to sleep. When I finally did, it was too late to spirit her back to her room."

"You couldn't turn her away."

Roc found he was shaking his head at that notion. Amazed at the idea. "I couldn't turn her away," he admitted thinking perhaps he should do as she wished and bring her home, to his house.

Privacy to sort out their relationship was needed. He could not take her back to the portal. She needed to make the decision to stay with him.

"If it's any consolation, I would have never been able to turn

Maisie away. She is everything to me."

"What would you think if Lainie lived with me? I don't want to tarnish her reputation. She tells me she doesn't care. In her time, if two people care about each other, they often live together. I know that sounds strange also. She insists it is true."

"I take it, she sees you as being too stubborn to deal with."

"Old-fashioned is the word she uses. Which by her standards, I am. She doesn't understand how people will talk about her. Label her."

"Have you asked for her hand?"

"No, as you assumed, she wants to find the portal. Go back. I'm not taking her until I convince her she wants me more than she wants all the comforts of her other life."

"So many?" Hawk asked.

"More than a million."

~ * ~

"They are floundering," Elliott said to his wife who was drying the breakfast dishes. "Cameron doesn't know if he's coming or going. Lainie is pushing him willy-nilly in too many directions for him to have one rational thought in his head. Though I don't believe she is doing it on purpose. She also appears confused. One minute she wants Roc to take her back to the falls. The next she doesn't."

Harris was listening to her father expound on her brother's ineptness. "He wants to give her the world. Seems she's held more than Roc could ever give her in the palms of her hands. There is no reason she would wish to give all that up. I wouldn't. What would you do if you were transported to a place where everything is done for you?" As she was drying dishes, she looked a bit perplexed. "They even have machines that wash then dry dishes. Can you imagine that? I would go back to that time if I had the choice."

Elliott barked his laughter before tossing her something else to think about. "You, my dear, don't have a choice. By the way, when is your beau, Ashton, going to appear? He said he'd return. Where is the man?"

She sighed, her heart heavy, wishing this wasn't a conversation she was going to have with her father. "He writes. Told me he would send money so I could go to London. I, however, told him a resounding no to that bit of nonsense. If he wants me, he can come here. I'm not travelling alone that far. I mean to be his wife before I give... Never mind."

"Good girl. The man needs to care enough about you to come here and marry you in all the ways of the clan. If he can't do that, he can't possibly be your mate. Ashton can bring any family that he wishes to accompany him. I'm in full approval of your decision."

"Agreed. I want to have a wedding at the McKenna keep. He's only implied he wants to marry me. There has been no proposal. For all I know he might have another lady on his arm at this moment."

Harris recalled the day he seduced her, gave her what he called her woman's pleasure. She would never forget that moment when all her senses erupted then her body fragmented into thousands of pieces. Harris also understood he could have taken her innocence that day. In some ways he did. Ashton ruined her for any other man even though she was still a virgin.

"If it's any consolation, you are doing the right thing by holding back."

"It's hard." Harris didn't want to think about all that she was giving up. She refused to let him make love to her a year ago because she didn't want to end up pregnant. Dear Lord, if she had let him and if she did conceive, the child would be almost a year old. Ashton couldn't get the time off from his duties to come see her. Would he act the same if she had a child? Harris didn't want to find out. Ashton needed to make a commitment before she would go anywhere with him chaperoned or unchaperoned.

"It's parliament," he tells me in his letters. "He has a seat and since he is a new member, he can't take leave of his duties. Not certain I wish to be married to an Englishman, especially one who has a hand at making laws."

"You don't believe him?" Elliott sat back, stretching out his long legs, his glass of brandy settled on his stomach.

"I think there is more. Something he isn't telling me."

"Perhaps. We will have to wait."

"I'm surprised Cameron acquiesced without saying more than a few words of displeasure. Wouldn't be surprised if he showed up there after he spoke with Hawk."

"Neither would I. He is a very possessive man."

Harris wished Ashton would act that way toward her. She let air rush from her lungs. The man did tell her not to see anyone else. The dictator. The fact of the matter was, she didn't want to see anyone but Ashton. She didn't see him either. He was nowhere to be found. Too busy to be part of her life. Too many obligations. Shouldn't she be one of those obligations?

Chapter Four

Reluctant steps brought Lainie, accompanied by Heather, back to the Frasier home. She should have insisted Heather take her to his shop. Going there by herself wasn't possible. She didn't know where it was located. "I don't wish to stay here. You understand that. Right? Has nothing to do with you or your husband. You've both been wonderful to me," Lainie ventured to say. Her arms were filled with packages. "I'll never be able to repay Roc. I can't leave until I do."

Lainie wasn't at all certain that hadn't been Heather's plan from the very beginning having known her intentions to pay him back. She would make it as hard on her as possible. The woman ordered multiples of everything. She had gowns, slippers, reticules, bonnets as well as gloves. She had several corsets along with more than one chemise. She wasn't going to wear the damn corset! There were stockings and garters. No wonder Roc believed a woman took a long time to dress. Her leggings, bra as well as panties were ever more practical. She didn't need to have a maid to lace her up.

"Would you rather we had the garments delivered to Cameron's home? I can send someone to change the directions." Heather appeared amused.

Lainie understood her amusement was not at her distress. During the time at the dress shop, Heather made certain she knew she would never be judged by her decisions. Still after what Roc told her, she didn't know if she believed anything he told to her.

"You wouldn't mind?"

Lainie was quite shocked by Heather's comment. It seemed she was attempting to put them in a compromising situation. Were mothers supposed to do that? Heather would if the final outcome would meet her approval. Her own mother never cared what she did. Lainie didn't understand. Nonetheless she liked the caring.

Stopping for a moment, Heather turned to her. "It's not what I would mind that makes a difference here. Cameron is certain to have an opinion. Do you mind if the two of you are at tenterhooks? Arguing both night and day? The two of you must have a chance to work out the huge differences separating you. The only way the two of you can do that is to have privacy. After that, it follows that you should live with him."

"No...yes...I do care but I believe he will come around to my way of thinking, given time. He wants me to be with him. I do know he won't stay another night at his old home. I don't want him to leave me. It's not that I'm afraid anymore. I trust you. You're family."

She understood he would be just down the street. If she felt lonely, she couldn't go to him in the middle of the night. When her feet were cold, she would have nothing to warm them with...except memories. After she returned to her century, she wouldn't... Lainie gulped air.

"We will have the completed articles taken to his address. Now, if we gather up your things as soon as we reach my house, I'll have Elliott take you to Cameron's home. After that, he will go to Cameron's place of business and tell him where you are. It will be up to him to see that you are not ostracized."

Ostracized?

If she wasn't going to be around in a few months, what did it matter? "Does Roc want me to help him at his work? Is he just placating me with a job? Half the time I don't understand how he thinks. He doesn't think or act like any man I've met before."

Heather chuckled, her voice soft when she spoke, "If it's any consolation, more than half the time he doesn't understand you or your motives. Not only are you female, which confounds most men, but you have memories that have nothing to do with him or this century. He will have to learn much as will you. The both of you will have to adjust to your abnormalities."

Was she abnormal? Did Roc look at her as being strange? "I don't know what to do? He thinks I want to go back to my century," Lainie paused for several seconds expecting Heather to say something. She kept quiet waiting, it seemed, for her to finish her thoughts. "I don't understand my thoughts. While I should feel the need to return, should hope and pray to find a way, I don't want to leave Roc. In this short time, I've come to..."

I love him.

The revelation was both unexpected as well as unwanted. Life would be so much easier if she didn't have such strong feelings for the man. What if he doesn't love me? He wants me. Want is not love.

"Have you told my son your thoughts?" Heather's question was spoken in a quiet voice. "You need to explain how you think about him. The facts would go a long way to sooth his autocratic demeanor. His unwillingness to give into your demands. If he wished for you to find that portal again, he would have taken you before he brought you home to meet his family. Cameron has never brought a woman to meet us. I believe he will put that journey off as long as humanly possible. It's obvious to anyone who is looking, he doesn't want you to leave him. What do you think?"

"I never brought any one to meet my mother and father either. Now, I never will. I just don't know. Do you believe he wants me here? Yesterday, I felt as if I was a burden to everyone. All we did during the day was argue."

Yes, I argued about leaving him.

"There is not a doubt in my mind. Your Roc has a lot of explaining to do, mostly about our ways. How we select the woman who will be his forever woman. What you need to consider and examine are what the arguments were about."

"You speak in riddles." Lainie was stymied by all Heather was trying to tell her without telling her anything at all.

"As once a long time ago, Elliott spoke to me in riddles. All his words were a puzzle to me. I would tell you more except it is not my place. It's Cameron's. That's why I'm not objecting to you staying with him. There is much for the two of you to talk about. Come, we are almost to my house. You can decide what you want. Know that the Frasier clan will support your decisions. Whatever they might be. We will all stand beside you."

When they stepped inside the Frasier home, Roc sat in his father's office talking. When the pair looked up then saw her, they stopped almost as if they were talking about her. The huge smile he greeted her with left her heart pounding, blood rushing through her veins. Her breath vanished in a puff of air. She thought he might be happy to see her.

He stood...so tall...his shoulders so very broad, hips narrow. Perfect. "Are you going to show me everything you bought? I would like you to do so."

His smile was broad also indulgent. His gaze upon her was tender. She saw no anger. Confusion swept through her. This was not what she expected.

Her eyes were transfixed on him. "Hardly. I'm wearing one of the gowns as well as so many underthings I lost count. My way of dressing was much simpler. Took all of two minutes for me to be ready to go out."

By the broad grin on Roc's face, Lainie was positive she knew what he was thinking even though he'd never undressed her except for the nettle incident. He didn't remove all her clothing...he unhooked her bra.

He touched her.

The touch was clinical. No, it wasn't. Not entirely.

She breathed in long, deep breaths while she tried to put the bewildering memory behind her. It would not do for her to become reliant on him in so many more ways. She always depended on herself. Would it hurt to depend on him?

"We are having her clothing sent to your address when the articles are completed," Heather told him. "Now, Lainie and I are going upstairs to gather her things. I'm happy you came here. You can escort Lainie to her new home. We should have insisted yesterday when it was obvious how much she means to you. Come along..." Heather took her by the arm then propelled her up the steps.

As Lainie looked over her shoulder at him, he was gaping, his mouth open. A momentary thought fluttered through her head that she should close it for him. Roc looked as if he meant to form a rebuttal.

Heather whisked her upstairs so quickly they disappeared from his view before words could be formed. Lainie expected him to waylay them before they reached her room. It was beyond Lainie's comprehension that Heather would promote the idea that she live in sin with her son. This was something few mothers or fathers approved of in her time. This was the eighteenth century.

She found herself flabbergasted by the thought. Who were these people?

By the time they returned to the office, Roc was perched, half sitting on his father's desk, half standing beside the huge desk. He was sipping a glass of brandy. His body was tense, his features unreadable. The steel-gray of his eyes darkened when he saw her. To the tips of her toes, she felt the heat from his gaze. Lainie found she wanted his approval.

Elliott saluted them with his whiskey glass when they stepped inside, "Cameron needed a stiff drink. Can't believe my conservative wife is allowing this. Neither can my son. Seems you've no care for his future, wife."

Lainie never agreed to marriage. These people saw them as man and wife. What mattered to her now was why?

"Before you leave with Cameron, would you like a sherry? Lainie might be in need of some added fortification also," Heather asked her before turning her attention to Roc. "Do you have anything that can be fixed for dinner? If not, you will..." she paused with her thoughts hanging in midair. "I will send something over."

"I don't know. I've food that can be prepared," he said sardonically as he watched her his gaze riveted on her eyes. After staring at her for several seconds, he asked, "Can you cook?"

Lainie shook her head sending him a bright smile. Tossing her unbound hair over her shoulder, she replied with sweetness that would leave Roc groaning, "I can boil water. If that's what you mean by cooking. Otherwise, no."

The lie would become evident if there was anything in his pantry that could be put together as a meal. She was an excellent cook. She loved creating new dishes out of the contents of her pantry and fridge.

"Though..." she sought the right words while she tapped one finger on her chin. "I would know how to turn on the stove so I can boil anything. Don't care too much for tea. Nonetheless, I enjoy a heady cup of coffee, usually black."

"I can start the stove," Roc growled as if he was discouraged with the thought his future meals might all windup scorched. "You don't need to overtax yourself. We will not starve. I'm well-versed in cooking beans. My mother will be pleased to help you learn." Roc turned to her. "Won't you?"

"Yes, I could learn."

She ventured that perhaps she pushed him too far. She never knew how he would react to her quips. He didn't always believe her. This time it appeared he did.

"To cook or to start the stove." His words were curt as well as abrasive.

"Both."

She'd done that to him. She wasn't at all proud of the fact. She would have to counter the affect with something nice. Somehow, she would try to find a way to make this up to him.

"You two go on. I'll send over some of the stew I'm making for dinner. Perhaps hiring a cook would be in order. Before now, Cameron took most of his meals here, with us," Heather said as she winked at Lainie seeming either to guess at the ruse or plan on being the instructor.

Part of their discussion when she was getting poked, prodded and measured for her new wardrobe was the cooking situation. Heather gave her a few pointers as to the foods Roc enjoyed the most. Nonetheless, she had several recipes in mind that he might appreciate. She wondered if ground venison would work for hamburger. She imagined it with noodles coupled with an alfredo sauce. She loved small boiled potatoes. The chicken cooked in wine sauce and sautéed mushrooms she created was divine. She was certain Roc would enjoy her cooking. Breakfast would be the easiest meal to prepare.

On the way to his house, she carried her bag. He didn't mention taking it from her. For some reason Lainie didn't understand, she would have refused if he insisted. Perhaps in this time, men didn't carry parcels for women. Maybe Roc could read her mind. He could be angry. They didn't speak until they stood inside his home. Except for the furniture the floor plan was the same as when Rafe bought the house. There was a room for bathing she found interesting, the tub small. She wondered if they would both fit inside, supposing after the thought she was managing to put the cart in front of the horse.

"When he bought it, Rafe always told me this house called to him. That it was somehow special. Strange, but I felt the same calling. Now here I am. In a different century. In the same home. I'm going to live here for a few months. I would have never lived in Rafe's home," she added when she noticed his changing features. The scowl. She wondered how many times this beautiful old home had been remodeled from the foundation up.

Roc stood beside her, his hand resting on her shoulder as if he meant to give reassurance. "It is not strange, Lainie. There is nothing weird about any of this. Tonight, I want to take you to the bonfire. We can speak of some...some important matters that you need to know about me. I will tell you more about myself, my family. Maybe even something about your Rafe. I'm making assumptions here but I'm certain I'm right."

"You are sounding so mysterious. Roc." She turned so she faced him now concerned by the lines of stress radiating from his eyes. "I lied to you. I feel terrible about doing so."

His expression turned blank, brows drawing together in well-defined lines. "Lied? I don't understand."

With the tip of her finger, she touched his bottom lip, smoothed her finger across it. Smiled. "About cooking. I'm a very good chef. I will need help with the stove, however, until I learn. Yours is nothing like the ones I am used to. I love to create new dishes."

Roc slanted her a blank look while he rubbed his chin. "About cooking? You lied to me about cooking?" He held her hand, with a languid stroke then another, he moved his thumb across her wrist, grinned with wicked delight when she shivered from the contact. "Why? Why would you tell me something that is not true?"

She lifted her shoulders, a small gesture under the circumstances.

He looked so hurt as if she betrayed him in the worst sort of way. "The thought just popped into my head. So, I went with it. Thought you could be teased and not hate me. Was I wrong?"

"You have the strangest way of saying things."

She imagined there might be a compliment in there somewhere. "Heather won't be sending food. She knew what I said wasn't true. If you have..."

He cut her off with the pressure of his finger to her lips. "I have fresh baked bread that Mother sent over this morning. There are thin slices of venison steak. We have a round of cheese we can cut."

"No vegetable? We have to eat our greens."

"Greens?"

"Yes, some peas, perhaps, or mushrooms. If you see me to the kitchen, I can get started."

Lainie was ready to make amends for her lie. She had big ideas. Pleasing his palate was foremost in her mind.

"Not so fast. First, I'm going to give you a tour of the home." Roc clasped her hand in his then started through the house pulling her with him.

"I know this house, I don't need a tour," Lainie told him. "It doesn't seem anything has changed too dramatically. Rafe lives here in another time. When I knew the home, there was a third floor." She didn't think she should tell him about posing nude for Rafe.

Roc's breath seemed to quiver with displeasure as he inhaled. She wondered if she shouldn't talk about Rafe anymore. He seemed to have a negative reaction whenever she mentioned anything concerning the first man she ever cared about.

"He wasn't my lover," she blurted as if the words were necessary. "There was never anything between us sexually." She paused as she grabbed a *wee* bit of air. "I'm a virgin. I thought you understood that."

His fingers drifted down her cheek. "Hush, love, I understand you have a past just as I do. Nonetheless, when you mention him, I..." He touched her gently again, holding a few strands of her hair between his fingers. "Knowing you care so much about this man angers me. Fuels jealousy that I've never felt before."

"You've no right to your anger. We were never anything except friends."

"I've every right, Lainie. You are mine. I don't share what is mine."

"I understand that is what you think..."

His lips touched the corners of her mouth. Strong fingers held her head still so he could explore. With his teeth he gently tugged on her lower lip, pulling when she opened for his quest. He ran his tongue along her bottom lip then the upper one, leaving her mouth wet as well as wanting. Roc explored the sensitive undersides of her mouth, after that the smooth ridge of her teeth were met by his tongue.

A humming sound captured by his mouth burst from her. His fingers wound into her hair, tightening then releasing. Her hands roamed their way to his neck, nails rasping across his nape. The fine hair at the back of his neck intoxicated her. His lips found a delicate spot behind her ear then lower to place small nibbling kisses down her neck. At her pulse point he lingered, nipping, sucking, exploring with his mouth. Shivers wracked her body. Flames ignited. Her hands wrapped around his neck.

"Hang on to me," he encouraged as his hands ran the length of her arms then back to wind into her hair again.

He found his way back to her mouth, resuming the gentle kiss he began, nips from corner to corner. Then pressed, laved, suckled then nipped moving her lips to part for him. When she complied and opened for him, he touched his tongue to hers, the caress gentle. He pushed his tongue in then out, searching the inside. Feeling him in the dark secret places he sought within her mouth they danced together, tongue to tongue until he sipped her into the heat of his mouth. His hands found purchase at her waist drawing her into the cradle of his thighs. She felt the evidence of his erection, hard, pulsing against her.

Sparks flew between them. She'd never felt such intense heat. When Rafe kissed her those few times there was nothing like this. With all her strength she clung to Roc. Her knees seemed to be giving out beneath her. He steadied her. She whimpered. A small broken sound caught in the back of her throat. More sounds she didn't recognize spilled from her splintering into his mouth.

His lips teeth and tongue lodged on her neck again. Creating havoc and flames within her body. While he laved then nipped at the same spot. She was trapped within his strong arms, unable to move. She cried out. "You're giving me a hickey!"

When he looked up, he spoke, his smile wide, his words soft. "I've no idea what that is but I suppose I am. Do you have any objections?"

Everyone will see."

"True."

"I'll have to wear a scarf to hide it."

"Your new dresses will not? See, you should have allowed me to go to the dressmakers with you. I would have made certain no one would be the wiser for the kisses I intend to share with you. There is always a good reason for a gown to cover a woman's neck."

She punched his chest. Annoyance flared. Punched harder the second time, shouting, "Beast!"

His mouth found hers again, the contact so very light her breath was stolen for her, trapped within his. While seconds ticked away on the hall clock, he searched and explored while her body quivered with need, flamed with the heat.

He ended the kiss, touching her swollen mouth with his thumb, rubbing the pad along her lips. "One day soon, I'll show you my inner beast. For the present, let's see to dinner. I want to walk you to the bonfire when we're done. We can roast marshmallows."

She pushed away from him so she could see his face better. "You have marshmallows? I have graham crackers and a chocolate bar in my bag. We can have s'mores. Did you not see them?" She was excited to share this with him, surprised he would have marshmallows. Astonished.

The wicked chuckle she heard unnerved her a bit. He cleared his throat to ask the next question. "What's a s'more?"

Of course, that would be something he wouldn't know about, wouldn't have a name for the hearty treat. She was surprised he had marshmallows. "A desert I'm sure you will love. At this bonfire of yours, I'll make you one. You have to roast the marshmallows though. I always burn mine."

"Ah...impatience. A trait I'm well aware of in you." He placed his hand where he'd been showing so much attention on her neck. "Something else we have in common. I like this mark. Tells everyone you belong to me." His hand wrapped around her neck tugging her close again. He kissed her hard on the mouth then let her go. "The more I taste you, the more I want you. I just can't get enough of you."

"What is it you need to tell me?"

She needed to change the subject. The kisses disconcerted her, felt so different than anything she knew. Her fingertip touched upon the mark he gave her. Heat spiraled. More insecurities arose. She wanted him so much. The desire rising with each mercuric touch of his hands and lips on her body.

"Things."

His voice was husky, raw vibrating to the tips of her toes.

"That is something I would say. I can wait though." Staring into his eyes wishing for another kiss, she held his hand, gazing into the silver shimmer of his eyes. He elicited blinding hunger along with raw passion within her. Enchantment eternal.

They walked to the kitchen. "Are you hungry?" he asked still looking at her as if he wanted to consume her. He spoke with a soft whisper of longing, bringing her hand to his mouth. "I don't have any wish for a meal. Unless the meal is you. The way I feel now is that I could devour all of you. Stopping the kiss where I did, left my starvation for you simmering in the hardest part of me."

"Oh, my..."

Devour?

"Where are these graham crackers and chocolates you mentioned. Don't tell me I missed examining something in your bag." His tone changed to lighthearted while she still ached for more from him. To Lainie it seemed he abandoned the earlier topic with too much ease.

"You must have missed them." She touched her finger to her mouth, wishing she dared trace his lips. "You were much too interested in other things to notice food." He was more fascinated in both sexual items in her bag, the birth control as well as the condoms.

"Was I not gentle enough?" Now, he sounded too concerned about the kiss. "I would not hurt you for the world."

She'd known several kisses. None that moved her as his did. There was something...a trigger...that's what it was. She never felt that stimulus with Rafe. "You didn't hurt me if that's what you're asking. Though, I've never known anything...quite like the sensation...your mouth ravishing mine."

"Go get the crackers and chocolate," he told her, his voice so husky the words were difficult to discern.

Though she understood the gist of what he said. In the kitchen, he put cheese along with the bread and some slices of venison in a container. On what seemed to be a second thought, he added a container of coffee.

The walk to the bonfire was pleasant. The sky filled with stars. He held her close, his arm wrapped around her shoulders. She couldn't help thinking of the kiss. Another one would be nice. His was the first kiss that generated sensual emotions.

Dare she ask him? No, even in her time she would never ask a man to kiss her a second time...or a first. Either he wanted or didn't want to put their lips together. Pushing those thoughts aside, she concentrated on Roc, on what he would say to her. She was curious. "What do you want to talk to me about?"

"Impatient, are we?" He drew her closer, his hand circling her waist, his finger caressing her hip. "I like that. Promise you will listen then not draw conclusions until you've heard everything. This is important."

"Yes..." She gripped his arm as he pulled her even closer. "I'm too curious. Always have been. Impatient too. You are right about me. Even in this short time, you know me better than anyone ever has."

Once at the bonfire, he spoke to her "I feel as if I've known you my entire life. I've never brought a *lass* here before. You are special to me, Lainie. You do *ken* that don't you?" He laid out a blanket for her then bade her sit. "I'll start the fire. We can talk. Roast the marshmallows. Make your s'mores."

Lainie nodded her head, understanding that he thought it was so.

After the kiss she also thought what he told her was true. "Maybe."

"I'm going to have to endeavor harder to change your mind."

~ * ~

With the fire blazing he set out the packed food. "What would you like?"

"You..." she whispered her voice so soft she wasn't at all certain he heard.

"What was that you said? I didn't hear."

He did hear her though. Was pleased that she felt much the same about him that he felt about her. He wanted her too, in every way. Even though at times she was bluntly honest as well as shocking with her words, she was never completely truthful with her feelings. Lainie hid something from him. He would discover all her truths. She seemed to keep her most secret feelings close to her heart. Perhaps she was coming around, falling in love with him.

Trying to keep her words to the back of his muddled brain, Roc went about fixing a plate for her then one for himself. He poured them both a cup of coffee. Sitting against the log, they ate in silence. She seemed to have more patience than he expected. He would have her eager to learn about his heritage. She didn't know that was what they would speak of tonight.

"Did you go to school? Do women in the era you were born in seek schooling?" he asked as he stared at the fire.

He'd eaten his fill and set his plate aside while he waited for her. Knowing a little bit more about her would always serve him well. Truth be told, he yearned to know everything about her from her birth to the present.

"High school as well as college. I understand from the history of this time it's unusual for a female to attend the university. I graduated from the University of Glasgow in photography. Of all things, there is no photography in this time period. Should have been a nurse. Every century could use nurses. What about you?"

"Me too, graduated from University of Glasgow in literature. The newspaper I started is small. We mostly write articles about the happenings in town. Sometimes I take on a controversial issue. Not often though. With the Sassenach around, don't wish to risk my life or my freedom. Suppose I'm a bit of a coward."

"That wasn't what you wished to speak with me about, was it? As you wish, I'm prepared to listen."

"No, it wasn't. I hesitate because I don't know where to begin. There is so much to tell you. So much you might not believe."

He could show her his cat. However, that needed to be done in private. Revealing to her his other form might frighten her if she didn't understand he would never hurt her. If she didn't have the essential knowledge before that could happen, she might be terrified. He should tell before he showed.

"Start at the beginning or where you feel comfortable," Lainie told him, watching him with worry in her eyes. The deep blue color lightened as she waited. "Am I not going to like what you tell me? There isn't another woman in your life. Is there?"

"Did Rafe ever speak to you about...about...never mind. We live in the highlands. Right?" He didn't know what he expected. While the question wasn't irrelevant, it was stupid. "The highlands are known to be magical. Rumors abound about all types of things mystical."

Her brows drew together. Her lips pursed. "Right," she told him with hesitation. "All my life I've lived here. Why? Does this have something to do with the secret you keep from me. Does it have something to do with Rafe? It must because with the mention of his name you didn't scowl at me." She pulled the blanket he brought for her around her shoulders.

"Are you cold?"

"No, just...shivery."

He didn't think she would guess he'd been keeping secrets. This came as the first surprise to him. "We've talked about the Kinnel Stones. Have you ever heard rumors of shape shifters?"

The first question was cautious. He watched her eyes cross while her brows drew together with what he perceived to be inquisitiveness. She questioned.

She touched his mouth with her index finger. Lightly, wishing he could do more, he touched the tip with his tongue wetting the flesh she offered up to him. This was not the time to lose himself in her kisses.

"Everyone has. I've heard tell of the Clan Chattan who once lived and roamed the hills around here. Heard how the Sassenach, chased them, offering rewards to hand the shifters over to them. All old wives' tales. Nothing more. Rumors with no realism."

"All true. I've an old handbill on my second floor in one of the back rooms to remind me to caution. Shifters need to be watchful."

He watched her changing expressions cognizant that he held no preconceived ideas as to how she would accept the information he thrust her way. Though he understood she would question.

"Now you're teasing me." She grinned as she reached out to him only to pull her hand back then settle it beneath the blanket.

"No, I wouldn't do that about this subject. Just as you should not have teased about your ability to cook. When something concerns a man's stomach..." As if he needed to lighten the atmosphere, Roc patted a space between his legs. "Come here. I want to hold you." He needed to feel her warmth along with her trust against him. She would accept him in either form. He felt certain about that. Lainie was his mate.

"What is it exactly that you're trying to tell me?" She moved between his legs, cradled by his hard thighs.

He wished it could be the other way around. "Most of the Frasiers along with the Stewarts and the McKennas are shifters. I am as is Houston. Harris is also but Heather is not. Massie, Hawk's wife, is not a shifter while Leah, Houston's, wife is."

His arms circled her waist. Her head settled against his chest while he rested his chin on the top of her hair. As he waited for her to comment, he watched the flames of the fire sparkle into the dark velvet backdrop surrounding the fire. High above stars tipped their sparkling light toward earth.

Perhaps they should have tried those s'mores before he brought up the reality of shifters. Maybe she needed to digest this information before he continued the story. He paused waiting for her to hold out a clue for him to go forward with.

"Is that all?" she asked turning in his arms, her mouth slanted toward his.

She was looking at him, her mouth so close, her mint scented breath whispered across him, tempting him to take her mouth within his for another kiss. If they kissed, there would be no more talk. Roc wasn't certain he cared.

"You know it isn't. There is ever so much more to tell you, to show you too." He wanted her to question, to test his words. "I won't ever lie to you...not even about something so insignificant as the ability to cook."

He saw her response in the firm set of her jaw. She didn't appreciate his comment.

"I apologized for that insignificant *faux pas*. It was done to tease not hurt. Won't do it again," she mumbled. She looked back to him as if trying to erase the feelings. "What form do you change to? How do I believe you honestly can do such an unusual thing? Does it hurt? What does this ability have to do with me? I don't think I'm one. Am I and just don't know it. Is that what you're trying to tell me?"

Roc enjoyed the fact she was inquiring. It meant she was willing to believe in him. To listen to what he had to say. "You have a lot of questions. This is good. I'll begin with your first question. I change to a black panther. When we are alone as well as in a secure place, I'll show you my cat."

"I'd like that. Do you purr?" She grinned then touched his mouth. "Do you have long whiskers here?" She touched his cheek lightly with the tip of her finger, ran the tip along his jaw then down his neck. "What about your ears?" She circled his ears with the tip of her fingers. "Then there is your teeth...do you bite?"

Catching her hand in his, he brought her fingers to his mouth, nipped the tip then did the same to all her fingers. She trembled. Her eyes darkened. He turned her hand over then kissed the heart of her palm, running his tongue across some of the lines there until he felt the quivering of her luscious form.

"I've not finished the first questions and now you have more. As to how you can believe me, I've already told you I'll show you. No, changing form doesn't hurt. The act is exhilarating, life changing. As a little boy, I delighted in showing off my abilities to my brother and cousins. We all did. Bath time was the best. Mother let us change after the bath then return to human before bedtime. Father took us to the loch to teach us how to swim."

"I see," Lainie told him, her lashes blinking, lowering to her cheek then back to stare at him.

Trying to be as gentle as possible, Roc set his mouth on hers for a swift, undemanding contact. "What does it have to do with you? Lainie, shifters mate not only for life but for all of eternity. You are my mate. I think that is why you and Rafe didn't feel sparks fly when you were with him. If we wed, in the future you will feel the flashes with him that you do with me."

"I wasn't his mate? Was he a shifter?"

"You aren't his mate just as you are mine. He's a Frasier. So, it figures he is a shifter. Since he would understand you weren't his, he would never mention that fact to you. With that knowledge, I'm trying not to be jealous of the man because in some ways he is me in another century."

"I don't see anything at all. Don't understand what you are telling me. This is too bizarre to comprehend." Lainie snuggled back against his chest. His arms were beneath her breasts. He felt the rapid rise and fall of them as she tugged in air. She was thinking about what he told her. He wished he could be inside her head.

"That doesn't surprise me. Somehow, we weren't able to meet in this time. I don't know why. Something terrible must have happened to one of us. I believe it was you. We never met. Until now. Until you fell into that vortex that brought you to me. You've come back to rectify the accident that took you away from me. That's why you were sent here. If you try to move though time again, you will not only keep us from realizing our love now, in none or our future lives will we be able to mate."

"Oh..." Startled by his tale, she sat up. The top of her head hit his chin. "Well..."

He grunted. Rubbed his jaw.

The fire crackled and sparked, the flames leaping high into the air. After she leaned against him again, he knew she was struggling for air, fighting to understand his words. Making sense of this when she never lived among shifters would be difficult. Roc understood the gravity of all he told her. The thoughts were a lot to absorb especially when shifters were thought to be tall tales. Even in this century there were many disbelievers. Maisie, his brother's wife, never believed until Riley Stewart came into her sister's life.

"What are you thinking, Lainie? Talk to me. Don't leave me in the dark. What you think is far too important to keep to yourself."

Roc stroked her hair, ran his hands down her arms. Inside the blanket he once again wrapped his arms around her. Silence etched into his brain, filled his soul with fear.

"We should have those s'mores now." She pushed away from him then strode to the sticks he set out for them to roast the marshmallows. She looked through the trappings until she found the makings for her treat. After pushing two marshmallows on the end of one of the sticks she handed it to him. "You can roast. Don't burn them."

Roc supposed she had good reason to change the subject. It would take her time to digest all that was said. She would need time to think. Though he wished she would ask more questions. Instead of bringing the topic back to the point he'd been endeavoring to make, he hunkered on his haunches with the marshmallows next to the coals. The fire was a fine one for roasting, perfect coals. Because of the conversation coupled with the intensity, he wasn't hungry. For Lainie's benefit, he would pretend.

They each finished two of the treats which he conceded to her were delicious. Now, she sat cradled in his arms again. Her warmth touched him. At least at this moment, she wasn't running her cold feet along his calves. He heard the soft sigh of pleasure or relief perhaps even resignation. Pressuring her for more of her feelings would not happen tonight. Whenever she wished to talk, he would be here for her. If she posed more questions, he would answer. How much and when was up to Lainie.

"I'm your mate. Are you telling me if I return to the twenty-first century, neither you or anyone else who is supposed to be me, will marry then have children?"

"That's the crux of the problem."

"Did you know it's not fair."

"To who? You or me? I want you to stay. If, after this conversation, you still want to locate this portal, I will take you. As much as I don't want to, I'll let you go."

With his words, his gut tightened, his stomach turning sour with the thought of losing her so soon. The devil, he just found her. He was just beginning to get to know her. Not even a week had passed. Now that he tasted her, learned the smooth texture of her lips, felt the suppleness of her breasts pushed with beguiling softness against him, felt the tender flesh of her well-rounded rump, she'd become part of him. A part he could not live without.

"Do you mean that?" Lainie asked, the tenor of her sweetly soft voice tentative.

"I won't lie to you," he repeated his earlier sentiment. "If that is your choice, I will take you. I just pray it will not be so. I also pray this portal through time will no longer work for you. I believe the vortex will go only one way."

"What happens if I stay here?"

Good, she was asking questions again. This query was more to his liking. He tapped her on the nose, kissing her at the moment was more prevalent in his thoughts. Tasting her again, savoring the taste of marshmallows and coffee coupled with the sweet dark chocolate that was part of her treat, tempted him more than he could withstand.

"If you stay here...we will be married in the Catholic church as well as the way of the Clan Chattan. They are both ceremonies that are intricate to our way of life. After we are married, I will claim you as mine. I'm told you will see some of our past lives together. I won't. So, you will have to tell me about them."

"I'll have to think about it."

He barked a shout of laughter. "Thinking is good." Roc turned her, brought her legs over his so she sat on his thighs. "I've been thinking about doing this since we came here, since before we ate, since before we had s'mores. You have a bit of marshmallow here," His tongue touched upon the bow of her upper lip. "Good, just as fine as the first time...and here..." He found the corner of her mouth, nipped at the treat. The real delight was her mouth, her lips. If he kept kissing her, he might not ever come up for air.

"Roc...you don't have to be so..."

"So what?"

"Gentle. I won't break. I want you to make love to me. I want to feel more than your tongue inside me."

His back stiffened, his fingers that were wound into the silken length of her hair tightened in the silken strands. Not here, not tonight though he would sleep with her. "You need to make a different decision first. If you were to decide to leave me, I can't send you back pregnant. I won't."

"I can't get pregnant!" She sounded frustrated with him.

"Nothing is infallible. I will wager your doctor told you as much."

Lainie didn't answer. Her silence was answer enough for him. Without him asking and without his encouragement, she opened for him. This meeting was sweeter than the first, deeper as well as hotter. She reciprocated every move he made with one of her own. Heat shot straight to his groin. Lust spiraled and spun out of control. Though he understood he needed to tamp down the sexual need rushing through him, he could not. If she continued to kiss him in this manner, he might never stop. Might take privileges that he could come to regret.

Roc found the small brand at the base of her neck his lips and teeth created. Increased the pressure there. A fractured sound rippling from her lips touched him to the core.

Control.

Lainie ran her hands along his chest touching ever part of him he tried with desperation to control. He sipped in a deep breath of fire scented air. She tugged on his shirttails pulling them from his buckskins. Hands upon his naked chest sent him spiraling with sexual hunger he didn't want to ignore. Lainie was willing. The deep breaths he pulled into his lungs were necessary. His fingers itched to taste more tender parts of her. She ran her fingers across his nipples. Passed over them once then twice.

He deepened the kiss, thrusting into her then out just as he wished to do in the heated depths of her core. His hand cradled one breast as he slipped his tongue within the sultry confines of her mouth then out. His groan of pleasure didn't go unnoticed by Lainie.

She lowered her hand. He brought it back from his belly to the broad expanse of his chest.

Through the fabric of her gown, he held the palm of his hand on top of the tight hard tip of her breast. Rubbed the center across her taut nipple. Toyed with the tips until he heard the soft hum of desire he was beginning to adore slip from the back of her throat.

She arched against him, silently begging for more.

He pulled away, staring at the kiss swollen lips that called to him. They were slightly red. If he kept kissing her, he would make love to her. In the aftermath, he would regret his actions. His body ached to delve inside her, to bring her to a woman's pleasure. To possess as well as share his love.

He set his course and would stick with it as long as doing so was humanly possible. Once more he turned her so she sat against him, nestled tightly between his thighs, pressed against his swollen sex.

"You don't want me?" Lainie asked, her voice soft, restrained.

He heard the roughness in it along with the hurt while she attempted to keep her disappointment from him.

"More than I want anything else." He tweaked her nose. "Even more than I wish to have another treat. You are the most delicious treat of all. Wish to savor your sweetness for as long as we both live."

The silence between them was broken by the chatter coming their way. Without acknowledging to Lainie what was happening, Roc groaned though he understood this was for the best. His brother along with Houston and Leah were walking up the hill. Their presence put an end to any thoughts of lovemaking he might still harbor. For tonight his cousin and brother would be his savior.

"Should we share the s'mores?" he asked wondering what she would decide.

The devil, this would be the only time they would have the new treat.

"We can. That means there will be less for us. We can get more chocolate. What about the graham crackers?" Lainie asked.

"If I ask mother, she might be able to figure something out. She's an exceptional baker. We must save at least one to show her. We do have graham flour. Is that what your crackers are made from?"

"Most likely," she agreed as she lifted her shoulders in a delicate shrug.

She snuggled in closer to Roc while he made the new introductions. He wondered if Hawk spoke to his partner about the contraceptive he showed him this morning. If he did, Houston would have an opinion.

"What are the two of you up to?" Hawk asked, the two couples seemed to spy the marshmallows.

The s'mores were explained. The chatter along with the laughter continued. All was eaten except the portion Roc expounded needed to be saved. As the night progressed the couples settled into different places around the fire, attending to the sounds of the night. Roc listened to Lainie's raspy breathing as he leisurely explored some of her hidden treasures that were covered by the blanket.

"Who's looking after the children?" Roc asked even while he guessed the answer.

He wanted to investigate the possibility of children with Lainie. That was putting the cart before the horse. Before he could do that, she would need to commit to him. If he pursued too quickly, she would try to bolt. If she did, there was only one place she could run...the falls or the portal he thought to be there. Taking his time with her, charming and sweet-talking her would gain him more ground than a frontal attack. Though the latter had possibilities that were difficult to ignore. Her front was exquisite as was her back.

"The same people who will look after yours when they arrive," Hawk said with a dry laugh. "Who do you think? Mother and Father. They won't take no for an answer. Won't allow us to hire a sitter. Say they enjoy the time with the little hellions."

In his arms, Lainie wiggled with each new and bold caress. The palms of his hands smoothed over her breasts. His thoughts drifted backward while he wondered if she wanted children. The birth control pills didn't hold all the answers nor did the condoms. While he responded to her questions tonight, he didn't pose any to her. Thoughts of her lying with another man, even if that man had been Rafe disturbed him more than he could imagine. Jealousy exploded in him with each supposed innuendo.

While all shifters understood about the future, he had a name for her lover in another century. That seemed to put a different kind of stamp on his assumptions than when there was no name attached. No face. No history. No jealousy.

"Everyone here is a shifter except you and Maisie. Do you wish to ask questions?" Roc asked while his hands explored from her rounded belly to the sweet tips of her ripe breasts. He didn't dare touch her anywhere else.

"What is claiming? Does that hurt?" She uttered the question that Roc didn't wish to pursue.

He'd heard from his brothers and cousins. Both spoke little of what transpired though he understood there would be some pain.

Leah reached out to her. Her hand covering hers. "That question is best left to the wedding night. As to the pain, there is some but it is over with before you know it. In time you won't remember anything except the visions of your man in another time and place."

"That's because you are also a shifter though she is right about how quickly the hurt disappears." Maisie pointed out. "We should not say anything more. If you ask Roc, he will tell you what he believes best. How much knowledge you have is up to your husband. The claiming won't happen until you are married."

"Does that mean Mother is planning a wedding? She will be verra pleased." Hawk asked with a chuckle Roc didn't ignore.

"No!" Lainie cried out too quickly for Roc's appreciation.

She sat up straight, the blanket sliding from her shoulders. With a huffed breath of air, she settled back against him covering herself.

Roc added his feelings to Lainie's. "I hope so. As you can tell, we are divided on the issue. A wedding tomorrow would not be too soon for me. However, Lainie and I have much to discuss. Sounds as if I have a *wee* bit of convincing to do."

Beneath the blanket as well as her clothing, Roc's hands cupped her breasts. Touched her. Played and toyed with the tight hard buds veiled beneath the fabric of her gown. He understood her need was rising as the seconds passed. With each caress, she moved against him. The lushness of her delectable backside pushed against the hard ridge of his penis. Small hums of mushrooming passion burst from her throat. He knew her eyes were closed. He could see the fan of her lashes across her cheeks.

"Roc doesn't speak for m-me..." Lainie stuttered while he enjoyed the wonderful heat they were sharing.

He was arousing himself as well as Lainie. By the time all left and they went back to his home, that would be good too. His father told him he should do everything possible to convince her this was where she belonged. His plans might need to deviate.

If in a week or two if she still wished to see if the portal existed for her, they would travel there. Though the thought sent anger rolling in his gut. He needed her to trust him, and to love him enough to want to stay here.

Before that happened, he was going to paint her. If she left him, he needed a memory of what he would miss throughout eternity. If what she told him was accurate about the house where he lived, he might find the painting of her in his future. He would tuck it away in a safe place. No one except himself would ever see it.

Hand in hand they walked down the hill, both seeming to need more privacy than what they shared at the bonfire. The others stayed to watch the flames. They fed the fire. In time they would wander to more private places then make love. If he changed his mind about his course of action with Lainie, that was what he would do too.

In the master chamber upstairs, Roc turned her in his arms. Moonlight washed her delicate features with silver beams. He traced her eyebrows with a gentle fingertip then down her nose to caress her mouth. He kissed her not wishing to generate more fire until the unfinished business of the evening was seen to. Coaxing her to him would be heaven. Time and patience would be his guide. He didn't want to take too much too soon. When he ended the kiss, he touched her cheek with the back of his hand. "Would you like to see my cat?"

Lainie ran her sweet pink tongue along her lips. Dewy moisture was left behind. He wanted to taste. Her hands clasped under her chin. She nodded her consent. "Yes, my curiosity is brimming, threatening to runover."

"Your eyes are so wide, I'm afraid you will jump out of your skin when you see me. I'm rather large. Understand, I would never hurt you. Despite my size, I'm as docile as a kitty unless provoked."

Now, that the time was upon them he was terrified of her reaction. He prayed she prepared herself for him by listening.

"I'm ready." Inquisitiveness rampant in her eyes, she stared at him. "I want to see you. Need to know everything about you." She was breathless. Her breasts rising, falling with agitation or excitement. Perhaps both. "I'm...want to understand what you can do. You said things. Implied other things. Nothing made sense. All you told me made sense even when the words didn't. I was so confused. Still am." Lainie set her palm against the contour of his cheek.

He sucked in a huge breath of air. This could break whatever fragile trust there was between them. Roc understood he needed to proceed with caution. "When I disrobe do you want me to turn my back? I'll be naked. Have you ever seen a fully naked man?" The look in her eyes both amused him and endeared her more to him. He pulled his shirt over his head. She gaped. He closed her mouth with a finger.

"You have to t-take all-all your clothes o-off?" She struggled for control. Seemed to find a small measure. "I've seen men in bathing suits, with their shirt off. Nothing more." Lainie stared at him, her gaze roaming the length of his bared chest.

She ran the sweet tongue he loved to taste along her slightly swollen lips, swollen from his ardent attention. Inflamed from the kisses they shared at the bonfire.

"Not even Rafe?"

Roc didn't understand why he asked that question. As her eyes narrowed in what he was beginning to understand was anger, he wanted to kick himself.

"No!" Her fists were clenched tight. She punched him. He deserved her anger.

He needed to smooth his *faux pas*. "Would you like to watch me undress?" He enjoyed himself. Teasing her was a delight. "I would let you see me naked. You know that. Right? You should get used to seeing me wearing nothing. Though the kisses we've shared have aroused me."

"I-I d-don't know."

Lainie closed her eyes seeming to strive for control. He waited. Her hands were folded beneath her chin. When she opened them again, his fingers were wrestling with the fastening of his buckskins.

Roc didn't intend to wait for an answer. He wasn't certain if she would be able to say *yay* or *nay*. With little fanfare, he divested himself of his clothing. While he watched her eyes along with her changing expressions, he stood in front of her fully naked. Her thoughts were impossible to read. His body was hard with need. His arousal evident.

"It's time."

When he began to change, his body quivered then shook. Over the years he mastered the process. Only a few seconds later he sat in front of her as a fully grown black panther. He remained as if frozen in time. His heart accelerated as her hesitation grew. She didn't appear frightened of him. Roc needed to wait for a reaction from Lainie.

"Oh my... You are so beautiful. I-I mean handsome. Magnificent. You are quite large." She started forward then stopped while she was holding out her hand. She brought her fingers back to rest between her breasts. "Do you understand me? Can I pet you?"

The devil, he would love to have her pet him. Stroke his fur. Cuddle with him. Push her breasts against his face. If he wasn't so large, he would love to curl cat like on her lap. He would purr for his Lainie. Her doing so would be much better in his human form. Nonetheless, as a cat he could appreciate the attention from his mate.

With a hesitant step she moved closer. When she reached out, her fingers trembled. He wanted to take the fear away from her. The first touch to the top of his head was nearly his undoing. She rubbed her long slender fingers behind his ears before touching his sensitive whiskers. Scratching. Stroking. He shivered with each contact, wishing he was human and she was doing the same to his body. He needed to let her explore. Hoped she would become comfortable with him as his cat. She knelt. Their eyes met. Lainie wrapped her arm around him before moving back to better look at his cat. Roc would have loved all this attention from her when he was in human form.

"You do have whiskers." She scratched him under his chin then along his neck. He moved against her leg, purring.

He thought he'd died and gone to heaven. His body still reacted to her voice as well as each stroke of her hand. His purring brought her hand back to her breasts, clasped tight between them. Wide-eyed she stared at him. Her mouth gaped open. He wanted to nudge it closed.

"Nice cat? Nice kitty? What are you?"

Her hand ran along his back again. He arched, begging for so much more.

"What are you? Cat or Kitty? Nice or wicked?"

He certainly wasn't a kitty. Lainie should know that by looking at him. He could be both nice as well as wicked. With her he thought a little bit of both was appropriate. The inflection of her voice tantalized his cat senses. He grinned at her, barring his teeth.

Startled by the sight of his teeth, she jumped back. "Oh my! You won't bite me, will you? You already have." She touched the small mark at the base of her neck.

His grin grew as he realized what she was doing as well as her thoughts. Yes, he'd bitten her. While this was entertaining, they should stop. He understood he needed to put an end to the show. The knocking on the door below caught his attention. He didn't understand who it could be at this hour unless it was his father...or his mother. They wouldn't bother him unless there was an emergency. Who the devil?

Hawk along with Houston were probably still at the bonfire. When he looked at her, he tried to communicate with his eyes. Her hand rested adorably on her breast. He wished to lay his head where her hand was positioned. Perhaps another time. Now he had to change back.

With as little fanfare as possible he changed form. Picking up his pants, he began to dress. "We have company," he told her while he pulled on his buckskins then his boots. "I'll get the door. You stay here." Even while he ordered her to stay put, he didn't believe she would follow that command.

Lainie looked as if she wanted to yell at him. Her lips pursed together in an adorable pout that he wished he had time to kiss. Her fists tightened in that sweet spot between her breasts. Roc hoped she would behave herself and do what he asked. He realized what he said was more of a directive than asking. That was why she bristled. Why she would fight him, he didn't understand. It would take him years to get used to this woman. With all her modern ideas she was an enigma to him. Independent as well as determined, she seemed to think she could do as she pleased. In this century, she could not. Lainie would need to comes to terms with that fact. He would have to figure out how to explain the dangers to her.

"Who is it?" she queried as she followed behind him in obvious defiance of his orders. At this point, he didn't have time to argue. The pounding grew louder. The voices behind the door stronger. His heart flew to his throat.

If he knew, he wouldn't be racing down the steps to discover the truth. He shrugged calling to her over his shoulder. "Don't know." At the bottom of the steps, he turned to her. "Thought I told you to stay upstairs."

"I don't take orders." Her voice was firm. She wouldn't do anything of the sort. "I can make decisions about myself."

"No, I've figured that out." In frustration, he rammed his hand through his hair. She was such a defiant little thing. "Shall we see who's knocking at our door? Can you stay behind me?" He knew the answer before she blasted her response to his question.

"You are going to allow me to stand beside you?" Lainie shot her response back at him. She would expect nothing less than complete equality. He couldn't give that to her as much as he would like it to be so. This was a different time. She didn't understand the necessity of listening to him. There were so many things she didn't understand.

The way she tilted her chin in the air had him wondering about the issued words that sounded more like a statement than a hated question. The answer had to be everything she yearned to hear. Doing a complete about face, he spoke, "You're standing beside me would please me immeasurably. Was that the right answer?" He nearly laughed when he watched her eyes cross then she stiffened.

"Yes. Why? Are you making fun of me?"

No, he would never make fun of her though he might tease. In this case he was doing neither.

~ * ~

The man on the other side of the door was Hawk. His emotions taut with worry. He and Houston needed all the help he could find. Roc was always willing even though he had little practical experience. "We've some injured folks out of town. Got to go for them. You coming?"

Roc thought Hawk and Maisie would still be trysting by the bonfire. Seeming to sense this was an emergency, he grabbed his hat from the coat stand then slipped on his jacket. Laine grabbed for her shawl. If Roc thought to stop her, it appeared he had second thoughts.

"What happened?" Roc asked as he pulled his hat down then looked to help Lainie.

"If you come with me, you will follow orders. No questions asked. If you can't agree, I won't allow you to come."

Without speaking, Lainie nodded.

"There's been a carriage accident. Houston and Leah went on ahead. I'm going as soon as the two of you get to my office. Four of the five people riding on the coach are injured. One dead. Appears someone tried to hold up the coach. The men who stopped it got away with everyone's valuables."

Hawk looked to Lainie wondering about the girl who came from another time. He wished she had practical knowledge. "Can you help? Do you know anything about medicine?"

"Yes." She spoke quickly. "Though if you are asking if I'm a nurse or a doctor, I'm not. I know my first aid. I don't faint at the sight of blood. I still remember my CPR. Yes, I can be of assistance. I promise you," her words tumbled from her lips fast and furious. "I'm good under pressure. Don't faint..."

Hawk didn't have time to decipher the meaning of her statements. He would have to trust in her word. "Good, go with Roc. We will need as much help as possible. Stay at the office. We'll bring in the injured as soon as possible."

"I can help set up the office for the patients. Bandages will be needed. What else?" she asked. "Do you have anything for pain?"

"Roc will tell you. He's been through this drill before. You can boil some willow bark to make tea. That's the best we have for pain. It's not addictive." Hawk started from the porch, talking over his shoulder as he rushed to his stallion.

"I could go with you," Lainie said, following with quick foot steps behind Hawk. "I'm good in emergencies. I can tend to those who are not seriously hurt."

"No!" Roc sounded all too adamant as well as furious. "Heed me in this, Lainie. You're not going even if Hawk is stupid enough to allow it. I don't want you in danger. You just told me you would follow my directives then you decide you would give assistance at the scene of the accident. I won't allow it."

She bristled, her back straightening, her chin tilting. "Very well," Lainie told him through gritted teeth. "Know this, all I did was ask a question. I didn't go against your instructions. You failed to give an order. Now that you told me no..." she didn't finish. Roc cut her off with a wave of his hand coupled with a shake of his head. He grabbed her hand as they started through the door.

Hawk smiled from one to the other, thinking the two fueled each other's anger with very little provocation. "It shouldn't be more than a half hour before the first patients arrive. Father has a wagon headed that way as does Alistair and Connal."

Hawk rode Windwalker toward Inverness. Passed his father as well as Alistair and Connal. The accident was about three miles up the road. He didn't know what he would find. Leah and Houston should be there by now. If he'd needed Lainie to tend those with minor injuries he might have argued with Roc. As it stood now, Leah tended those with only scrapes and bruises. He'd alerted Alistair as well as Connal telling them the details along with what was needed before he raced from them to Roc's home.

As he rode his big stallion, he smiled halfheartedly. The relationship between his little brother and the woman was flammable. When they disagreed, a bystander could see the smoke. Though Lainie embodied the physical attributes of the type of woman his brother lusted after. He imagined that pair were in for a rocky ride. Nothing was easy where securing a mate was concerned. This woman was opinionated as well as far from biddable. She was independent. Lainie wasn't shy. No, she spoke her mind. Hawk didn't comprehend how his brother would handle that.

Lainie came from the future. He would have to ask her about this first aid as well as CPR. Was always thirsty for medical information. There might be something to be learned from her knowledge, minimal as she told him it was. What he knew about Lainie would fit in a thimble. Though he also understood there were advances in medicine all the time. It would be a surprise to discover she held expertise in her beautiful head that neither he or Houston knew about. What might be common knowledge in the future might be unheard of in this time.

Fifteen minutes later he arrived at the accident. Houston shouted directions while Leah tended to a child. A blanket covered one man. Hawk prayed he was the only casualty. Leah and Houston worked alongside each other in perfect harmony. Hawk always marveled at that. His Maisie was tending the children while they worked.

After he settled down next to a man who was lying on the ground, he felt for his pulse. It was slow and uneven. His breath rasped in and out of his chest. He was having trouble breathing. "Where do you hurt?" Hawk ran his hands down the man's sides noting when he flinched.

"Feels as if I hurt everywhere. The other doc is seeing to my wife. I need to know..." he gripped Hawk's jacket in his hand, tugging him close to his face. "Go find out if she's going to live. She was hurt real bad. She was unconscious for a while. My son is with the lady. She told me he's just got a few bruises. Thank the merciful heavens."

"I'll be right back," Hawk said.

It had been his experience that patients did better if their anxiety was relieved. In this case, he didn't know if he could do that. When he reached the lady, he saw the extent of her injuries. It didn't look good.

"How is she?" he asked Houston who was tending the woman. "Husband needs to know. In this case, doesn't look as if it's going to be good news."

"She's losing blood from a gash in her upper thigh as well from her head. It's her thigh that I'm worried about. Doing all that I can while we are not at the office, I've slowed the bleeding. She'll be the first on the wagon into town. I want you to go with her. She'll need extensive care when she gets to the office. More than Roc can give her."

"Roc and Lainie are at the office waiting for us," Hawk told him. "They will have everything ready for the incoming patients."

"Can Lainie do anything?" There was a great deal of skepticism in Houston's voice. "Don't want her getting in the way either."

Hawk didn't know what to tell him. All he could do now was to state the facts that Lainie gave him. "The little gal says she doesn't faint at the sight of blood. She knows CPR and first aid. Didn't question her further. No time. If she can fetch and carry without being a burden, that's all that matters to me."

"All right," Houston shook his head appearing as perplexed over the comments as he was. "Suppose we both need to decipher her words. What do you think? Can we rely on her?"

"Believe she'll be efficient as well as helpful. As soon as the first wagon gets here, I'm on my way back."

Hawk walked back to the man.

Once more he hunkered down beside him, speaking in a low voice. "I'm not going to lie to you. She's hurt but she's alive. We'll do our best to keep her that way. What she needs now is for you to be at her side. So, tell me where you hurt and maybe we can get the two of you to help each other out until the wagon leaves for town."

My shoulder, think I pulled my arm from the socket. Might have broken my ankle, could just be sprained. I don't know. My ribs are bruised. *Dinna* hurt bad enough for any to be broken." He winced when he spoke. "Had a broken rib before."

"I can fix your shoulder as soon as another person gets here to hold you while I put it back in place. Right now, I'll take a look at your ankle."

Moving down to his feet, Hawk lifted the man's ankle, touching the swollen area. He flinched. "What's your name?" Hawk continued to touch lightly while he assessed. "Mine's Hawk."

"Birk. My wife's name is Garia. Can I ride into town with her? My son too? We'd be...?" he stopped, seeming to understand by the expression on his face that wasn't going to be possible.

"No, there is not enough room in the wagon for the three of you as well as me. She will need constant attention. You would get in the way. Now, your son needs you. I'll bring him over here. The two of you will stay together. We'll get the both of you back as soon as possible. After that you can be with your wife." *If she is still alive.*

It was then that Elliott brought the wagon to a stop in the middle of the clearing. He jumped from the wagon. Long strides took him to Houston who stood, waving his hand to get his attention.

"Bring the wagon over here," Houston called out, still waving with his arm. "Need to get this woman into the back. Hawk's going to ride with you."

With the three of them working together, they loaded her into the wagon. While they worked with her, she moaned. Houston covered her with a blanket explaining once more the extent of the wounds. Elliott looked to Hawk for direction. He understood moving her was painful. Was glad she wasn't awake to feel the pain. If she had been she'd be screaming.

"Before we leave, I need your help with a dislocated shoulder." Hawk told his father, gesturing for him to follow him. "You can hold the man still."

Elliott followed his son.

"This is going to hurt," Hawk said as he took the man's arm.

The man cried out when the injured limb was set in place. "Tell me she's going to be all right. My wife has to live. What will I do without her?" Birk wiped tears from his eyes. He sat up watching the scene.

His son was beside Birk when they left, holding his father's hand.

The woman, Garia, was still bleeding when they brought her into the office. "Put her in surgery. She's going to need stitches. Lainie, get me some whiskey."

Hawk didn't like the appearance of her skin which was white, pasty. When he looked into her eyes they were glazed over.

"Roc, I need bandages. Now!" I'm going to need you to hold her down when I stitch her up. Even though she's not awake her body is likely to jerk."

Chapter Five

Roc sat in the wing chair in his home, his head held in hands. Lainie didn't feel any better than Roc looked. Tears she didn't have time to shed when they were working over the woman, slipped from her eyes now. She knew Roc felt much the same. In a different century the woman might have survived.

In a different century...

The night had been long, gruelingly difficult. They were both exhausted. The woman didn't make it despite all the care given to her. Lainie understood Garia lost too much blood. In this time, there was no way for a person to receive a transfusion. If the woman's home had been in a different century she might have lived. This time was so primitive. She was meant to live here. She didn't know how. The devil, some doctors bled their patients as if they needed to lose more of the life-giving substance. That notion was preposterous.

Recalling the previous events along with the words she said to Birk, "She will be in heaven and no longer in pain."

Lainie didn't possess a strong faith. She'd seen more than her share of radicals who thought some religions were better than others. Under the name of their god, they persecuted those who didn't believe as they did. When she spoke to the woman's husband, she tried to reassure him that his wife was now in good hands. She was in heaven. There would be no more pain for her. It was hard when she didn't know if she believed what she told him.

Birk's sobs tore through her, lodged within her. The loss was potent. She wished for a love like he seemed to have with his wife. When two people married, they should love each other. While her thoughts flew through her head at lightning speed, her attention focused on Roc. He told her she was his eternal mate. Did that mean he loved her? What she knew was he fanned sensual sparks in her body she never knew existed. The passion she felt for him was very raw and very real. This desire for Roc...wasn't that lust? In no way could he love her. It was too soon. What was it now, six days? Or was it seven? She'd lost count.

"I want to be with her. Can't live without her."

Tears still ran down his cheeks. He held onto his son's hand, squeezing.

Lainie looked from the man called Birk to his son. She wanted to shake the man who needed to think of someone other than himself. Needed to find some means to convince him that life was preferable to death. "Your boy needs you too. He's lost his mother. Don't make him lose his father also."

Birk opened his arms for his boy who rushed into them. They held onto each other while they both sobbed for the loss of the woman one called wife, the other called mother.

The driver of the carriage was the man who died at the scene. The rest of the passengers had broken arms or legs, nothing life threatening. One of the passengers told her the robbers went by the names Scratch and Geordie. They said they were looking for a woman. Those were the men who attacked her. Some way, she didn't know how, she was linked to him. Did that fact have something to with her travel through time?

Lainie basked in the praise Houston heaped on her. He went as far as to ask her to teach him CPR. Houston told her if he'd known what to do, he might have saved the driver who suffered from what he thought was a heart attack. He'd been alive when they reached him.

"Come here," Roc beckoned to her. "Sit by me. I need to hold you."

Lainie sat down beside him. She wanted him to hold her too. He wrapped his arm around her, her head resting on his chest. She found she was in need of his warmth, his strength as well. The hectic evening taught her more about what her life would be missing if she remained with Roc. She tried to sort out the gains from the losses. In the face of the woman bleeding out because they could not give her blood, it was hard to see the positive reasons for remaining in this time. Her feelings didn't have anything to do with creature comforts, just the practical side of life and death. Could she love Roc enough to overlook what she was losing?

"We couldn't help her. She should have been able to live to watch her son grow up."

Torn between two worlds, Lainie sought comfort in Roc's arms. Comfort food was what she needed; a large bowl of macaroni and cheese. Tomorrow...today, she amended, she would make some for dinner. She did have a recipe in her head though she would have to make do with regular milk instead of the condensed variety.

Even though there were things she vividly recalled, her past life began to fade. What once was her life seemed to be a distant past. Faces dimmed. Rafe's handsome face became intwined with Roc's. When she closed her eyes, she didn't know which one she saw, Roc or Rafe. She no longer recalled the names of her friends. Maisie and Leah replaced those people as did Hawk and Houston. When she looked in the mirror, she saw distinct differences in both her face as well as her form.

"You did well." His hand running along her arm soothed her. "You were always there when Hawk or Houston asked for you. I wasn't certain about the fainting part. You never once wavered. I'm proud of you. Maybe you found a calling in this time since you cannot photograph anything."

She thought on his words. Understood the truths. "We did save those two people." The hurt would never go away. She would never forget the way the woman looked when Hawk covered her with the sheet. Nor would she forget the harsh sobs of loss from her husband and son. She never considered herself nurse material. Hated needles. Didn't do well when she saw them. Never liked to see anyone in pain. Tonight wasn't something she wished to remember. Knew she would never forget.

"No, we didn't." Roc let his hand settle on the curve of her hip. Lainie was beginning to savor his touch, to look forward to the way his hands so sweetly caressed her.

Lainie held out her shaking hands. "Look at them. You know what I see?" She didn't give him a chance to answer. "Blood. I see oodles of blood. More blood than I've ever seen before. When I told Hawk I didn't faint at the sight of blood, I was right. What I couldn't tell him was that even though my hands look clean, I still see the blood. Will I always see it?" Tears slid from her eyes.

"I do too," Roc whispered, his words so soft Lainie had to look into his eyes to realize what the words were. "I do too. Don't know the answer to your question."

To be close to Roc was of utmost importance. Lainie set her head in the hollow of his shoulder. She heard the steady, reassuring beat of his heart. Listened to his breath as he slowly breathed in then out. Lainie set her hand on his chest to confirm Roc was here.

She was here.

Here in this home, there was no portal to fall through. They were safe. Lainie felt she would always be safe as well as loved if she was with Roc.

After going through the gateway to this time, she could have died. Geordie or Scratch could have done... She gulped down the bile rising to her throat. They were the men who held up the stage. Those two men were looking for her. Surely as she was sitting here in Roc's home and in his arms, Lainie understood. Those two horrible men still wanted her. They were not affected by Roc's threats.

She shivered, the tremors running through her to the tips of her toes.

Roc saved her. She owed him. Her life was no longer hers. He tried to see her point of view. She understood how incredibly difficult that would be. Though she knew he tried, he didn't understand her fears. How could he? She wasn't certain she understood.

Lainie pushed away from Roc. His eyes had been closed. After she moved away from him, they opened. "Why are my memories fading? I don't want to forget my past. I cared for Rafe. I know as the time is passing, I won't remember him. I don't understand how I know this. I just do." Lainie pushed farther away, tilting her chin so she could see into the steel-blue of his eyes. "I don't want to forget."

With his hand in hers, he squeezed as if to give the reassurance she was desperate for. "I don't know. What is fading?"

He sounded both curious as well as confused. She supposed that was good.

"Rafe's face is looking more like yours with every passing day. Though the two of you are so similar, the fact steals my breath from my lungs. My parents are difficult to recall. The friends I once had are now replaced with Maisie and Leah. I can't recollect a single name. There are other things too. Everything I once seemed to remember is now intermingling with the present. I don't like that."

"Perhaps that is the way it is meant to be if you are going to stay here with me." With tender care, he stroked her hair, played with the long silken strands that fell lose from her pony tail. The ones that were as brilliant as the sunset on a clear day. "Eventually, you might lose all the images you once knew in your future time. Would that be so bad?"

Lainie shuddered at the thought. She didn't want to lose any memories or knowledge. That was all she had of her old life. Did it mean so little that the past would be wiped clean from her head?

"I don't like that idea. Now, it seems it's just the small details that are gone. I can't tell you what color Rafe's eyes are though I believe they must be the same color as yours. You have a perfect dimple on this side of your mouth. On the other side, the indentation is only half of what it could be. It's all that keeps you from being...perfect."

His hoot of laughter caught her attention. "I would think that dimples or lack thereof have nothing to do with perfection. Before you, no one has ever called me perfect or nearly there. You must always remember, I'm not a perfect man."

"You are though. To me anyway."

"No, let's take you if we're going to speak of perfection. This face of yours..." he lifted her chin, "is the most beautiful face I've ever seen. The way you care about others befuddles my mind. You were wonderful today even though what you saw hurt you. I hope you never forget all the practical things you've learned. Though I wouldn't be averse to your forgetting Rafe."

"You were just as good if not better. You are smart. Determined." So, they were exchanging compliments. Lainie didn't recall the last time a man, any man complimented her. She liked the feeling. "Why do you want me to forget about Rafe?"

"You know things no one in this time knows about healing, even

Hawk and Houston. When you showed them how to breathe life into another person then keep the heart muscles going so it would continue to pump blood, I was astonished as well as impressed. It is so simple. Logical. One shouldn't forget those things."

"Will I forget that information? Will you have to teach me?"

The thought of losing the knowledge that was so important dismayed. There were so many unanswered questions. What if she saved someone or Houston or Hawk saved a patient because she taught them CPR? Would that change the history of the world? If she stayed, she would have to be careful. Perhaps that was why her expertise was also meant to fade away. Why, in time, she wouldn't remember anything from her earlier life.

"I have no idea. Does it matter?"

"Yes, it matters!" Lainie was exhausted, her frustration with Roc turning to anger. She needed to breathe deeply, needed to calm herself. In her mind, the only way she could do so would be to change the topic. "What time is it? It seems as if we've been awake forever."

"Nearly dawn."

She swept a deep breath of air into her lungs, determined to forget the worst part of the evening. Determined to remember everything that was good as well as beautiful. "Your cat is amazing. The sight electrified me."

Both the vision of him naked as well as in his other form was breathtaking.

"Lainie, you excite me, thrill me. Your breasts overflow my large hands. Your hips are wide, your belly rounded with sweet perfection." It seemed they didn't want to stop talking. "If you would commit to me, I would like to kiss all those places on your body. Need to see you naked. Right now, all I've got to go on is my imagination as well as the way you feel when you nestle yourself against me at night. I fear my imagination doesn't do you justice."

While she was delighted with his words, she needed to put an end to this as she realized the new day would be upon them soon. Undressing for him was frightening. No man...except Rafe...had ever seen her naked. Though her swimsuits did little to hide her body, the fabric did cover certain strategic spots. Committing to him was even more frightening. If she married him, she would never leave this time. "Do you want to sleep with me tonight? Just sleep?"

Lainie understood she wasn't ready for more than the comfort of his arms around her.

"Yes," his voice was ruff, husky. "I will always prefer to sleep with you. "Did you think different?"

She was beginning to understand the ruff sound of his voice meant he wanted her, desired her in ways that Rafe never did. "Would it be too much to ask for a bath before I retire for the night? If it's too much work, I understand."

She felt unclean. Dirty to the tips of her toes. Still felt as if blood covered her hands. She needed to scrub every inch of her.

"No, I'd like one too? Do you want to share?" He waggled his eye brows at her, his wide grin infectious.

Laughing at his antics, she punched him on his chest. "We *cannae* share. We are not married. Besides, I doubt if your bath is large enough for the two of us."

Lainie realized then that even her speech was changing. She was beginning to take on a more Scottish brogue befitting the time she landed in. "A hot shower would be nicer." Lainie didn't know where that thought came from.

"A shower?" He shook his head. "We can share. I'll make room." He kissed her lightly, his lips touching tenderly upon hers, once then twice. With a masculine sigh, he moved away from her. "I will start the water heating. You go upstairs. I'll bring you the heated water as soon as it's ready."

"You should not have to carry it that far." She was used to hot running water. A shower would be heavenly. A shower they could share. Lainie wasn't at all certain why she was thinking in that manner. She understood he didn't want to make love to her until she told him she would stay here. Perhaps there was some rational reasoning in his thoughts. He knew she could not get pregnant. In her mind sex between them would not result in an unwanted child. When or if she left the eighteenth century, she would not return to her time an unwed mother.

"If you don't want to share..." Roc left the sentence hanging midair. "I'm only a man, a man who wants you more than his next breath. We need to be separate for the bathing. If you stayed downstairs and I knew you were naked..." He held out his hands to her. She stepped back, unwilling to walk into his arms.

"I understand." She did comprehend what he tried to say to her. When she saw him wearing nothing, heat swirled inside her. A pulsing ache centered between her thighs swept thoughts other than Roc away from her mind. Golden butterflies dance and flitted in the most secret parts of her. "I'll go upstairs and wait. You can bring it to me as soon as it is hot enough."

She would sleep with him tonight. He would hold her just as she had all the other nights. How long would it be before she would again give into the impulse and asked him to make love to her. Not long. One time she asked him to make love to her. He refused. He would refuse again. The man believed in traditions. He wanted their first time together to be on their wedding night.

Before she left the room, he kissed her, his lips touched lightly on hers. She felt the hesitancy as she also understood that she had many decisions to make. It didn't seem he wanted to walk away. With his hand behind her head, he deepened the kiss, his tongue probing, searching for her heat, for her passion. Desire flamed to life. As her future life seemed to grow less and less important to her, she wondered...wondered what she would decide.

Roc wanted her. No one in her time felt that way about her. He was willing to take her to the portal. Maybe he was less than willing. They tarried here, in Carnoch. What would happen if she traveled back to the century she was born in and remembered nothing of this time? The thought gave her reason to pause. If she regretted leaving him behind, she would forever seek a new way to find him. Would risk everything to return. While thoughts of living with Roc tugged her one way, thoughts of returning to a century where life was so much easier pulled her in an entirely different direction.

Roc set her away from him. "Go...go before I change my mind. I'm a weak man. If you keep returning my kisses, we'll never get baths."

"Change your mind about what, pray tell?" She liked the way he looked at her, the way his lips cherished hers. Now, he had the fiercest expression on his handsome features. Lightly she touched the dimple that formed with his smile. She wanted to kiss his dimples. The perfect one along with the one that was not quite so perfect.

"Sharing a bath, what else could it be?" Roc asked. "I could wash your back. You could wash mine."

"I'm not ready to be intimate with you," Lainie lied to him.

It wasn't that she wasn't ready. Over time, her feelings changed. She was afraid of intimacy as well as commitment. To her they went hand in hand. Seemed that Roc felt the same.

Sporting a heavy heart, she walked up the steps. Exhaustion seemed to almost take over the need to wash the events of the night from her body and mind. In the bathing room on the second floor, she placed a towel close to the bathtub. The nightgown Heather gave her to take with her, she placed next to the towel. When all that was done, she sat in the bed chamber and watched the embers in the fireplace as they found the wood Roc set next to them. Flames rose from the new wood. Heat surged into the room. She hugged herself wishing she had all the answers, wishing she had even one. Wishing she didn't keep changing her mind about Roc along with what she wanted from him. Desire and passion played such a resounding role in her new life. Desire along with passion were both new emotions to her. Lainie didn't understand how to deal with the emotions she'd never experienced...until now.

Could she tell him she would marry him? Would she become his wife in all the ways he wished. A few words of love would do a lot to make the transition easier. She couldn't ask him for something that she couldn't return. Perhaps if she knew she loved him, the decisions would be easier.

Roc brought the water. The task took him several trips up the steps to get enough to heat it to her satisfaction. She didn't mean to be picky. She just didn't want a tepid bath. Once everything was ready, she sunk into the heated liquid. The warmth soothed as well as calmed the energy that had been seething within her for too many hours to count. She set her head on the lip of the tub then closed her eyes. Memories washed through her at a blinding pace.

The images that flitted across her mind were all of the present not the future she came from. The life she once knew was vanishing. Diminished in her mind. She didn't understand the images. She saw Roc in his cat form, loping toward her, his cat grin wide. She waited for him, seeming pleased. Watching him strut through the field, her hands were clasped between her breasts.

The attack came without warning. She cried out when the arms circled her from behind. Lainie found herself thrust into the arms of a different man. A hand covered her mouth, stopping the scream. She struggled, trying to dislodge herself from her captor.

A shot fired.

Roc's cat fell to the ground. She reached out to him unable to touch him. The man kept her from running to him. Held her arms behind her back. Tears slipped down her cheeks. He was hurt. Unmoving, Roc lay in the field where he'd just been running. His blood soaked the earth. She had to get to him, needed to stop the blood from spilling onto the earth.

This was her fault. She asked him to return her to the portal. She should have been satisfied with her life now. Always, she yearned for something better, for what she couldn't have, never being satisfied. She didn't want him to die. She needed for Roc to live.

I love you!

"No!" she cried out struggling against the man.

Her nails ripped across his arm. Blood filled the scratches. She screamed and screamed Roc's name.

"He can't help you now." The man grabbed her by the hair, his fingers biting into her scalp. "He's dead. You're mine. When I'm finished with you, I'll give you over to Geordie for his fun. You're a grand plaything. You won't be so high and mighty after you've had us between your thighs."

Lainie recognized the voice. *Scratch.* She fought from his hold, rushing to Roc. Holding his head in her hands she saw the blood. Just like in the carriage accident. If she couldn't bind the wound enough, he would bleed to death.

All the blood. More and more blood. Blood everywhere.

"Lainie..."

The voice whispered in her head, the gentle tones soothing her fear. It was Roc's voice she heard. She shivered. The scene vanished. Lainie no longer held his head on her lap. The field of grass and flowers grew dim. As she opened her eyes, she blinked a few times.

"Lainie..." The pressure on her shoulder slowly brought her back to the present. "Wake up. It was just a bad dream. A nightmare...nothing more."

When she opened her eyes, Roc stood in front of the tub holding out a towel. She crossed her arms in front of her. "Roc?" She was naked. He'd never seen her completely naked. At least not from the front. "You can't be here. I'm..."

"Naked? I see that." He was grinning. "I like what I see. You will have to get used to being naked around me. When we're married, I'm going to insist on a few things."

"Can't we talk about that later...when I'm dressed?"

He nodded his agreement. "You were screaming. I had to come see. Yes, we'll talk later. After we've slept. Here," he told her then held out the towel. "I'll leave you now. Call me when you're dressed." His hands trembled when he held up the towel. She saw the tight lines around his eyes and mouth.

Roc was giving her a small measure of privacy. She understood. As he turned away to leave the room, he set the towel where she left it. While he walked away, she watched his long strides. His shoulders were so broad, his hips narrow. He was all man, not an ounce of fat possessed his hard lean body.

She dried herself then slipped the gown over her head. "Roc," she did call out to him.

He must have been waiting outside the door. His large body filled the opening as he stepped back into the room. Once he was close enough, he folded her in his arms. "You smell of gardenia. Don't know what we'll do when you run out of the soap as well as the perfume. I'm used to the scent. The flower suits you."

"I could wear lavender," she said as she nestled against him. His scent pleased her too, all male as well as a bit spicey. She looked at him, "I need to talk now. Don't know if I'll be able to sleep if I don't."

Scooping her into his arms, he strode with her to the fireplace. Roc set her down on the hearth. At least she hoped he had time for his bath. Roc must have bathed downstairs. His hair was damp, the long ends curling around his neck and over his ears.

"You need to dry your hair. I'll brush it for you." He sat down behind her. With the brush and comb his mother gave her, he began to work the tangles out, his fingers winding through the length ahead of the comb. With infinite care, he pulled the comb through the long strands. While her hair wasn't as long as it once was, it still reached below her shoulders. She didn't understand that thought.

His strokes continued with deliberate slowness and caution. The movement soothing, embracing her. Shivers filled her with each exquisite stroke of the brush. She sighed, air whispering from her lungs, leaning into him. When he held her hair away from her nape, his knuckles brushed across her flesh. She shivered with need. Golden butterflies danced in her belly. She wanted to lean against him. Stroke after stroke she felt the tender glide of his fingers. Her hair dried. He continued with the brush. Her hair seemed to take on a life all its own, winding around his hands, clinging to his face, the day's growth of whiskers.

"You have beautiful hair. For me would you let it grow?" he asked as he continued to brush.

She sighed with the pleasure streaking through her. If he would always brush her hair, she would promise him anything. "My hair tangles with the least provocation," she murmured sleepily thinking at this rate she would fall asleep sitting here. "It's a nuisance I'd rather do without."

"I will comb and brush it every night," he murmured as if trying to convince her. He brought a long strand to his face. The length tangled again in the day's growth of beard stubble, clinging to him. "It is so cool to the touch, silken when it passes over me. It seems to follow my hands. Caresses me."

In the back of her throat, she purred. If she could change to a cat, would her purr sound the same? "It's the static electricity. How did you learn to brush hair?"

"My sister's hair is almost as unruly as yours. While it isn't naturally curly, it's so thick she curses it. Since she was a little girl and mother didn't have time to brush it at night, I would do it for her." Roc set the brush on the hearth while he ran his fingers through her hair, letting the strands sift between his fingers.

Silent shivers wracked her body. Aching shivers. She burned in dark secret places that seemed to come to life whenever Roc touched or kissed her. He pushed her hair aside so it fell over one shoulder. His mouth touched upon her neck while his hands warmed her arms. An ember in the fireplace popped. She jumped.

"Shh... It's all right. Let's go to bed." He picked her up in his arms, walking the short distance to the bed. He set her down. "We need to sleep."

Before he joined her, he closed the curtains, darkening the room. The soft glide of fabric being removed then the plop as his buckskins hit the wood floor followed. He would be naked. He would hold her through the night, keep her fears at bay. He was her rock. No one else would do.

After the tread of his footsteps stopped, she felt the covers as he lifted them. He slid into the bed, joining her. She scooted next to him, understanding the heat from his body would keep her warm. She would be in his arms while she fell asleep. She ran her feet along the length of his leg. The small gesture in such a short time had become a ritual. Tonight, she didn't think her feet were cold. He would tell her if they were.

With her head on his shoulder, she began to explain to him about her dream. She was drowsy from the warm bath coupled with the heat from the fire. The need to say a few words made sleep impossible. "I don't *ken* if I...I don't *ken* if dreams tell of the future. I'm afraid if we go to the field where you found me, you'll die. It was Scratch and Geordie who were there waiting for me. Scratch shot you. You were in your cat. I don't understand that part. Why would you change?"

"I'm not afraid of those two. I want you to know that I will never change to my cat out in the open. The dream cannot possibly come true. We don't do that. If we want to frolic or swim the clan goes farther into the highlands to places where few people live. Even if I do take you to the portal, I would not be in my cat form. There would be no reason."

His words did little to make her feel better. She was still afraid for him. Still terrified she would lose him.

He held her so close to him, she felt protected. Even Roc couldn't protect himself from a gunshot.

"*Dinnae* worry for me, *Lass*." He stroked her hair, holding the length in his hands. "I'm not going to die."

~ * ~

Her dream terrified him more for her sake than for his. All he told her was true leaving out the part...unless he was provoked...unless her life was in danger. Only in those cases would he ever change to his cat so close to Inverness. While the area was fairly remote, too many people traveled the roads nearby.

When she told him of her memories fading, he was both pleased as well as disappointed. Pleased for himself, disappointed for her. He understood one wouldn't want to lose years of their life. There would be no memories of her childhood. If she forgot everything, she couldn't return. In the future she described to him, she would be lost with no memories.

What would he do if he no longer recalled his family, if he no longer had the joys of wrestling with his cousins and his brother? Life would be less than what it should be. There was nothing he could do about it though. What would happen would happen. The thought sent a wave of frustration through him. While he didn't want to ever take her back to the field where he first set eyes on her, he knew he would. He would need to give her every available option. If she was going to live here with no regrets, he would have to give her every opportunity to decide for herself. Nothing could be left to chance.

He grimaced yet smiled too. It seemed his Lainie could not get to sleep unless she set her cold feet on his legs. The gesture never failed to bring him to attention in every way possible. The rush of desire would send him to his knees if he'd been standing. When next he felt her cold feet, small streaks of light filtered between the curtains and the windowsill. A squinted look at the clock near the bed told him the time was just past two in the afternoon.

He groaned. The warmth of the bed, the feel of her full ripe woman's body nestled next to him would be gone in a few minutes. He should let her sleep. If he did, she would never get to sleep tonight. As it was, sleep this evening would still be difficult. He lifted himself so he could see her face. She'd been sleeping with her delicious bottom pressed tightly against his groin. When she moved, thoughts of seducing her clouded his judgement. He found he was spending his days in constant semi-arousal.

"Do we have to get up?" she murmured, her voice thick with sleep.

She turned over, her chin resting on his shoulder. The delicate tips of her fingers slid along his breastbone burning him with fire.

The whisper against his neck and chest sent another surge of desire racing through him as the warmth of her breath always did. Sleeping with her without the possibility of sex was pure torture. He couldn't take her. Not until she agreed with his wishes. As long as the idea of returning played in her head, he couldn't have her beneath him. If he believed the sooner they went back to the portal the better, he would do so. However, with the fading of her memory, time was on his side. She would understand that also. It seemed it was just a matter of time before she voiced her need.

This was a living nightmare, a hell of his making. He'd not been celibate for this long since he turned eighteen. In the village there was always a willing widow. In Inverness he had his mistress. He'd not told Lainie about the woman he kept in the city for his pleasure. He supposed a quick trip there in the guise of business to dismiss her should be done soon. She would be upset with this turn of events even though she understood that eventually he would find a woman he wished to marry.

What if Lainie left him while he was gone? What if she made the trip to the portal without him...on her own. She could ask his brother or one of his cousins to take her. They would never do that.

No, the trip would have to be put off. It wasn't in his nature to act too quickly. If she left him, what then? Would he marry and have children? The thought turned his stomach sour. What he didn't understand was why she didn't feel the same as he did? Maisie felt the connection immediately to Hawk. Leah to Houston. Aila to Kit. Shawna to Riley. The list went on. Lainie didn't understand how precious this time was. Did she feel no sensual connection to him.

He needed to understand why Lainie was so damn hesitant where her feelings for him were concerned. Why didn't she feel linked to him? It tormented him to think she didn't want him so badly she burned with the same fire that scorched him.

"Yes." The answer was adamant though it came at a great expense. "I've work to do. Have to get going." He rose from the bed, leaving the covers over her. He didn't make any attempts to hide his nakedness but strode to the armoire to pull out clean clothing. He felt the heat from her eyes while he walked. She looked at him. She liked to watch him. He would have to capitalize on that notion.

Facing her, he began to dress. Again, he felt her watching him, could sense the way her gaze traveled the length of him numerous times. She didn't know where to stop. His smile, he didn't know if she would be able to see the wide grin. With the curtains drawn tight it was dark in the room, there was some light for her to see him. The thought of her watching him dress sent another striking bolt of energy through him. His body hardened with the need to possess her, to stroke all of her, to know her intimately.

"You are so handsome," she murmured as she sat up in bed, pushing the fall of her glorious golden-red hair from her face while still keeping the covers to her chin. She was still modest. Except for a few hints in the bath, he'd not seen her naked. He would soon. When he painted her, she would pose wearing nothing at all. Though she had yet to agree. For a reason he didn't quite understand, he knew she would agree.

Her eyes were sleepy lidded. The darkened lashes fell over her eyes for a moment. "You should get dressed then come down for something to eat. If we don't get up now, we'll have the devil's own time falling asleep at a decent hour tonight."

Tonight, after he made his first preliminary sketches, he wanted to hold her. Sitting next to the fire, he would explore her curves more intimately. He didn't know if she would agree to pose nude.

"I know."

When she pulled her hair back from her face, the covers slipped and her breasts pushed against the fabric of her nightdress. The thin batiste fabric did little to hide the dark pink tips of her breasts. Did little to keep his arousal at bay.

The tight hard buds he so needed to taste pushed with enticing hunger toward him. He pulled in a hard breath of air. Persecuting himself further wasn't wise. He needed all his self-control to keep from tossing the covers then coming down on top of her, exploring all of her. "I'll meet you downstairs." His voice was curt, tensed from the ragged desire he held in check. He couldn't take her. He told himself over then over again. He had to wait. Needed patience. Seemed where Lainie was concerned he had none. In all his life, he'd never wanted a woman so damn much he hurt.

"In a few minutes. Give me time to dress. I'll be down." Her soft voice hummed through the room. His tortured mind needed that humming sound to be made from her passion. He needed to feel her sultry rain drench his fingers as well as his sex.

She would think he was angry with her. He wasn't. He just couldn't stay there and watch her innocence beguile him. Every gesture, every move of her arms, of her hands aroused his senses. Every breath she inhaled sent her breasts swaying provocatively. Heaving deep breaths, he strode down the stairs surprised to be greeted with the scent of bacon frying in a pan in the kitchen.

When he stepped inside, it was to see his mother at the stove. "Did you forget where you live?" he asked sardonically while he inhaled the tantalizing scents that filled the small room. The pan on the stove was piled high with bacon. Fried potatoes sat on a nearby plate. Scrambled eggs were waiting in a bowl for the bacon to cook.

"Of course not. I made your father breakfast first. Now, since both you and your...both you and Lanie helped out last night, I trotted myself right over here to make certain you didn't starve. Knew the two of you would be in need of a hearty breakfast after you roused yourselves. Will Lainie be down soon?"

With his arms crossed over his chest Roc leaned against the frame of the door, watching, evaluating his mother's words. "She is dressing as we speak." He thought his mother would turn pale or voice some objection. What he said implied they did more than just sleep together in the same bed.

They had not. Though with each passing night, his determination faded.

"Good. I'm certain she will be hungry. As your father told the tale, the night was long as well as grueling. Two people died. That was a shame, a young mother. When are the two of you going to speak with Father Damian? Don't you think it's time to make Lainie your wife? You are not getting any younger."

The question was far from innocent. His mother had an agenda. She wanted more grandchildren. Soon his father would be in competition with Alistair and Connal. Roc didn't doubt for a moment his thoughts weren't true. More than he wanted to settle this with Lainie, his mother did. She was far from patient. Though Roc did think they should talk to the priest. Perhaps he could shed a modicum of light on their situation. Reconsidering was always an option.

"I will speak to Lainie about riding to see him at the McKenna keep."

"You should set a date for the wedding. Don't appreciate the rushed affairs when everything has to be taken care of within twenty-four hours or less. I'd like to take her to the dressmakers so she will have a wedding dress. She deserves the best."

Heather turned the bacon then beat the eggs waiting in the bowl one more time.

Roc held up his hands in warning, trying to caution his mother. "Don't get ahead of yourself. Lainie hasn't agreed to anything, especially not a wedding. She is still thinking strongly of an attempt to return herself to the time she was born to." He didn't want to say anything more to his mother.

"You're sleeping with her." Heather's voice was accusatory.

"Yes."

That was all his mother should know about their sleeping arrangements. The less she understood about their relationship the better. He wasn't about to explain anything to either of his parents.

Lainie stepped through the door. She was scowling, her brows drawn together so tight he had the urge to run his fingertip across them, ease the discomfort. The expression on her face told him she'd heard her mother's accusations. She started to turn away. Lainie would hide before she faced their truths. Perhaps that was what she was doing all along. Hiding. Perhaps running.

"Come here, Lainie. Mother has fixed more food than the entire family would have eaten when we were growing up. You've got to be starving." Roc eyed the growing pile of bacon before noticing the stack of pancakes, the plate of potatoes along with the eggs she was about to add to the pan. Shaking his head, he spoke up. "We can't eat that much."

"Some of the food will save," Heather protested. "You don't have to eat it all right now. Are you going into work?"

"It's late. I'm certain that whatever new jobs find their way to the printers will wait. The paper isn't due out for three more days. Plenty of time." He dished up a plate of food for Lainie who seemed to be hovering as far from the table as she could and still be inside the room. After that, one for himself.

Roc set the plate down then looked up. "This is for you." He turned to his mother. "Will you eat with us? We can always use the company."

"I'd be delighted to."

Lainie sat. For a few seconds she toyed with the food, pushing what he gave her around on the plate. The conversation she overheard needed to be addressed. "You have to eat something. I understand you heard some of Mother's questions. No one is rushing you to the altar. I understand your confusion, at least I'm trying to appreciate what you are going through."

He tried to be gentle with his words even while he was as impatient as his mother.

She was nodding her head as if she agreed with him. Her face still appeared a death mask, her voice held a wealth of uncertainty. "Father Damian is the priest in this area?" she asked as she gingerly began to eat her food. "Why would we wish to see him. We've no future plans of a marriage. I *dinnae* wish for counseling. I'm not Catholic." After she set her fork down then looked at his mother, she spoke. "I don't want a wedding dress or a cake or flowers. Since we've made no decisions, there will be no expenditure of money. I will not..." She caught her lip between her teeth as she seemed to think about what to say. She never finished, leaving Roc with more uncertainty than he needed.

"Can't blame a mother for trying," Heather laughed followed with a slight lift of her shoulders. "Eat up now. You have to keep up your strength. These all-night adventures can take their toll on a girl. One never knows when we'll be called on by our doctor son to help out. Heard the two of you did a marvelous job. Also heard Lainie taught Hawk and Houston a few things."

A smile broke across Lainie's mouth. Roc had an immediate urge to kiss those lips. "You're right. Last night was exhausting. It was also exhilarating. For the first time in a very long time, I felt useful. Nonetheless, we should have been able to..." she bit off the rest of the comment, her expression changing.

Roc saw Lainie's frown of remorse the moment when all that happened last night came back to haunt. As if he was inside her mind, he knew she was thinking about the woman who lost her life. Was also thinking about the fact Scratch and Geordie still looked for her. That image in his head sent ice through his blood.

She poured honey on a pancake letting the thick sweetener make delicate circles within the melting butter. After she set the container on the table, she spoke. "We always have maple syrup," she murmured then ate a bite, her words trembling from her soft lips. "I don't remember exactly what that is."

"If you concentrate..."

She stared at him. Her brows furrowed tighter than before. Waved her fork his way, "I don't know what anything is anymore. I've forgotten so much. I'm afraid I'm going to lose all that I was. If that happens, who am I? I'll have no identity."

She stood so quickly the chair she'd been sitting on fell to the floor with a resounding crash. Rushing through the room, she left the kitchen. The door banged shut behind her. Roc understood she might want to be alone with her thoughts. He didn't want that. If he left her alone too long, she might decide she couldn't stay in this time. The devil!

"Go after her," his mother said reaching out to touch his hand. "Your woman needs you. Be there for her. This must be so hard on her. You know she can never go back. I don't think it works that way."

"Kit came back," Roc told her succinctly. "Kit came back. It took months but he came back to the time he was supposed to live. How do we know Lainie is predestined to live here? From everything she has told us, this must be a terrible shock."

"We both understand she is meant to live in this time. She is your mate."

Roc's hands were fisted tight, his lips set in a grim, determined line. "She doesn't feel the kind of connection the others do. She doesn't believe she is my mate. There are..."

He cut off the comment with a slash of his hand. This was his mother he spoke to. He could have told his father. His father wasn't here.

"Lainie does. She just hasn't told you or she doesn't realize the connection. The joining between the two of you is strong, stronger than most. She is frightened near to death as I was when I first met your father. I can tell when she looks at you, when she watches you, she's in love."

His hand landed hard on the table. If she loved him, why didn't she tell him? Would that be so difficult? *Probably for the same reason you haven't told her you love her.* Roc knew he didn't speak of love to her because he was afraid she'd tell him she didn't share that love. Once she told him it was too soon to know how they felt. They didn't know each other well enough. He told her in time they would finish each other's sentences.

"What's in a look?" Roc shrugged wishing he understood the answer. "A look will not warm the nights, will not create children as well as grandchildren. A look will not hold her in this time. There has to be more. Something tangible I can hold on to."

"Do you recall the way Riley looks at Shawna? Even when he

thought she lied to him, his eyes heated with desire."

"Yes, well, I'm certain Lainie wouldn't believe the tale if I told it to her. I should go after her." He was afraid if left alone too long, she would enlist help to get her back to the doorway to another time. His mother was right about most things. This one she was not.

"Stay here for a few more minutes. I believe your instincts were right in the first place. She needs time to think. It can't be easy to forget what you are most familiar with. I know how frightened I would be if my past life faded away in ribbons of loss."

His mother was right. How would he feel if he forgot all the little things that were a part of his life? What if he forgot how to change form? Instinct. That was something he would never lose the ability to achieve.

"Tomorrow, you will see Father Damian. You don't have to take Lainie with you. If nothing else you will have a neutral party to talk to. She said she didn't want counseling. Do you? Could you use someone to listen to your story? I've found the good Father has had many experiences with shifters that you might find interesting."

He was nodding, watching the door, eager to see Lainie return. As the minutes ticked by, she didn't walk through the entrance. Roc finished his breakfast even though he no longer felt hungry. He helped his mother clean up the dishes then stored the leftovers for later tonight. His gut turned. His mind seemed filled with confusion.

She'd been gone two hours when he decided to search for her. She did need to be found. Needed to be held by him. Reassured. While he didn't know where she ran off to, he felt certain the first place he should look for her was the bonfire. After he reached the top, he saw her sitting in the same place he held her next to him the night before.

A wan smile crossed her delicate features when she heard his approach and looked up. "Hello," she managed then patted a place beside her for him to sit down. "I apologize for running out on you and Heather."

"Hello to you too. Nothing to apologize for."

While he ticked off the seconds in his head, he looked into the clear blue of her eyes, wishing he could read her thoughts behind them.

"Thank you for giving me time. I acted the fool over maple syrup.

While I thought long and hard about it, I remembered the sweet taste of maple."

After he sat down, Roc picked up her hand then turned it over. Understanding he had more than enough time to be patient, he traced the lines on the palm. He had never had maple syrup. Didn't know what it was. What he needed now was to boost her spirits from the weighty depression he sensed. "You aren't a fool."

"A terrified fool."

"If you'll let me know what's bothering you, I can chase away the terror. Keep the fear hidden at night when shadows fill your heart. In the bright sunlight of the day, I will hold on to you so you won't stumble and fall. You are my sun. Did you know that?"

He brought her hand to his lips, kissed the palm, touched the sensitive skin with the tip of his tongue. Turned his attention to each finger, gently nipping then stroking with the moistness of his lips.

"That makes all the butterflies in my stomach fly then soar as if there is no ceiling." Her shudder pleased him.

He nipped the tender skin on her wrist. Saw the pulse leap to life, throbbing. "I like butterflies."

To generate a need in her so great, she would never wish to leave him was his goal.

"Do you have them? Here in the pit of your stomach?"

She closed her eyes when he kissed further along her arm.

"Butterflies are with me all the time when you are near, when I can look at you, inhale the scent of you. Will you allow me to paint you?"

The soft sound of pleasure rippling from the back of her throat pleased him immensely. Cat like she arched her back. "Rafe painted me. He wasn't finished. That night we disagreed. I haven't seen him since. I walked away from him. I never meant to lose him. He was the best friend I ever had."

Roc wanted to be her best friend as well as her lover, her only lover. "Lainie, if I paint you it has to be on my terms."

"What are those?" she inquired as she touched the dimple by his mouth. "I always wondered what a man's terms are. What that means." She was trying to clarify. That pleased him.

"Naked, covered only by your hair." He let go of her hand as he reached up to run the silken length through his fingers.

"That's how Rafe painted me too. It's alright. You won't look at me except to sketch then paint. Rafe never looked at me with lust in his eyes. I was his model. Nothing more." She sighed leaning into him, absorbing his warmth.

The rise of anger was so fast and furious it startled him. His teeth clamped together, his jaw twitching. He had to remind himself that he was more than likely Rafe in her next life or the one after that. The reminder didn't help him come to terms with the boiling jealousy or the annoyance of hearing about the man. He would be better off if she forgot Rafe altogether.

"We will begin tonight?" It was a question simply because she'd not answered him. "After you eat a hearty dinner since mother upset you and you ate very little at the last meal. We will go to my studio. It is located in the back of the house then up some stairs. It's more the attic than anything else."

"Tonight," she murmured as he stood then extended his hand to help her up. "Will you have a pink satin robe for me to wear?"

The agreement as well as the question was made with a breathy little whisper of air. Thoughts of seeing her unveiled, wearing nothing but her hair made his blood rush through his body hardening him to steel.

"No pink satin but I have a black robe that I'll bring from our bedroom. You can wear that."

He would welcome the scent of gardenia hugging the robe when he wore it again.

Hand in hand they walked down the hill.

"Tonight."

~ * ~

Rafe opened the door, startled to see Dallas standing on the doorstep, a big bag slung over her shoulder. He hadn't seen her for almost a month. After he had her car towed back to her house, he felt guilty. She might have left the vehicle at the falls for a reason. She might have needed transportation and expected it to be waiting for her when she returned. He acted impulsively and without thought for her. Today, he would make it up to her.

"Dallas."

His heart caught in his throat when he watched her closely. The woman was Dallas. Nonetheless, there was something undefinable about her that made her seem different. "Where have you been all this time? The other day...the other day I thought I saw you in the city. I followed you but couldn't catch up to you."

"Rafe, I know why you didn't call me or text. I lost my phone along with my camera. My bag... I've...I had to come see you. Tell you what is happening with me. I couldn't find my car. Had to hitchhike to Edinburgh. A very nice man picked me up." She paused then, fidgeting, her hands running up then down the bag she carried on her shoulder. "Thought you would want to show me the painting."

He fought back the anger when she mentioned hitchhiking along with some man picking her up off the road. The fury was more for himself than the fact she risked herself. If she lost her phone, she couldn't call him. If he took her car, she didn't have transportation. He filed a missing person report. Nothing came of that. No one saw her. "Come in. Yes, you say you would like to see the painting."

Rafe saw a sparkle in her eyes that had never been there before. The blue was brighter. Her hair seemed to be darker, a darker red than he recalled. She was different. His Dallas was the same yet... "Why didn't you hitchhike here?"

She stumbled at the entryway. The board that stuck up there needed to be fixed. When she fell into him, grasping at his arm, heat bounced between them. "Rafe?" Dallas looked at him with curious eyes. He felt flames radiate from her directly into him. It was a fire that burned him. "I had a job interview in Edinburgh. Didn't want to be late."

He wanted to kiss her, pull her into his arms. See if the blaze would continue to burn. Knew he would be disappointed if he did so. Once a long time ago, he'd thought they were meant to be together. They both discovered there was nothing there for them. He righted her. Set her on her feet. Dropped his hands from around her shoulders.

"You know you need to watch that step." He pointed at the offending piece of wood. Years ago, he should have fixed it. "What kind of interview. You never spoke of it."

She blushed, the color heating her face. She placed her hands there as if to cool the skin. "I forgot about the step. The job is for a photographer working for a magazine. I got there on time only because of Steven. He bought me a new dress then took me there. Because I couldn't find my car, I didn't have anything, no clothes, no money, no ID, no bag with essentials. The dress I'd worn that day was filthy as well as torn."

Dallas followed him up the long winding steps to his studio. While he thought about all she told him, he felt her presence behind him. The feeling was unusual. He was eager to show her his work. Needed her approval. Her trained eye would always pick out things he could improve. On the third floor, he unveiled the painting. "Here it is. What do you think?"

"It's wonderful," she clasped her hands in front of her and beneath her chin.

Dallas stepped back, tilting her head as if she meant to view it from a fresh angle. She moved to a different spot in the room, assessing and evaluating. "It's more than wonderful. This is your best ever." She turned on him, her eyes blazing. "You better not sell this one. It's obvious the model is me."

Unable to help himself, he touched her cheek with his knuckles. Thoughts of further exploration surged in him with blinding speed. He caught himself wondering. The small touch ignited him. Dallas gasped. He inhaled sharply as desire shot to his groin so rapidly the sensation stole his breath. "Did you feel that? Is it my imagination?"

"Sparks?" She touched the place where his hand had been. "I don't...I don't understand. It can't be. It's all wrong. We've never felt this before."

"Neither do I. For me, there is nothing wrong about the flames, burning, igniting. Why would what we feel for each other change so dramatically."

He placed his hand behind her neck, drawing her closer to him.

His thumb made gentle circles at her nape. The shiver racing through her sped into him. Rafe was afraid to kiss her, afraid not to. His body hummed to life with the brief touch.

When she stared at him with those deep blue eyes of hers, her tongue slid majestically across her lips. Talons of hungry passion raced inside, his blood heating and speeding through him, surging to his aroused flesh. The moisture on her mouth beckoned to him. As if in a trance, he lowered his face to hers. The first few kisses were light, nearly nonexistent. He explored the corners of her mouth then the slight bow of her upper lip. With his teeth, he tugged on the bottom one, silently asking her to open for him. His tongue traced a path across her lips, the top then the bottom. She sighed, her hum of satisfaction giving him reason to continue. She leaned into him when he probed for entrance, opening for him as if he was a beacon for her light. A slight catch in the back of her throat sent air sifting with no sound.

Her fingers clung to his shoulders, nails biting into flesh through the fabric of his shirt. She stood on the tips of her toes, trying to get closer to him. He pulled her hips against him, knowing she would feel the solid evidence of his desire. Her breasts were flush against his chest. He scooped her into his arms. A few seconds later she sat on his lap in the oversized chair in his studio.

Rafe was shocked by the intensity of the contact between them. He wanted her. Needed her tonight. Dallas was his woman; had always thought she would be. This is the way it should have always been between them.

They weren't suited for each other.

Until now.

Until now, he'd not felt the raging desire ignite between them. Raw passion surged through him. It seemed she felt it too. He kissed her thoroughly then deepened the kiss with more intensity. His hands curled around her waist, inching to move higher, to explore more tender, soft flesh. The feel of her soft breasts pushed against his chest would be his undoing. He lifted her tank top until he could undo her bra. The clasps undone, he ran his fingers down her spine then back up to the nape of her neck.

Dallas moved her hands along his chest. "Do you think this is too fast?" She sounded breathless. "I don't know if..."

She moaned low in the back of her throat when he brought his hands around to cup the fullness of her breasts. He flicked the tip with his thumb needing to taste her. Her scent, gardenia and woman teased his senses.

"If it is, we can slow down. I don't want to rush you. This is elemental, fragile. You are so delicate. I never noticed that before now. Don't be frightened."

No, but he needed to be inside her now. He sent his tongue deep inside her mouth while he played with her breasts, savoring the silken flesh as if it was the first time or the last time. He couldn't let her go. Rafe sensed her hesitancy. He needed to bind her to him.

"Me neither. After all this time, why now? We should wait. See if this is real or not real. This could be a mistake." She refastened her bra then pulled the tank top down. "I have to think about this, Rafe. What if this thing that flared between us is all wrong. We've been so positive that we aren't right for each other."

"I understand." He said the words but he didn't understand anything. What Rafe did know was that something happened to change their connection. Dallas was his mate. He couldn't let her go now.

"Rafe," she paused in thought touching his chest where the buttons of his shirt were undone. "I've...I'm living with a man in Edinburgh. Though we are serious about the arrangement, we haven't had sex. Now...now this...the kisses...changes everything. I told him I wanted to live with him, wanted to be with him. We didn't...we... I don't know."

Fury coupled with jealousy erupted in Rafe. "No...no you can't. We need to figure out what just happened here before you do something that cannot be taken back." He never told her he was a shifter. Never told her they mated for eternity. If she was his mate, she could never give herself to another man. "Don't live with him. Whatever you do, don't..."

He stopped. He had no right to dictate terms to her.

She wiggled from his lap, her breath ragged. "At the moment, I don't have anywhere else to live. I'm going now. He's waiting for me outside. Told him I needed to see you before I could go with him."

"No!"

Dallas left. There was nothing he could do to stop her rapid flight from his home. She was running scared as was he.

Chapter Six

Lainie stood by what looked like the same table where Roc would position her each night when they retired to the studio. A month passed while he sketched then painted. He was almost finished. She decided that she would leave when the painting was completed. If he wouldn't take her to the doorway she tumbled through, she would find someone who would. Lainie's arms came around herself as if she could shed the cold sweeping within.

I don't want to leave.

Beneath the black robe she always wore, she was naked. Cool air from the window caressed skin that wasn't covered by the robe. He'd seen all of her but never touched except to kiss her in a few places. She saw raw hunger in his eyes when he painted her. Knew his control was more than she thought any man possessed.

All the things he told her about himself frightened her. What he said about Rafe scared her as much. Though to her, Rafe was a safe haven. She didn't have to give herself to him. He didn't want her in a sexual way. Roc wanted to possess her body and soul along with her heart. Believed he had every right to do so. His mother still moved forward with the possibility of a wedding that would never be. She didn't wish to remain in this primitive time even though her feelings for Roc deepened every day. He didn't love her. She needed a love that went soul deep. He couldn't give her that. Rafe couldn't either.

She thought back on that first day when she tumbled down the slope practically into his arms. She'd been unable to stop herself from plummeting through time. It had come as a shock to her. In this time no one would miss her...except possibly Roc. The century she traveled from; Rafe would miss her. Life would always go on with or without her. With Rafe there was no chemistry.

The first time she stood by the table where Roc set her, she remembered sitting for Rafe. Recalled the first flush of embarrassment when the pink satin robe slipped from her shoulders. The two men were so alike, twins from different centuries. Her body shivered at the memory but not from the cold. Thoughts of his gentle touch caused the vibrations. He stirred her passion until she burned. No man had ever kissed her as thoroughly, or touched her so sweetly.

Frightened, she stood by the table running her finger along the small wood then into the soft warm rug that covered the planking. Lainie had been there before. Somehow when it was Rafe looking at her, she didn't feel anything. With Roc, she knew heat would surge through her when his eyes turned to pewter. She bit back a nervous giggle. She'd never wanted a man before, never expected to feel the need for his kisses, his touch, the whisper of his breath across her when he talked.

At the first words he spoke, she jumped, startled by the rough timbre of his voice. She whirled to stare wide-eyed at him. When she recalled the first night she was with him, thoughts tumbled into her head. He'd never seen her completely naked. Tonight, in a few seconds, he would.

"You can take the robe off...unless you want me to do it. I wouldn't mind. In fact, I would rather do it myself than watch."

His words where husky, smooth as whiskey the sound was one she understood to be desire. Stepping back, he pointed to the table as well as the markings where she would put her hands and her legs. The ones that indicated where she would sit.

"No, I will..."

With the three words, her voice fractured while air shuffled from her lips. Unable to face him when she disrobed, she turned her back to him. She heard the sexy chuckle while he watched her. As if she could see him, she felt the tenderness of his smile behind her, the amusement at her reticence. Could imagine his nearly identical twin dimples on either side of his lips growing deeper.

"Good, if I removed it, I might not be able to keep my hands to myself. You're all silk and satin, warm woman. I need you in my arms. The devil knows I've had a difficult time not giving in to my desire."

His warmth behind her flowed from him into her. Heat rippled in languid waves through her. She imagined the way the muscles of his arms would move when he held her.

The lump in her throat seemed to stay there as she swallowed hard to push it down. She didn't mean to tease but the time it took for her to loosen the tie at her waist seemed to take an eternity. When the robe slipped from her body, she would be vulnerable to his gaze. Another giggle passed through her. She thought he should have to paint naked. That would be fair.

Earlier, he'd opened the window to cool off the attic room which basked in the heat of the warm spring day. When the fabric slipped down her back, she felt the breeze flutter through the opening. Tonight, the temperature was no longer hot. She shivered from the cooler air. Her nipples tightened even though they'd just been uncovered. She imagined his touch on her breasts, how he held them in his large hands when they slept.

Tension radiated inside the room. She heard the hissed in breath of air Roc sucked into his lungs when the robe pooled at her feet. Her nipples hardened in reaction to that sip of air. Her knees threatened to give way. After that, all she heard was the whisper of the curtains at the window when the breeze stirred them.

"You have to turn around sometime. If I'm going to paint you, I will have to look at you. Can't promise anything else," the soft amusement in his voice didn't go unnoticed. "I would it be sooner than later that you turn. I will have to put you in the right position. What do you think? The first time is always the most difficult."

How would he know? He wasn't the model. "What if you just paint my back?" she asked as she thought she would never be able to present herself to him. When she felt the heat of his hand on her shoulder, she gasped. With languid slowness, he caressed her arm, touched her hip then higher to stop beneath her breast. The sultry glide of his fingers stirred her to a point where she was certain she couldn't inhale another breath of air.

"I can do that another time. This session, well, it is your front I wish to capture in oils forever. I want to show the sweet shadow between your breasts, the rose bud tips that I've held. Not as often as I would wish. The lush curve of your nicely rounded hips. The swell of your belly." He touched the nape of her neck with his mouth, nipped while she shuddered. His fingers wound into her hair as he continued the play of his lips across her. She jumped when his teeth closed over the lobe of her ear. Shuddered, when he sucked then laved. His teeth scraped down her neck setting waves of fire fencing inside.

Lainie could barely think let alone stand. Flames ignited with violence writhing in the most secret parts of her. Thought her knees would buckle if he continued the satin smooth seduction of her body. He did know what he was about. "You said you would not...touch me."

She heard the heavy expulsion of air behind her, felt the breath sweep across the dampness of her skin where his lips had been. Knew when he stepped away from her, by the sound of his shoes on the wood floor. Felt his anger when she asked him to stop. If she gave in, she would never be able to leave. He would hold her heart in the palms of his hands.

Now that a month passed from the first time she sat for him, she felt so very different. If he took her, she would hold the memory close to her heart for the rest of her life. If he made love to her, she would never regret the joining.

"I should not have agreed to something so ridiculous. We both want each other. Neither of us can deny the attraction that tugs at us each night as well as during the day," he bit out, his voice harsh. He gripped the charcoal in one hand. "Come, turn around. I'll show you how I want to position you. The pose will be discreet as well as compelling. I want to capture your sensuality. All anyone will see of your femininity is the tip of one breast peeking through the fall of your hair." His pause struck her as something he didn't usually do. "That would be nice if your hair was long enough. I will have to improvise." Before this night he sketched her from different angles. This was the position he would capture with oils.

Lainie sat down on the table then tossed her hair behind her. She wasn't going to hide from him. This wasn't her first job. She'd been naked in front of other men besides Rafe. She modeled for her art class in college. Somehow that felt different, impersonal. This time was very intimate. She understood what Roc wanted from her. If she was honest with herself, she wanted intimacy too.

The air she held in the back of her throat burned until she let it go in a silent rush. She never felt this hesitant with Rafe. It was easy to be naked around him. She'd known him, loved him as a friend forever. Rafe was her confident. Roc scared her. He held such a claim to her heart. Everything here was new to her. "I'm...frightened," she told him her voice paper thin. "I...I didn't mean to make you angry. It's just that..."

His smile left one dimple showing and one that did not. "Don't want to frighten you, sweetheart. Take a few deep breaths of air. You'll feel better when you do. Try to relax."

In what could only be described as clinical, he proceeded to place her, move arms and legs until he had her the way he wanted. After that he arranged her hair, he stepped back, gazing at her, the hunger in his eyes was easily readable. She was frightened and pleased all at the same time. He moved back to her, swept one side of her hair behind her back. This time his touch wasn't clinical at all. As if he was unable to stop himself, he swept his fingers down her arm. She burned, heating from the inside out. A broken sound left her lips. If he kept that up, she would splinter into a thousand pieces.

"You're very beautiful this way. Every beautiful curve you possess is defined and accented by the light." He ran his finger around the outside of the exposed breast then lightly touched the nipple. Watched as it peeked to a hard bud. "Is this anything like the way you posed for Rafe?" he asked sounding as if he tried to be disinterested.

"Much, almost identical. He never touched me." *He did. I just didn't feel anything.*

Her words whispered a soft cadence. She could not talk, could not breathe when he touched her, when he looked at her. Lainie wanted more. Understood she needed him to teach her about the ways between a man and a woman.

The charcoal he used to draw the strategic places on the table for her to place herself after breaks, tickled her flesh. She laughed knowing this touch was not intentional. It was both nerves as well as embarrassment that caused the laughter. When he finished with the marks, he turned his attention to the canvass.

"You tell me when you need a break. I'm afraid when I work, I get absorbed in what I'm doing. In the process, I lose all thought of time. If allowed to do so I could work all night. You can't sit there all night. I've only you to rely on. Don't want to overtax you."

"So...I'm not your first model."

She didn't know if she was annoyed by the thought that he painted other women who were naked. She wondered about the paintings, where they went. He would sell them. Would he sell this one of her? Startling herself, she blurted, "You will not sell this painting. Will you? If you say yes, I'll get up right now. Put that robe on and never come back."

"No one as beautiful as you," his reply was smooth as well as disconcerting.

Nonetheless, she felt warmed by the compliment. He was smiling and shaking his head at her. "No, I won't sell this one. Don't want another man in this world to see you the way I'm seeing you now. This painting is for me...only me. My eyes only."

"You probably say that to everyone."

Lainie recalled Rafe telling her the same. For some reason both men liked women who were larger than the norm. Her breasts were larger than most women her age. Instead of a flat belly, hers was rounded. Plump would describe her abdomen best. She had dimples on her thighs which she detested. Cellulite. Though many women, even thin ones had the detested cellulite. She thought it strange that of all things she recalled that word. She was forgetting so much.

"Never have said that to another woman. Never will again except to you." Now Roc stood behind the easel, his fingers roaming over the canvas he prepared an hour ago. "Never have spoken to any of my models about how they appeared. They were simply here to do a job. That's not the case with you. You're here because I cannot resist the temptation you bring to me. I need to know all of you. To see all of you. By your bashfulness, I was certain I might never be able to do so." He was working now, seeming to be able to talk while he sketched. "I will though, Lainie. Never doubt that fact."

"Oh...what did you do with the other paintings? I'd like to see them."

She puffed some air upward to move a ticklish piece of hair from her face. While she tried to distract her thoughts from the words he spoke, she stared out the window. Focused on the dying sunlight. He would light the lanterns soon.

"Sold them. Even if you wished, you wouldn't be able to see them. Don't know who bought the paintings. They've all sold. You *ken* this is just a hobby for me."

He turned to the window he'd opened earlier then closed it. Rain sluiced from the sky. The rapid staccato of water against the roof as well as the glass eased her mind. She shivered wishing she could warm herself.

"You moved." With a smile on his face, he strode to her. "Can't have that."

His touch was neutral when he repositioned her arm then her hair. She jumped, startled when the back of his hand brushed across the hardened tip of her breast. It seemed he used every chance he could find to touch her. He stepped back to study his creation. Rubbed his hand along the back of his neck as he turned his head one way then the other as if to unkink the muscles. At the easel he compared her against the sketch. He seemed satisfied.

"Easy...I won't touch you again. That was an accident."

His feral grin told Lainie the caress was no accident.

That was what Rafe always told her when he touched her. With Rafe, she never felt the fire or the butterflies dancing inside her. She imagined that with Rafe as with Roc the caresses were no coincidence. Rafe wanted to see if there would be a spark. Roc just wanted to seduce and charm her to his way. He'd told her he wouldn't make love to her until they wed. She was certain now that he had a change of heart.

"It's alright. I know it was an accident. I like the way your touch makes me feel. You know that though. It's no secret how I respond to your kisses. The way your hand moves on my hip when we are in bed."

While she spoke, her voice was shaking. Her feelings were so mixed she needed to scream. He didn't respond. He was absorbed in his art.

For another hour they worked without speaking. Lainie knew now the companionable silence was something she would treasure after she left him. She had to find her way home. He confused her to no end. She didn't like having the terrifying feelings that centered deep inside her. Didn't want to burn when he touched her, when he looked at her. Her mother spoke so many times of men who only wanted to rut between a woman's legs. Rafe wasn't like that. She didn't think Roc lied to her when he told her she was his mate. Spoke to her of eternity. Lainie found herself torn. He showed her his cat. Made himself vulnerable.

She didn't think Roc would take her innocence then leave her as her mother said men did. However, he wanted her that way. His feelings were nobler than most men. Under the guise of the word mate, he made it clear they belonged together. He offered marriage but never proposed in a romantic way. She didn't know what to believe.

What Lainie did believe was that she needed to return before she forgot everything she'd ever known. Every day some little piece of her mind along with her soul vanished. There were times she forgot her first name was Dallas. When she complained, Roc told her she was only forming new memories. She was learning about this time, about the people, the politics and shifters. He told her given time she wouldn't miss the things and people she knew before she met him. Roc had an answer for everything.

If all that Roc told her was true, Rafe had to be a shifter. He never showed her his cat. *Fool, he never did because he didn't believe you were his mate.* What Roc told her was that if she left him, Rafe would never find that eternal woman. If she stayed here, everything would proceed as it should. The world would return to the way it was supposed to be.

"I need to get up," she told him stretching as she tried to get her muscles to work.

She sat in that position too long. Arching her back, she swung her legs over the side of the table. He handed her the robe that she left on the floor before helping her slip the garment over her shoulders. She couldn't move her arms yet.

"I don't think I can stand. Waited too long."

She'd been so lost in her thoughts; she didn't pay attention to herself. The robe over her shoulders, she leaned on the table, drinking in the air until she would be able to move again.

"Walk around a bit. Get the kinks out. You'll feel better before you know it." Roc encouraged.

He watched her as she pulled the robe closer then tied the belt.

"Easy for you to say," she gritted out between stabs of needles biting into her legs and arms.

Lainie walked a few hesitant steps. She stopped every time a chair presented itself. At the window she stared out at the grey, rainy day. This morning the sky had been bright with sunshine. He stood behind her, his hands resting on her shoulders. His fingers were strong as he massaged the knots from her back and neck. He worked on her arms then lowered himself so he could give attention to her legs. Her head against cold window pane, she sighed at the wonderful feelings coursing through her, relaxing her. His hands were efficient. He knew where to massage.

Despite her chagrin, her stomach rumbled. He wrapped his arms around her, settling his hands on her angry belly. She didn't eat much today. Her stomach rolled each time food was brought to her. Nervous energy consumed her earlier in the day.

"You hungry?" he asked chuckling at the sounds she was making. "There is food on the table over there along with some hot tea. Maybe not too hot any longer. Though with the coaster around the pot the liquid will be warm. Put a little honey and milk in it. The tea will sooth what's ailing you."

Lainie helped herself to a few things thinking if she didn't eat as much, she wouldn't be so round. Both Rafe and Roc liked her curves. She didn't. That didn't seem to make a difference to either man. "Thank you."

She nodded her head in approval as she bit into the one of the sweet confections that had been left for them.

"You need to keep up your strength. Eat some more. You lose your temper too easily when you're hungry."

How did he know that? She imagined she lost her temper over

the last weeks too many times. "Eat so she could do nothing but sit? That's a novel idea," she said blandly thinking about how it was so much easier to gain weight than to lose it.

She hated that fact. Most of her adult life she'd been hungry.

"Yes. Can you sit for another half hour? I'll be in a good place to stop by then. If not...I'll bow down to your wishes. My model's comfort comes first." He fixed the collar on the robe before adjusting the belt around her waist. Even with those simple touches, she burned for him. Her body ached in secret dark places. Roc made her so aware of her body's dark yearnings.

"I can sit longer. Rafe never gave me a choice. If he needed to work another hour, we took more breaks."

Rafe didn't pretend to love her. Neither did Roc. If he would say...if he loved her, she could stay here.

Ah, that had been the first night. They worked almost every night after that. He wouldn't let her see the painting. After the first week, he began with the oils. Roc worked much the same way as Rafe. They were so much alike yet different. Roc's hair was lighter, a burnished blond, more brown than gold. His eyes weren't as icy as Rafe's. When Roc looked at her, the blue deepened to a startling pewter with hints of blue. His gaze upon her was always warm.

During the day, she cleaned his house. While he wanted her to work with him at his paper, she held back. She enjoyed the tasks of keeping a home clean and sparkling. Loved the times when he came home then raved over the meals she created. She introduced him to new ways of baking the same dish. She fixed chicken in so many different ways then experimented with the rainbow trout he caught. He brought her venison. She'd never cooked venison. So, she went to his mother for some recipes which she made her own.

When they sat down to dinner, he would tell her about his day, all the little things that happened. They spoke of his likes and dislikes concerning the politics of the time. Much of what he told her she had no experience with, hence no opinion. She listened to him. The handbills he worked on, the invitations for parties that the citizens of the small village paid for. At night after dinner, they would sit in front of the fire until he coaxed her upstairs to pose for him. He would light the lanterns then place them in the exact spot as he did the night before. If he found a chance to touch her, he would.

Except for the random caresses along with the massage after each session, he worked just as Rafe did. After she posed for Rafe, she went home. After she posed for Roc, she went to his bed. He would hold her. Sometimes he would caress different parts of her until she wanted to scream with her arousal.

Though the two men looked much the same, they were different. Rafe didn't have two dimples, only the one. Roc, she thought, was taller his shoulders broader, the muscles of his thighs more pronounced. Rafe was quieter than Roc. Roc loved his family to distraction always taking time to visit. Rafe had no immediate family. Heather was more like a mother to her than her own, who rarely found time for her. Roc's mother would visit weekly bringing some delicacy with her to eat over a cup of tea.

Lainie didn't think she'd ever been happier. Still, she missed the creature comforts of the century she was born into. She never felt this was the right place for her. Somedays she couldn't remember to take her birth control pills, somedays she didn't know what they were. Roc would have to remind her.

After he was through for the evening, they would go to bed. He would hold her through the night. When they woke in the morning her legs were usually entangled with his. He laughed when she ran her cold feet on his legs to warm them. Roc told her when the time was right he would kiss each and every one of her toes. The thought burned her. Evidently, the time had not as yet been right.

One day, they visited the McKenna keep and Father Damian. She protested all the way there. Whined was more like it. Though Roc was teaching her how to ride a horse, she feared the big animals. The way they moved beneath her terrified her, left her grabbing onto the saddle horn to stay upright. He would laugh then tell her she was getting the hang of riding. In time, she would be able to ride anything. She understood he was speaking about something else. When she would send him a scowl, he would hoot with laughter.

She knew she never rode a horse before but she couldn't remember how people got around in her time. When Roc would remind her of cars, all she held in her memory was the picture he painted. The words were what he told her.

"Come along," he spoke. His voice soft, "We're going to bed now." He finished the painting of her. She would leave tomorrow if she could find a time when he wouldn't watch.

She shivered. The look in eyes told her a wealth of things. He wanted her. It would be nice if he made love to her tonight. She would have something to remember him by. The thought she could treasure in her lonely single bed, when the winds blew down the craigs into her lonely home.

Now, looking back on that visit to Father Damian, it wasn't so bad. The priest was nice. He was the only priest she knew. He laughed easily when the two men spoke of the brothers along with the cousins he wed.

"I'm not going to become a catholic," were her first words to Father Damian. "I'm not very religious."

The man sat back in his chair, his hands over his rounding belly a frown line creasing his brows. "No one has asked that of you. Your religion is up to you, child. Nonetheless, if the two of you wed, there are certain ceremonies that must be fulfilled."

She bristled at his condescending words. "True." She got her back up, recoiling with his statement.

"I would like my wife, my mate, to be a catholic. What do you have against the religion. Frasiers have been catholic from the beginning of time." Roc was holding her hand, squeezing a *wee* bit as he spoke. She saw the deep creases around his eyes. His eyes were more ice than steel.

Lainie could do nothing except send him a withering glare. He grinned at the scowl and the drawn brows as if her wishes meant nothing. By the new look on his face, Roc appeared certain he would have his way.

"Have the two of you come to an agreement about the date of the wedding? I assume there is no rush." Father Damian accepted the cup of tea one of his servants set in front of him. "Would either or both of you like tea?"

He didn't have to say the words. She wasn't with child. If she was, Roc's demeanor would be different. "There are no agreements as to the date or to a wedding. He has not asked and I have not accepted." Her back was stiff, her shoulders rigid.

"I see." The good father tapped his fingers on his desk his gaze moving from one to the other. "Why are the two of you here? If not to plan a wedding...what are your intentions?"

"I'd like for you to speak to Lainie about the clan ceremony...if you can. I..." Roc was struggling for words.

"You understand I cannot do that. The ceremony is sacred. The two of you are not engaged. Nor are you wed. Later, if your circumstances change, I can be freer with the descriptions."

They were getting nowhere with this line of questioning.

Clearing his throat, Roc began to speak. "You should be ready for the wedding next week. By then I hope to convince Lainie she belongs with me. I will have secured a proposal. Mother will have put finishing touches on a wedding between the two of us. She will have spoken with Wynnie about the festivities afterward."

Lainie shot him another frosty glare that she hoped would put ice in his arrogant bones. "I'm not..."

He turned to her. His dimpled smile heating her all the way to her core, stretching nerves she thought to be at a breaking point. "We're not arguing about this here. We'll speak later at home. You can tell me all your misconstrued notions about marrying me. Again, I will explain why you have to."

If he touched her, she would burn.

The memories seared through her. They were into the next week now. She'd been here more than a month. The container with her birth control pills was not empty. She had two prescriptions. A pregnancy could happen if they were to become intimate. The wedding was being planned without her approval. His hand resting possessively on her back, he walked her from the studio. He bent over her, his lips close to her ear. "I'm going to make love to you tonight."

Beneath the robe she wore nothing. Where his large hand rested, his fingers seemed to heat her flesh. They stopped at the closed door to the studio. She swallowed a fiery breath of air. He ran his fingers along her arm. She would soar to the sun then burn and fall. They walked down the stairs. Her pulse thundered violently in anticipation.

"No protest?" he asked as if he expected one.

She found herself shaking her head. "No protest. I want you. I think you know that for a fact."

She needed to feel him inside her before she left. Tonight might be the only time they would have if her plans came to fruition.

Tomorrow, she would find someone... Lainie hoped Hawk would take her to the small glen where she miraculously appeared in this time. She knew no one else who she trusted. Hawk might give her plans away to his brother. If he did, she would find another way to get there.

Inside the bedroom they shared, he closed the door. Leaning against the wood frame, he watched her at his leisure. She sat down on a chair facing the fire, closing the robe over her legs. How to proceed with this was something Lainie never considered. The ragged breath she inhaled didn't reach her lungs.

"Wine?" he asked as he strode toward them. "You need to relax. You look tense. Drink the wine then I'll massage your stiff, aching muscles. I know you are sore from holding the position. Don't know how you can do it."

"I am," she admitted to him, nodding while she thought about the way his hands and fingers would move over her to ease the distress. "I don't...I've never..." She looked down at her hands as they wound into the fabric of his robe. "Never been with a man. You know that." She waved her arm in the air frustrated by her fears.

He poured her a glass of wine. Handed it to her. "Drink when you finish that one, I'll pour you another. As many as you want." He turned his back on her in order to pour himself wine. "Don't want you to be afraid of me."

She caught a fragmented sound in the back of her throat. "I'm not afraid of you. Never you. It's what we are going to do."

When he sat in the chair beside hers, he stretched out his long legs. "Tomorrow," he began, his voice soft. "We'll have a picnic. I'm not going to work. We'll spend the day together. Only you and me. What do you think? We can explore all our feelings, the emotions you've kept inside yourself all this time."

"No work?"

The thought panicked her. The glass she held shook. A few drops of wine slid down the crystal. She licked the drops.

"It's Sunday. We could go to church first. Would you like that better?"

~ * ~

Roc had never seen Lainie stretched so thin. Her fingers were moving constantly as she popped her knuckles over then over again. When she looked at him, her eyes held a strange expression, one he couldn't decipher. Her steady silence unnerved him, set his own nerves shaking. If he didn't miss his guess, she planned something for tomorrow. Something he wouldn't like. He needed either for her to confess or to get ahead of her in the deadly game she played with their lives. He would ask his siblings. If they knew nothing, he would go to his cousins. He didn't doubt that one of them would know the exact nature of her plans.

Over the last few days, she acted both distant as well as needy. When he was close, she clung to him as if she would never see him again. Her actions terrified him. When she thought he wasn't looking, she stared at him as if this was the last time for them to be together, as if she sought to memorize his face and form. She asked to go to the bonfire. All those uncharacteristic actions sent shivers of dread coursing through him. If she planned her escape, she would have to ask someone for help. As long as they'd been together, she didn't know very many people, mostly his family. He went over all that he knew, all that he guessed.

"You wanted trout for dinner tomorrow?"

He rose one eyebrow in speculation, understanding she was planning their last meal together. He wasn't going to allow that to happen. Roc intended to pull out all the stops to keep her with him. "We'll go together. The day will be fun. I've not seen enough of you over this last week."

He needed to see more of her not less. As to convincing her to remain here, it seemed the more she forgot about the century she'd been born into the more she longed to return.

"I despise fishing."

Her smile was weak, no longer as brilliant as the sun. Her body seemed strung tight as a bow. "You've seen more of me than any other living soul while you painted me. Well, except Rafe. He saw as much."

The reminder that another man saw her naked sent a fierce rage through him. He needed to think with clear purpose. She could hide nothing from him. In this, he would be one step ahead of her. It would be made easy when he spoke to his family. One of them would come forward with the truth. She would risk a lot if she asked Hawk to take her to the portal. His Lainie was an only child. She would know nothing of the dynamics of a close-knit family. From what she told him she wasn't close with her mother or father. The only person she was close to was Rafe. She wanted to return to that man more than she wished to stay with him. His fists clenched tight around the stem of his glass.

"Ah, one can relax, lean back against a tree then let the water and the fish do most of the work. We can have a lazy day the two of us together. I'll bring food. Lots of things you love to eat, a bottle or two of wine. What don't you like about fishing?"

He realized the description of fishing was not accurate if they went fly fishing. She would have to be involved.

"The worms."

She cringed when she said the word. A small shudder sent her breasts swaying against the black robe. The tight hard buds of her breasts were defined, the rounded curves enticing. It seemed the fabric clung lovingly to her. He didn't understand how she so easily sent blood pounding through his veins; a look, a smile, the slightest movement sent longing so fierce the sensations shook him.

"I fish with flies."

He wondered what possible objection to that she would have. She didn't disappoint. Once more she shivered her objections.

"Insects? You fish with an insect?"

His laughter cracked loudly in the room. Lainie had no idea. "They are not alive. I tie them with colorful threads to attract the fish. They can't resist."

She was so beautiful. When she bent over at the waist to reach for her glass of wine, the dark silk of his robe gaped open giving him an unhindered view of the rose bud tip of one breast. More blood surged. Heated. Boiled. He made a quick adjustment to his buckskins.

"You are making fun of my ignorance."

She strode to him. Breathing in a huge breath of air which sent her generous breasts swinging again, she poked him in the chest. Her gaze held a hint of fire when she spoke to him through gritted teeth. "That's not fair! I don't know anything about fishing. Don't think I want to know either. So, you can just take your laughter and stuff it!"

In every way, Lainie was an obvious delight to his senses. Her unfettered words never failed to surprise him. She said things in the most unusual ways. Lainie was unique. What was it, he wondered, she wanted him to stuff. Oh, it was his laughter. Maybe he could stuff his tongue...no, he wasn't going to do that right now. He wasn't about to stuff his sex.

Roc didn't know what tomorrow would bring. What he did know was that he intended to taste her tonight. Savor. Cherish until neither one of them could move. Together they would burn down the night. This might be his last chance to convince her she belonged to him, to this time. With no hesitation, he pulled her onto his lap. She gasped, surprised by the sudden loss of balance. Her deep blue eyes widened. His lips met hers, framing them, sealing his raw hunger with hers. His tongue swept across her mouth leaving behind moisture as he absorbed all that she was. The devil, she tasted sweet, tasted of the wine along with her passion. Fierce with raw hunger, her heat ripped through him.

She gasped. Her lips opened wider as if in anticipation of more. She moved against him, her rounded breasts pushing against his chest.

He took advantage of the small opening she offered him. His tongue slid inside her mouth, rubbed, appreciating, learning the texture of her, heating with each small mewl of pleasure escaping into his mouth along with each splintered sound. She ran her tongue across his. The raspy texture sent spirals of burning heat simmering inside. He plunged then retreated needing the kiss to be hot as well as deep. Hard as well as one that could last a lifetime. Deep to convince her to stay with him. His hand rested on her hip, pressed, traced the contours, learning her body. He slipped his hand inside the robe where it separated across her legs. His hand slid up her thigh testing warm, womanly flesh, moving higher. She inhaled a sharp sound. Moaned as their lips forged, bonded as if one.

"Kiss me back, Lainie. Kiss me as if you never want to stop. As if you would never leave me. What would I do without you? You belong to me, to this time," he murmured as his teeth raked along her neck then back to hover above her mint scented mouth. "Kiss me like I like it. Rub your sweet little tongue across mine. I want to burn. Wish to feel the winds of the tempest you create soar. Need you to burn right along with me."

He wanted to yell at her if she left, she would never know ecstasy such as this. She would be alone as well as lonely in a life she would come to regret. Roc understood just as he understood their passion if she left, they would never know each other again, this life or the next. She would never be with Rafe.

At the first contact a fractured sound broke from the back of her throat. He absorbed the tiny sound inside his mouth while he tested sensitive flesh behind her bottom lip. Bit gently. Explored with intimate meticulousness. Her hands rose to his shoulders, pushing at his shirt, playing with the laces that tangled beneath her clumsy fingers.

"I need to feel you," she whispered hoarsely against his neck.

Roc broke away long enough to whip his white muslin shirt off his body. She ran her hands along his chest, his muscles contracting and rippling at the sweet contact of her hands against his skin. He stifled the intense groan threatening to consume him with each tender caress of her small fingers. A lifetime would not be long enough for him. He needed the promise of eternity. She kissed her way across his collarbone, running her hands along his chest, touching the palms of her hands to his nipples.

"As I need to feel all of you." His hand clenched on her upper thigh while his other hand cupped a soft breast, rubbed a hard crest.

"I don't know what to do," she whispered close to his ear. She blew gently. Ripples of pleasure slid through him at the contact. "Can I bite you here?" She touched the tip of her tongue to the lobe. "Like you did to me."

If she did, he would lose control. He prided himself on his control. It seemed with Lainie he had none. She pleasured him so violently and thoroughly; his body reacted with raw passion. "Bite me anywhere you like. Kiss me. Taste me. Do whatever you wish. I would never tell you no." He inhaled a long deep breath of gardenia scented air.

"I want to see all of you..." his voice was unnatural, husky with his desire. If she explored further, Roc didn't know if he could maintain the discipline he needed to keep from taking her.

With fumbling fingers, he untied the belt holding his robe in place, revealing creamy white skin he needed to touch. Watching, demanding to see then feel, the silken textures that were so exquisite they stole his breath. He pushed the fabric aside then down her shoulders. She clung to the material as if the fabric was some type of lifeline.

"Let it go," he breathed with soft passion. "You know I've seen every beautiful inch of you. Don't be shy. You have nothing to hide from my eyes."

The robe fell from her body. She shivered. Her beautiful breasts swayed. The tips hardening, growing larger as he stared at her. He didn't know if the reaction was from a chill in the room or hungry desire.

"I..." Her head fell back. His teeth scraped the exposed flesh. She purred. Moaned. Sweet sounds of desire splintered. Her nails bit into his muscled shoulder.

He kissed her again. His tongue pulsed within her heated, sultry depths. Hers fenced with his. Danced. Played. Withdrew then returned. He slid his hands along her spine while her nails scraped along his shoulders sending tremors into his body. He found he was shaking. "You have tiny little claws. Use them on me. I would like to see the marks."

"Oh!"

Lainie repeated the caress up then down his spine, across his shoulders.

When she turned, her breasts swept across his body. Blood pulsed violently. His body hardened until he felt the painful pleasure she instigated. He shivered with the flames that small movement ignited. He could resist no longer. Roc bent his head to her breast. His tongue traced the circle where pale satin skin became a pink temptation begging for him. He was trying to resist for a few seconds longer. Needed this union to be slow as well as filled with intense pleasure. His tongue flicked the hardening bud before his teeth bit with great delicacy. Cream and honey was the taste of her, gardenia her scent, silk and satin the texture.

She looked down where his mouth held her, sucked until he withdrew leaving her nipple swollen and damp from moisture left there by his mouth. When he stared up at her, Lainie's eyes were wide, her mouth trembling. Her back arched seeming to beg for more. He'd known from their first kiss she was a passionate little being. He turned his attention to her other breast, drawing the tip out, suckling until it was elongated and wet with his hunger.

Roc didn't know if the trembling was from fear or passion. "Don't be frightened. I won't hurt you. Not ever."

He knew his words to be false. When he took her innocence, he would cause pain. While he claimed her as his, she would feel the bite of his claws break through her soft flesh. He cringed with the knowledge he could never change.

Still, he hoped his words were true. If she wasn't a virgin there would be no pain when they joined. One less thing to worry about. He hoped she was as innocent as she seemed now despite the threat of hurting her.

His lips molded to her breast. Roc knifed sensually with his tongue at the severe crown he roused from Lainie's breast. She moaned and heaved against him. Tiny little mewls of her pleasure echoed into the firelit night. Silent silver moonbeams slanted through the window caressing the fullness of her body. He sheathed the edges of his teeth in his lips and tested the hardness of her nipple. Sensations shattered, spurring a harsh, impassioned cry from her. Roc didn't raise his head until her breathing was fragmented and she was twisting as well as arching gently underneath the onslaught of his lips. She was begging him for more. With infinite care he released her captive breast before admiring the high ruby crown his mouth created. "You draw even tighter for my mouth than you did for the cold wind against you when you sat before me with nothing on."

"What?" she asked, her eyes dazed with raw desire.

The blue so deep he could barely breathe looking at her, Lainie's eyes never failed to captivate him. They changed color with every shift of mood. They were so dark now, his breath caught in the back of his throat. "What did you say?"

"This." Roc took one of Lainie's hands and swept it over her breast, keeping the palm flattened against the tight hard bud he drew to stiffness with his mouth. "Feel your passion. Such a velvet hardness. It begs for my mouth, my fingers. Do you beg for me too?"

She gasped, her eyes widening even more than when he moved his head to meet the steady gaze of her eyes. He wished he could read her mind, understand her thoughts. He could not as yet. He would have to settle.

Chuckling, pleased with himself along with her vibrant response, Roc bit gently the base of her hand. Her body jerked with the unexpected contact. Still amazed at her swift rise to passion, he needed to keep her so aroused she would think only of staying with him. He captured her nipples between his fingers then plucked until she was once more writhing beneath him. Her moan was soft, languorous, a sound he wanted to hear into eternity.

When one of his hands slid down the length of her body, Lainie didn't protest. She sighed, the sound soft, pleasure filled him with confidence along with trust. His warm hands stroked her legs, heated her as she trembled beneath his caress. With each tug of his mouth at her breast, she moved, opening herself more completely to him. She was vulnerable and wanting. Soon to be his in every way possible that a man could possess a woman. Tonight, they would explore, sightsee each other until they both understood each other's wants as well as needs.

"Tell me how it feels when sunlight touches you. Your smile is my sunshine. His voice was deep, raspy. More fire flared within him, burning him as he stroked her. She didn't seem to notice that with each tender pressure of his palm her legs shifted then shifted again until nothing of her softness was shielded from him. His hand rested just above the tangle of red-gold curls guarding her most secret place. He needed to slip his fingers through the feminine petals he hoped were swollen and wet, waiting for him.

With awe, Lainie whispered, "Warmth. Complete warmth. Lazy as if nothing matters except the heat. I want you, Roc."

"Heat that stokes the flames. Is the warmth everywhere? I want you, too, sweetheart."

Understanding came as he fulfilled his wildest dreams, touching her where her heat blossomed, where her woman's scent rose to beckon him. "Dear God, Roc, even there."

"Especially here." He pressed gently to the softness between her legs, the hot swollen folds she allowed him to caress when she parted her legs. "You're going to come as sweetly unwrapped as a gardenia opening to the rays of a southern sun, baring its petals for the first time."

Motionless, eyes glazed over with the raw desire that he provoked, Lainie stared at him. She reached up to touch the line of his lips. After she touched him, he bit gently on the soft fingertip that caressed his mouth with such intimate care. She inhaled. Her gasp sharp. Would have pulled away but he caught her wrist with his hand. Held her in place.

"Don't be frightened. Your body is telling me you want this. Do you, Lanie? Do you want me inside you? I can see your desire even if you can't feel the hunger. You are already unraveling for me. Let me come inside you, become one with you."

Roc slanted his mouth over Lainie's once more, allowing the increasing waves of desire to spin delightfully back and forth between them, melding them in a quest that could have only one end...a uniting of their bodies. More than anything he needed to bind her to him, make it impossible for her to leave. If they created a child tonight, that would be one more factor that would keep her with him.

Lainie's fingers slid deeply into Roc's hair. The bite of her nails against his scalp sent fissions of heat pummeling his hard body. The low sound he emitted was both the reward as well as the goal. She flexed her fingers again and again while her body arched and writhed against his, sending rivers of heat stopping hunger coursing through him. His body rippled with the sensual pleasure she spurred.

"Such sweet little claws," Roc said.

With careful restraint, he bit Lainie's lip. She made a sound that he interpreted as both surprise as well as pleasure. In his arms, she was this man's dream of heaven. Grinning, he let go of her lips so slowly she curved against him, begging him in the most elemental of all ways for more of the same. With each movement she made, her breasts touched him, caressed him with their warmth and softness. He wanted to cover her, to lay her down on his bed then thrust into her making her his.

She leaned closer as he withdrew. By the subtle gesture he understood she wanted more of the gentle torment. He laughed a tender chuckle then turned aside depriving her of his mouth. After she turned to follow him, he held her face still between his hands. Her lips were parted, swollen from the sweet attention he gave them. They sparkled with moisture trembling as she waited for him to kiss her one more time.

"Roc?" she questioned him.

He made an enquiring sound that was rather like a male purr of satisfaction, pleased with what transpired. He would wait and see what she did next. He was not to be disappointed. The sensual game they played would end in complete fulfilment.

"Don't you want to kiss me?" Lainie whispered as if she waited for the right answer. She was holding his head between her hands, staring into his eyes.

"I don't know. What is it that you want?" He held his breath praying for the response he sought. "You should tell me. If you don't, I won't know. A man shouldn't be left to guess at such an important time."

"Another kiss then one more after that until...until I can't breathe another breath of air." She moistened her mouth with the tip of her small pink tongue. He wanted to suck on it, play with it some more. He wanted her to rub it over his again then one more time. Yet, he sensed her need. The raw desire that pirouetted around them, touching on all his hopes as well as fears.

"If that's what you want. Another kiss, one to last until the morning sunlight bursts through the window."

Sunset strands slid over his hands, caressing him with cool fire.

His suddenly indrawn breath filled his throat.

"Then do it, sweetheart. Do it now. Kiss me until I can't take in a breath of air for wanting you."

It seemed she tried to choke back the sensual cry that resonated deep in her throat. "Do you want to taste me?" she whispered. "Is that how you want it? I don't know...I want it to...please you."

"Oh, you please me more than you could ever imagine. Yes, I want to savor every part of you. Is that how you feel about kissing me? Do you hope to cherish as well as taste every part of me? There are places I would taste that might very well shock you." The devil he prayed for this. These sensations he never felt with another woman. He never rose so hot and fast. He was feverish with need. His blood thundered in his rapidly hardening body.

When he tried to speak again, he could not. Lainie fused her mouth to his. The hesitant and oh so delicate exploration of her tongue made him groan with the waves of pleasure streaming through him. She could have no idea what those small attempts to create pleasure did to him. Her innocence heightened the enjoyment, the novelty. He could die and go to heaven knowing her secrets.

She lifted her head, her eyes so blue and wide they beckoned to him.

"More," he told her huskily. "Kiss me some more."

Lainie gave Roc what he asked for. He hoped it was what she wanted also. Sensed that it was by the raw desire that seemed to escalate within her small body with each stroke of his tongue against hers. The taste of her was familiar from the other more chaste kisses they shared. Her textures lured him, making him feel both powerful and uniquely satisfied. She strained against him. He held her closer needing an even deeper sampling of her. He wanted to hold her so tight that she would become a part of him, never to be wholly separate again.

With an urgency he didn't understand, Roc felt Lainie's hands stroking him from his head to his shoulders then down to his hips as she tried to pull herself closer and closer to him. He neither advanced or retreated letting her come to him. Her arms tightened around his neck.

An exquisite sensation shot through Roc as her soft breast

touched his hard chest again. Heat spilled. Flames ignited. He hadn't known how he ached for that contact until he once more felt the brush of hardened peaks against his body. The sound Lainie made at the repeated contact was both encouragement and sensual demand. She sank her nails into the tightly corded muscles of his back.

"Hold me. Wrap your arms around me. Don't let me go," her whispered words were a murmur and a sigh in the heated air.

When he didn't respond as she asked, she made a frustrated noise that he knew was unraveling, creating her raw desire. She was almost there, almost to the place he needed her to be before he entered her. Before he made her his.

"What?" Roc asked in a low voice needing to coax all her truths from her before it was too late.

Once more, Lainie tried to draw his mouth down to hers. He was far stronger than she was. He held his lips above hers, teasing her with the kiss he withheld just as he was withholding his strength form her passionate demands. He knew what she wanted as well as needed.

"Tell me what you want. If you do that we can go on from there," he whispered.

"To kiss you. For you to hold me as if you never want to let me go."

Her pause filled the silence. "I want you inside me in every way possible."

That was so true for him too. He could do both. He would never let her go. He brushed her mouth with his, teasing, tantalizing more of a reaction than Lainie knew how to give. He would teach her.

"Like that?" he asked waiting for the backlash as he knew she wanted more.

"No. Yes. No."

Pleased with her seeming confusion, Roc's tongue teased Lanie's lips encouraging them to part one more time while she strained to be closer.

"Yes," she told him. She was shivering with the gentle touch of his tongue.

He withdrew to look into her eyes, to evaluate her passion, her needs.

"No," she said quickly.

"Yes and no. Make up your mind, sweetheart. A man can get so confused as well as frustrated."

"Roc," Lainie said urgently. "I want...more. More than just your kisses. More than your touch on my breast."

His breath stomped into his lungs as if she punched him in the chest. This was what he wished for, what he needed from her. He wished for even more, much, much more than a kiss and a touch of soft flesh.

"Open for me," Roc said in a deep voice. "Kiss me that way. Let me see that you want it as much as I do. Show me."

Moonbeams glistened on Lainie's lips and on the tip of her tongue. Sultry moisture covered the places he kissed, the places she touched with her tongue. Roc made a low sound and tightened his arms, lifting her face up to his.

"Again," he said brushing his parted lips over hers.

Lainie shivered then did as he asked.

Roc's mouth closed over hers. His tongue slid into the warmth that opened to him. He took her mouth as he meant to take her body, completely, a seamless melding of flesh and honeyed heat.

When roc looked at her, saw the stark evidence of her desire, he felt the vibrations within her small form reach fiercely into his soul. Shaking with her need, she was ready for him. He wished he dared claim her tonight. He could not. Not until they wed in the way of the clan. He understood that if this was a matter of life or death, he could claim her. It was not.

Lainie made a sound that could have been his name as he eased his hand lower, cupped her between her thighs that were parted sweetly for him. Quickly, he withdrew his hand, waiting, waiting for the right time. It was almost upon them.

~ * ~

Roc swept her into his arms before carrying her to the soft bed waiting for them. It was what she wanted from the moment he stepped up beside her in the studio, from the moment she decided she had to have him before she left. With gentle care, he set her on his bed. Stepping back, he disrobed letting his boots fall to the floor, kicking his buckskins out of the way.

Raw and blatant evidence of his desire made her breath catch in the back of her throat. Lainie had never seen a fully aroused man. She saw one now. If possible, her body heated more, pulsed with shivering vibrations deep in her core. He lay down beside her, stroking her gently with calloused fingertips.

Lainie didn't know how much her breasts ached to be stroked again until Roc's hands cupped and his thumbs nudged nipples into jutting crests. She didn't know when he moved from her side and was now lying half over her. Until his nimble fingers tweaked the rigid nipples and ribbon after ribbon of fire flowed through her, making her body curve and reach to get closer to the man who wanted her to stay with him. The man who told her they were destined to be together through eternity. She wanted to believe him. Didn't see how she could. His words were outlandish. They went beyond the pale delved into the supernatural. She'd seen his cat. That should be enough to convince her there were unexplainable things in this world.

What she did know was that the anticipated contact of his body against hers thrilled her to the marrow of her bones. She would have cried out at the sensual desire of her body pressed against his. Warmth and heat enveloped her, protected. Moonlight slanted across the masculine features she admired. The only cries the deep mating of mouths allowed were small mewls of hungry desire from the farthest recesses of her throat. They rose from deep in her belly. He gulped the fervent moans and soundlessly insisted on more, teasing and kneading her sensitive breasts. Long fingers fondled then shaped and tugged until she twisted wildly beneath him.

Only then did Roc shift again, flowing completely over Lainie, giving her what she needed without knowing it. His hips pressed against the cradle of her thighs. She understood that fire whirled wildly, burning her. Her nails dug heedlessly into the flexed muscles of his back as she gasped in the grip of pleasure that flamed so potently, she was unable to restrain her body.

Roc made no complaint to her nails. Instead, he groaned his response then rocked his hips over her in passionate reflex. The melting fire of her response spread between their bodies.

Surprise froze Lanie until Roc's hips moved again, sending raw passion raging through her body in a burst of heat she could neither deny nor conceal. When he repeated the movement, his tongue shot into her mouth in a possession that was totally yet so tantalizing in its lack of completion that tears formed in Lanie's eyes. With a desperate need she searched for more. She'd read enough to know the climax should be earthshattering and all-encompassing. She was not there yet...still she writhed, reached for that elusive thread he held away from her. She was so close.

One of Roc's hands moved between their bodies. "It's all right, sweetheart. Soon," Roc said, his voice thick as he spread his fingers low across her belly. "This is what we both want. Easy..."

Lainie barely heard his words. She knew only that she wanted him to never leave her. His weight covering her gave her the feeling he protected her would guard her always. The thought jolted her but she was too involved with the hungry mercuric passion he ignited to realize what those thoughts meant.

Gently, the weight of his body settled over her, his forearms braced on either side of her head. From his lofty height above her, he smiled down at her. She twisted against him, rocked her hips, searching upward for more contact than he was giving her. No matter how she moved, he managed to evade her. She wanted to hit him. Yell at him. He was still smiling at her.

"Roc," she said raggedly, her voice a hoarse whisper. "Please."

"What is it?" he asked when she didn't speak again.

"Please do something more."

Lainie had no useful words. Her mind was a blank slate. She struggled for air while he continued his gentle assault on her body. His teeth raked lightly over her neck then downward to taste a nipple again. She never felt as she did now, the sensations he provoked were hot and wild, her body responding hungrily as if she was famished. When she looked into his brooding eyes, Roc smiled darkly. She was certain he knew what was missing. What she needed from him. What he held back.

"Tell me..."

Then he cocked his head, listening to the disintegrating of Lainie's voice as he his teeth closed with more intensity on the satin of her flesh.

"I c-can't...I d-don't..." Helpless to form words or thoughts, she gasped for a single breath of air then another.

He trapped the tight hard tips of her breasts in his fingers and pulled drawing the peaks tighter and harder. Her breath rushed out in a husky sound as she arched frantic to be closer to him. The motion made him settle more deeply between her legs. He still wasn't where she wanted him. Against his shoulders, her fingers dug into him with unbearable frustration. She curved up against him in unknowing demand.

"Spread your legs apart," he whispered while he nipped at her ear, bit gently. "Move them for me. Open yourself to me. Give me all you have."

Shuddering in his embrace, she cried out, overtaken by the pulsing desire that overpowered her deep inside. As Roc spoke, he moved his hips just enough to brush against Lainie's heat. The caress drew a tattered shriek and a flood of heat from her. She shifted, wanting more of the sweet violence he tormented from her. Torture flamed.

"Wider," he whispered. "I need to see that you want me. I need to know."

Lainie did as he requested, opening more for him. Exposing every part of her.

"Wider, sweetheart. You know you'll like it. Draw your knees up on either side of me. I need to see all your secrets. All that I will be part of soon."

Much to her surprise she did as he commanded, opening her legs until he lay easily between her thighs. Slowly once again he was teasing her nipples, watching her as he plucked the sensitive peaks.

"That's right," Roc said when Lainie lifted her hips blindly toward him. "Just like that. Tell me you want me. I'm not going to do anything you don't ask for."

The sensual torment of his hands on her breasts was no longer enough. Lainie's head moved as restlessly as her hips, seeking release from the vise of need that was closing around her.

"Roc, please...I," She swallowed hard on a searing gasp of pleasure.

"I know. I can see it. You are slick with your nectar."

Roc's fingertips flicked over her unprotected secrets, touching her driving her higher.

"...and, I can feel it," he spoke in a low voice.

Lainie gasped in a combination of fear and passion as she realized that she lay vulnerable and defenseless before Roc. She trusted him. But...

Deliberately he plucked a sensitive spot that sent her writing, bolting up to moan low in the back of her throat when she fell back to the bed. He used his thumb to massage with languid movements in that same spot. The rush of pleasure Lanie encountered was so intense she cried out sharply then melted into the bed. She arched begging him for more. Writhed beneath the onslaught of his caress. He withheld himself from her.

"Again," Roc said, rubbing his thumb all around her, teasing her with what he was once again withholding. He skirted the edges and around the most sensitive spot.

Sounds from the back of her throat fragmented then whispered in a sigh.

"Let me feel your pleasure," he murmured. "Now."

Without waiting for words that would never come, he touched her again. She gave him what he demanded. The husky sound of his satisfaction was another light caress, another delicate flick of passion's whip across her intensely sensitive flesh. Sounds, mewls of pleasure echoed through her.

"I will remember the expression on your beautiful face until the day I pass from this earth," Roc said, his voice low, filled with passion.

His fingertip caressed again, drawing forth another rush of pleasure.

"I like that sweetheart. I like it the way I like to breathe, breathe in the scent of you, all woman and gardenia." His fingers moved barely brushing her slick, hot flesh.

Lanie wept and writhed with the honeyed teasing that sent savage streamers of fire through her. She didn't know when Roc's fingertips were replaced by blunt, satin flesh. She knew only that he wasn't touching her the one place she must be touched. Her nails raked down his back in a demand she couldn't help making.

No matter how hard she twisted and fought to make him touch the hungry bud he drew from her softness, he eluded her. Danced away from her writhing begging hips.

"Why?" Lainie finally asked.

"I like hearing you ask for more."

A frustrated sound spilled from her. She twisted again and again. It wasn't enough. It seemed what she did, what she asked for was never enough. Lainie trembled with her need, with the passion she could not tamp down.

"More."

Roc brushed against her swollen, sultry flesh.

"Harder," she said raggedly.

She hit him, striking his shoulder while she strained toward the unattainable fire that he withdrew each time she almost reached for that culmination of flames. She needed to soar higher and longer, brighter with the intensity she knew he kept from her.

"You know that's not enough."

"What if I tell you that's all there is?"

"No! I know there is more. There has to be something else. I've read..." she stopped knowing he wouldn't understand.

She could tell him more though... The thoughts vanished as quickly as they came to her.

Roc touched her again, drawing his nails with exquisite care over the swollen bud. She gulped as her body responded heatedly, reaching for him, searching for that sweep of pleasure she'd heard about but never experienced.

Lips pulled back, teeth barred as if he sought restraint. She watched him with shuttered eyes. Roc inhaled a deep breath before he spoke. "Ah...sweetheart... I feel as if I'm breathing fire. Your scent...your feel..."

"Roc," she whispered. "I..."

"This?" he asked.

Flesh that was both smooth as well as hard pressed sensually against her, parting her secretly even as she felt as if she melted over him.

"Yes," she said brokenly. "Yes."

With a smooth powerful motion, Roc pushed into Lainie until he stopped. "Your maidenhead." He spoke with a soft cadence, kissing her gently. "I pray this will not hurt." With that said he drove into her, seemingly intent on making swift work of her virginity.

Lainie's eyes flew open, no longer absorbed in the pleasure or the frustrated need he induced. Pain rather than pleasure jabbed through her entire body. Her nails bit into his muscles as she willed herself to keep still. She closed her eyes in an attempt to think of something pleasant. When she opened her eyes to look at him, he was staring down at her, his body deep inside hers.

He froze. Held himself still while he waited for her pain to end. He pushed long strands of silken hair from her face while he placed gentle kisses across her lips asking for nothing only giving.

"You're hurting me, Roc. I expected that but..."

She closed her eyes understanding how stupid it was to expect no pain from the mating. She pushed on his shoulders. Tried to move from beneath him. He was an immovable force. His big body filled hers. She inhaled deeply wanting nothing more to do with him. Forgetting the past pleasure that swamped her with ease.

The motion of Lainie's body as she tried to dislodge him stripped away any semblance of control he might have felt. She knew only that she needed to be free of him. His hands gripped her hips, keeping himself deeply within her. All she wanted was for him to leave her body. They could do this another time. It was too late. He groaned before he pushed even deeper, thrust with hard purpose to touch her womb. Release swept through him. With a guttural cry he emptied himself inside her. His forehead rested against hers. She heard the raspy breaths, felt the whisper as the oxygen caressed her.

This was not at all what she expected. Unable to do anything but stare at him, she focused on the steel hue of his eyes.

"I'm sorry, sweetheart. I never wanted to hurt you."

"I understand." She was still pushing on his shoulders. "You need to get off me!"

When he bent his head to kiss her again, she felt the now familiar stirring of her body. Felt the heat at the apex of her thighs. The pain vanished; only pleasure awaited. She tried to shrug it off.

"I'm not leaving you, Lainie. Your pleasure comes first." He framed her mouth with his lips, sucked on her tongue then thrust his into her mouth. He moved as a shivering pulse sent now familiar flames licking at her.

The pain was gone as if the small hurt had never been. His fingers found the slick bud, flicked it, rubbed it as his tongue swept over hers in the age-old primal dance between man and woman. Heat blazed with new life as he moved within her. The mewl of pleasure surprised her as much as the lightning bolt of heat that streaked through her. Her hips arched against his, demanded. He rocked her as he brought the blinding pleasure back. Violent sensations flooded her, swept with secret intimacy within as he brought her to a place where her body spasmed and nerve endings shattered.

"Roc!"

Her nails raked across his shoulders. She cried out again and again. His mouth covered hers absorbing the sounds of her raw hunger into him.

"Hang on to me sweetheart," he whispered to her while he kissed her again, hard and deep. "That's it. Ride the sweet tempest of fire and light. The sunshine you give me when I look at you cannot be lost on a whim."

Her body spilled over him. Blinding waves of pleasure pitched her body into a frenzy of lost control. She was beside herself. As more time passed, she began to ease, the pulsing slowed. He gathered her in his arms, holding her close, tight as if he didn't ever wish to let her go. Her arms wrapped around his sweat sheened body knowing how much she would miss this man, thinking a second along with a third time about her intentions.

Chapter Seven

Roc didn't intend to let Lainie out of his site today. It came of no surprise when Hawk came to him with her request. He swore, cursed in the ancient language that had always been so much a part of his life. While he understood he could not guard her day in and day out, he also knew none of his family would take her to the glen. No one he knew would be the catalyst that would ruin his life, that would take Lainie away from him.

He would have to do it.

You're a blind fool.

Yes, he was that. There was no other way.

Last night they made love tenderly as well as fiercely. This morning he woke to her legs wrapped around him, her luscious body sprawled across his chest. All the while he prayed the lovemaking would be enough to convince her she wanted to stay with him. She didn't speak of leaving. Nor did she speak of staying. His thoughts were bittersweet. Nothing changed. His last desperate means to keep her bound to him failed. The final decision lay in her tiny hands. He would have to abide with that decision no matter how desperate he was to bind her to him.

Now, he fished while she waded in a narrow part of the creek upstream from him. Her long skirts were tucked into the waistband of her skirt. The legs he saw were long and white. They tapered to trim ankles. He wanted nothing more than to make love to her again. Tonight, she would be in his bed. This afternoon they could dally on the blanket by the tree after they ate the lunch he packed for them. Perhaps with a few glasses of wine, she would admit she no longer wished to leave him. That was wishful thinking on his part.

She stayed upstream well away from the fishing poles he set out. Today he opted not to fly fish as he wished to spend as much time with her as heavenly possible. Lainie didn't want to be a part of the fishing process even though she liked the taste of fresh caught rainbow trout.

At any time, he could put the fishing rod down. He could go to her. Wrap his arms around her. Kiss her until she was breathless, until the soft sighs of her pleasure he heard last night masked all other sounds. He caught enough for dinner and some to have with breakfast in the morning. Earlier today, he brought her to church with him. She told him she never went to church. That she wasn't positive she believed in God. Her words shocked him. He supposed she would believe what she wished to believe. Perhaps in time she would come to accept his God. In this situation, when they wed, they would wed in the Catholic church. He would hold her while Father Damian performed the clan ceremony. There was still a lot for her to learn about his family.

The two of them were so different, singular in most every way. Since they were intimate, he'd not mentioned marriage or staying with him. Roc didn't think she was bound to him in any way except his wishes. Tomorrow would come whether or not he wanted it to. He shuffled in a long deep breath of air, searching the sky. Tomorrow, he would test her, would offer her the freedom she told him she craved. Abiding by her wishes if she chose to search for the portal would prove to be difficult.

After church this morning, the sky was clear blue, nearly the color of her eyes. The blue of her eyes was darker, deeper than the light spring sky. A gentle breeze shuffled dry leaves that had fallen last autumn and during the winter along the forest floor. Puff balls from the huge oaks, popped when he stepped on them. When he was a child, he and his siblings used to race to step then hear the pop. He supposed that was a silly inconsequential game that meant nothing to him now except a vague memory. She was losing all her memories.

With a soft sigh of frustration, he set the pole aside. He wasn't in the mood for fishing. Striding toward Lainie, he kept his smile in check. He wanted to walk with her for a while. Hold her in his arms while he kissed her. The devil, her body fit him to perfection. Every delicious curve she possessed fit snug against the hard planes of his body.

"Lainie, come here, please," he spoke his words a soft whisper, his body tightening with the thought of last night's shared, hungry passion.

How could she ever dismiss the fact they belonged together? He didn't know. There were no answers. If the portal accepted her, she would go back to Rafe. The thought turned his gut sour. He needed her here, in this time, sharing his life.

When she looked up her eyes were bright, her smile brilliant. Sunlight filtering through the leaves above her landed on her face. Her beauty glowed from her like the sunshine above. *Ma petite rayon de soleil.* She was so unique. His body tightened with the arousal he could never deny. He adjusted his buckskins hoping to forget how the sight of her aroused him.

"What?" she asked as she skipped toward him.

Her skirts billowed around the long white legs that were wrapped around him a few hours past. Her body moved sensuously with the lithe movements. She bent over to grab her shoes then walked toward him.

"Walk with me?" He held out his hand, palm up. When the palm of hers touched his, he brought her fingers to his lips, stroking each one carefully with his tongue, shadowing the wetness between each finger that he wanted to create within her tight sheathe. He felt her body's response as her hand vibrated within the warmth of his.

"That sounds dangerous."

She grinned at him, a fabulous smile forming on her lips. What do you have in mind? I'd like to know. A girl must have a choice." Her words trilled in a breathy whisper as if she anticipated his wicked thoughts.

"Naughty girl, what do you have in mind that has you breathless with anticipation this afternoon. Are you remembering what we did last night...this morning? Would you like to do it again? Here? In the sunlight? Beneath the canopy of trees?" He lifted an eyebrow while he watched the darkening of her eyes, the swift caress of her tongue across her lips.

"Where would you like to walk? I'd go with you anywhere. So...suppose the where does make a bit of difference to me. Do you have something in mind?"

She pulled her hand back from his before sitting down to slip on her shoes and stockings.

Where Lainie was concerned, he always had something in mind.

Lainie didn't even try to be discreet. He supposed that was as much her upbringing in a century that allowed their women folk to run around almost naked. Thinking of the strap marks on her beautiful body...the nearly nonexistent swimsuit she told him covered her, a surge of raw anger ripped through him. He couldn't stand the idea of men seeing her wearing so little. While she'd been hesitant in bed, she exposed her body easily. When she modeled for him, she had little trouble with her nudity.

"Down the path. No place in particular."

He lifted his shoulders, focusing on the flowing water then back to Lainie.

By the time she tied the garters of her stocking her legs were bared to her thighs. She didn't push her gown down while she slipped on her shoes. Roc appreciated the view. While watching, lust shot fiercely to his groin. The speed with which she so easily aroused him both startled as well as pleased him. Deep inside, he laughed at his behavior. This was not a place for him to toss her skirts. A kiss or two or even three would be appropriate. Anything else would flirt with discovery. He wasn't the only man in the village to come fishing here.

"I need to walk. Though I would rather stretch out on the blanket to soak up the sun. Would like to strip to my bathing suit so I could tan. My skin is too white. I need a bit of color." She laughed at his frown. "You can be a prude. You know that don't you? I've never gone to a nude beach. Nor would I ever."

Nude beach?

"Yes."

The things she now remembered then didn't remember surprised him. In an hour, she would most likely forget mentioning nude beaches.

After she stood, she pressed against him as if seeking his warmth. He felt the curves of her breasts he learned last night. Felt the soft motion of them against his arm. Her breasts were more beautiful than any he'd ever seen. Single handedly, she put the moon and the stars to shame.

"I'm sorry," she murmured. "You can't possibly understand a time where women are much more equal than they are now. No one cares if they..."

She fell off her speech. Small frown lines formed. When she shook her head as if attempting to remember, he felt a strange sense of sorrow for her.

Roc understood she forgot. He didn't want her to forget. Nonetheless, her memories seemed to be slipping away from her at an alarming pace. While he understood what she was going to say, she didn't remember. They spoke long hours about the various benefits that could be found in the later century. She even tried to convince him he would enjoy all the niceties. He would never leave his family.

"You forgot," Roc said as he watched the ever-changing expressions on her face, his heart going out to her.

With a gentle stroke, he traced the line of her jaw then down her neck. Her neck was long and white, beautiful. "I like your creamy white skin, the way you flush when I embarrass you."

"It's so frustrating," she bit out, her fists tight beside her.

Her whispered words quivered when she spoke again. "I start to talk about something then it's gone from my mind. I can't call the thoughts back. They just are no longer in my head."

"You would be lost in the twenty-first century. If you go back, would your memories return? Would you then marvel over all the things you took for granted? Would you wish to return to a simpler life? One that is not so fast paced a body can barely breathe. I for one don't wish to hurtle down a road at sixty miles per hour or through the air at an even faster speed."

"It's where I belong!" she argued vehemently. Once more she was shaking her head, "I...I don't know any longer. You say I belong here."

As far as he was concerned there wasn't going to be an argument. He was resigned in this. Roc was also pleased she wasn't positive about returning. There was doubt in her mind. That, he decided, was a good sign. She might not continue to wish for something he prayed could never be if he didn't allow her to see if she had a chance of succeeding in her mission to return. Roc didn't think fate would take her away from him after destiny sent her hurtling through time so they could be together.

Their mating was written in the stars. The eternal union between them couldn't be denied. The more he thought on the fact, the more he prayed his notion was correct.

"It's where you think you belong. It's not where you truly belong. Should we find out? Should we tempt fate?"

Even though the words blurted from his mouth, he didn't intend to regret them. Roc understood taking her to the glen, giving into her wishes was the only way to move forward. Lainie needed to discover the truth for herself. His words would never convince her.

"What do you mean?" she asked, clinging to him, her fingers biting into his muscles. "I don't understand what you are trying to tell me. You want to take me to the portal?"

"Let's walk. Want to steal a kiss or two. Would you like that?" Turning her, he wrapped an arm around her shoulders. He guided her along a path that paralleled the stream where they fished. While they walked the only sound he heard was of the wind whispering through the leaves above. When they strolled by a small fall of water, the gurgle of the cold liquid rushing to the sea was louder than the wind. Later a squirrel darted in front of them, the scolding chatter from the animal's perch high up echoed between the branches.

He breathed in deeply of the fragrant air. Knew this was where he belonged, where he was supposed to share his life with the woman walking beside him. He couldn't fathom anything else.

Gardenia was the heady aroma coupled with the woman scent of the vibrant lady who walked beside him. He needed her to walk beside him for the rest of their lives. First, she needed to discover destiny's truth for herself.

"I love your kisses," her words were thick, throaty when she spoke. "I like the way you make me feel when you are deep inside me. When you touch my very soul..."

Roc recognized the desire evident in the honeyed flow of her words, in the darkening of her gorgeous eyes. Capturing that raw hunger thrilled him. In another time, she wouldn't have those sensations of love and desire. She would find no pleasure if she didn't fulfil her destiny here, neither would Rafe with the woman called Dallas. He would make love to her again tonight. She had not been taking the pills that would control her monthly flow or stop her from conceiving. He wondered if she didn't already carry his child.

One night... He breathed deeply. If she conceived, he would be a man well-pleased. One night, anything was possible though hardly probable. If she did, he would know before she did.

In hopes of discovering one truth, he dropped his hand to her hip then spread his fingers across her belly. Nothing met his fingertips. Not even a quiver of life. If he felt his *bairn* there in her womb, he would never be able to take her to the glen. Would never allow her to leave him. Roc didn't know if he was relieved or disappointed.

When he withdrew his hands, she started as if she was disenchanted. Her passion and hunger for him overwhelmed him. Lainie could not know why he set his hand on her belly just above her womb.

"Do you worry about a child? What if you conceived?" Roc asked, curious as to her answer. It had been several weeks since she stopped with the birth control. He never said anything to her. When he spoke of things from the other century that she no longer comprehended, he didn't like the way her eyes grew sad. He knew she was afraid she would lose the very essence of herself.

"I..." She ran her tongue across her lips then focused on him. "Should I be? I've been taking..." she cut herself off. "I haven't...I forgot."

His gut tightened while he watched her eyes fill with sadness. Even in this time a woman would surely understand what they did together, could create a child. Roc wasn't certain what to say next.

"We've only...it was just one night." She creased her brows together creating that tiny line in the middle of her forehead he wanted to run his finger along. "Would it...it would only take once..." She was thinking so hard he didn't know if he needed to laugh or cry. "Pills...there was something about pills. I should remember."

At first when they spoke of being together, she'd known things no woman in his century would know. They would not have been taught so many things. Now...he couldn't help but shake his head. Now, she was more innocent than he would have ever thought possible.

"Once is enough," he told her, tracing the eyebrows that had furrowed in concentration. "Takes only one time if the day is right." He lifted his shoulders, a smile tugging at the corners of his mouth. "With us creating that child might take a few more times. The pleasure is worth it. Don't you think? Would you like my child?"

They were walking again. She set her head on his shoulder, his arm swept around her waist to keep her closer. He needed to hear her answer. Wanted to know if she gave any thought to the possibility of a child.

"How do you know that I'm not carrying your child?" Lainie brought her head up to better look at him. She leaned into him, pressing her body close.

He absorbed her softness, the lush flare of her hips, the soft movement of her breasts against him. Never in all the lifetimes ahead of them, would he ever grow tired of her. He had to figure out a way to have more lifetimes together. The previous ones were not enough for fulfillment.

After all the talking, all the information he gave her, she still didn't believe. He was more convinced than ever the only way to proceed was to take her to the portal then see if it would accept her.

He prayed it would not.

Clearing his throat, he decided to express only the truth. Even though grim reality seemed difficult for her to believe. "Shifters possess a sixth sense. Just as I knew the moment I saw you that you are my mate, I also know you don't carry my child. Don't think I could let you go if you did. Don't want any child, especially not mine, to be born a bastard in any century. Don't want some other man to be the father." Roc gritted out the last words, barely able to spit them out or acknowledge the possibility. If they continued as they carried on last night, she would find herself increasing.

"I don't want that either."

With wide blue eyes, Lainie stared with sincere trust into the steel gray of his.

"Good, we agree about something." Roc didn't want to think or talk any longer. For this moment, he needed to feel. Wanted her body close to his. Needed to taste her again then again.

Lifting her chin his eyes focused on hers, he brought his lips to surround her mouth. She parted for him. Set her tongue against his. Rubbed. The tiny moan of the first blossoming of her pleasure sifted into his mouth. His hand on her waist flexed.

Hunger soared.

Desire flared with impatience of newly blossoming intimacies.

The raging tempest she so easily provoked in him flamed to vivid life.

A drop of rain hit him. After that another. He flinched, unable to pull away from the humid heat of her mouth. Dark secrets wove through his head. Silently, he swore. He should have been watching the clouds. Instead, he only had thoughts of Lainie, of burying himself deep inside her. Ideas of ways to keep her here with him.

"We've got to leave here before we're drenched all the way to the skin." He pulled away, staring into her dazed eyes. The devil, he didn't want to leave her now. She was aroused. Ready for him. "Don't want you to take a chill." He grabbed her hand then raced down the trail to where he set a picnic basket which they'd failed to enjoy. Perhaps he could spread the blanket in his attic studio then pretend.

Taking his poncho from one saddle bag, he draped it around her shoulders. "Stay here where it's a bit protected. I'll gather our things." He placed her under a stone overhang. Wind threw raindrops her way. She shivered holding the poncho close to her. If Hawk had taken her to the glen, to the portal this morning, she would either be drenched to the skin or gone. Storms always traveled inland from the ocean. Was this a warning of what could happen? He didn't think so. Though he wasn't about to discount any signs from nature.

As quick as possible, Roc gathered their belongings then secured them to his horse. He was tempted to huddle with her beneath the overhang until the storm ceased. When he looked to the horizon, he didn't think the rain and blustering wind would stop any time soon.

He was a damn fool. He called himself three kinds of an idiot.

He traded her safety for a walk and a kiss. Besotted was the only way to describe himself. She cast a magical enchantment over him he could never deny. If this was going to be one of the last times he was with her, he meant to enjoy every second.

"Come." Once again, he held out his hand to her. "Believe in us."

Roc wasn't at all certain he said the words aloud or only to himself. It was what he wished for. Longed to have her believe in the life they could have together.

With trust showing in her face, Lainie walked to him, her arms outstretched. He tossed her into the saddle before mounting behind her. She was so small, so delicately built. All her curves overshadowed the fact that she weighed half his weight. He needed to protect her from any and every type of harm. Deathly afraid of what might happen, he urged his horse to a faster pace.

Just as he was afraid that by the time they reached their home, they would be soaked through to the skin, they were. When he lifted her off the horse, she laughed holding her hands on his shoulders. After he set her on the ground, her soft fingertips moved dripping hair from his forehead. She looked very pleased with herself, with the storm. "I feel as if I jumped into that creek wearing all my clothing. I remember a time when I was out walking. A logging truck passed by spilling a pool full of water on me and my..."

She looked to him for help. Her eyes narrowed in concentration. It was obvious she forgot.

"That must have been something."

The ache in his belly intensified. Lainie looked so lost, so very alone. Forlorn. Defenseless. His heart cried out to her. It would be best for her if she forgot everything from her other life. He felt certain she wouldn't agree.

Seeming to have nothing more to say, she nodded her head before lifting her shoulders in a feminine manner.

"I should take you to the loft. We could make love there." He eyed the ladder to the perch above where the horses were stabled. Thinking better of the notion, "Perhaps another time we can bring food and drink there. Sometime when we are dry as well as warm." He touched his lips to her forehead. "You are freezing. Your lips seem to be turning blue and you're shivering." He picked up her hand, "As are your fingertips. Your feet must be ice. Need to get you heated up."

"Yes. Would rather go to the house where it is warm," she murmured, clinging to the poncho. "I'm not as wet as you..."

Her smile was soft, naked in its meaning. Her mind seemed to drift in the same direction as his.

He understood her thoughts were far from chaste. "Your hair is dripping with all the rainwater that found its way under the hood. Got to get you warmed up before we do anything. Health first, as my brother the good doctor would tell me."

"You are a soggy mess," she retorted as she ran her hands across his chest where his shirt was plastered to him. "There is no part of you that is dry. You needed to be warmed up."

"A hot bath we could share." His thoughts were wicked. If she remembered anything from her past, she might be willing to share the tub.

As if startled, Lainie blinked a few times. "Share a bath? Rafe once wanted to share a shower with... No... What's a shower?"

Once more her brows furrowed together showing both her concentration on the topic as well as the frustration. Moisture filled her eyes. A silver tear slipped down her cheek, mingling with the rain water.

"Believe a shower is what we just encountered."

This time he didn't get angry with the fact Rafe wanted to bathe with her.

The devil! He wasn't going to have to show his hand tonight. Tomorrow would be soon enough to discuss the trip that would either solidify their relationship here or demolish it. If the weather improved, they would travel together. If she was swallowed into another time, he damn sure was going to be with her. The thought gave him a shudder he couldn't repress. That wasn't something he wanted. Staying in this time was just fine by him. How on earth would it be for two males who sought the same woman as a mate? Fate would never be so cruel to put them together. Despite doubts, he needed to keep reassuring himself.

Jacob appeared from a back room to take care of his mount.

"Thank you," he told the young man. With her hand in his, he ran the distance from the stable to the house, banging the doors as they rushed for the cover and warmth of his home. He should have carried her.

Inside, he pulled her into his arms for another kiss. This brief contact was soft and sweet, heady in its own right. Rain drops sluiced down her face to mingle with the sweetness of her kiss. Powerless to resist, he deepened the contact. She opened for him. The buttons on her gown melted away. He ran his hands along her spine as his body seemed to take over his mind. He sipped water that was sliding down her neck to pool in the shadowed valley between her breasts. Licked. Teased tender flesh.

Heat unfurled.

She ignited him, testing his control, his restraint. Blood rushed to his groin. Where she was concerned, he had no resistance. He wanted to be inside her. Needed to see the pleasure in her eyes when she climaxed. Wanted his mate. Needed to get on with his life. Didn't want to take her to the damn valley. For his peace of mind, he needed to do so.

"Roc..."

She touched him, traced the taunt line of his jaw. Her hands smoothed his damp shirt, touching muscles that jerked with the pressure of her fingers. She was unfastening the buttons, tugging on the shirttails. Her hands ran across hot, wet skin. He lifted his arms then bent at the waist so she could pull the fabric from him.

"Yes, sweetheart." His voice was thick with the desire raging through him. "Yes, I want you too. Now. On the kitchen table if we can't make it to the bedroom."

Lainie was shaking her head. She rubbed her face across his chest before she looked at him, sincerity in her eyes. "I don't know if I want to go back. I might want to stay here. With you." She touched her lips to bared flesh, her tongue flicked across a nipple. Her hands roamed along his spine.

His heart jerked from her words, just as his body did from the sweet passion of her touch. His mind splintered into a thousand pieces. Hope flared.

"It's just that..."

She was about to tell him, she needed to return. All hope died. "Just that what?"

He tried to temper his emotions. Tried to tell himself not to hope. There was fear and disenchantment in hope. The disappointment would send him to his knees.

"I don't know," she said, lifting her mouth to his once again. "I don't know what I want. Except. Except, I want you. I don't want to leave you. Don't want to live this life or any life without you."

He pushed at her clothing, her gown, her petticoats, her stockings until they were pooled on the floor around her tiny feet. Her fingers made short work of his pants. Before he could remove his buckskins, he tugged off his boots. Damn, he didn't even have water heating on the stove for that bath he hoped to share.

"Don't go away."

He wrestled with the buckets. By the time water was set upon the stove, she'd wrapped a quilt around her shoulders. He wanted to join her beneath the blanket. Fondle ever exquisite part. "You want to share."

If they shared, they would both burst into flames. That was not a bad thought.

There would be no bath. At least not for a while. He pulled out the copper tub. While the water heated, he poured them both a goblet of wine. He locked the front door as well as the back door to the kitchen.

"I'm going to take the food to the studio."

Roc planned on a gentle seduction. Needed to feel her sultry heat as the moisture rained down upon him. In his studio he set out the blanket then the basket of leftovers. He took out the plates along with the food which he arranged on the modeling table. Next, he hung the drawing of her on the wall. Stepping back, he studied his work. He would always remember. She told him Rafe painted her. He lived in this same house.

After he entered the kitchen, he saw her. She was still encased in the blanket, sitting at the kitchen table. Naked beneath. Quick sex on the kitchen table was not part of his plan. However...while they waited for the water to boil, his blood already reached that temperature. A slow grin formed. He tracked her as she sipped her wine.

She stood. The blanket fell to the floor. It seemed she offered herself to him. His mouth was so dry, words wouldn't form. Perhaps sex on the table held merits all its own. Ones he could not foresee. Her hands rose as she reached out to him.

He stepped forward. Pulled her into his arms. Waiting was over. They would burn down the kitchen then the night. By morning, if anything but ashes existed, he would make arrangements to take her to the cave then on to the little glen where the portal awaited them. She would see for herself there was no going back. Lainie was where she belonged.

With him.

"I want you now," she murmured as her lips traced a path along his neck. Her arms were around him, fingers winding into his hair, nails scraping his scalp. She stood on the tips of her toes. The sweet sashaying of her breasts across his chest held promises of delight. He needed to taste all of her. Would start with her mouth. After that he would move on to more exotic places.

Without preamble he swept his arm across the table, emptying the solid wood of napkins and silverware that clattered on the floor.

"Wrap your legs around me."

She did.

When his tongue pushed into her mouth, he thrust into her humid core. Lainie pulsed around him, kissing him with the spasm of her release. She cried out into his mouth as he climaxed with her. Later tonight, he meant for the loving to be slow, languorous. Before the night ended, she would beg.

He would give her everything she wanted. If she wished for him to travel through time with her despite his fears coupled with his reluctance, he would do so. They would meet each hurdle then vanquish that obstacle.

~ * ~

Roc told her he would take her to the cave. Rain got in the way. Day after day of relentless rain poured down. Water pooled on the roads. Anything trying to get through sunk into the knee high mud. She didn't think the water would ever stop falling from the sky. Not that she was anxious to leave Carnoch. So much of her past was forgotten. What she remembered were things she'd told Roc then he repeated them for her. The facts were no longer in her head. She no longer knew who she was. What she did understand was that she wasn't Dallas. At times she forgot her first name.

Lainie didn't know what she wanted any longer. There was so little she recalled about her other life. What she did remember came at great expense to her well-being. Day after day she forgot more of the past. Frustration ate at her, drug her to her knees when she least expected. With more patience than Lainie thought she could give him credit for, Roc explained things to her when the subject came up and all that was in her musty brain were cobwebs. If she didn't remember the future, she would be terrified when she encountered it.

With her elbows on the windowsill, in the parlor, she stared out at the torrential weather. She was sitting on an oversized chair, wishing she knew what she wanted to do about her life. What she did understand was that she never wanted to lose Roc. He'd become part of her. Their growing intimacy amazed her. While she treasured Rafe, she never understood what loving a man could do.

She wasn't pregnant. Heather had to help her with her needs when she had her first period in this time. She didn't say anything to Roc. It was his sixth sense. He knew. Told her he would know pretty much the moment she conceived. She would never be able to run to him, with the news. He would *ken* the truth before she did. For some reason that didn't seem right to her. The woman should tell her man the blessed news. He told her he would even comprehend the sex of the child. That part she didn't mind.

Roc didn't believe the conception would be that wonderful unless they were married. He hoped she would not become pregnant before they were married. Understood if they continued with the course they settled on, she might very well be increasing at the time. Did she want to marry him? Go through with this clan ritual? She didn't think she could be a good Catholic. Her faith had never been a strong part of her life.

Cleaning his house and cooking for him was more than she

expected. Washing clothes was hard work though he offered to hire a housekeeper to do the hardest chores. Ah, but she didn't know what she fantasized about. The cooking she enjoyed more than the cleaning. What she discovered was that she wasn't much for dusting and sweeping. Dishwashing left her hands red and chapped. In the time she'd been here, she used up all her hand lotion. Roc told her his mother would teach her how to make it. *What? You can't go to the village store to buy some?* Nor did she enjoy gardening. Hated the dirt beneath her fingernails. If she had to stay here, she thought she could find a job as a chef. She thought possibly at the Tea and Crumpets Inn. Roc told her a resounding no when she brokered the idea to him.

Lainie thought she presented reasonable arguments. Still, no matter what she said, Roc wouldn't allow that. When she mentioned it in passing a second time, the grim set of his lips as well as his jaw told her he hadn't change his mind. She reminded herself he had no say in her life. Not until she married him. If, she married him. As it stood now, he was hell-bent on making her see reason by taking her to the place where she appeared. The more she heard about the Kinnel Stones and how they were used, the more afraid she became of returning to this portal. At least a person could see the stones. Would decide whether or not they walked inside. Ending up in some other time than this one or the one she came from terrified her. Even though she told him that she didn't want to go, he now insisted.

What a quandary.

Pig-headed man.

"What are you thinking?" Roc pulled up a chair to sit beside her. Since he was smiling at her, she relaxed. He picked up her hand. Traced the lines in her palm creating a heated shiver that rippled through her. Excited her. His touch burned. She didn't want to live without him. Each day brought them closer than the one before. All he had to do to make her want him was to look at her with the silver heat of his eyes. When he touched her, she melted. When she tugged on her hand, he refused to release her fingers.

"Will it ever stop raining?" she asked on a half-sigh. Lainie puffed a dangling piece of hair from her face not liking the scowl on

Roc's. "I think we might be in need of another arc."

His laughter at her comment was a soft chuckle, not his usual boisterous laughter. "You in that big of a hurry to test the portal?" He placed a kiss on her palm. Instead of tracing the lines with a fingertip, he did so with his tongue. Closing her eyes, she let the sensations ripple through her.

"Not in a hurry at all. Don't want to go there." Lainie shuddered with the contact, her body quivering from the top of her head to her toes. She tugged. With delicacy for such a big man, he bit the pad at the base of her hand. "Don't want to go," she repeated. "How many times do I have to say the words for you to believe me?" she told him for what had to be the fourth or fifth time in as many days. She didn't understand what it would take for him to accept her word as fact.

"I'm not going to live the rest of my life afraid I might lose you. We have to test the portal or I'll forever live in fear of something taking you away from me." His thumbs massaged gentle circles on her wrists. "If you go to the spot and nothing happens, I'll breathe easier knowing you will always stay with me. After that we can make arrangements for the marriage."

"What if the opposite happens?" She quivered with dread of just such an event. "What if that horrible place takes me away from you?"

"It won't."

"That's what you are hoping. I repeat, what if it sucks me right up then tosses me somewhere I don't want to be?" Lainie found herself shaking her head at the stubborn man who refused to listen to reason.

"I'll be with you wherever we end up."

"Stubborn, irritating man!"

His easy laughter annoyed her more. "*Aye*. 'Tis me alright."

Every night they made love until her monthly got in the way that one time. Since then... Those nights he held her. Tucked her head close to his chest. His heart beat was always steady and strong. She was terrified if he took her to the portal, she would never feel his arms around her again. He was certain nothing would happen. Convinced that once they put to the test his theory, there would be no more worries between them.

Lainie didn't remember when so much changed for her. Didn't know when she adjusted so completely to this life she didn't want to leave. Now, she was resigned. With little fanfare, she learned that once Roc made up his mind there would be no arguing. When they returned, she would marry him. All would be right with the world.

"That's good there is no hurry. Do you want to go?"

The request in his eyes was always there. He would continue to ask the same question. She would continue to tell him no. She didn't want to leave Carnoch or him.

"Do I have a choice?" she bit out, furious with him for insisting.

The last few days he made certain she would understand that the portal would reject her. She didn't agree with his assessment. How could it be so particular? "Why do you keep asking then not listening. You are stubborn, a stubborn, stubborn mon. I don't wish to go to the portal or leave you."

"No!" he bit out waving his hand in the air.

The anger in his voice was unmistakable. His voice carried all his fury with the simple word. "I don't want to always question as well as wonder about you going back. What if we had an argument? Afterward you decided to leave me? We can't live that way. Always wondering. If the portal takes you, it will take me also. I promise you. I will never leave you."

"You don't want to go!"

Neither did she. She could vent her anger too. It seemed he wasn't giving her a choice.

"Do you want me out of your life so much?"

The thought of rejection hurt as well as terrified. Except for his insistence she do this, she had no reason to believe her question. After she blurted the words, he looked stunned. His brows narrowed as he seemed to search her for answers.

Roc recoiled as if she hit him. Schooling his features, he pulled her against him before settling her on his thighs. The top of her head was tucked beneath his chin. "Want you to marry me. Want all this nonsense to stop building a bridge between us. Once we learn the truth, we will both be happier. We can go on with our lives no longer in fear of the unexpected. It's something I have to do...have to know before we can marry then settle down to raising a family. I want to teach little shifters how it is done. Want to raise beautiful girls that look just like you."

He stroked her hair, sending pins sliding to the floor. His long fingers massaged her scalp, easing the tension.

"What is that truth you think you will comprehend?"

She knew the answer before he spoke. Roc told her before. Would tell her again. She should learn to listen better.

"Ah, the truth, sweetheart. The reality of us, of our lives together is that you belong with me. You won't come to terms with that fact until you realize that you can never return to the time you appeared from. You are my mate, returned from the future so we can move on with our lives as well as the ones that will come after. Kit's mate moved forward through the Kinnel Stones so she could live with him. As soon as it stops raining, we will go. I want this to be solved, sooner than later."

Just as Roc wished, she also wanted this to be over sooner. "There are breaks in the rain. We could have safely traveled yesterday. We could this afternoon. We would be at the cave before the night darkens. We could return tomorrow." Since he insisted, she wanted this done and over with yesterday, not tomorrow or the next. Her nerves were stretched to the breaking point. Waiting unraveled her nerves one thin strand at a time.

"Yes." His hands ran along her back, touched each vertebra. "Yes." He kissed her forehead, then closed her eyes with kisses. "Tomorrow. Tomorrow we will travel east to the sacred grounds that brought you to me."

"If it's not pouring in the morning, let's leave first thing. It's Saturday. You don't have to work unless you want to do so."

Leaning into his hard body, she let a puff of air slip from her lungs, memorizing his scent, the strength of his body. Her hands tripped across his muscled shoulder.

"All right." His hand slid upward to hold her breast. He flicked the tightening bud with his thumb. "Tomorrow."

"Are you going to seduce me?"

She rested against him, feeling the evidence of his arousal where she sat on him. His hand traveled down her ribcage then back to her breast. He flipped a few buttons before sliding his hand beneath the fabric of her gown.

"No. Don't have to. I'm guessing you're ready for me."

She gasped as his other hand lifted her skirt then slid along her leg. Getting used to wearing nothing beneath her skirts had been difficult at first. All women wore in this time were petticoats, multiple crinolines and stays. Now, she liked the fact it made it easier for Roc to stroke her intimately. His fingers settled on her belly. He was questioning. After that, they slipped between her opened legs.

He found her g-spot, touched, massaged until she opened wider beckoning him into her dark secret warmth. He laughed when she told her what it was called in her time. Time and again he reminded her so she wouldn't forget. With his calloused fingertips, he teased her, caressed the inside of her leg then higher to cup her mound. "You are already weeping for my touch. Your nectar rains...spills onto my fingers. Do you want me inside you?" He asked as he lifted her then turned her so she straddled him.

"Yes, please."

She licked her lips. Anticipation. Desire. Hunger. All swept through her as she waited for him, for the blinding rush of pleasure, the fragmenting of her nerves she knew would come. "I think I'm always ready for you."

Lainie unfastened his pants. He was free of the confines. Hard. Aroused. She touched the satin top, feeling the tiny spurt of liquid. She set her hands on his shoulders, waiting. Her eyes closed knowing what would come next. She felt the smooth blunt tip, touching her, teasing her folds. In one fluid motion, he slipped inside her. His hands on her hips he held her still. "Don't want you to climax too fast. That wouldn't do. No, ecstasy too fast is not acceptable. Hold real still. Do not move."

With her top teeth she clamped down on her bottom lip, trying to do as he told her. His fingers made quick work of the bodice of her gown, drawing the fabric over her arms then down to her waist. Covered only by her thin chemise, he sucked on a nipple. Talons of fire clawed at her, fanning the inferno he created. His lips were drawn back. His expression feral. Still, with one hand he held her, kept her from moving. She wanted to cry out with her need. Needed for him to move inside her.

"What do you have cooking for dinner?" he asked as his attention shifted to her other breast, sucking then delicately biting. His hand beneath her skirt, stroking sensitive places over then over again. She never wanted to leave him. Was terrified of this test he insisted on doing. Experimenting with the unknown could be dangerous.

I love you, Roc Frasier!

Lainie wanted to yell at him one more time. Tell him how she felt. Wished she dared. She squirmed, needing more, knowing that with time when he was satisfied, he would see to their pleasure. Hungry desire built. The enchantment mercuric. She couldn't think. He asked her something. On a whisper of ecstasy as he moved inside her. "Food," she murmured, tossing her head back. Giving his questing mouth access to more sensitive places along her neck. She ran her hands along his chest, pulling on his shirt tugging, wishing the fabric to vanish.

"Food, sounds delicious. Right now, you are tastier." With infinite care and taking his time, he slid the laces of her chemise from the eyelets. When the laces hung free, he moved the fabric away from her breasts. "Can you be more specific about dinner?" In the light of the passion, his request seemed absurd to her.

"No..." The tiny wail was thin and thready as she searched for her release. Desperate to get closer to Roc, she arched, sending him deeper into her body. "I—I c-can't think."

Roc laughed as he rocked her against him. He captured her mouth with his. His tongue swept inside, touching her intimately. "You're burning me alive." One hand flicked a tender bud. The other massaged the tight hard jewel between her legs. "Inside you are kissing me. The pulses feel like tiny little kisses pulsing along my shaft. You are so hot, so wet, so soft."

"Please..." Her whisper was contained by his mouth. His tongue explored inside while he moved. He took her lower lip between his teeth then tugged. His tongue ran along the sensitive inner lining. Her sigh of pleasure filled him. She felt the first wave of her climax. Closing her eyes, she let him lead, allowed him the power to bring her to the ecstasy she always enjoyed.

"Tell me what you want." He nipped on her ear then touched on the lobe, kissed behind. Inside her he still moved prolonging heightening desire, urging passion to build.

The friction of his body deep inside her sent strong vibrations to her body. "You, just you. All I want is you, Roc."

He was enchantment to her soul. Like magic his fire swept through her. She whimpered when he thrust deep and hard inside her.

A fragmented sound broke inside her mouth to be swallowed by his. His lips moved along hers, nibbling then biting with expert skill. His finger gently twisted a tender bud. His body shuddered when she stroked his neck with her teeth. She wanted to move to feel him glide deep inside her. Wanted him to touch her all the way to her womb.

It seemed he could not hold back. Felt the same. He moved harder then faster. His body penetrated deeper, touching all of her. He took her with him when his body jerked. Inside, her womb's spasms erupted, blinding uncontrollable pulses flooded her. She cried out as her body shook with the blinding sensations overtaking her.

Lainie fell against him, her head resting on his shoulder. His hands soothed her running along her back. She whimpered, her body weak and trembling in the aftermath of her climax. For several minutes neither moved. The breaths she inhaled were deep as she fought to bring oxygen inside her lungs. Lainie reveled in the strong steady beat of his heart. Her eyes closed. She wished she could stay here surrounded by the warmth of him.

Her gasp of surprise came when he swatted her on her rear. "Roc!"

"I'm hungry." He grinned at her, his hand soothing where he swatted her. "What's for dinner?"

"Dinner is most likely burned thanks to you," Lainie told him petulantly as she tried to remove herself from his thighs. She pulled her chemise together, lacing where he unlaced then setting her dress back to its original place, fastening everything. "If you wish to eat, you need to let me up." She sounded peevish.

"We've company coming tonight." His smile widened as if the

surprise pleased him immensely.

"What?" she gasped out, realizing what they just did as well as where. "Who?"

They just made love in the drawing room. Anyone could have walked up to the front door and seen them. Heat rose to her cheeks. She pounded him on his chest, disturbed that he thought this so amusing.

"Hawk and Maisie...Harris too. They should be here in about ten minutes. You've absolutely nothing to worry over. They didn't see us. I assume there is plenty of food. The discussion we will be having is important."

Lainie was straightening her gown wishing she had time for a bath. The fact he waited so long to tell her sent a wave of resentment to her muddled brain. She'd been working all day, sweating in the kitchen. This was unfair of him to spring the news on her. "You should have told me sooner. We might not have enough for three more people."

They would though. She made noodles this morning. There was more than enough for his entire family. She could add more vegetables to the cream sauce that was even now simmering on the stove.

"Of course we'll have enough food. There is always enough left over to feed an army. I would have told you sooner if I'd known sooner. Saw Hawk on the way home from work just before I got here. When I came into the drawing room, you distracted me. That wasn't my fault. You have this way..." He winked at her, his gaze wandering over her body. She ignited with the touchless caress.

"I distracted you?" she asked, her hands fisted on her hips knowing the opposite was true.

He purposely set out to seduce her which didn't take much. She was terribly easy. Fell into his arms when he smiled or his eyes lit up with hunger.

"*Aye*." He wasn't going to give over to any other scenario. "You sashayed your pretty little butt right in front of me. This man doesn't stand a chance when he sees your delicious curves. Want to taste...and feel...then drive inside your heat."

"So, you thought you would just ask him without telling me first?" She was shaking a finger at him while she tapped one foot. "You need to consider me when you make propositions to your family as well as your friends that concern me.

"*Aye.*"

"Oh! Now you're agreeable. The least you could do is apologize for being so high-handed. You will have to help me with the dinner. You can cut more asparagus and snap peas. It's the least you can do."

Lainie wasn't certain what else needed to be done. She would have to allow her temper to cool before she could think straight.

"Hawk said they would bring bread as well as a desert. Pie, I'm hoping. Maisie makes delicious pies. Is that good enough to soothe your temper?"

He laughed again, looking as if he enjoyed himself at her expense. He still sat, both hands on his thighs, his grin stretching wider with each passing second. He had not fastened his pants. She saw him. Heated anew. She had to ignore his blatant masculine display.

Lainie strode to the door then turned. "It will have to be good enough. Since I've no say in the matter. Now, I'm going upstairs for a moment. You can join me in the kitchen when I come down or you can go to work now. Now would be for the best."

"Why?" He looked at her a puzzled expression on his face. Then set his gaze to the upstairs. "Don't understand."

"If we are having company, I need to change my gown. I've been working today. Would have liked a bath too. Could have if you told me the moment you walked in the door. I'll wash without benefit of a tub."

She was in a royal snit because he didn't tell her. He made love to her where anyone might have come up to the door and knocked. Before she started up the steps, she shook her finger at him, "I'm not going to forgive you anytime soon for this. I'll wait for an apology."

His hoot of laughter followed her up the stairs. She picked up her skirts then ran thinking of some way to get even with him. This would never do. Haste in the back of her mind, she poured water into a bowl, washing herself the best she could without getting a bath. She dressed. Smoothed the gown. Combed her hair, pushing some strands behind her ears. It was longer now. He forbade her to cut it. Hah! She would cut her hair if she wished to do so. What did she care? Hair always grew back.

She needed to make a point.

His way of telling her what she could and couldn't do ignited a spark of anger as well as mischief. While she didn't mind growing her hair out, his order that she not cut it rankled. The order provoked her to do the opposite. For a few wistful seconds, she eyed the scissors sitting on her dresser. Would love to see the look on his face if she cut her hair then came down the stairs with a short bob.

When she stepped into the kitchen, she found him cutting vegetables. She'd taught him how she wanted them cut. He was a quick learner. There were carrots from the cellar as well as snow peas from the little garden out back. Fresh asparagus sat on the counter waiting to be sliced. While she would have preferred dinner to be meatless, Roc would not go without his protein. He always thought it amusing when she called the meat protein. Every night he brought her meat. Tonight, they would have chunks of ham in the cream sauce along with the vegetables. The ham came from his parents. Lainie wondered how long she would remember that she always called meat, protein. She wondered, too, if she would recall how to cook; the sauces she made, the breads from scratch, the noodles...the list went on. So far, she forgot nothing about her skills in the kitchen. Seemed odd to her. Maybe for her cooking was instinctive. Still...nothing she prepared for Roc could be found in this time. All her dishes were unique.

For a few seconds, Lainie paused in the doorway, her gaze focused on his broad back, his trim hips. The muscled thighs and well-shaped rear. Watching him was always a delight to her senses. She'd never get tired of looking at him. The muscles of his back rippled. Even through the fabric of his shirt she could see them flex with each movement. He rolled up the sleeves of his shirt. His forearms were large covered by crisp brown hair.

This man is beautiful.

"You going to stand there and keep admiring me all night or are you going to help?" Roc didn't turn around. "While I can slice and dice the vegetables, I've no idea what to do with that sauce you've got simmering. Is it enough? Should you make a bit more?"

"How did you know..." her voice trailed off.

He always knew where she was as well as what she was doing.

His broad shoulders lifted in a very masculine shrug of indifference. "Always *ken* when you are around. Most of the time, yes. It's part of being a shifter. Since you're my mate, it's my duty to make certain you are protected. Can't do that if I don't *ken* where you are. Come tell me what to do next. I've a feeling our guests will be arriving very soon. I do wish to help."

She stepped up next to him, her hand resting on his shoulder. "It's not as if I'm in danger here. I've nothing to fear in Carnoch."

"You could be. I'd be remiss if I didn't take care of my woman."

"Tell me the truth. Why did you invite your brother and his wife for dinner, Harris too? Does it have something to do with tomorrow? With our trip?" The reason would be obvious if she thought long enough. It would be much easier to let him explain. She didn't appreciate guessing games.

"Yes. Want someone at my back tomorrow. We don't *ken* what will wait for us there. Not taking any chances with your life. Remember Geordie and Scratch?"

One dark eyebrow lifted in question.

"All right, so we are going to provoke the portal? What then?" she asked still dismayed that he was now insisting on this trip that she no longer wished to take. She would try one more time to dissuade him. After that she didn't know what to do. "We *dinna* need to go. *Dinna* need to worry about anyone's safety. I'm happy here, with you. *Dinna* want another life in a different time."

"Interesting way of putting it. So, yes. Harris was a mistake. When she heard Hawk was coming to dinner, she invited herself. I ran into her on my way home from work. Harris will want to go too. Told her no. Don't expect her to comply to my wishes. Just like you, my little sister seems to have a will of her own."

"You couldn't say no? You've no trouble saying no to me." Lainie asked wondering why he wouldn't just explain the truth to his sister.

Again, one of his eyebrows lifted to the sky. "My little sister has never been told no in her entire life. At least I don't recall a time. She is spoiled. Willful. Will continue to remain spoiled. It's just the way of things with the Frasiers."

"I need a glass of wine," Lainie muttered while she opened a bottle then poured herself a hefty glass. She tipped back her head drinking most of it.

"Pour me one too." Harris waltzed into the room grinning widely. "I've barely seen you. How are you doing?"

Roc handed her a glass. "Don't you ever knock, lil sis? You might stumble in on something..."

Lainie poked him in the chest.

"Why should I?" she asked on a giggle then a sip. "I *ken* I'm always welcome. What might I walk in on?"

She was naïve. An innocent. What would Roc tell her?

Because you might interrupt something that would embarrass you.

The crack of laughter from Roc startled her. "Because you might discover two people intimately involved with each other. That's why. You need to knock before you skip into my home. You never know what you might discover."

Lainie sent him a scowl that she hoped he would understand that he told his sister too much. He didn't have to be that blunt. Oversharing could get a person into trouble. Though perhaps that was the only way to proceed with his little sister. She would concede the truth that Roc knew Harris better than she did. Since she didn't know her at all. Lainie noticed that Harris turned a blushing shade of rose as if she understood Roc's words.

Harris shouldn't understand.

"Put the noodles in the boiling water, Roc. Harris, you sit down and enjoy yourself along with that glass of wine."

Lainie bustled around the kitchen making certain everything would be cooked to perfection. She didn't mind the added company. The conversation would help take her mind off tomorrow. When she thought about the following day, her stomach somersaulted.

"Anyone home?" Hawk called out from the front door.

At least Hawk didn't traipse inside unannounced. He was a

married man. It was likely he knew better. Would expect two people who lived together to be intimate with each other in more places than the bedroom. Not in the front room of the house or the kitchen. Oh my, Lainie remembered when he made love to her on top the kitchen table. She would have to put a stop to his amorous adventures in any room of the house. Heat rushed to her face. To cool herself, she set her hands on her cheeks.

Once dinner was served, little was spoken except mundane conversation about the weather. Business was spoken of. Roc printed invitations announcing the marriage of a wealthy landowner who lived farther west. Hawk spoke of his shared practice with Houston.

They talked of the Kinnel Stones which intrigued Lainie. Setting down her fork, she looked to both men for answers. "Why didn't I come through the stones? Seems that would have been more appropriate. We wouldn't have to worry about my accidentally returning to my time. I would either walk in or I would not."

"Appropriate? Perhaps," Hawk looked as if he was thinking. "Perhaps not. You found your way here. You didn't know of the stones. Some other force was behind your traveling through time. We would not change that. Magic is not something to toy with. This is magic. Hopefully, good magic is at play here."

It seemed to Lainie that by making her travel with them to the falls was playing with the supernatural. Inviting bad magic. Terrified shivers ripped through her. She didn't like the fact any better now than she did a few minutes ago. "I didn't know the hill behind the waterfall had magical properties either," Lainie pointed out with a bit of sarcasm in her voice. "I was pushed from behind then slid down the steep hillside. Ended up sitting on my bottom staring Roc in the face. To my misfortune, there were other men there too. Who, well..."

She pushed a strand of hair behind her ear not wishing to say anything else.

"They were afraid of me," Roc smiled at her then faced his brother. "That brings me to the point I wanted to make today. Would you go with Lainie and me tomorrow? We're going to retrace that day. In the process what happened there will be put to rest. I need someone at my back. The two men who thought she was theirs to play with might make another appearance. A chance or a mistake I will not make. Don't wish to have Lainie put in jeopardy of any sort."

"You're thinking about Geordie and Scratch?" Lainie asked with fear making her voice quiver. She wrapped her arms around herself in an attempt to ward off the shivers.

"I am."

Startled, she sucked in a gulp of air. Heat fled her body. A splintering of fear rushed through her as she recalled the looks on their faces when they saw her. Remembered what they intended. It had been weeks since she thought of those two men. When she mentioned them in the earlier conversation, she didn't think they would be a problem when it came to the quest they were embarking upon. It was obvious to her that Roc wasn't intending to trust to luck. Lainie had to appreciate that fact.

Roc's eyes were icy, steel-gray, hard as well. Hawk's eyes weren't much different. Masie reached out to touch Hawk's hand. Maisie's lavender eyes were filled with concern when she turned her attention toward her.

"You have to go with them," Maisie told Hawk. "I'll do whatever I can to help at the office. Houston along with Leah will be there. This is your family. They need you. I'll be fine as you well know."

Hawk nodded as he looked from her then back to Roc. "Yes, I'll go with you. Understand you might need help. We have no expectant birth mothers waiting for attention. This is not the worst time of year for the clan to fall sick. As my wife mentioned, Houston along with her and Leah should be able to handle the office with ease."

Beneath the table, Roc held her hand, squeezed as if he meant to give encouragement. She sucked in another breath of air. When she closed her eyes, shaking her head, willing all the issues away, she wanted to scream. Needed to tell him she didn't want to go. Would never willingly leave him.

I love you.

Roc was a tenacious man. He would do things his way. Curse him. He had to prove every point. They didn't need to do this.

"Everything will be fine. You'll see," Maisie said as if she recalled another time, a time when she'd been at risk.

Yes, if I don't return all will be just as it should be. Depression settled around her. Lainie tried to come to grips with the fear rolling through her. She didn't want to leave Roc. She loved him.

~ * ~

Rafe walked along the hallway in the McKenna keep that housed the portraits of hundreds of years of the Clan Chattan. The pictures were arranged by families. He stood in front of the Frasiers, walking, memorizing each picture. They were all familiar from other times he perused them thinking of his heritage. He knew he should find his mate. Knew also that finding that right person sometimes took time. His patience was wearing thin.

The fact that Dallas refused to see him disturbed him deeply. Since he could remember they'd been close, shared everything, feelings, disappointments, accomplishment. He needed to figure out why she now seemed so aloof after the brief kiss they shared. The intimacy was something he never experienced with her or with any other woman. The spark they often talked about in the negative was there this time. The flash between them was so intense he thought he would ignite. As if terrified of the brief but potent contact she ran off, fled to the arms of another man. He had to figure out a means to get her back, to make her see they were meant to be together.

Intrigued with one painting in particular, Rafe stopped to gaze at the portrait of Cameron Petrock Frasier, a relative of his. His wife sitting beside him gave him pause. She was beautiful, so very similar to Dallas the woman stole his breath. If born at the same time they could have easily passed for sisters...nay, twins. Maybe not, there were subtle differences between them.

"Rumor has it that the woman, Lainie Frasier, came from the future to be with her soul mate." Case McKenna the laird of the McKenna's as well as the head of the Clan Chattan, spoke with a soft measured voice. "Do you believe in rumors?"

Staring, mesmerized he couldn't shake his gaze from the woman sitting next to Cameron Frasier. "I don't know. Haven't heard many of late. Suppose I would also have to believe in time travel," Rafe said while he rubbed the back of his neck where a prickling of hair told him he should listen to the McKenna. In passing, he'd also heard of the Kinnel Stones, rumors of their magic.

"The Kinnel Stones," Case reminded him. "The stones have brought many a mate to a member of the clan as well as sent an enemy through time. Some say to eternal damnation." Case lifted his shoulders in a small shrug of indifference as he seemed to study Rafe. "I trust you've heard of the stones. All in this area should understand them, the magic, the enchantment. They are just as supernatural as our abilities to shift."

"Eternal damnation, is there such a thing?"

Rafe wasn't certain about any of this. What he did feel strongly about was that he needed to find a way to retrieve his mate before she made the biggest mistake of her life. The man she meant to live with was not a good person. She could be harmed. "Last time I saw Dallas, she told me she was moving to Edinburgh. She had a new job along with a new man. Gordon was his name, Mathew Gordon. I can't find her anywhere. She doesn't answer the phone when I call. I'm terrified something has happened to her again."

"Why?" Case asked, his voice curious while he listened to a good friend. "If you figure out why she wants to leave you, you'll have a better chance of finding her. Do you believe she is your mate?"

Rafe stiffened when he heard the question. For years he'd been asking himself that same question. Once he thought no. Now, after the last kiss, he had a different answer. "I didn't. Now, I do. With all my heart and soul, I know what I should have known years ago when we were floundering."

The two men strode down the rows of pictures, each man and woman staring down at them as if they had a story to tell. Rafe felt the emptiness to the tips of his toes. He understood he had to find Dallas. Needed to discover her whereabouts soon. Before it was too late for them. He just didn't have any more ideas as to where to begin his hunt.

This morning when dawn was barely breaking, Dallas called to him. With her clear honeyed voice, he heard her. She needed him. He didn't know where she was. The clues to her whereabouts were few.

"I have to drive to the city," Rafe said.

"Did she tell you where this new job was supposed to be?" Case asked. "You could start there. They might have an address or a number where you can reach her."

"Yes, it's a magazine. The Highland Experience. She is the main photographer. Told me she would be in the highlands most of the time, on assignment. Cell service might be the only problem, a bit sketchy in the countryside. There are parts of the highlands that are isolated, unreachable. When I found her car at the falls, I drove it back to her apartment. She would have been on foot." He paused to rub the back of his neck again. "She hitchhiked. By my reckless actions, I put her in danger."

"You had no way of knowing. That was a month? Two months ago? Where has she been all that time? Have you asked her?"

"McKenna, Sir, I had no way of knowing what happened? How do you explain her disappearance then as well as now? None of this makes sense to me."

Cold shivers swept through him. "After that, her sudden appearance. I'm baffled. If my guess is correct, Dallas is avoiding me. We were both shocked when I kissed her. I knew then the opposite of what I thought before. Dallas is my mate. Something about her changed. I don't understand that either." When he kissed her that day, mercuric feeling swamped him.

"I don't have an explanation for you," Case said as he too seemed to feel the coldness sweeping through the keep. "There is something terribly wrong."

"The rumors concerning this woman? Rafe nodded to the portrait. "She is so like Dallas. This woman could be a twin from another time."

All kinds of scenarios swept through him. If Dallas traveled back in time, which was highly improbable, who was the woman he now sensed as his mate? Was the woman sitting in that picture Dallas or Lainie as it said? If she was Dallas, who was the woman he kissed? The woman he knew was his mate?

She couldn't be in two places at the same time. The thought stopped him cold. A wave of frost swept down his spine.

It wasn't the same time.

Lainie Frasier lived in the eighteenth century. Dallas Shaw is alive now. Was she? His stomach lurched.

"Don't suppose you will ever have the answer. Go find Dallas before it's too late. Go to the highlands. I'm certain the magazine she works for knows where she is. Tell them you're her husband if they won't give out the information."

That was just the point. Rafe was violently afraid he was too late. He gulped in a breath of cold air. To him it wouldn't matter if this Gordon fellow took her innocence. He would still love her. She would still be his mate. What mattered was if he could convince Dallas of that fact. So many years passed them by while they believed they weren't meant for each other.

"You know," Case began stroking his chin as if in thought. "We both understand that if something happens and a member of the clan is not able to wed and claim his mate, the line dies. What if Lainie...Dallas traveled back in time to rectify that mistake? What if Lainie had to be with Cameron Fraiser?"

The thought rifled through Rafe's brain. The explosion of questions in his mind weren't answered. "Yes...what if?" He struggled with all the possibilities, unable to put everything into its proper perspective.

"If Cameron claimed Lainie, if the girl was Dallas, then all would be set right? Now, you will be able to claim your woman. If what I'm thinking is true, everything has changed for you and your woman. Dallas somehow must have changed to Lainie. Subtle differences. She was chosen because they are so similar. Maybe Dallas went there then returned. One can only speculate. I doubt if anyone in this time has answers. Least of all me."

Chapter Eight

A torrential downpour stopped them from leaving at dawn as was planned. Roc hoped to go then return in the same day. All problems would be solved by this evening if they could just be on their way. That wasn't going to happen. The entourage would have to spend one night in the cave. He packed food as well as blankets. He needed to leave the cave prepared for the next arrivals. It was on Clan Chattan land. All in the clan were welcome to use the well-stocked cavern.

When the sun finally broke through the dense clouds to warm the Scottish countryside, Lainie was pacing and wringing her hands. Roc understood her nerves were disintegrating. It was all he could do to relax and accept the inevitability of the night surrounded by a brother as well as a sister. That wasn't why Lainie paced. She'd told him she was afraid of what might happen in the morning. She didn't know how he could be so certain she would remain in this time. Now he had second thoughts of inviting his siblings. Ah, well, what would one night sleeping alone matter in the scope of the rest of their lives together.

The ride with Lainie in front of him tested his restraint. The moment she settled between his thighs, he could think of nothing except enjoying her, seeing to her pleasure. Hawk laughed as if he understood.

"Why don't you take a cart? It would be more comfortable for both of you." When Hawk made the suggestion, they were only a quarter mile from the house and passing by their parent's home. Hawk was right. Nonetheless, he'd rather hold her close, savor her scent coupled with the sweetness of her lush curves. If she sat next to him on a wagon, she would still arouse every male part of him.

"We could take the cart?" Lainie turned in his arms to see if he was willing. Frown lines marred her perfect features.

"True."

Roc didn't want to elaborate. Didn't want to tell her how much he preferred her just where she sat even though he realized she was still terrified of horses.

She tilted her head to the side as if examining him. After that she lifted her small delicate shoulders. "Suit yourself. We did this once before, remember? Seemed to work out just fine. Though if I recollect correctly, your mood was sour by the time you got me to your parent's home. Is that the way it's going to be now?"

He would suit himself. While he told himself nothing was going to change, he was afraid for her. The closer they came to the cave, more fear coursed into his veins. The fear didn't come from the portal. No, there was something else at work here this day, something sinister that he couldn't grasp. When rain started falling about a mile from the cave, he cursed anew. The sky was dark, the ground sodden. Mud splashed with each hoofbeat.

"Are you cold, *lass*?" he asked afraid for her. She snuggled into him pulling her cloak tight as if accepting his warmth.

"No, just tired." Lainie leaned into him, closing her eyes. "It seems lately I've been tired all the time.

"Go to sleep. I'll wake you when we get there."

Roc understood exactly why she was tired. She conceived a few days ago. Lainie carried a son, a shifter. He decided he wouldn't tell her that he knew about her condition. After an earlier conversation, he understood she was disappointed he would know before her. He could wait until she figured it out. He grinned, so very pleased she was going to have his child. The portal would never take her away from him. It wouldn't dare.

"Are you sure? I wouldn't, well, it doesn't seem right to fall asleep."

"You're not much company when you can't keep your eyes open. Rest so you'll have more energy when we get there." He watched his brother and sister riding ahead of him. He'd deliberately pulled behind them so he could fondle her, caress tender flesh when they weren't looking. His hand cupped her breast while he guided the big stallion with his knees. His thumb brushed across the tight hard bud, coaxing, sightseeing. He wanted to raise her skirt. See if she was damp and swollen ready for him.

"Are you seducing me?" her voice was a breathy whisper. "It's working. Not fair of you to do that when you *cannae* finish."

"Didn't we figure out that I didn't need to seduce you? You seem to be always ready for me. Just attempting to keep my hands warm." Roc touched her with his teeth before kissing the sensitive spot behind the lobe.

"One of them will turn around then see what you are doing," she protested yet the words weren't fierce enough for him to stop. "You will not be embarrassed but I will. Don't want anyone to see what you are doing."

"I enjoy touching all of you, just as you enjoy the sensations my gentle caresses generate. You want me just as much as I want you. Don't deny it, *lass*."

His teeth raked along her neck. He pulled the black rain poncho she wore more securely, making sure the hood fit snuggly on her head. Once again, he gave attention to her breasts, his hands hidden beneath the poncho.

Hawk waited for them. He pulled up beside his brother, looking at him as if he knew what he was doing beneath the cloak. "We'll be there in a few minutes. What do you plan? Did you want to go to the glen now or tomorrow."

"To the cave, not the glen. It will take another hour to reach that spot where Lainie appeared. Darkness will fall before then. Won't take that risk."

"So," Hawk pushed his hat back on his head seeming to think over all that was said. Rain dripped onto his shoulders. "We won't be able to test your theories out until tomorrow. Is that going to be all right? You say you won't do this once the sun sets."

"Even with cat eyes, don't want to do anything after dusk. Doing so is too dangerous for Lainie. Won't risk Lainie or Harris. Too bad we won't be able to convince our sister to remain here when we go to the glen." The tightening of Roc's skin didn't surprise him nor did the prickle on the back of his neck making his hair stand on end. He wanted nothing more than to reach the safety of the cave where he could protect Lainie better.

"What's wrong?" Hawk asked seeming to have noticed the tension sweeping through him. "You look worried. Care telling me what's bothering you? It might be easier to have your back if I'm not surprised by something you forgot to tell me."

"Only my sixth sense kicking in where Lainie is concerned. Someone is watching us. Know it for a fact. Sure, as the hairs on the back of my neck are standing on end."

His mind went to Geordie and Scratch. He urged his horse to a faster gait. In his arms she shifted, her fingers clinging to his forearm. Frightening her was not part of his plans.

"Roc?"

"I'm sorry to wake you," he spoke knowing the urgency he felt was clear in the tenor of his voice. "Hang on. Need to get to the cave before dusk." He passed Harris who slanted him a sideways look of disapproval. The hooves of his horse pounding on the damp earth, he raced past his siblings.

"It's not raining that hard," Harris called out as she followed her brothers, pushing her horse to a faster pace. Pins flying from her hair as it flowed behind her.

Roc understood Lainie's fear. He cursed himself for not taking the time to teach her to ride and not to fear the horse. In this time, her horse should be her friend as well as her means of transportation. Not that bizarre thing she called a car.

With the rain pounding them, they reached the cave. He helped her dismount, lifting her from the mount. Hawk took care of the horses. Once inside the cave, Harris started a fire. Lainie stood in front of the heat, rubbing her hands. Roc put water with ground coffee beans on the fire to heat.

Lainie looked to him with wide eyes. "I'm not useless. I can help. I could have made the coffee. I can start dinner if you point me in the right direction," Lainie said while Roc helped her from the poncho then shook off the water hanging it on a hook to dry.

Yes, she would manage dinner quite nicely. He needed to

delegate better. Lainie would need something to keep her hands busy and her mind occupied. Roc didn't like seeing the fear in her eyes. "As soon as the supplies are unloaded you can put something together for us to eat. Looking around the room, he recalled the first time they were here. She showed him and spoke of things that he never knew existed before he met her. She sat on nettles. He spread ointment on her butt. Took his time rubbing the medicine across her deliciously rounded bottom. Memories slammed around in his head. Most of the things she spoke to him about were forgotten.

Lainie stared at him with eyes that seemed to be recalling the same things. At least she had not forgotten what happened in this century. Her beautiful white face flushed to a lovely rose as she seemed to be recalling that first time they spent the night together. From experience he knew the tops of her bountiful breasts would be the same color as her cheeks. Lightly, he tapped her nose with his fingertip. His feelings intense, he worried about her. Hated the fact that she couldn't remember her life before depressed her. This was her new life. It was all that mattered.

"You remembering too?" he asked wishing for a kiss, not a chaste one but a deep hard kiss that would lead to other things.

She nodded. "I recall everything we did here. I wanted you from the first moment I saw you. Somehow, I understood we were connected. Just didn't know how deeply those connections were." Her sudden attempt at a breath of air was shaky. "Not everything I told you about, those things...most of those things, I don't recall. I *dinna* want to forget. Gradually, I'm losing a part of who I am. I'll never get it back. Is that the way it's supposed to be? Am I not supposed to have a past that is the future? If what you say is true, I must have a past that is part of this time. Who was I before? I'm not even certain I *ken* who I am now."

Moisture clouded her beautiful eyes. With the backs of her hands, she swiped at the moisture.

Roc wished he could give her an explanation. He couldn't. "You can't help it. Wish I could tell you I understand. Want to be able to tell you the reasons. Just know that this is where you are supposed to live." He pulled her into his arms, hugging her to lend comfort nothing else.

She rubbed her cheek along his chest. His fingers held her head close, winding into the silk of her hair. When she backed away, he spoke again. "Why don't you make some biscuits to go with the venison stew I'm going to heat up. Cooking might keep your mind off other things."

Lainie nodded seeming to agree with him.

When he heard Hawk walking into the cave, he turned. Hawk's arms were filled with supplies for tonight as well as the next time someone came from Inverness. There was more on the packhorse they brought with them. He tested the pot of coffee that was beginning to boil.

While Lainie cooked the biscuits, Harris made up the pallets with fresh bedding. Hawk stored the provisions. When all was finished, they sat around the fire. Hawk made several trips to the opening of the cave. His brother felt it too. Felt the evil on the wind. Currents of madness seemed to float around him. Tomorrow they would take great care. He didn't intend to risk anyone's life. This was just the period to end any thoughts Lainie might harbor about her past life. One she could barely recall.

Despite feeling some measure of relief this would be finished on the 'morrow, his gut tightened knowing dawn of the next day would arrive sooner than later. Roc could not chase the feeling that something was terribly wrong from his mind. He'd been so certain the portal would reject her. Tonight, he wasn't as certain. Experiencing indecision was not something Roc was used to. He didn't enjoy harboring doubts where once there had been certainty.

Leaning back against the wall he pulled her between his crossed legs. Her body against his was warm, pliant. He wished they could make love. His hands squeezed her waist, inviting, telling her he wanted her.

"What has you so tense, Roc? You're frightening me. Talk to me. Won't you?" Lainie asked.

Turning in his arms, she touched his jaw, ran her finger down his neck. Stopped at the pulse point throbbing. Telling her he wanted her. "I would know the truth. Are you having reservations about doing this. I tell you now. I don't want to go there. Don't want any part of this test you speak of. Even though the trip would have been made for nothing, I would happily return to Carnoch in the morning rather going to the glen where all this began. The waiting, the fear, is stretching my nerves tight. I feel as if each one is about to snap."

"The prickling of my neck, the feeling of evil abounds, tells me we should be twice as aware when we step into the glade. We are not turning back or avoiding this scenario. If not for you, I want to know with certainty for myself that you will always be here with me. Besides, there is something else in action here. Something that is beyond our imagination. I know that fact as well as I *ken* my next breath."

"We're going there anyway. What is this second scenario you're speaking about?" she asked, her words dry, clearly displeased with his decision. "Even though I've told you I don't want to do this. You're a stubborn man, Roc Frasier. Can't say that I like that about you. Stubborn, intractable man!" Lainie hit him on the arm.

"Yes, you can also call me pigheaded if you wish."

His breath he'd been holding he let ease from his body. He didn't like upsetting Lainie. Didn't know how to explain to her why this had to be done. He wished he could reassure her. "It's the only way we will be secure in our life together. If the portal takes you, you are not my mate." She was. She carried his child. For her sake he had to remain calm. It was the feeling something else was happening that drove him wild.

"What if that isn't the only reason you are feeling this prickling of your senses? What if there is other evil out there and the portal doesn't have anything to do with it? There could be factors out of your control, driving this. You will never convince me this is necessary. Needless to say, you will persevere. I accept that."

The question she asked was valid. Scratch and Geordie had been on his mind as well as Hawk's.

"I believe that might be the case." Roc did think there were other factors. "Hawk senses it too. We need to watch out for the men who found you that first day. They thought of you as theirs. They might...they might try to take you again. If I have my wish, I'll send those two through the portal."

Roc ran his fingers through his hair wishing there was no reason to take precautions. The devil there were always reasons to take safeguards. If necessary, he would change to his cat. In that form he was even more aware of his surroundings, the hidden, unsuspected dangers. His sixth sense heightened by his change of form.

"Won't you change your mind? If you do, I promise I'll never argue with you again," she spoke, her words quiet while she ran her hand along his chest inviting intimacy they couldn't share.

Her eyes were wide pools of blue beckoning him to see this scenario her way. She lowered her lashes for a second.

He hooted his laughter. Kissed her on the forehead then her nose, lifted her chin so she stared into his eyes. He brushed soft kisses along her mouth from corner to corner. "That is a promise you would never be able to keep. Though I appreciate the effort. How do you feel?" Roc asked wondering when she would realize she carried his child.

Even though he knew it was too soon for her to guess. He was heartily pleased she stopped taking the birth control she brought with her. After the first month in this century, she didn't even know what the pills were meant for.

I shouldn't be risking her this way. Am I a fool? An idiot?

Roc didn't think the risk was to her. He was neither fool nor idiot. Though he couldn't be certain who was at risk. As if she gave up on her quest to deter him from his path, she inclined against him. He felt her breathing slow as she drifted to sleep. He ran his fingers through the silken strands of her hair, pleased she was allowing it to grow. Though when he first mentioned it, she glowered at him. When he saw her chin tilt upward with defiance in her eyes, he would not have been surprised to come home one day and find her beautiful hair short.

In everything she would maintain her independence. There were few things he would be able to dictate to her.

Hawk handed him a cup of coffee before sitting down near him, a grim expression on his well-chiseled features. "She asleep? Probably a good thing. Tomorrow could be harrowing for all involved. By the end of the day, she'll be exhausted." His voice was low, resonating softly among the shadows cast by the fire.

"Already is. She's carrying a babe."

Harris sat on her pallet, sipping her drink watching intently. Her mind seeming to splinter in a thousand different directions. As if something drew her, she wandered to the opening of the cavern. Roc watched his sister, wanting to call out to her to stay inside. He didn't wish for anyone to roam the woods this night. Danger. Madness. All abounded.

"What's your plan for tomorrow?" Hawk asked while he also seemed to keep his attention focused on Harris.

She didn't step outside. Was leaning against the rocks holding her cup with both hands. She looked pensive. Roc figured she was thinking about her lost love, Ashton Wolcott.

"Tomorrow," Roc paused in thought. "Let me see. Get up. Eat. Ride to the glen. Wait for what? We don't know." Roc lifted his shoulders in thought. "If nothing happens, we can walk around to the waterfall then take this from the same angle that Lainie did that first day."

"What happens if...could be an unwelcome shock to all of us. My heart pounds thinking of the possible loss to you."

"Nothing is going to happen to Lainie. It's the other part I'm feeling that I'm worried about. Geordie and Scratch play some role I don't understand." Roc was shaking his head terrified of the thoughts revolving in his head. "I'm not going to let go of her hand. If the worst things happen, I'll be with her. I will be with her," he repeated.

"You don't think...she will be sucked up by the portal," Hawk finished on the worst-case scenario.

"It can't. It won't. She belongs with me. Lainie doesn't know it yet, but she carries our child. There is no way in hell I'll let her leave me now. I'm ecstatic that she doesn't want to return to her time."

"Why are you here?" Hawk asked, posing the question Roc had been asking himself since she arrived to turn his world upside down. "Why don't you let everything stand as it is? I'm not sympathetic to this need of yours."

"The devil, now that I'm here my reasons don't seem so important. Lainie tried to change my mind about going through with this. For my benefit, I ignored her. She's terrified of tomorrow." As if she sensed he was talking about her, she moved in his arms, pressing her head into the hollow of his shoulder. Roc ran his hand along her back. The gesture was one that always seemed to soothe her when she was upset.

"We don't have to go to the falls in the morning. You've all night to think about this crazy plan of yours. No decisions need to be made this moment. I do not mind turning around and going home tomorrow without resolving this."

"I would have to do this at a later date, if not today."

"Your choice." Hawk lifted his shoulders in a resigned shrug.

Roc felt the same way, bristling at his brother's suggestion that he felt when Lainie made the same proposal. "I don't know why but I feel as if this has to be carried out for everything in the universe to be set right. There is more at stake here than the fate of Lainie and myself. I can't say for certain what it is. Just know that this has to come full circle."

"Uh...huh..." Hawk looked quizzically at him telling him he needed to give a better explanation of his thoughts. "Explain."

He let out a deep breath of air while he searched his mind for the necessary words. "Suppose one could say my sixth sense is kicking in to take charge. Lainie has been changing...subtly...since she arrived here. She is not the same woman who slammed into my life on that spring day. The differences are small. Her hair, her eyes...all are the same yet different. Her breasts are larger, her waist smaller, while her hips are rounder. I don't believe she would fit into the dress she wore when I found her or anything else she carried in that huge bag of hers. Half of what she brought with her, she doesn't comprehend though that first day she told me everything about her life in the future. The universe is at play here, madness, attempting to set all right that went terribly awry at some point in time."

"She might just be eating better," Hawk proposed, a silly grin on his face. "From what you've told me, she's a marvelous cook."

"No, it's not that. Food doesn't account for the slight change of her hair and eye color or the slow loss of her memories. When she came, she bemoaned the fact that she was overweight. She told me about the diets meant to help her lose weight. She no longer *kens* any of those facts. When the word diet is brought up, she looks confused."

"She isn't overweight now nor was she then. Why does a woman want to withhold food?" Hawk asked clearly baffled.

"No, but she is nicely round, very womanly. My preference in a woman is generous curves."

Roc could never get enough of looking at her, touching her. Now, holding her in his arms, thinking about her body, lust shot through him hardening him in an instant. That's all it took. A thought. An image in his mind.

"Yes. Just the way you like your women," Hawk laughed at his words. "You've got exactly what you wished for. When are you going to speak to Katy? You remember. Your mistress. Needs to be done the sooner the better."

"Yes. No argument there. She's also lost many of her memories of the future, her life there. When I remind her, she gives me a blank face before she scrunches her features as if she's thinking I'm daft. After I put everything together, I understand she won't go forward. Someone will though. A place will have to be taken to make up for the loss of Lainie. I think somehow the woman..." Once again Roc was shaking his head in confusion or disbelieving his thoughts. He didn't understand how any of this could take place. This was all conjecture. He felt as if he wrote a story he didn't know the ending to. Perhaps it wasn't his place to understand. "The Lainie I hold in my arms was born to this time. Something happened to her over the last few months. The woman who came through the portal belongs in the future. That woman has to go back. Tomorrow has to play out."

"Ashton!"

The shriek coming from the cave opening was torn from Harris. The scream caught his attention as well as his brother's. Hawk stood. Lainie moved in his arms, pushing hair from her sleepy eyes. He tensed.

"Ashton is here?" Roc asked in disbelief as he watched Hawk stride with purpose to the front.

There now is another person we will have to look out for. Another person to watch his back and Lainie's. Perhaps his sudden appearance was not such a bad thing.

What the devil was Ashton doing here? There could only be one reason. He returned for Harris just as he told her he would do. They would be chaperoned here. Roc held the distinct feeling they'd been intimately involved at one time. Even though when he questioned his sister, she adamantly denied it. Something besides a few kisses went on between the two of them. Harris told him she would never risk the same fate as what befell Crissie McKenna. She didn't want the stigma of bearing a bastard. Ashton would have to marry her before she gave herself to him. Sometimes fate stepped in to change things. Ashton needed to prove himself before he would be accepted by Clan Chattan.

Hand in hand the couple walked inside, Hawk behind them, a grim expression on his face. All the while, Harris' grin was besotted. She looked like a small cat who found the cream she wanted to lick up. He supposed if Lainie had been gone from him for more than a year, he would be feeling the same.

"Coffee?" Roc asked blandly giving nothing of his true feelings away until he spoke. "What are you doing here? Thought you would stay in London where all Sassenach belong."

"I can understand your animosity. Yes, I'd like coffee." He reached for a cup. "Surprised to see you as well as Harris at the cave. She took a few seconds to explain what you were doing here. Though there was more than one hole in her explanation."

Harris intercepted Roc, grabbing the cup then pouring for him. Roc noted the wide smile, the eagerness in his sister to please this man. In his mind, there were too many reservations to count. In his mind recalling the times over a year ago, Ashton needed to do everything in his power to make his absence up to her. His sister would do as she pleased. Whatever she wanted with this man, she would pursue. He only prayed she would not be hurt again.

"So, you came back to Carnoch. I assume that is where you are headed," Hawk said. "You will wait then travel with us. We will leave tomorrow after our business here is finished."

"All my obligations have been tied up. Now..."

He picked up Harris' hand then brought the back to his lips. He kissed then held her hand, twining his fingers through hers. His sentence was left unfinished.

Roc thought his sister would swoon from the brief yet obvious mercuric contact. A brother wasn't intended to watch the seduction of his little sister. Perhaps the man was her mate. Time would tell the full tale. Harris deserved happiness. Needed to find that man who was meant for her. "Now?" One of Roc's dark brows launched upward speculating. "Now what?"

"I came to court your sister." He smiled at her again. Harris smiled wider. "I'm not going to leave until I've won her heart. Harris will be mine."

Lainie snuggled in closer. Roc supposed he didn't have an argument. Lainie was pregnant with his child. They weren't married though it wasn't from his lack of trying to make it so. Roc understood by the way Harris acted a year ago when the man left her, that something happened between them. At least, Ashton didn't leave her alone as well as pregnant while he spent a year tying up his affairs. By the way Harris looked, the man would not have to work too hard to win Harris' hand.

Now the man was back. They would all need to keep a closer eye on his sister. He wondered how much time it would take until Harris would succumb to Ashton's many charms. The man was handsome, charismatic. He was tall with broad shoulders tapering to a narrow waist. He was taller than any of the Frasiers or the McKennas. His eyes a brilliant compelling deep blue.

"How long do you plan on staying this time?" Hawk asked as his brows were also creased with concern for the youngest sibling. "Don't want to see Harris hurt again." Hawk put his thoughts to words. "You're leaving..." Hawk stopped seeming to think this wasn't his place to speak.

"As long as it takes to undo the damage of my hasty exit. You should all understand I didn't want to leave without her. I was given no choice. Family business."

Brazenly, as if he wasn't standing in front of two brothers, he wrapped his arm around Harris' waist while he focused on Hawk. Ashton kissed her forehead before tapping her nose with his finger.

"I see. You will be here for a long time."

Roc heard all the moans and groans from his sister after Ashton left. Hawk had been busy courting Maisie as well as dealing with the Earl of Blevins. Furious would not come close to describe his sister's feelings toward the man. At the present time, she didn't appear to remember any of them. He prayed she would hold off the bedding until after the wedding. If the man proposed, he didn't have a single doubt she would agree.

His sister was a shifter. How would Ashton feel about her when he discovered the truth. Harris would have to do some fast talking. Roc wondered if Ashton knew that tiny little fact. It was a fact that needed addressing...before the wedding...not after. Ashton had been stationed at the fort in the highlands. That fort's sole purpose was to capture shifters. To his knowledge, they'd not been successful in a single case. Ashton had been allowed at Hawk's wedding. That in itself was unusual. Sassenach were never invited. He would press Hawk to discover the truth. There might be more to this man than one saw at first glance.

It seemed the couple had a great deal to talk about. Most of which would not be said in the company of two brothers. They should allow some discussion between the pair. Though Roc didn't doubt talk was the only thing on Ashton's mind or his sister's for that matter. Ashton would seek a kiss or two, maybe more. A little sweet seduction must be on his mind.

Ashton swallowed the last of his coffee. "We'd like to go for a walk if you don't mind." Asking for permission was a start in the right direction. "Harris and I have a great deal to hash over before we can come to terms with a possible wedding. I need to convince her she wants me. She will undoubtedly make doing so difficult."

Harris visibly bristled upon hearing the accusation. Though all Ashton mentioned was true. When Harris told her truth, he would run the other direction. Roc spoke up not wishing for them to have time together. Ashton would have to work for those kisses. "No more than ten minutes."

The devil, if he wanted to make love to her, they would need no more than five minutes. No one could say the things that Harris needed to explain to her beau in five minutes. Probably not ten either. She would be hesitant as well as hopeful Ashton would understand.

He might not.

"Stay by the opening of the cave. That will give you privacy of sorts. None of us will follow you though I want to be able to look up and see the two of you. I'll set up a pallet for you on the other side of the room," Hawk said to Ashton, seeming to take over this new situation.

Hawk would not allow them to sleep together. That was good.

"We'll need more than ten minutes," Ashton said, his voice deep with emotion. He touched Harris' chin. "You're unusually quiet. Any reason?"

"Yes and no. I cannot explain in ten minutes, nor can I..." she broke off turning her head to the side.

~ * ~

While Harris was pleased to see the man she loved, she needed to tell him that he was to keep his hands to himself. She wasn't about to let him seduce her as he did the last time she saw him. Though he didn't take her maidenhead, he did teach her a woman's pleasure. He did that a year ago despite the fact she told him no. Though he didn't force her. Merely gave her the promise of something more with sweet kisses then tender caresses. Now, might be different for any number of reasons. A few kisses were fine. Nothing else. After he helped her from her seat, he tucked her hand around his arm. She knew her brothers were leery of this relationship. Understood Ashton would have to learn about her family. Knew too that when he discovered the truth, he might not wish to court her. Might not want anything to do with her. He couldn't be that shallow. Could he? There were others who thought of shifters as beings that were less than human.

How much honesty could the man handle? That was the question of the moment. She had no idea. After they stepped outside, he wrapped his arm around her shoulders, tugging her closer to him. His heat emanated from him into her. Her head on his chest, she heard the strong beating of his heart coupled with long deep breaths.

"You know how much I want to kiss you?"

His voice rumbled next to her ear. With gentleness that never ceased to amaze her, he squeezed her shoulder. His thumb found naked skin at the base of her neck. "Will you let me? I don't care if your brothers are watching. Do you?"

"Yes, I care. We need to wait. I..."

She swallowed the words that were on her tongue. She didn't want to wait to kiss him. If they kissed though, he would have the upper hand that she didn't want to give him. She needed to persist, to stay the course she planned. She would not give on this decision.

While she was excited to have him back here, she wasn't going to fall into his arms as easily as she did the last time she saw him. There were going to be no repeat performances. Guidelines would need to be set. When he turned her and her back was to the rock wall of the cave, she understood she would have to be stronger if she was going to get her point across.

Ducking beneath his arm, she stepped away. Her hands were fisted, nails biting into soft skin to help remind her. "No kisses, no fondling, no..." She sucked in a deep breath of air so deep the act burned her. After she finally let the air go, she challenged. "You can't just waltz back into my life then expect to pick up where you left off. I was hurt. You hurt me. While I'm happy your business has been culminated, I won't be your whore."

He slashed his hand through the air. His expression furious. His deep blue eyes turned cold. Her words angered him. "You know bloody well I never thought of you as my whore. I came back for you, to make you my wife if you'll have me."

She cleared her throat continuing while she was shaking her head, "How do I know you aren't lying? You were here courting me then you were gone. How do I know you won't do the same after you seduce me? You left me dazed as well as unsettled. I cried thinking of my loss. I won't allow that again. You need to do things my way or leave now."

"If I don't?" A brow arched in speculation as if he didn't believe anything she told him.

"The devil! You can go home. See if I stop you? My way," she gritted out through tight clenched teeth. *Not yours.*

His grin was wicked and pure male. Arrogant. Filled with the sense of power that came with his sexuality. The deep blue of his eyes, penetrated her defenses. They turned dark as they always did before he kissed her.

Stay strong. I have to tell him no then tell him no again.

It didn't seem he meant to back off. For every step she took away from him, he closed the distance. "I want you, *lass*. I'm not going to force you. If you tell me no, I'll heed your words. A kiss is just a kiss, nothing more. What has you holding back? It's just a kiss I'm asking for. A welcome back kiss? A chaste kiss if necessary. A peck to your cheek if that is all you'll allow. Do you understand? Do I need more explanation?"

He caught up to her, his hand holding her around her neck drawing her to him. He ran his finger along the side of her face. His gaze focused on her eyes then her mouth. She couldn't help but moisten her lips. Knew that was an invitation of sorts. They were so dry, so parched. Her breathing hitched. His thumb made lazy circles on her neck. "You want me. I can see it in your eyes. You are burning for me. Your pulse quickens...here...where my thumb rests."

"No," she whispered, her voice so thin she didn't recognize the sound. "No...I d-don't want this. Please, Ash."

"Yes. Yes, you do want this kiss as well as another one after that."

"You've been gone more than a year. I don't know you. You can't expect me to...to fall into your arms."

For several seconds while she counted to ten, her lashes fluttered closed. When she opened them again, she found herself mesmerized by the blue simmer of his eyes. She gulped for air. Drug air inside her lungs for courage. Her hands were placed on his chest but they weren't pushing him away. The curling of her fingers into his coat told her she was lost.

Though he didn't kiss her. Instead, he spoke in a soft sigh of pleasure. This was his challenge to her. "You made a promise to me. Have you seen anyone? If you have...I would not be pleased."

His voice turned into a low growl of fury as if he thought she would tell him of all the men she'd been with.

Until now she forgot her promise. She stiffened, once more stepping away from him. She needed distance. Wished for space between them. By the question coupled with his anger he demeaned her integrity. She didn't intend to answer. Resented the question. "Have you?" she countered, hoping his answer would also be no. "Have there been women in your bed? I'm not going to replace your lovers or your mistress. I won't spread my legs for you to have you leave again."

Harris was unexpectedly so furious she was shaking.

The sudden shock in his eyes told her all she needed to know. Her body drained of heat. Chills ran the length of her spine. She walked away from him pain filling her to overflowing. Her stomach catapulted. Every breath was a strain. The moisture that teared in her eyes, she fought to push back not wishing for him to see the pain his words caused. Strength was what was needed. She walked farther from the cave. Heard his steps as he followed her.

"You can't expect a man to remain celibate for an entire year. A man has needs. Still...I would tell you...I've not..."

He was beside her. His hands on her shoulders were gentle yet she knew he wanted her to turn and look at him. She could not. Her lashes fluttered momentarily against her cheeks. This new information was too much for her to understand. The thought of another woman in his arms was drowning her. Swamping her. It was all she could do to keep standing.

Once more she distanced herself from him. Whirling, she spoke heatedly her feelings. "Why not? You expect that of me. Yet, you kept a mistress. I know you did. Did you have other dalliances? Did you? You've just said you have needs! Maybe I do too!"

"Yes and no to your questions." Instead of approaching her again, he leaned against the stone wall. "Yes, I do expect my woman to remain chaste. I am the only man who will know you intimately. What I did or did not do over the past year has nothing to do with us. There was no one I wished to take to my bed. Though I will never let you dictate to me. If I wanted a woman, I would bed her."

If he slept with her today, he could say the same about her tomorrow. This was not the start she hoped for. *Distance. I need distance.* "I'm not your woman."

She wanted to be his woman, his wife, his lover, his friend as well as his confident. He didn't ask. All he did was accuse then make demands. He was the only man she wanted. Harris understood it would not do for her to give herself over to him without making herself clear.

She needed to keep telling herself that she couldn't fall into his arms. She'd believed him to be her mate for eternity.

"You will be soon. It will be so." His harsh voice resonated, echoed through her. His fingers clenched then unclenched, again and again.

The devil, there was so much he didn't know. So much she had to tell him before anything else could happen between them. Tomorrow, he might see who her brothers were. She understood they would never shift unless doing so was necessary...if there was no other choice. Just as her brothers had the fine-tuned senses of a shifter, so did she. She sensed the danger on the wind. The madness that was so close one could smell evil.

Hawk stood beside her. She understood he was angry. His jaw taut, his eyes blazing. "Your time is up. Harris, get inside."

She bristled. Didn't want to be spoken to in that manner even though to some degree she agreed with her brother. She needed to end this conversation on her terms. Speaking to him about her family a necessity. Hawk didn't intend to give her the time. In ways she appreciated the protection as well as despised it.

"I'm a grown woman, big brother. We haven't finished talking." Her body shook with the realization she was defying Hawk. Something she'd never done before. "We are trying to come to terms with our future. Will you deny me?"

"You have the rest of your lives to figure things out if you choose to wed. For now, your time is up."

~ * ~

Geordie tossed a small stick on the campfire watching the flames catch before licking the stem to vanish into the dark sky. "What do you think they are doing here? It can't be good. He brought the girl here."

He turned to Scratch seeking an answer. While he wanted the woman, wanted her the first time he saw her, he never expected Cameron Frasier to play into his hands. Until now the girl had been protected and sheltered.

"Don't know. Seems we should stay away from them. They got that Sassenach soldier with them now. Don't look good to me. Don't have a death wish. Sassenach can't be trusted."

"You afraid of a few shifters?" Geordie asked while he drank deeply from the scotch bottle. He pulled on the liquid again reveling as it burned its way down his throat to his belly. "I'm not. What can they do to us? Seems to me if we don't rile them, they'll leave us alone. Do you want to rile them, Scratch? We could have the girl. That's always a possibility."

"*Aye*, you want that woman as much as I do, maybe more. Gonna have her. Come hell or high water I'm gonna taste that sweetness between her legs. We can share. Always have. This time won't be any different." He scratched his belly then moved lower while he seemed to savor the thoughts whirling in his head.

"The shifter's sister is here too. Maybe while we're at it with the one that's sweet on Cameron, we can taste her too," Geordie pointed out one bony finger directed at Scratch. "Though I don't see how we're going to get the women away from their men. That won't be an easy task. Will have to look for an opening. That Sassenach sure is big. Biggest man I ever seen."

"Kill em, I say. Who's going to miss a worthless shifter? Everyone knows they're not human. Got my pistol primed and ready for the deed." He scratched his belly then beneath his arm. "What do you say?"

"What about the third man? What are we going to do about the Sassenach? Don't like the odds. All three of those men are big. The Englishman's even larger." Geordie felt worried about the situation. They were outnumbered if you counted the Englishman. "Maybe we should wait for another time. We can always find a way to get the girl alone. The shifter can't protect her forever."

"Today, we'll try today. If it doesn't work out, we can do it your way. We need to separate them. Create a diversion so they won't all be together." Scratch grabbed the scotch from Geordie. Drank long and deep.

"We'll see tomorrow. Well, it's almost tomorrow as we sit here speakin'. Morning sun goin' to be pokin' its head above the craigs anytime. Sun's trying to soak up all the mist."

"Just like were goin' to poke those *lassies*."

~ * ~

Lainie woke to the smell of bacon sizzling and coffee brewing. Coffee always gave her a fresh jolt of adrenalin to begin the new day. She recalled thinking that many times. She didn't know what adrenalin was. Whatever it was, coffee did the trick. Gave her a burst of energy. She could smell it. Now, she could almost taste the brew. She liked her coffee strong, so did Roc. Sometimes she believed the morning coffee with him was the best part of beginning the day. Other times the best part was when he made love to her before they rose. After that before he left for work.

When she opened her eyes, her head was nestled on Roc's chest. He was holding her close, his warmth surrounding her, giving her peace. She heard the steady beating of his heart, listened to each breath. Her hand lay on his belly. She moved her fingers across him relishing the changing textures of flesh and curling dark hair. During the night she unfastened his shirt. She rubbed her cheek on his chest before biting his shoulder. He groaned as she raked her teeth across him touching a hardened nipple. She wished they could make love. She wished she dared more seduction.

He stopped her hand as her fingers brushed beneath the band of his buckskins. Thinking about all the previous times with him, she wiggled her fingers, maneuvering. Mischievous. Her body hummed with the same heat that her teasing generated within Roc. "Don't play with fire. We both can wait until this afternoon after we are in the privacy of our home."

"You are hot, blazing beneath my caress. Do you burn for me? I find I'm in flames. You are melting me."

She should never have been so bold. He taught her what he liked, how he loved to be touched.

The sound of Hawk clearing his throat stopped her, brought her up short. Her fingers touching aroused flesh beneath the fabric of his clothing, she froze. With a heavy sigh she removed her hand. This was not the place or the time to pursue carnal knowledge of Roc. As he said there would be another more appropriate time. "Of course, you are right. How silly of me." Unable to stop herself, she touched his shoulder with her tongue. A second time she used her teeth to delicately bite.

"I'm getting up while I still can. You need to eat before we leave." His voice was raw, husky with desire. "Can you be ready in fifteen minutes?" He stood over her, staring down at her flushed features.

Her head jerked up at the sound of his voice. Her soft sigh didn't go unnoticed. He grinned. She did need to eat. Didn't need him telling her she should do so. "Yes. First, I want a cup of coffee."

In haste, fastening the buttons on her gown that Roc undid during the night hours, she sat up. Pushing the covers down she stretched. The palms of her hands were on the small of her back. She groaned slightly when the pressure of sleeping on the hard pallet was relieved. Harris and Ashton were sitting beside the fire talking in hushed whispers. Harris didn't seem pleased with the direction of the conversation. She wanted to know what they spoke of. While she knew Harris missed the man, she also understood Harris made some vows to herself. She would never again fall so easily into the man's arms.

Lainie wasn't here when Ashton left for London. Roc told her a bit of the story, the things he knew as fact coupled with his guesses. He'd been certain there was some shared intimacy between the two. He didn't know exactly how much or if they made love. What both he and Hawk knew, they both held their breath waiting to see if she would find herself carrying the Englishman's child. She did not.

Her heart went out to Harris. To have the man she loved ripped away from her, not knowing if he would return could never have been easy. Even though the man told her he would return. It had taken him more than a year to do so. The thought brought back the intent of this day. Roc could be torn away from her. She sucked in a deep breath of air. Fear coiled deep and dark in her belly. She felt loss. Didn't understand why. She seemed to possess some of that sixth sense shifters enjoyed. Lainie didn't know why.

She pushed that notion to the back of her mind. After smoothing her skirts and making sure everything was fastened correctly, she walked outside to see to her needs. When she returned, Roc handed her a cup of coffee then kissed her on the forehead. His gentle smile reduced some of the fears she harbored. Nothing could make all of them vanish. At least not until the outcome was known.

"It's almost over. In a few hours, we'll know what is meant to be as well as what is not. You will stay close. Don't want to have you wandering anywhere by yourself. While my feelings are hopeful, I don't want you to take chances with yourself." He held her next to him, his arm around her as if he didn't want to let her go.

Staying near would not be difficult. She didn't wish to let him out of her sight either. With her eyes closed, she imagined the scene unfolding before her. She recalled the floating sensations when she was tugged through time. Her stomach lurched. The dizziness in her head increased. For a few horrible seconds she thought she might lose her breakfast. Earth and sky seemed to blend together. On her feet she swayed, believed her knees would give out. The memories were far from pleasant.

"What's wrong?"

Roc stood beside her, his hands on her shoulders. His fingers brushed across her cheek. His halting words took her by surprise. The concern she read in his eyes brought her back to the present with jarring haste. "You look pale. I would know what you recalled. This might be important."

He lifted her chin so she stared into the steel blue of his eyes that seemed to be turning icy with each passing second. She shivered. Her lips twitched as she fought the sensations still swamping her. "I remembered. The dark hole. The blurring of everything around me. The tugging and pulling until I couldn't resist. My stomach turned queasy. Then I saw Scratch and Geordie. After that you..."

Her heart seemed to pound in her throat. She tugged in air that didn't want to follow her orders.

"What? All that? Is there anything else" His eyes narrowed while his mouth thinned. "Memories of your past life?" he ventured a guess.

Lainie found herself shaking her head in denial. While she tried to absorb the heat from Roc to vanquish the frost surrounding her, the feat was impossible. She was so cold she was shivering within his embrace. He pulled her close rubbing her arms with his hands. Nothing erased the chill that seemed to drown her. That brought her deeper into its hold with each breath she inhaled.

"I.." She swallowed hard trying to dislodge the lump of fear that settled in the middle of her throat. "I..."

"I?" he encouraged her seeming to need words. "You weren't reliving your past. What did you see? Your travel into another dimension?"

"Remembered the sensations when I landed here as well as just before. I was terrified when I lost my balance. All control was lost to me. My footing gone." She turned to look in the direction of the glen. "That's all. Nothing to be worried about. Just as I didn't remember my life before now, I still don't." Lainie didn't like the fact he appeared relieved at her loss. "I would that I could recall everything."

"All right, I'm trying to understand. If you could live your life before here, I would wish for it too if I could live it with you. As it stands, we must play with the cards we've been dealt," he said smoothly as if trying to hide his relief.

"Why don't you want me to remember? Despite what you just said, I know you don't. I can sense your relief. Why am I sensing and feeling things I never did before?"

With his hand on around the back of her neck, he tugged her close to his chest. "It's simple. I'm afraid of losing you. If you wished to go back to a life that was far easier than this one, I'm afraid you would find a means to return despite my efforts."

She hit him on the chest. Heard his soft grunt that meant nothing. "During the last month, you haven't listened to one word I've told you. It would be nice if you learned how to pay attention. I don't wish to spend the rest of our lives with you making up my mind for me. And..." she paused thinking. "You didn't answer my question."

"I listened. Still doesn't dissolve my fears. While I cannot be inside your head all the time, I would like to be there. While I will never be able to spend every moment, waking or asleep next to you, I would like it to be so. If I didn't wish to..." he looked at her thoughtfully. "I was going to let you give me the news."

"What are you talking about?"

"You carry our child, Lainie. He is a shifter. That is why you are sensing and feeling things you never did before."

With her hands against his chest, she pushed slightly away. "I'm increasing? You know?"

"I told you I would know as soon as it happened. Only a few days ago. I was going to wait and not tell you. You forced my hand."

"I don't understand."

She was trying though. He was right. She would have liked to be the one to give him the good news.

"You have to marry me."

The small crease line in the middle of her forehead formed. Her brows drew together. She wanted to go back to the fact he knew what she was thinking. To the fact she didn't want to leave him. Now more than ever, she would stay forever with him. To convince him impossible. "You are in my head? All the time? I wouldn't..." She thought that had to be an invasion of her privacy. "How? What do you mean? You hear my thoughts?" Heat flooded her face. Embarrassment tore at her. "No! You cannot be inside my head. I won't stand for that!"

"Unfortunate for you, yes. Fortunate for me, sometimes I am privy to your thoughts as well as your feelings. Understand the emotions you are afraid to tell me. The things seething and simmering in the back of your head. You need to learn to be honest about your thoughts, especially with your future husband. I will never hurt you. Will always put you first in everything I do as well as think." Roc brushed hair from her face to tuck behind her ears. She saw in his eyes that he meant his words. Saw too the fear that hovered close to the surface. Liking the facts and seeing them were different.

She turned from him, walking away. When she whirled, she shook her fist at him. He smiled at her. "You would listen to my thoughts and not tell me? You would come to conclusions about me that are not true? You would... Oh!" For several fleeting seconds, she thought to stamp her foot from vexation. "I don't know what to say."

He nodded, seeming to understand her anger. "I'm thinking perhaps I should have told you more about a shifter's sixth sense. If you are honest with me and I'm touching you, I know what is playing out in your agile sweet mind. If you are distressed, I hear your pain. When you want me inside your heat, I know without asking. I think that is what brought me to the glen the day you arrived in my life. You were distressed. I felt that as clearly as I'm sensing that suffering now. You were calling my name, waiting for me to find you."

Unable to remain standing, her knees seeming to buckle, she sat. Roc joined her, engulfing her in his arms. Holding her so close she felt as if their hearts beat as one. "Truly? I was calling your name? You will put me first? I would do the same for you. I would cherish being able to see into your mind." What he told her was poignant. She never thought another person let alone a man would be so sincere.

"We need to get you fed then be on our way. I want this to be finished as soon as possible. When we are at home, we can continue this conversation. We can also make love. Would you like one or both?"

"Can I stay here? At the cave?"

Though hopeful, Lainie understood what his answer would be. He would never let her out of his site. Earlier, he said as much. Told her to stay close. She couldn't risk it either. It was just...

"No, Geordie and Scratch are wild cards in this scenario. If I knew where they were and staying here alone would not put you in danger, I would consider the possibility. However, without you, there is no reason for the rest of us to seek out the portal." At her hopeful look, he placed a fingertip on her lips. "Considered. Not agreed."

Fleetingly, she touched her tongue to his finger. "Let's get this over with. I see that Hawk is outside with the horses waiting for us. Where are Harris and Ashton? Are they coming or remaining here?" The question was silly. "No, they must be with us. Hawk would never leave those two alone. They are a powder keg waiting to be set off. Our little sister could just as easily succumb to Ashton's easy manner as resist. We need to be helpful to Harris. Take the choice from her."

Beside Hawk, Ashton made it clear he would protect Harris as best he could. Lainie heard the whispers between the two men, tried to decipher them. Even though both men looked relaxed the exchange was heated.

"Though he treated Harris in a way I dislike, his intention is to make amends. He wants to be part of the family, of the Clan Chattan," Roc told her as if that made all that the man did to Harris amenable. "If there is to be restitution paid for his mistreatment, it will be up to Harris."

"Does he know who you are? What you can do? Don't you think before he becomes a husband in this family, he should *ken* the truth? You told me almost to the day you found me. How long has Harris known the Sassenach?"

"I believe so. Last night Hawk and I both sensed he is also a shifter. That fact is most likely the reason no shifters were caught in the highlands during his watch. He found ways to protect us. Was always around when some soldier decided to catch a cat. We all knew that he was more friend than foe even though Sassenach blood runs through his veins. Don't believe Harris knows about him. Suppose he will tell her when she trusts him enough to speak of the rest of the family. What do you think?"

"Is he also a black panther?" Lainie felt her eyes widen at Roc's words about Ashton. Another shifter... This sixth sense...shouldn't Harris be able to sense his abilities?"

"That, I do not know. To your second question, believe she is too enraged as well as confused to sense anything about the man."

"Harris should know the truth before she comes to any conclusions concerning them. Knowledge would help her understand his motives."

Although her role in this family was minute, Roc didn't keep his truth from her. He told her...showed her his cat soon into their relationship. She should have been terrified. He eased her way, explaining everything. After that he teased her. At the memory heat flooded her.

"As far as I know they have not spoken of abilities they possess. While I can sense emotions in you, I cannot in my sister. While Ashton understands who we are, he might not know about Harris though I'm guessing he does. Harris is too young to interpret all the things she might sense about Ashton. She's too engaged in protecting herself from his many charms. She doesn't want the man to seduce her then leave her."

"I see... So, Ashton knows what Harris is thinking and feeling?"

Lainie was coming to understand all that Roc told her. Most of the things he said, she had to take on faith. All in this time was so very different. He told her Rafe was a member of the Clan Chattan. Rafe never mentioned that fact. Oh, he did talk of mates and that she wasn't his. All the while she had no idea...absolutely no realization. Now, Harris was at a disadvantage in a fledgling relationship. The man would know how she felt about him, possibly before she did. There was nothing fair about any of this.

"Do you?" He tapped her on the chin. "I want to make love. Need to hold you in my arms while I'm deep inside your heat. Want you to burn me to my core. That's exactly what I'm thinking and feeling."

That fact gave her good reason to grin. Some of the chill that encompassed her warmed her heart. Lainie had the strong sensation by the time they reached the glen the cold would be within her again. In hopes of absorbing his heat, she leaned into him. He didn't disappoint.

"Let's join them. I'm eager to be done with this so we can get on with the rest of our lives."

His hand resting on her hip, he guided her outside. The sun was just rising. Colors streaked the sky. The day would be unseasonably warm. That would be nice after all the rain.

Mist swirled off the damp ground, steam rising into the air to vanish without a sound. It was the morning sun heating the dew coated earth. When she looked above the mist, the sun shone clear and bright. The sky was blue. A few white clouds hovered. It was much like the day she came here. A sense of *deja vous* ripped through her. The similarities were too frightening. She pushed them to the back of her mind.

With an easy motion, he tossed her on his horse then mounted behind her. After he grabbed the reins, she clung to his forearms. Lainie still didn't like to ride. Wasn't comfortable with the gait of the animal. Leaning into him, she closed her eyes trying to tamp down the rising nausea.

Since all choices were taken from her, she thought like Roc. The sooner this was over with the better. She didn't know what was to come yet she no longer feared the future events. She had the strong feeling all would be right with her world. This adventure would not change her life except to make it better. Time or portal would not claim her again. She would not find herself hurtled to some other place or time. Though deep in her soul, she understood the opening would claim someone. One hand rested on her belly. Until this moment, she'd not taken the time to absorb the fact she carried Roc's child. They weren't married. He would do something about that. Marriage with him was what she wanted.

Even though she sensed the culmination of events, she felt Roc's tension. The closer they got to the glen the stiffer he became, his heart pounding harder, his breath quickening. If she could trust her female instincts, she would say he was preparing himself for a fight. Perhaps the *bairn* was telling her that. Lainie wished she could figure out a way to soothe him to ease the building strain in his strong body. He wasn't frightened for himself. Roc feared for her safety.

As they approached the glen, the men stopped talking. Harris and Ashton fell behind them. They stopped, pulling up the horses. Tension splintered the air around her. Nerves she thought were rested awoke as if from a deep sleep. Energy charged air surrounded them. The scene was idyllic promising only peace. For someone there would be no peace today.

After Roc dismounted, he set his hands on her waist. In a second, she stood beside him. He vibrated with unleashed power. His body shook with anticipation. He geared himself for a fight. For a split second, she thought he would shift. Didn't understand why she sensed his changing form. She was so very different now that she spent a month with him. Now that she carried his child. To Lainie it seemed as if she sensed things she never could before.

"This is it," he whispered his breath sweeping across her cheek. His kiss was light barely a breath against her face. "Remember, stay close to me. Do not go anywhere without me. Whatever happens unless..." he paused as if in thought. "Unless I have to shift. If that happens, stay with Harris. Run. Don't look back. If I shift, so will Hawk." He placed her hand in his, squeezed gently, slipped his fingers between hers. "I don't want you anywhere near me if I have to change to my cat. It means the danger has escalated to a point I've no other choice. Do you understand?" His voice was harsh. He needed an answer. His hands tightened on her shoulders. His eyes blazed molten steel.

A gasp of air preceded her nod to him, hoping that was enough. Changed her mind and answered understanding he would appreciate the verbal exchange. "Yes. Yes, I do understand. If you unleash all the power within you, don't think I would like to be close to your cat. It was one thing when you teased then strutted around me showing off. This situation is something entirely different. I *ken* it." Her fear for him grew. She wrapped her hands around his wrists in an effort to ease the terror welling up within her. "Take care," she mouthed to him. "I couldn't bear it if I lost you."

"Good. I want you to stay close to Ashcroft as well as Harris. He won't shift unless the situation becomes dire. It won't." The following pause left her more unnerved than before. "If he does, mount with Harris then ride to the cave. If that is what happens, we will all be along shortly." He brought her hand to his lips, kissing the back while he continued to walk forward.

In her imagining mind, she saw Geordie and Scratch. With unwavering certainty, she understood they would be here today. They wanted her. Bile rose. She clamped her hand on her stomach thinking of the child he told her grew beneath her hand in her womb. "What do we do now?"

Despite her thoughts that this would not change her life, the words warbled out as if she was just learning to speak. Her heart sped faster than she could ever remember. Now, she set her hand on her chest as if that small gesture could slow her beating heart. The world seemed to spin. Green earth was blending with blue sky. She clutched his arm, steadying herself.

"We walk forward toward that spot where your delicious little butt sat the day I first saw you. The look on your face was both precious as well as startled. Your eyes were nearly crossed. Today, nothing should happen. After that we will ride to the falls then take the way down you did the first time." He brushed flyaway hair from her face. "All will be fine. I promise you."

He couldn't promise anything. Sucking in a deep breath of air, she agreed to his proposition by moving her feet toward to that spot she remembered landing on. Her nails bit into his arm. He didn't seem to care or notice. Her feet seemed to lag. They didn't want to move. His fingers on her hip squeezed, encouraging her to continue forward. She heard him in her mind telling her she could do this, put one foot in front of the other. Soon this would end. She also heard his fear for her. While they had to do this, he didn't want her here. She didn't want to be here either. He was watching for Geordie and Scratch. Expected them to make an appearance. His body was tense. She felt the explosive energy in his muscles as they constricted.

"You can do this." His words were soft spoken. He ran his hand along her arm warming her. Even with that warm contact, she shivered. Hawk strode along behind them and to the side.

"Yes, I know. Doesn't make this any easier."

"Do you feel anything?" he asked as they closed the distance he seemed to be focusing on. "Tell me if there is a change. Tell me anything. Everything. Do you recall how you felt the first time?"

"Just falling, tumbling through nothing. Through air. No gravity. Nothing to stop my fall. Was surprised when I landed as if I sat down." She didn't feel anything. Not a whisper of pain. "It was as if I was sucked from one dimension to another in a blink of time."

She thought he could sense all her emotions. Both curious as well as terrified, she looked to the glade in front of them.

"Not willing to take a chance on your life. If something occurs to you, tell me. Odds are I will know before you can speak the words."

His gaze searched the area. He swore softly. There was nothing to see. Nothing at all.

It was a strange feeling to understand his thoughts. Without speaking to her, he chastised her. She supposed she deserved that. After her thoughts he squeezed her hand again. Curse the man. With him there were no secrets. "Just your hand on me. Your body next to mine. The beat of your heart next to my cheek. The madness that is present and waiting for something or someone. I *dinnae ken*. There is evil here. To pursue this is foolishness. Though you tell me there is no choice. We should never have come here."

"I feel the same sensations. The evil will travel to another time. Not us."

His thoughts were now about her, centered on the baby she carried.

"I pray that is true."

Chapter Nine

When he saw Scratch and Geordie, he pushed Lainie behind him. A cold breath of air shimmered in his lungs. Tangible fear doused him with liquid ice. This was it. The confrontation that had been brewing for the last months. Both men held muskets pointing their way. After he looked from the corner of his eye, he saw Hawk who nodded at him. His brother was also aware of them.

The two men stood very nearly on the exact spot where Lainie landed that day. The portal. The two men both wore leering grins. He smelled their anticipation, their eagerness to possess Lainie. Knew the moment they saw Harris. Roc's gut tightened. His body tensed with the need to spring. Changing would have to be done with lightning speed. He didn't doubt for a second the men would shoot.

"Now, if ye be knowin what is good for you, hand the little *lass* over real slow. We'll just take her off your hands. Know you didn't bargain for the lady when you found her. She must be nothin' to you but trouble," Geordie said as he motioned with the musket for him to step aside. Scratch kept his weapon targeted on Hawk. "Don't think to shift. We'll shoot if you be doin' so. That's a promise. You'll die right here. No woman's worth the death of you."

Geordie had no idea how he felt. Roc was certain he could shift then spring at him. He heard Lainie's voice calling out to him. Against him, her body trembled harder. "You've only got one shot. Has to be accurate the first time. A second chance won't happen. If you decide on that route, you're a dead man," Roc said, his voice low keyed but menacing. Without words and in his mind, he was trying to tell Lainie to run. "If you don't kill with the first shot, as I just said, you're a dead man. Best you reconsider your alternatives."

Roc reigned in his temper while he kept one hand on Lainie. He felt the slight trembling of her body behind him. The scent of her fear washed over him, through him. He wished now she wasn't here. They would have been better off leaving her with Ashton and Harris at the cave.

For this to play out, she had to come.

"Yeah, well I'm a pretty good shot." Geordie moved the brown bess up and down then sideways as if to emphasize his promise. "Don't miss what I be aimin' at." He cackled then spit on the ground.

"No, Roc. Don't." Lainie's gentle plea didn't sway him. She clutched his arm as if she understood what he was about to do.

"Go, run back to Ashton," he whispered trying to make his voice calm. "Leave here!" His terror for her as well as his unborn child doubled. Hawk and I will take care of these men. You have nothing to fear."

She wasn't moving. He should hear the sound of her footsteps on the hard packed earth.

I won't leave you for them to shoot. I won't. Roc!

You have no choice. Run now! He couldn't sway her. She was determined to stand her ground, determined to protect him.

No. Her little voice held too much grit. She wasn't made to fight against men. Too small. Too fragile.

All the words were spoken silently between them. Arguing was wasting time. He couldn't take his focus from the men or the trigger finger. His breathing slowed as he felt the first stirrings. His body would change. She had to be away from him.

"My fingers be gettin' itchy," Geordie said glancing over at Scratch. "How about yours? You got this urge to shoot. Ask questions later. Send the *lass* over to us."

"Itchy," Scratch agreed as he rubbed his crotch. "Want to be findin' a bit of release for my itch. Who's got her first?"

Run.

No!

Get down! He cried out realizing she wasn't going anywhere. Stubborn, foolish woman. She called him stubborn. Hoping and praying she did as he ordered he prepared for battle. His body twinged. Shook.

Hawk was changing too.

In that instant he changed form. His body grew. Power filled his senses. The roar reverberated through the small glen. Hawk's roar melded with his, uniting as one entity. He watched Geordie's fingers. Knew the moment the man shot. As he started to leap to the side to avoid the ball, Lainie darted in front of him.

"Roc!"

Her scream terrified him. The devil what was she doing? Lainie! Beneath his feet, she crumpled. Anguish tore through him. He felt her pain. Knew she'd been hit. Rage took over common sense. Blood soaking her head. This time his roar was filled with pain not challenge. Was swamped with rage as well as fear for his mate's life. Geordie would pay with his life.

He had to end this so he could see to Lainie.

Roc leapt at Geordie who threw the now useless musket on the ground. Turning to run, he fell when Roc throttled him. Beneath him, twisting and turning, wiggling his thin body, Geordie scrambled to his feet, crawling on all fours away from him. Geordie cried out when one of Roc's large paws scratched him across his face. He raked his claws along the man's back as he struggled to get away. Against him the battle was useless.

"No! Didn't mean what I said. Mercy! Don't kill me. I beg of you! Won't ever do it again." He pleaded, begged for compassion he would never give. Geordie back pedaled as he tried to find a way from the wrath of the big cat. Roc stalked him, waiting for the right moment. The man needed to fight not run. He needed to act like a man. Despite the ever-present need to kill, Roc could not.

Roc saw the dark opening in front of him before he realized that Geordie was about to enter into what appeared to be the portal. Giving the man room, Roc sat back on his haunches watching the enfolding scene. Intrigued. Curious. He saw the dark opening grow wider. Felt as if the wickedness in the glen was about to be vanquished. Saw a woman inside. The woman looked so much like Lainie he had to turn to see. Lainie was on the ground. Ashton was over her, tending to her. She wasn't going anywhere.

Humming. The dark opening vibrated. Purred. The sound growing louder as the hole grew in size. It began as a black pinprick. Now it was the size of a large ball.

Larger still. Now, a man could find his way into the blackness. The buzzing and whirring was so loud, Roc felt a need to clamp his paws over his ears.

The circle continued to widen as it seemed to want to eat its prey. Hawk stalked Scratch in the direction of the bleak darkness. As Scratch scrambled toward Geordie and the blackness waiting for them beyond, sweat soaked his shirt. He hoped they were sending these two men to hell and they would never find a way to leave it behind. Without further warning, both men were sucked into the hole. Roc could see them, huddled together. Their mouths open in a scream that would never be heard.

Crack!

The noise bit the air before the sound echoed throughout the glade over then over again. The blackness vanished as did the men. The hole closed. In the ensuing silence, there was only brilliant light. Silence. In the small glen now, there was nothing remaining save an eerie, unnerving calm penetrating Roc deep into his core. He turned to see Ashton running to them, Harris behind.

The Sassenach dropped the clothing on the ground beside him. After that he returned to Harris, his arm around her shoulders he walked her into the trees where she would not see them dressing. Roc's deep breath of air warmed the chill he'd felt.

Lainie! He saw her sprawled on the ground. Her hair spilling around her a cloak of beautiful color.

With the swiftness of a cat, he changed back to human then pulled on his buckskins then his boots. Quick strides brought him beside Lainie. Concern mingled with terror. His hand shook when he reached out to her. Crimson soaked the ground around her head. *No!* She was supposed to fall to the ground not throw herself in front of him. She tried to shield him with her body. If she did as was told, she would not have been hit. Neither would he. Tearing off strips, he used his shirt to soak up the blood from the lesion on her head while he told himself all head wounds bled a lot.

The cut was clean and not too deep though it would require stitches. She was unconscious but she didn't appear to be hurt that badly. *Dear God, she jumped in front of the musket ball to save me.*

He would never doubt her word again. She told him too many times to count she wanted to stay with him. Did not want to travel through the portal. She said there was nothing for her in the alternate time.

"How is she?" Fully dressed, Hawk knelt beside him. He moved Lainie's hair to the side, used what was left of Roc's shirt to further stop the flow of blood. Her head was painted with the blood. "It's a flesh wound, nothing more. She'll recover nicely. When we get back to the cave, I'll stitch the cut closed."

"Where did the ball go?" Roc asked.

"Most likely in the ground behind where you were standing."

Hawk didn't seem to be concerned. He tore off several strips then wound the strips around her head.

"The devil, the foolish woman jumped in front of me. I told her to get down."

He cursed as he tried to calm the seething rage that brewed within him. He stroked her arm. She was so small, so fragile. How dare she put herself at risk? "I'm going to shake her until her teeth rattle when she recovers. Foolish woman," Roc gave voice to his thoughts.

"You said she was in front of you?" Hawk asked as he stared at him concern in the steel-gray of his eyes. A moment passed before Hawk spoke again. "Hate to tell you this. The ball is in your shoulder."

"No..." Roc looked down. Blood oozed from his shoulder. His stomach fluttered then rolled at the realization that he'd been hit after all. He'd felt no pain. Now, however with the knowledge came the searing heat where the ball lodged.

"I'm going to have to get it out. Can you ride to the cave?" Hawk's voice was calm, reassuring when necessary.

On his knees in front of Lainie, Roc swayed. He didn't know what he could or couldn't do. The earth tilted. Teeth clenched tight, he gritted back the throbbing that raced through him. "Funny," he said staring at his shoulder. "I didn't feel anything until you told me I was hit." He steadied himself, one hand on the ground.

"Can you ride?" Hawk asked again.

"Don't see that I've much of a choice. Though first I need to figure out how to stand." He closed his eyes, gripping his thighs with numb fingers. His gaze went to Lainie. "She can't ride without me."

"Will I have to tie you on the horse?" Hawk asked his voice rough. "Lainie isn't even conscious. What she doesn't know won't make a difference."

"Maybe," Roc laughed as another cloud of pain swamped him sending him reeling too unsteady to rise. "Who's going to take Lainie?" He couldn't hear her thoughts. She needed to wake.

"I will. Since she's out cold she won't be afraid. You, we'll have to tie on the horse. Don't see how you can ride pillion with anyone."

"Until she wakes up. What if she wakes on the ride back? She'll be afraid. Don't want that. I would, ah hell..." Roc could barely keep his eyes open let alone hold on to Lainie all the way back to the cave. When he started to crumple to the ground again, Hawk braced him.

"Ashton! Get over here. Need some help with Roc." Hawk waved his arm as he called out for the Englishman.

Together and with some help from Roc, they got him on his horse then tied him so he wouldn't fall off. Hawk took Lainie up to ride in front of him. For the first few minutes, Roc managed to keep his eyes open. After that he had trouble keeping himself in a semi-upright position. When he could see, he strained to see Lainie. Understood how dangerous head wounds were. What if she never woke?

In and out of consciousness the ride seemed to take forever. With each step of the horse, his shoulder burned, the throbbing intense. Penetrating sinew and bone. Every time he looked to Lainie she was still slumped in front of Hawk, her head drooping. He tried to keep his eyes open, tried to see how Lainie fared.

It was no use.

Before they reached the cave, he was slumped over in the saddle. His dreams dark and vivid. He woke when Hawk and Ashton took him into the cave.

"Lainie," he whispered hoarsely. "Lainie...!" Held by the two men, he struggled against them to see her.

"Still out cold. Breathing a bit erratic. Her heartbeat is steady. So far, Lainie hasn't opened her eyes. She's on your pallet now. Harris is cleaning the blood from her head with a bit of soap and water. I'm going to have to stich the cut. For me to do that, it's better that she is still asleep. She will never feel the pain," Hawk said, his voice gentle. "I'll see to her as soon as I get the ball out of your shoulder."

"No!" He reached up his fingers wound into his brother's shirt. His body was shaking both from anger as well as concern for Lainie. "No, see to Lainie first. As you said, if she doesn't wake up, she won't feel anything."

To Roc's chagrin, Hawk was shaking his head in disagreement, his mouth set in determined lines. "Can't do that. Got to get the ball out before infection sets in. Before it finds a blood vessel and you bleed to death. The ball in your flesh takes precedence over her cut. Lainie will be fine."

Roc grabbed his hand, stopping him. He didn't intend to give in on this issue. "I can wait. See to Lainie."

"You're in no condition to fight me, Cameron. The more time you waste in ridiculous arguments the longer it will take for me to see to Lainie."

Hawk went to his medical bag, removing items while Roc struggled to sit. Sweat beaded then dripped. Beneath his breath he swore at older brothers who thought they knew everything.

"If you say," Harris cleared her throat.

Her hands folded in her lap she appeared angelic. Roc knew the truth. However, when she spoke, he was forever grateful. "I can do the stitches. You know I've been working at your office. Studying what you do." She was looking from him to Hawk, asking for permission from both men. "I'm quite good. My stitches are small, neat. They won't leave a scar. Trust me with this."

Startled by her words, Roc stared hard at his brother, hope filling him. "Can she do it? Sewing someone is different than embroidery."

It seemed a solution. One that would satisfy him and hopefully

Hawk.

Hawk nodded with a nonchalant lift of his shoulders coupled with a thin smile. "True, Harris has been helping in the office. As she says, she is quite good at stitching. Nice neat little ones. Most women are."

Closing his eyes, he said a silent prayer of relief. He didn't want Lainie to feel pain. At least not any more than she had already. If Harris could do the job, he welcomed her. His sister had a steady hand.

"Ashton, I need you to hold Cameron down. He must be kept perfectly still. Don't want to cut a blood vessel or nerves." Hawk brought out a piece of leather. "Bite on this. It will help. If Lainie wakes up, don't want her to hear you screaming. Don't know what she will do if that happens."

Hawk handed him a bottle of whiskey he kept in his bag. "Medicinal purposes. Drink up. Half the bottle. You'll need this which Lainie won't unless she wakes up in the next ten minutes or so."

The groan was not surprising. All he needed now was to wake up with a blinding headache. "Just get on with it. The sooner it's done the sooner I can see to Lainie." Roc took another long pull of the whiskey.

"You won't be in any condition to see to Lainie. This is a serious wound." Hawk sorted through his supplies, picking out the most necessary items.

He poured whiskey on his knife then cleaned the wound. Feeling within the torn flesh for the ball with both his finger as well as the knife. Roc jerked with each penetrating stroke searing his body. He bit hard on the leather. Sweat beaded on his forehead. Slipped down his back. It was all he could do not to cry out.

After agonizing seconds that Roc thought would never end, "There it is."

Hawk found the forceps. Pulled the ball out of Roc's shoulder. Held the metal between his fingers then tossed the metal ball into his medical bag. "Now, it's time to sew you up."

He poured some of the whiskey into the gaping hole in his shoulder. Roc would have bolted if not for Ashton holding him down. He thought he was going to jump out of his skin. Hawk took needle as well as thread from his bag.

"Bloody hell, your wife jumped in front of you to take the bullet. I would say the woman loves you more than her life. What man or woman would do such a thing? Sacrifice her life for yours?" Ashton looked to Harris to see her reaction. She turned away.

"Lainie's not my wife," Roc's thin voice whispered in the silence of the cave. The tension between his sister and Ashcroft was tangible. "Not yet...she will be as soon as I can arrange the ceremonies."

Harris was humming a soft Scottish tune as she got needle and thread ready. Every so often, she glanced to the man who watched her through narrowed eyes. "This won't take long if you need me to help with Cameron when I'm done here." As if she waited for an answer, she looked up. Her gaze fastened on Ashcroft. Her lips pressed flat together, her body stiff. She looked as if she would throttle him if given a chance

Roc wondered what the two were thinking. What was truly going on between the pair. He knew she missed the man. By all appearances now, she wished him back to London.

With the first touch of the needle to his skin, Roc fainted. He'd been able to hold it together when Hawk probed for the ball. This was too much. Black darkness surrounded him. He floated in the air above his body. Looking down and with a shrug of indifference, he watched Hawk administer to him. After that he turned his attention to Lainie. She was still unmoving on the pallet they shared last night. The blood was gone from her hair; mostly gone, he amended. She looked so small and frail. Harris, finished biting the thread after tying if off. After that he saw nothing more.

When he woke, he heard Lainie's voice, clear as well as strong. She was speaking with Harris and Hawk. He struggled to sit. The pain was too great. He fell back in the tiny space he managed to put between him and the bedding. Sifting in a deep breath of air, he looked around the cavern. In an attempt to minimize the pain, he closed his eyes, using his senses to form the scene in his mind. The fire blazed. Flames shifted in the darkness. He caught the sounds of wind whispering around trees from outside. Heard the popping embers. The scent of coffee burned his nostrils. He tried to recall what happened.

With startling clarity, the scene rushed through him. "Lainie!" he cried out trying once more to sit. With intense urgency he never felt before, he needed to see her, to hold her. He wanted to run his hands over her body to make certain there was nothing more wrong.

She took a bullet for me.

"I'm here." She knelt beside him, smoothing back his hair, pushing longer strands behind his ears. She was smiling. "You're awake. We wondered how much longer you would wish to laze away the days. Thought you wanted to get back home as soon as possible."

Pain burned. His shoulder pounded. He ran his tongue across parched lips that felt as if they hadn't touched a drop of water in months. "What day is it?"

The answer was something he dreaded. Tensions scuttled around inside him. He didn't want to think. Only wished to hold Lainie. Her strength, her health, he needed to protect. Wanted to set his hand on her belly.

Lainie looked up as if to ask what she could tell him. When she turned her attention back to him, she gave him an answer he didn't like. "The day after we were shot. You slept last night as well as all of today. It's night now. Ashton returned with a wagon last night. He took Harris home. She is supposed to be with your parents. Ashton is here again. He's been a busy man. As soon as you're up to the journey we can return to Carnoch."

He touched her cheek with his hand. None of her words mattered. Now, that he was awake he had to know the truth. "How are you? You look just as beautiful as I remember." He trailed his fingertip along the neat stitches on her head.

"Better than you although I had a blazing headache most of last night as well as part of today. Your brother wouldn't let me sleep until early this morning. Of course, I couldn't pass his finger tests. My only consolation was that he didn't sleep either. When I was finally able to see straight, count the number of fingers he held up correctly, I fell asleep in an instant, next to you. Hawk let me curl up beside you so I could hear the beating of your heart. Where I could listen to each breath of air you inhaled and exhaled."

"You are fine now." His knuckles grazed her cheek. "So soft, velvet..." With no more energy, his hand dropped.

"Good as new. I was told Geordie and Scratch, to get away from you and Hawk, chose the portal instead of death. Sucked them right up. Closed with a crack so loud they probably heard the sound in Carnoch. What do you think? Did they go forward or backward in time? Suppose we'll never know the truth."

"Aye, I saw all that before I realized I was hit. Also saw a woman in that portal who looked a lot like you. Lainie, when I'm feeling better, I'm going to shake you until your teeth rattle. Foolish woman! You had no business jumping in front of me. You could have died."

"I didn't?" She turned her face away as if to ignore him. "Seems you should thank me. Hawk told me the ball might have gone through your heart if I hadn't done what I did. I deflected the bullet. When my body hit yours, I pushed you out of the way."

"The devil!" he gritted out between clenched teeth. Exhaustion swamping him, he relaxed into the blankets, for a moment closing his eyes. "Not going to argue with you until we're alone. Nothing to argue about. Damn fool thing for you to do."

What would he do without her? He couldn't live if he lost Lainie.

She would be alone.

Ah, she carried their child.

"The babe?"

Again, he had an urgent need to place his hand on her belly. Couldn't summon the strength.

"Don't know. However, I sense that your little shifter is doing better than either of us." She touched the bandage on his shoulder.

"Good." He drew in a long deep breath of air.

"I'll be happy as long as you don't ever make me come to that glade again. Don't like that place. The glen is evil. There is madness here. Wickedness abounds. Don't believe it discriminates. Just takes and takes." She smoothed her knuckles along his cheek pushed hair from his eyes.

"I won't."

"Promise?" she questioned him, her lips thinning as she watched him with intensity that surprised him.

In answer, he nodded then smiled.

His eyes closed, drifting into casual relaxation. Though he wasn't sleeping soundly, he caught bits and pieces of conversation. Ashton and Harris were once more involved in a heated discussion of some sort. He assumed it might be because she returned to the cave alone. Didn't Lainie tell him? Ashton took her home. Lainie sat beside him, sipping her drink. He wished he had the strength to pull her into his arms. As long as he could do so on their wedding night, he would accept this weakness today.

They were supposed to be home yesterday. He wanted to ask her to marry him again. Go to his mother to plan their wedding. She needed a dress. The white cloak was ready and waiting for their use. The celebratory feast would be planned by his mother along with Wynnie. Having waited for this most of his adult life, he smiled. She would understand fully when she saw them in their past lives.

"Are you awake now? You're smiling."

He opened his eyes to see Lainie staring down at him. She yawned then tried to hide her exhaustion behind her hand. "Lie down with me."

"I'll hurt you." She was shaking her head, silken skeins of her hair falling loose from the hastily tied bun.

"Not if you stay away from my wound." He patted his chest encouraging her to put her head there.

Warily, she settled next to him. He almost groaned as he felt the soft brush of her breasts against his chest. The arousal he expected didn't happen. He ran his hand along her back. She pulled the covers over both of them.

"Do you think you'll be ready to travel tomorrow?" she asked as her hand rested on the broad expanse of his chest. "You're breathing much easier tonight than this morning."

"I'll be ready. All I need do is lie in the wagon then let everyone else do the work. Want to be home. With you in my bed...with me."

His fingers threaded through her hair. The topic foremost on his mind was a proposal. To do so, he wanted to bend a knee to the ground. Presently, his entire back pressed against the earth. Privacy was needed for the question that would cement their lives together if she said yes.

She would say yes.

What if she told him no? What then? So far at every turn of events she implied she wouldn't wed. It had been weeks since he proffered the question. Everything about her changed. He prayed her answer would also be different.

She braced herself on an arm so she could look at his face, "A penny for your thoughts?"

"I was thinking now about our life together. Now that you're staying with me. We should make some plans... Don't you think?"

Hesitant, he wasn't going to ask yet. He would allow his statement to hover. Her eyes narrowed while she concentrated on his words.

"Our life together...?"

"Yes, little parrot."

He watched as she twisted then turned as if seeking some resolution to the question. In his arms, Roc felt her stiffen.

"I would hope that you still wish for me to live with you. You're not going to send me to your parents' home. I couldn't bear that. I need to be with you. In your bed."

Against his skin, he felt her lashes move. Her body relaxed. It seemed one moment they were talking the next she slept. Disappointment coupled with relief surged through him, shaking him to the core. If they continued the conversation even though it wasn't the setting he hoped for, she might have told him she would marry him. The proposal while he was flat on his back would not have been well done.

It seemed Hawk sensed Lainie's complete drift into sleep. He was sitting on his haunches a cup of coffee in his hand. "She needs the sleep. What about you? Would you like water? Something to eat?"

"Coffee would be appreciated."

With Hawk's help they moved Lainie so she slept on the pallet and not his chest. Again, with Hawk's help, Roc sat up, leaning against the wall of the cave. Thinking about his future...their future which looked promising.

"You can try a small amount of the thick juice from the stew. If you keep that down, I'll give you more. Sometimes surgery such as this makes the stomach not wish to work. We'll have to see."

"What about the biscuits I smelled earlier. Are there any left?"

"Again, if you keep the thick broth down, I'll give you a small amount of anything you want. After that we will proceed from there." Hawk handed him the coffee he held. He strode to the fire. When he returned, he held a bowl and spoon. "Try this."

Roc was an able patient. The broth settled in his stomach with ease. The stew and biscuit even better.

"I want to travel home tomorrow," Roc told his brother while he studied her, longed to hold her. "If Lainie is up to the travel, we can go first thing in the morning."

"She shouldn't have a problem," Hawk said as his attention was riveted to his sister.

"They have been like that all day?" Roc asked.

Hawk lifted a dark eyebrow. "Worse. Harris doesn't want to be controlled by Ashton. Says she's an independent thinker. Needs to do things her way. He wants to court her. She's holding him at arm's length which is frustrating him. believe she wants some type of commitment if not a proposal." With a slight lift of his shoulders, he continued, "Perhaps he deserves her cold shoulder."

He was furious when she came back to the cave, Roc thought. Laughing at the couple would do no good. Though their antics were amusing. "Harris doesn't trust the man to keep his hands to himself which solidifies my belief that something intimate happened before he left for London the first time."

"You're right, for whatever reason, she doesn't trust him. Nonetheless, Ashton is right about her riding all this way by herself. She risked more than she should have. There was no need for her to return. I would say if she can't live without him for more than a few hours, the two of them are in serious trouble."

"You've been away from Maisie for two days. That's on me," Roc said feeling guilt swell. "I should have reacted sooner. Should have made certain Lainie was not beside me."

"Maisie understands."

"I don't know if I would understand if someone pulled me away from Lainie for that long. I need her as I need air to breathe.

~ * ~

Harris tossed the contents of her cup into the fire. Swore. Running outside, she needed to escape Ashton, his burning gaze along with his blinding anger. As far as she was concerned, he could go back to London. She wasn't going to heed his commands. Wasn't going to give into the sensual pull of his lips on hers. The way his hands heated her when he touched her. His kisses... Determined, she would not become his victim again. He would have to earn her trust. He wasn't even attempting to meet her in the middle. Arrogant man, he just wanted to tell her what to do.

I'm a damn fool. Thought he would be pleased to see me. I rode all this way just for him. He has the audacity to lecture me about putting myself at risk. How dare the odious man? How dare he reprimand me. He had no rights where she was concerned. After she raced away from him, she didn't know what to do or where to go. For a few seconds that turned into at least a minute, she thought about mounting her tired horse and leaving. She wished she was far, far away from him.

Closing her eyes, listening to the voices in her head, she leaned against a boulder, watching the entrance to the cave. Understanding he would come after her, wishing he would as well as hoping he wouldn't, she waited on trembling legs. If she could figure out how to calm her racing, splintering nerves, she would. Single handedly, he did that to her. Sent her into a tailspin of indecision.

The devil, he expected her to fall into his plans without a question. A year...an entire year passed by. True, he wrote. She always wrote him back. He never explained what kept him away. Business.

Bah! Men!

Needing to vent her burgeoning anger, she threw a rock then another. The action made her feel better. When she imagined the pebbles pummeling his body, she dropped the rock she held in her hand. Her breath hitched. The broken sound startled her. She didn't want him hurt. She loved the odious man with all her heart. What she needed was for

Ash to understand her position, to make concessions. He thought only of himself. His way was the one and only right way. If he told her to do something, she was supposed to jump to his bidding. When he expected her to remain in one place, she better stay there.

I'm not that woman!

"Harris." His deep voice broke into her thoughts.

Her body lurched. Even though she understood this was inevitable, she wasn't ready to talk to him. Couldn't stomach another argument. "Go away." She understood he would never do her bidding.

"No. Not ever going away again. At least not without you by my side. We are meant to be together."

He stood so close she felt the heat from his body, his breath as he spoke washing across her cheek.

"Hell will freeze over first."

Her bitter words stole her breath. When she looked up his eyes singed her with the fire of his anger.

His finger rested beneath her chin, lifting. She shook it off, stomping away from him. He followed. The kiss he planned would unravel her, would tear at her very soul. She couldn't let him that close. Not now, not while she was still so angry with him. Why did he have to be such an authoritarian? Why did he have to affect her so easily?

"Your pique is getting tiring. I've apologized tried to explain in vivid detail my opinions. Still, you coldly turn your back on me as well as my overtures of good will. What you need is a good spanking. A good child's spanking."

Rage at his threats swamped her. "You wouldn't!"

"I would."

He was stalking her. Tiger eyes stared at her, burned as if they sent the message he would never back down.

"You can't lay a hand on me. Hawk would..."

He would hurt Ash if the man touched her in anger. She didn't want that. She held up her hands as if to keep him away, shaking her head, her hair spinning around her shoulders.

"Your little arms will do nothing to stop me," his voice was a low growl. "If I decide a child's punishment is in order, that is what you will receive. Your brothers understand our relationship better than you. They would never stand in my way."

His callous words outraged her, felt her shaking with fury as well as disgust at his presumptuous air. "You would purposely hurt me. I don't..." She licked her dry lips. Her heart in her throat, she had trouble forming words.

"Would rather kiss you. Touch your softness. Smell the fragrance of your arousal. Burn in your fiery heat. I remember your scent as clearly as the day I left. Recall how your body hummed to life when I stroked you."

"No..." her voice faltered with her answer. "No, a thousand times no."

She wanted that kiss along with the pleasure she knew he could give her. Understood in the deepest, darkest part of her soul, she could not allow that to happen. She would be his in every way if she allowed him just one kiss. Just as she was a year ago, she would melt to liquid. Would do whatever his clever hands wished.

"Be honest, you want that kiss. Don't deny us."

The husky timbre of his voice caressed her, filled all her senses until she needed to cry out that yes, she did want him to kiss her and so much more.

Her breath stumbled from her lungs while her body jerked in reaction to his hand gently tracing the column of her neck. He moved lower, along her arm then rested on her hip. Her breasts swelled with need, nipples hardening as if expectant.

"Yes, my body wants the kiss along with all that comes after. My mind does not. You will not force me. I would never forgive the transgression."

Her words must have hurt him. He drew away, his frown wedging into her soul. With his lips and teeth, he coerced her once.

"I see." He seemed to be recalling that time.

She didn't think he saw anything except his needs. In his mind, he would always come first. She couldn't live with that. She loved him. How could she not? She needed his love in return. "I'm not that kind of woman," she breathed softly. "I value myself, my body. A woman doesn't give herself, her body to any man who is asking. I'm not your whore or mistress to take whenever it pleases you. I'm nothing to you."

His curse startled her. Both his large hands raked through his hair leaving the strands disheveled. Her body shook. She ran her hands along her arms to warm the chill that was woven around her by the cast of his eyes. They blazed, changed color while he stared at her, raking her with the heat of his gaze.

"You're going to be my wife! I'm not just any man. You will never be my mistress or whore. In your righteous denial of me along with our feelings, don't demean yourself." He turned back to her, his tiger eyes no longer blazing with passion but anger, fury so intense she thought she would draw away from him. "You deny us pleasure for no reason."

"You've not asked. All you've done is shout and tell me what I can as well as what I cannot do. Besides..."

She didn't know what to say about the besides part. She wasn't going to cave to his demands. She wanted to be well and truly courted before she said yes to more than a chaste kiss. Wanted a ring on her finger, an announcement to the clan. Needed to see Father Damian at the keep. Talk about the rituals. He would need to understand the Clan Chattan traditions before he could say vows that would bind them through eternity.

"Bloody, bloody hell, I've asked several times! The devil take you woman... I know I've had enough of this nonsense. Grow up, Harris!"

"You had a mistress!" she accused then wished she hadn't said the words he admitted to.

"Yes!" When he turned his fists were clenched tight. "I've explained that too. Is there any wonder? You're as cold as ice. The mistress was years ago. Long before I met you. Trust in me. If you cannot do that, we've nothing!"

Tears slid from her closed eyes. Harris heard the pounding hooves as they faded into the distance. He left. Ran from the argument. Couldn't listen to her. He thought only of his needs and wishes.

~ * ~

Five long days passed since leaving the cave that morning. Laine was exhausted. She would be thrilled when Roc was finally able to see to all his needs. He'd been a bear of a patient. Irritable. Annoying. Frustrating. Except during the hours he slept, he was demanding. He apologized at least three times a day then he would go back to his obnoxious behavior. She understood he didn't like being bedridden. Neither did she.

When they arrived at Roc's home in Carnoch, both his parents were there, hovering. Lainie wanted to be alone with him. While she understood Hawk's need to settle him in a room where he could recover, she didn't understand why Elliott and Heather were at his home. Heather fixed dinner, invading her kitchen, leaving dirty pots and pans. Elliott chopped wood. That gesture was welcome.

Hawk and Elliott carried him into the downstairs bedroom. After that Hawk gave her directions to follow. She had to change the bandage twice a day for the first three. When that time passed once would be enough. Water was important. Roc needed to drink water...as much as she could get into him. If infection set in, she was to come to him immediately, night or day. The list went on and on. Hawk visited every morning to check on him as well as change the dressing. Which meant she only had to do the job once a day.

"You need to write down the instructions. I cannot be expected to remember everything you've told me. I'm not a nurse..." she paused as if remembering something.

Didn't know if there were nurses in this time. Didn't recall... When the portal closed, she saw herself inside the darkness. While the woman looked like her, she wasn't. The distinct feeling that the woman who belonged in the future was returning to the future. If Roc had seen the woman, he would have tried to save her. As it was, he was too worried about her. Nothing that happened was realistic or explainable.

Is my memory of my past returning?

She questioned herself, searched inside her head for more thoughts and found nothing except her time here with Roc. With a cup of tea in hand she sat down at the kitchen table. There were other things she found flitting around in her head. Her name was Lainie Dade Shaw. Fragments of her past were returning to haunt her. It was as if...as if she was this woman that until the last few days, she had no recollection of. The mother she didn't know, her surname was Dade. There were other strange things too. When she was young, she lived in a crofter's hut farther north in the highlands. When she turned fifteen, her mother died then her father. After that she was left alone to fend for herself. Yet, how her parent's died was not in her memories.

Lainie didn't know what brought her to the falls that day or how she exchanged places with this other woman. If indeed, she did change places. Maybe Lainie Dade Shaw just slipped down the side of the hill to end up at the bottom staring at Roc. She didn't know anything more. The sigh she emitted revealed all her doubts about herself. Hawk left several hours ago. Last time she looked in on Roc he was sleeping. The journey from the cave to Carnoch seemed to unravel his strength. Most days when he wasn't complaining or eating, he was sleeping.

Tonight, when he woke, she planned to feed him one of his favorite dinners. It was a concoction of vegetables fried with a tiny bit of oil along with a cut up chicken. She would serve it over rice. Every time one of the brothers traveled to Inverness, they would bring back a sack of rice for her along with various spices she enjoyed using.

When she poked her head into the sick room, he was snoring gently. She smiled; her heart filled with tenderness for him. He always told her he didn't snore. Well, she thought, surprising herself. If she had a tape recorder...

What the devil was a tape recorder? Another piece of her life vanished. Lainie found she no longer cared. Life was as it should be. She was where she should be. For her, life seemed to have returned to normal. A complaint would not leave her lips.

The knocking on the front door surprised her. Company wasn't expected. Hawk had come and gone hours ago. He never returned in the evenings. She lifted her skirts out of the way as she strode to the door. It was Harris sporting a nervous smile. Her fingers were weaving in and out of her skirts.

"Welcome. What brings you here?" Lainie stepped aside to give Harris room to walk through the door. "Would you like tea?"

"Wine? Could I have a glass of wine? A big one. You would join me." Harris shifted from one foot to the other. "I need to talk to someone...about... You will not tell Cameron what we say here."

What was going on here with Roc's sister? If she had to venture a guess, the problem revolved around Ashton. She certainly appeared nervous. "Of course. Let's go into the kitchen. You can cut vegetables with me while we talk. I do expect you to stay for dinner since you will be helping prepare it."

The wine was poured. Harris sipped. Made a face then drank down half the liquid. After she set the glass on the table, she let out a long breath of air. "It's Ash. I don't know what to do about him. He hasn't come back. He was so angry with me, he raced out of my life. I don't know what to do."

"Figured as much. Tell me whatever and as much as you like. Sometimes men can be puzzling. Don't know when Roc will wake up. Hawk told me he's to sleep as much as he needs. Though his time in bed has shortened. He insists on getting up, walking around the room. Tells me in one breath not to wait on him, in the next he yells for something he can't find. Yesterday he started asking for work. I had to make two trips to his shop to bring back things he could manage."

Lainie handed her the cutting board Roc fashioned for her before handing her spring peas along with a bowl of mushrooms to cut. "Bite sized pieces if you can. I'll cut the carrots then set the oil to heating."

The chicken had been cut earlier. She measured out water and rice to eventually bring to a boil. Set out an array of spices to make the dish hot to the pallet.

Harris set her knife down. She looked at her with eyes the color of ice. "That man is seeing another woman. I know it as I breathe. He as much as told me he saw women over the last year. He told me a man has needs. I cannot bear the fact that he couldn't wait for me."

Lainie's mind buzzed. She couldn't imagine how she would feel if confronted with the fact that Roc slept with someone else. "How does that make you feel?"

"Nauseous...jealous...guilty as hell. Want to shoot him where it would hurt the most, where he wouldn't be able to have another woman." She spit out multiple conjoining emotions in less than three seconds or so it seemed.

"I would feel the same if it was Roc. Did he tell you he saw other women?"

Lainie didn't understand how he could come back for her if he wasn't sincere in wanting her.

"He didn't deny it."

"Then...you don't know for certain."

"Before he left last year for London, he made me promise not to see anyone, not to do anything with another man." Harris' voice grew heated while she shook her head. Her knife tapped on the cutting board. "If I couldn't see another man, why does he feel he can sleep with another woman?"

Lainie heard the rage in every spoken word. She lifted her shoulders, wondering what Harris questioned. "To me it's obvious, the same rules don't apply to him. I gather. If there were no promises made between the two of you, he had no right to make demands of you. If he meant to flaunt..."

"If I have my way, they bloody do pertain to him also. He made no promises except to return. He took his bloody time in coming back. An entire year!" The knife seemed to be working overtime while she chopped.

"You imagining Ashton's head beneath that knife of yours?"

Lainie kept back the laughter as it threatened to bubble up. To Harris this was not amusing in any way, shape, or form. She loved the man. As far as she could tell, Ashton abused that love. Nonetheless, she imagined how Roc would react if she accused him. He might say nothing expecting her to realize he would never do what she was thinking.

"Yes, just a certain part of him. I could cut it off!"

Harris chopped harder and faster.

No comment came to mind. "Did his leaving you have something to do with your unbidden return to the cave? While I couldn't hear what was being said, we all knew the two of you were furious with each other."

"Yes. Everything to do with it. He thought he could play with my emotions. After I left the cavern, he followed me. Wanted me to kiss him." Harris sighed, sipped some of the red wine that was poured. When she looked up, her eyes were misty. "I wanted that too. More than anything I want to kiss him. He doesn't understand."

"What exactly doesn't the man understand?"

Lainie tried for a bland tone while she continued with dinner preparation. Judging this young woman's emotions was not going to happen. She slept with her brother. They weren't married. Roc's bairn was nestled in her womb. Lainie wiped her hands on her apron then drank some wine. Perhaps brandy would have been better for this unveiling. "Have you explained anything to him? It would help if the two of you could have a peaceful conversation. Something that didn't involve yelling."

"If he kisses me, I'll let him do whatever he wants. I *ken* that fact as does he. That's why he gets so upset with me when I refuse his kisses." The knife slapped on the board. Her fingers shook with escalating emotions. "He knows I wouldn't stop him after he's kissed me. The man believes he can control me with my body. I can't allow that to happen. Won't..." Harris was seething, the knife waving in the air.

Lainie was beginning to fear for Ashton's safety if he got anywhere near a knife wielding Harris. "I understand that sentiment. The same has happened to me with your brother. A woman must be careful who she trusts. Roc...well, it has always...no I wanted him from the first moment I saw him. Once Roc decided he'd done enough waiting for me to make up my mind, he did everything in his power to bring me to his bed. He teased with kisses, with the heat of his hands. I was vulnerable. Witless. Though now, I'm pleased."

"That is what I cannot allow Ash to do. He cannot succeed. I don't want to end up like Crissie McKenna."

"Crissie? Roc hasn't mentioned her. What happened?"

"Crissie McKenna, she fell in love with a Sassenach, an Irishman. She let him do things he shouldn't. After he left, she... The man got her pregnant the first time they made love. She was left for over a year...to bear the shame...to have the child without the father knowing. When

Walker returned, he took the babe with him. Took the child away from her. Told her she could do as she pleased but his son would live with him."

"Oh, my...that didn't happen to you. Thank God." Lainie's hand rose to her chest as if she could still the sudden pounding of her heart. "I better understand the way of it between you and Ashton."

"No, but it could have. I didn't let him make love to me but he..." She looked up from the battered snow peas.

"If you're uncomfortable, you don't have to tell me." Lainie set her hand on Harris' fingers. "Say only what you feel—" Lainie was cut off by the bellow behind her.

"No, but she better tell me!"

Roc stood in the doorway, his eyes blazing the anger Lainie understood he would be feeling. The man took advantage of his little sister. Roc's feet were braced apart. Hands on his hips. He was powerful, his shoulders broad. He stole her breath.

Lainie sipped in a good dose of air, calming herself to deal with the outraged brother. "Roc, this is private for her. It's not nice that you are eavesdropping." Lainie rose to help him into a chair. "Wine? Brandy?"

"Need to hear what the bounder did to my sister."

Harris turned a bright crimson. With her hands on her cheeks, she rushed from the room. The front door banged shut.

"See what you just did?" Lainie asked, furious with Roc for intruding on their privacy. "You had no business interrupting or listening. She was about to speak with me of that time."

"Me?" Roc appeared confused. "I had no business? The devil, she's my sister. I care what happens to her. Want Harris to be happy and with the right man."

"If you'd gone back to the bedroom and kept your mouth shut, Harris would have opened up to me. I don't have one doubt she would have told me everything. I might have even betrayed a confidence if it was in her best interest. In any case..." Lainie paused thoughtfully. "In this scenario, your sister is in love with Ashton Wolcott. Whatever happened a year ago did not result in a child. There is no shame in loving a man. The two of them are trying to sort out emotions from the sensations caused by the closeness that can happen between two people who are enamored of each other."

He crossed his arms over his naked chest. "Do you love me?"

Answering his question would not happen any time soon. Lainie wasn't about to delve into that topic until he voiced his love for her. In her mind, it wasn't a given that a shifter would always love his mate. Lainie knew and understood next to nothing about the Clan Chattan. As of this point in time, little had been explained to her.

"You need to finish cutting the vegetables since you sent Harris flying from here. She most likely won't come back for dinner. Are you hungry?"

"My question wasn't answered."

"The mushrooms are almost finished. Just cut off the ends of the peas then in half. That will be fine."

"You aren't going to give me an answer." One of his burnished eyebrows lifted. "Are you?"

Ignoring him now was in her best interest. She decided to take a page from Harris' book. She wasn't going to fall into line without him falling first. "I'm fixing one of your favorite dinners. I do hope she returns. However, I'm not about to hold my breath. If she does, you are not to question her about Ashton. It is not our business. As it seems right now, they have enough issues to contend with. If the two brothers enter the mix, nothing will be solved."

"Don't you think it strange he didn't blink at the fact both Hawk and I shifted?" he queried as he began to work on their dinner.

"You told me...didn't you, that your family believed he knew already that they were capable of changing form? That he protected you from discovery whenever you were north of here? Wherever did you go?"

"I did. Still seems strange to me. Most people have some reaction when they see shifters. He blandly handed me and Hawk our clothing. What about that? The Sassenach didn't question anything."

"If he ever returns from Inverness to court your sister, you can ask him. Until then you will have to continue to question."

"You know what I believe?" He leaned over the table tapping the knife. "That we should visit the cabin. We could be alone for days with only the housekeeper to make sure we've enough food."

"I'm certain you'll tell me what you believe," she said, watching him, knowing there must be some other reason for his sudden interest in the cabin.

"He's a shifter. I'm certain of that fact. Anyway, since we showed off our alternative shape, Harris is faced with one less discussion. She doesn't have to explain her family or what she can do."

"If he is as you say, why didn't he help out?"

"Didn't need his help. There was no reason to compromise himself." Roc lifted his shoulders with a masculine indifference. "Now, however, Ashton will need to show his true hand to Harris. Doing so should not be difficult. He will understand that she won't faint at the sight of his alternate form. He will know she lives with shifters, might even be one herself. She won't be terrified if she sees him change."

"Is she?"

"Yes. Much to her chagrin. She'd rather not be able to shift."

Lainie set his glass of wine on the table. "Drink up. This might be a long night."

He lifted his right burnished eyebrow in speculation. Wasn't certain what to think. "Hawk said lots of water, not wine."

"I just heard the door close in the front. Your sister is returning. Play nice. Don't demand answers that will drive her away. She deserves better from her brother. What is between her and Ashton is between the two of them. Not you and them or me and them."

Lainie walked from the kitchen. She took Harris' hands in hers after she stepped into the hallway. "Ignore your brother. He's not going to prod you for answers. Roc understands that if he tries, I'll beat him over the head with my rolling pin. I believe you both have had a shock."

"It's private. You understand. I would have told you."

Harris followed her back to the kitchen, speaking as she walked. "My brothers would decide they have to defend my honor which doesn't need defending. I've done nothing I'm ashamed of."

"You are right. Be strong. Besides, I'm certain your beau won't want what the two of you have done or not done known to family."

"I'm not going to tell parents or brothers what happened that day. I was blindsided. Experienced something I didn't know existed. Won't allow that to happen again unless we marry. It is part of what is making Ashton furious with me. He's a man who is confused as well as angry. Irritated and annoyed as he expects me to fall into his plans. Obey his every whim. Are all men like that? Obtuse? Unbearable when they don't get their way?"

"Sometimes a man is ruled by the wrong part of his body," Lainie said with little humor in her voice.

She did not have enough experience with the male beast to tell Harris what she wanted to learn.

Harris cleared her throat, her chin in the air. To Roc, she spoke softly, "I'm still a virgin. That's all I'm going to say on the incident that took place a year ago. Don't ask me anything else. It's not yours to know."

Roc grunted his displeasure, obvious by her lack of an answer. Knew enough to hold his tongue on the topic.

"Since you are both here, I'm going to put the rice on then cook the rest of the food. We will eat. Nothing more will be discussed about Harris or Ashton unless Harris brings the topic up. Understood?"

Lainie turned to hide her smile before she busied her hands. Roc was so much better. His second grunt of annoyance didn't come as a surprise.

In a few minutes oil simmered in the frying pan. She set the chicken to fry then the vegetables along with seasoning. The aroma filled the room. Lainie hummed. Listened to the bland conversation going on between Roc and Harris. They spoke of the weather. His business. The fact the Carlson's were going to have a party to celebrate their thirtieth wedding anniversary. She smiled when she thought about Roc along with the possibilities of her future. Since he was on the mend, he would be getting back to his normal self. He would want to sleep with her again. Maybe she should take a page out of Harris' book. Refuse until they were wed.

She felt his heated stare on her back. Knew his gaze traveled the length of her. He wished she was naked. Lord, she couldn't cook naked. His laughter didn't startle her as it should have. She set her hands on her belly understanding why she was able to see into his mind. Wished she dared turn around. If her guess was correct, he was thinking about ways to propose to her. That was all nice. She enjoyed the fact that through the child she carried, she was privy to his thoughts.

Harris walked home before darkness fell. Lainie finished with the dishes as well as storing the leftover food. This dinner would be good tomorrow night too. From the kitchen table, Roc watched her with shuttered eyes.

He drummed his fingers before picking up his glass of wine, twirling the contents. He set the glass on the table before walking to her. He stood behind her now. She felt heat generated by his big body while the scent of him blanketed her like the morning mist. "How long are you going to put off going to bed with me. There is no reason that I can think of for you to walk to the upstairs room each night."

The gasp of surprise didn't stop Roc from nuzzling her neck. His teeth grazed her skin then his tongue licked in a sensual swirl, burning all of her. "It's been too long," he murmured as she leaned into him. She wanted to lie down with him. Needed to feel his big body wrapped around her. Needed to warm her feet.

"My brother didn't say anything about foregoing sex. The wound is healing. He's taking stitches out in a few days."

His large hands cupped her breasts, brushed over the covered tips, bringing them to a hard pout. She shivered from the contact even though clothing separated him from her.

Turning in his arms, she wanted to laugh at his expression. Without her breasts to explore he turned his attention to her bottom. Discovering the curves. "That's because he thought we had enough good sense to understand sex might open the stitches. It is too soon. You said a few days or do you wish to have new stitches put in? If that were to happen, you would have to wait longer. Not until Hawk tells us it's okay."

Heat rose to her face. That was the last topic she wanted to discuss with his brother. She would let Roc confront Hawk about the sex they would soon share again.

"Another glass of wine then? We can sit in the drawing room. There are things we need to speak of," Roc said as he stood to lead the way. "I want everything I'm feeling clear. Don't want confusion of any sort. Need to secure out future."

Secure our future?

"You sound so serious."

She knew he wanted to talk about marriage again. Didn't know what else was pending. Unlike the other times she was ready for the conversation.

"I am." He scooped up the bottle of wine. "You take the goblets."

After they sat down, he topped off the glasses. Staring into the fire, he waited for what seemed an eternity to her. Silence greeted her ears until she began to hear sounds around her. She heard the ticking of the clock. The soft breeze blowing in through the open window. The day had been unseasonably warm. The rooms upstairs would be too hot to sleep in until the night cooled them off.

"You should sleep downstairs tonight. With me. I won't do anything you don't want me to do. It would be just like the nights when we first met and all I did was hold you."

With a soft sigh that brought his attention to her. "We just discussed that."

Lainie missed the warmth of his body pressed next to hers. She didn't dare give into his proposition. He would never be able to keep his hands to himself. She would never be able to tell him no.

"I'll keep my hands to myself," he laughed as his gaze delved into hers, his eyes warm with passion again, seeming to know what she was thinking. It was disconcerting to have her thoughts read so easily. "Yes, I'm reading your mind. Not too difficult with my little shifter helping me out."

"What if I can't?" she asked dryly wondering if her questions were fact or fiction. "I'll survive the heat upstairs. Until your stitches are removed. No chances will be taken by me or you. This topic is no longer open for discussion."

Roc set his glass on the table. Pulled out a small box. In front of her, he got down on one knee then he opened the box. When he looked up at her, his smile didn't reach his eyes. His fingers were shaking as he held the ring toward her.

She gasped, her hand to her chest as if she could still the rapid beating of her heart. This moment was something she waited for, hoped for. "Roc?" she questioned, reaching out to him before withdrawing.

The diamond ring in the dark blue velvet sparkled. Light from the fireplace created prisms of color.

He inhaled a deep ragged breath before he spoke with so much tenderness the sound shocked her, "Will you marry me? I want you to be my wife. You are my mate through all time. Our child lies secure within you, growing in your womb. If you say yes, we'll plan the wedding. You'd make me the happiest man alive."

Tears welled in her eyes. She didn't want to cry. At one time she never thought to find a person to love, to marry. Roc gave her so much. She found herself trying to swallow the huge lump in her throat. She couldn't talk. Could barely breathe. She wanted to tell him yes, the word didn't want to form.

"Don't cry. You are supposed to be happy. If you don't..." His strong voice dwindled to nothing as he seemed to doubt her answer. "Lainie? You need to say something. If you keep me suspended in time, I might not survive."

"No! Yes! Yes Roc! I will marry you. All you had to do was ask." With the back of her hands, she wiped the spilled tears from her cheeks.

"I have asked," he said dryly. "Too many times I'm not counting. You've always told me no."

"It wasn't the right time. I didn't know who I was. Didn't understand I'm meant to be here with you." She hoped as well as prayed he hadn't given up on her. This was what she wished for. "What do we do now?"

"Give me your hand."

She did. He slipped the ring on her finger. Held her fingers for a few seconds while he admired it.

"Now, as soon as I'm healed enough to ride to the McKenna keep, we'll see Father Damian. Should be about the time I'm healed enough to make love to you, to sleep in the same bed with you."

"A Catholic wedding," she murmured wondering why she hesitated about that.

Her expression must have alerted Roc to her vacillation.

"You once told me you weren't religious. You didn't think you could become a Catholic. Is that still true. For my family there is no alternative. Though you would not have to take the religion as your own. If you don't wish it, I won't say anything."

"Oh..."

She touched her finger to her lips, trying to recount the conversation. In her life, she never remembered a church. When they lived so far from the city, there were few churches and less time to visit even on Sundays. "I don't recall. I'm feeling as if I don't have a strong opinion."

"No objections?" he asked as he groaned trying to find his way back to his chair. "No reason to say no?"

"None."

"Tomorrow I'll send for mother. You two have a great deal to accomplish in a short amount of time. I'm guessing the wedding will take place in about ten days. Believe my stitches will be removed by then. I'll be in fine form to go through with the ceremonies. To dance with you to the bagpipes. To seduce you beneath the table. To consummate the marriage. All of that is tradition."

"Plural? Traditions?" she wasn't at all certain about that. "Are you going to tell me about them?"

"Not tonight."

"Please...what is it I have to look forward too?"

~ * ~

Both Geordie and Scratch ended up in the glen where they were when the darkness sucked them up spinning and whirling them end over end into what Geordie thought was eternity or hell. Bent over at the waist, he heaved. Lost the whiskey that had been boiling in his gut.

"What happened?" Scratch asked while he rubbed his hand on

his belly then lower as if to make sure his vital parts were still as they were supposed to be. "Don't like the feel of this one bit. Don't feel right if you ask me." He didn't think anyone was going to ask him.

"I don't know. Feel as if I've been ripped through time. The girl came with us. I swear I saw a girl." Geordie stood, feeling his arms and legs to see if everything was there. "Don't feel right. No, something's all wrong." He stood up to look around. "I don't feel so good. Think I might pass out."

"The woman wasn't Lainie. She's not here now. Do you see her? Where did they all go? I swear I hit one of them."

Scratch looked at himself. He wasn't wearing the clothes he wore earlier in the day. His pants were short, hair trimmed, no beard. He wore a shirt with short sleeves. Something he'd never seen before. He was different. Didn't even feel the same.

"Don't feel right," Geordie murmured agreeing with his friend his eyes widening as if he just realized this was a different world even though in so many ways it was the same. His gaze shifted from Scratch to himself.

"No, this isn't at all the way it's supposed to be. Where do you think we are?"

Scratch was looking at the trail up the hill. A fence skirted both sides. The trail wasn't terrible. It was topped with some material he'd never seen. He began to walk, seeking some answers. He felt different. His thoughts were altered. His knowledge of life was not the same. He thought about things he didn't know existed a few minutes ago.

"Where you going?" Geordie asked.

"To check out the lay of the land. Want to see what else has changed."

Thoughts collided in his head, melded with notions that were too far from realization to take seriously. From his pocket he pulled out items he'd never seen before but somehow knew what they were used for.

"Don't go anywhere without me." Geordie scrambled to catch up to Scratch. "Don't like this a'tall. Don't understand anything."

"What do you think of this?"

Scratch looked out on a parking lot filled with cars. He pulled keys out of his pocket, his wallet too. A cell phone next appeared. "Don't understand. Want to discover the truth of all this."

"Didn't we come here this afternoon?" Geordie held out his hands. "What I thought I knew and understood seems to be at war with my mind. I have notions about my life that seem real, unexplainable."

"What kind of notions?"

Scratch was feeling the same. He understood he owned a nice car. Just bought it two months ago. His home was in Edinburgh in an apartment building. Geordie lived nearby in a different building. They'd always been friends.

"That the means of transportation doesn't involve a horse. You've a car parked over there. It's next to that fancy black one. We drove here this morning." Where the hell did all those notions come from?

Scratch's hands tangled in his pocket with keys. He pulled out keys to a car as well as what he knew to be his apartment. In his wallet there were cards of all sorts. He knew what they were. He read his name on a dark blue card, Tinnely Scratch.

"What's your name?"

"You know my name," Geordie said.

"Find your wallet and look," Scratch challenged.

He did, "It says, Mathew Gordon."

Chapter Ten

The wedding planning took ten days. Roc laughed at Lainie when she told him she wasn't going to sleep with him until after the ceremony. When he tried to charm her into forgetting, she told him it was a promise she made to his mother. The first few days of their lives together, he never intended to sleep with her at all until after the event that would make them husband and wife. Now that he knew her taste, the sweet way she sighed with her pleasure, he was hard pressed to forego the sensuality and passion that was Lainie. Her allure was irresistible. As one stolen kiss led to another, his hands wandered over not so virgin territory. He couldn't help but discover the liquid heat that was Lainie. She called to him as no other woman ever before. Since a promise was made, to his mother no less, he grudgingly agreed.

During the ten-day hiatus, his mother dragged her from the modiste to the McKenna keep with constant regularity. They planned the feast for the celebration of their vows. She taught the chef several recipes she favored. The feast included some of her favorite dishes as well as Roc's, the rest of the food would include traditional Scottish faire, some of the clan's favorites.

At the modiste they went over fashion plates, picking out a white creation. She told him the special gown was simple. All he knew about the dress was that she would wear the Frasier tartan as a sash around her waist. When he asked from curiosity, Lainie wouldn't let him see the dress, saying something about bad luck. He didn't understand how viewing a dress would cause bad fortune. Since he found her, convinced her to be his, Roc didn't think anything could go wrong.

After they visited Father Damian, he understood the religious conversion would not be difficult. She seemed to understand everything that would be expected of her. She had no questions for him. The day before the wedding they spoke. Roc had not been certain this was a good idea. His brother urged him to do so. His mother told him he should not. The contradictory opinions frustrated and confused him.

"Forewarned is prepared," Roc began by picking up her hand.

He held their palms together. She was so small, fragile. She needed to understand what would happen on the eve of their wedding. She had no idea. Hurting her would not be something he would remember with pleasure. He reminded himself the pain didn't last forever. Just as the breaching of her maidenhead this would also vanish in a few seconds. He'd seen the Clan Chattan ceremony performed several times over the last years. Always wondering what the woman saw as well as how the married lady felt. Only the female could tell the male. The traditional ritual was experienced differently by male and female.

"What do you mean? You look so serious. What is it? Need to speak about what?" She ran her tongue across her lips watching him watching her. "I don't like the look in your eyes."

Heat exploded inside himself as he sensed her arousal. He never stopped wanting her. Ten days seemed an eternity. Tomorrow night would be a blessing in many ways. He would know her again in the way a man knows the woman he loves. The scent of gardenia, spring rain coupled with vivid sunshine always floated around her. When she walked into a room, he sensed her, caught the scent of her.

He drummed his fingers on the arm of his chair, searching for a means to begin the conversation he wasn't at all certain they should have. "Wine?"

Her smile was shyly sweet. She looked a bit disconcerted when she answered. "I *dinna ken*...Hawk told me I should limit what I drink or stop altogether. For the sake of the little shifter you're so fond of."

"Did he say why?"

Her answer surprised Roc. He'd heard nothing of the mother foregoing wine while increasing.

In a pretty, very feminine lift of her shoulders, her eyes sparkling mischievously she began, "He didn't know why. It was just a guess. Maisie didn't drink spirits during her pregnancy. Tonight, perhaps a small glass would relax me."

He would like her relaxed. What he was going to tell her would most likely be a shock. "There are things I want you to understand before tomorrow night. Don't let what I mention frighten you. All the women who marry into the Clan Chattan go through the ceremonies, the traditions." He paused, thinking, searching for the right words. "All survive to smile and laugh again. I'll do everything in my power to ease the way."

Her eyes widened to huge lovely circles. He saw her swallow as if he already said too much. His mother might have mentioned something. "Heather told me you needed to speak with me. She also said she warned you against doing so. Your mother didn't believe you would heed her advice."

"I've had reservations, too many to count. Don't want you to run in the opposite direction. Though what I've got to say is important. We've tried to be honest with each other...about everything."

His laugh wasn't at all joined by hers. The devil he didn't feel like laughing either.

"Perhaps I should wait until after we are married. Until we are in the tower room. I don't want you to dread the evening. Also don't want you too shocked when things happen that you've no control over."

"No. You've already told me too much to leave me wondering. You cannot poke the dragon then leave it be to wonder and worry." Lainie set her hand on his thigh. "Tell me what it is that has you wound into knots that will not come undone. Tell me why I might dread the evening that should be one of the best nights of my life. Until a few moments ago, I was looking in a forward direction. Now, you are putting a damper on those feelings."

"I promise you the night will meet all your expectations." His voice was strong when he said the words that he meant with all his heart. Though he could make no promises. Once the claiming was finished, there would be nothing left for her to worry about or face as a challenge. They could proceed with their lives.

Her little hand on his leg brought him to instant attention. Blood pounded so close to the touch of her hand wishing for more. The gesture wasn't meant to arouse. Nonetheless, it did, having been without her for days now, anything she did struck him as if lightening splintered the sky.

He would need to continue with great caution if he wasn't going to terrify her. "The first ceremony is normal. Nothing to worry about. We will be wed in front of the church for the clan to witness. The procedure is brief as well as to the point. After that we will go into the church where only family along with close friends will be permitted. This is the Catholic ritual, most of the versus are spoken in Latin. Do you know any Latin? We will be on our knees in front of Father Damian who will marry us for a second time."

"That doesn't sound like anything that would have you sweating or have me running in the opposite direction. What is it that will terrify me into not wanting to marry you? You do understand, I don't' have a choice if I wish to keep my good name."

She ran her hand along his arm. Brought his fingers to her lips, kissing the palm as he'd done so many times to her small hand. His pulse leapt to his groin. He didn't know how he would survive this last night of celibacy. He wanted her more than he'd ever wanted her before.

"No, it's not. Nothing so far to be leery of." He took control of their hands, bringing them to his lips so he could return the small kisses.

"What happens next? I'm eager to have this conversation finished. Despite the need to understand, you seem to be hedging. Did you mean to bring me this far then turn away without speaking your heart." She stood walking into the kitchen. Before she got to the door, she turned. "Would you like anything more to eat. I'll bring some of the shortbread cookies your mother made for us."

"Cookies would be nice, yes, just the thing to go with the wine."

He agreed with her. Tension he was feeling needed to be eased. He sat back, waiting for her then sipping the wine. In the kitchen she was humming. He liked the sound of her voice. It was low and husky when she sang. Not at all like her speaking voice.

While she was still rummaging around in the kitchen, he leaned his head on the back of the chair. Closing his eyes, he listened for the soft footfalls that would signal her return, the rustle of her skirts against her legs. For the few minutes she was gone, he repeated in his mind all he needed to tell her. The explanation could send her running back to the glen and the portal. Could make her change her mind about the ceremonies. Her scent caught his attention first spring rain, gardenias, and sensual arousal. He felt her presence. She was standing in the doorway, holding the tray she prepared. His little shifter was at it again. The baby would let him know if he terrified her.

No, she was made of sterner stuff. He didn't believe the Clan Chattan ceremony would frighten her away from him, would make her run back to the life she knew before her existence here. No, she remembered nothing from that time. Except perhaps the fact he would disrobe her. First, he should tell her no one would see her naked save him. He'd already touched and kissed every place on her body. Knew her as he knew his body.

The claiming is what terrified him. Maybe the women were correct in not allowing the information to reach the bride until all was said and done. Once it was done, it was finished. There might be tears at the time. After that there would be nothing except pleasure. It seemed from what he heard from those who experienced the ritual, the women, told them enough to ease their fears. Earlier he thought he might have told her he had to claim her. Perhaps those words were enough. She would know something would happen in the privacy of their room but she would not understand the details.

The whisper of her dress around her ankles alerted him to the fact she now stood over him. She was no longer watching him from the shelter of distance. He opened his eyes, smiling. She poured more wine for him. Handed him a glass. She sipped hers. The cookies were on a platter where he could reach them.

"What now?" her voice held a hint of dread coupled with a slight quivering. "I would know everything. When you are finished, you will hold me."

If he held her, he would make love to her. If he held her, the vow to his mother would be broken. He couldn't deny her the comfort of his arms if that was something she needed.

"The Clan Chattan ceremony. I wondered if you would speak about that. I gather it is different from the religious ones. I would know what will happen. Only immediate family is allowed to watch. Why?"

He supposed because the newly married couple would wear nothing. He needed to ease into that fact. "The tradition goes back through ancient times. One might say it is pagan in nature. Goes back farther than anyone can remember. The tradition can never be forgotten. That would be bad luck, taking chances that should never be taken."

"Is this the part I will see you in other times?" she asked while she swirled the contents of her glass seeming to watch the dark red pick up the lights from the fire rather than drinking the liquid. Before sipping, she set the glass on the table beside her. "Perhaps tea would have suited me better."

"Yes."

His thoughts caught in the back of his head. Stayed there while he studied her profile, intrigued by the pensive expression on her lovely features. "It is not the only time you will see us together in a different time. There will be one more time. I've been told what you see is different."

"Tell me, tell me everything you believe I should know. Nothing you say can make me change my mind about wanting you...or about the marriage. If this is something that must be suffered through, I'll endure."

He flinched from the one word. *Endure.* There it was, wanting not loving. When he asked a few days ago if she loved him, she didn't answer. Chose to remain silent, unable to meet his eyes. While he loved her, all shifters loved their mates. She wasn't a shifter. She might not love him. Care and wanting were not the same as love. Was she incapable of loving another person? Her early days were not filled with love along with laughter as his were. The thought was too much to bear. He tried to tell himself love didn't matter in this equation. If all she did was care for him, that would have to do until he found a means to change her feelings to love.

"The Clan Chattan ceremony, yes, everyone except immediate family will leave the church. The tradition is private to only the people who are the most connected to the couple exchanging their vows."

"It happens inside the church? Couldn't that be construed as blasphemous if the tradition is pagan?" Lainie asked tilting her head a bit to look at him sideways.

Her grin was askance. The expression told him more than anything that he wasn't frightening her.

He wasn't at the frightening part yet. "No, never sacrilegious. The part you won't like is that you will be naked. The devil!"

Roc knew he overstepped, changed the lighthearted banter between them. He was saying first that which should be explained last.

At her gasp, he realized his mistake was graver than his first impression or his *faux pas*. Holding up his hands to stop the ensuing comment or to keep her from telling him he should go to the devil, Roc started to explain again. "I will disrobe you."

Once more he missed the step he should have taken by shooting ahead to something she would take issue with.

Now, she was shaking her head, her eyes narrowed, brows furrowed. "Not in front of everyone you won't!"

Now that he blew the explanation, he would make certain she paid close attention to the rest. "Yes," he'd continue now as he planned. Even though he failed miserably. "That is what the white cloak is for."

He thought he should explain everything necessary to ease the way to the next step in their journey.

"So?" her voice was curt as well as angry. She was trembling. Her speech nearly shrill. "After the fact, after everyone has seen me naked you will cover me with the cloak. How gentlemanly of you. This puts a damper on everything. You were right to think I might refuse to finish with all your so-called traditions. Only you will ever see me naked. Damn all your clan's traditions."

At least she seemed determined not to back down. He could deal with her anger. If she remained silent and fuming, he would not have done well. "Before I remove your wedding gown along with the other clothes you might choose to wear, the cloak will be wrapped snuggly around both of us. You understand. I will also be naked. No one will see you except me. No one will see me except your eyes. I would suppose we would feel each other rather than see. It will be as if we are wrapped in a blanket. I will support you through the ordeal. A woman is weakened by the ceremony. Sometimes to the point she cannot remain standing by herself. I won't let you fall. Won't allow anything to happen to you. Will support as well as protect you in this along with the rest of your life."

"Oh."

Her lips formed a perfect circle, her eyes wider than the China saucer her cup of tea sat on. "You will also be naked. Will I remove your clothing?" she asked with a tiny smirk. "I might enjoy that."

The mood changed back to what he needed it to be. He let out a silent breath of relief as he tried to figure out what else needed to be said. How best to make the explanations. Telling her about earth, wind, fire then water was part of the tale he knew little about. The experiences were never repeated outside the couple who faced them. He wasn't at all certain if there was an earth element.

"Where is your mind traveling, sweetheart. Yes, if your little fingers don't fail you, you will remove my clothing. I believe that is a precursor to the feasting. Unfortunate for me, you will dress when everything is completed."

"Let me get this right. Sheltered by the cloak, by the white cloak, we will both be naked. What will you do? You can't..."

"I would not. I will support you. That is all the male does."

Time and again her thoughts as well as fears were being revealed. His little shifter was reading her naughty mind then telling him what she was thinking. She didn't know how to fix that. For the time being he meant to ignore the images rattling around in her head at an alarming rate. "I suppose what comes next for you, I don't understand. I've heard the women are caught up in the elements of the earth. Most spectacularly, wind, fire then water. You will feel all, the wind blowing hard, fanning the fire and flames burning around you. In the end water will douse the fire just as the wind fanned the flames."

"Oh." Her tongue touched her top lip as if she was concentrating. "At this time, I will see you in our past. Will you always look the same?"

Roc was pleased with her curiosity. "I've heard similar. Not the same." Just as she no longer appeared as the woman he found that first day. Lainie changed to become the exact woman he was supposed to wed in this century. The differences subtle. "I believe you will see me in both my cat form as well as my human. You will tell me about the experience.

Will you not?"

She nodded, now her bottom lip was caught between her teeth. A violent urge to do the same surged into his blood stream. With slow finesse she sipped her wine, her eyes gazing at him over the rim. He needed to hold her. Didn't trust himself if she was in his arms.

"I will tell you whatever I can."

Before he could protest, not that he wanted to deny her, she sat down on his lap. Her arms went around his neck. Soft breasts pushing against his chest sent another swamping of heated desire inflaming him.

"This is not wise if you intend to keep your promise to Mother."

His voice deepened, turning husky. He thought he'd done well the last few days after the stitches were removed. He managed to stay away from her. This was not going to work with her sitting on him, so close.

Lainie brushed a quick kiss across his lips. Her smile wicked, she said without a look of guilt, "I know. I lied about the vow." She placed a fingertip on his lips when he thought to protest. He touched the finger with his tongue unable to refuse the invitation. "While she asked, I never promised. Didn't trust you not to seduce me. When we touch you *ken* I cannot say no. I could never give a promise I knew could not be kept when challenged."

Delicately, he bit on the tip of her finger. As if she heard his desire, she presented each finger to his mouth for his tender attention. His hands on her waist he could feel the tremors plunging through her.

Despite the urgent need to possess, Roc set her aside. "We should wait until tomorrow night. We managed to remain chaste far too long to fall back on that promise of sweet delight after the wedding and the feast."

Lainie puffed in another breath of air. As if resigned to his statement, "While I do want to wait..." it seemed to take her several deep breaths before she could continue talking. "...tomorrow is so far away. What happens next?"

"The feast you've helped plan. We will eat then dance. At first you will be too tired to do anything but watch. I'll seduce you at the table while all the clan is celebrating. Your woman's pleasure will be obvious only to me because you'll hide your pretty face against my chest."

"You..." She was speechless. "You will do something like that? Where everyone will know what you are about?"

He liked that he shocked her to the tips of her petty little toes. The same cold toes she loved to rub on his leg. He continued. "Tradition. Once I've fed you and you've recovered from my careful seduction, we will dance. My father will want a dance, Hawk too. After the cake is cut, the women will take you to the tower room they've prepared for our use."

"Why?"

Roc boosted his shoulders considering her question carefully. "Assume they do it to torture the men. Why else? They will lay out all sorts of delicacies for us to eat during the night hours while we more thoroughly discover each other. There will be wine to relax us so we can," he paused at her look of confusion.

"That can't be." She was shaking her head, curls dancing around her face. "No wine."

"Very well," he didn't intend to argue the point. Wine would help her relax. One night couldn't hurt the *wee* shifter. "They dress you in a filmy negligée. One I will be able to see all your sweet curves, the tips of your breasts, the thatch of hair guarding your most intimate secrets. I will enjoy the beautiful site of you. The women will explain things about the wedding night, a few restrained words about the claiming and about the breeching of the maidenhead."

"I'm no longer a virgin," she said with blunt honesty. "That advice will not be necessary."

"I suppose you will miss out on that topic. Mother knows you are increasing. Rest assured you are not the first women in the Clan Chattan to come to her wedding carrying a child. Once we've identified our mate, there is no reason to wait for the vows."

He was skirting the edges of the claiming ritual having decided he'd rather not explain what was going to happen. That once again he would hurt her. He wasn't going to allow the fear of the joining to take away all the other pleasures of the evening. She reclaimed his lap.

"How do you go about this claiming?" she asked as she ran her finger along his neck, circled his ear while she once more held her bottom lip within her teeth.

Lainie was persistent. He gave her credit for that. "Believe that specific information is better left for the future. A conversation to be held later rather than now."

"It's going to hurt."

"Yes."

"I would learn more about this claiming business. As you said before not in these words but the more I know the better prepared I'll be. Do you no longer think that is a good idea? I promise you I will not run from the wedding," she queried.

"I did say that, didn't I? In this case..." He couldn't help shaking his head. He tapped her on the nose before kissing the same spot. "In this case, no. Learning about the process will not make you better prepared."

He liked her when she was playful, when she let down her shy inhibitions.

"You've explained everything else the best you can. I appreciate that." Lainie brushed a sweet soft kiss on his mouth.

"You understand my other form is black panther." He hesitated, watching her eyes for fear. "I'm a large cat."

She stiffened, vibrations running through her. "You said you couldn't do that. Is that not true? You can?"

He wanted to hit the side of his head with his hand. Her questions made no earthly sense. "What the devil are you talking about?"

"You know...making love..." Her face turned a brilliant shade of red. "In your cat...I *dinna*..."

After understanding knocked him on the side of his face, his sharp crack of laughter created that little vertical crease in the middle of her forehead that told him that now she didn't understand. She looked as if hitting him would give her pleasure. "No, that is not the claiming ritual though it does have to do with my being a cat along with my claws. In my cat form, I can tease you. Touch you. Even caress you with my tongue if it is something you would enjoy."

Immediate and with fierce knowledge, he knew he said too much.

Her face paled from the vivid blush to the color of a perfect pearl. "C—cl—claws?" She could barely get the single word from her mouth.

She was shaking. "You're going to use your claws on me? You told me you would never hurt me. Why?"

Unable to help the rage he felt at himself he looked away. Explain or not to explain. If he said too much... As to the why, it never made a great deal of sense to him either. She would have his mark on her beautiful white skin for the rest of her life. Each time they came together in a new life, he would do the same. To him, it seemed that once should easily be enough to satisfy whatever pagan god who created the shifter.

Heaving in a deep breath of air, girding himself for questions he wasn't about to damn himself further by answering, he spoke... "When the women are ready for me, my mother will come down to the feast then beckon me. The men will talk bawdy while they heft me onto their shoulders. They carry me to the prepared room then set me down. They will take everything off me except my kilt. For a moment they will wait. After that we will be alone for as long as we want to stay in the room."

"As long as we want?" She ran her fingers across his shoulders then his neck. Heat pounded in his veins. "You aren't going to answer my other question, are you?"

His besotted grin brought a small smile to her lips, replaced the lack of color with a tinge of pink. "A night, a day, a week. I would like to return home in the morning after I've made love to you one more time. Unless you have reason to stay sequestered. We will be more comfortable in my bed."

"I would also enjoy returning home, to our home. I want to cook for you. I truly don't understand why I remember the cooking and nothing else."

Her smile was wide and soft. Her lips dewy with moisture.

He groaned understanding he needed to wait for her one more night. A small price for the most beautiful woman he'd ever known. "Most likely because the dishes you prepare please me immensely. That fact doesn't confuse me at all."

"You know I don't remember anything else. Did you see the woman who disappeared with Scratch and Geordie? I saw her before the bullet hit me."

The abrupt change of subject surprised him. Speaking of the

portal now was much easier than explaining what would happen on the wedding night. "There was a moment where I tried to go after her. Thought she was you. I realized you were lying at my feet, unconscious because you protected me. One woman arrived here. One woman left. I believe it is as it should be. The universe has righted itself."

"So, you think that was my old me returning to the future? It could be."

"In this crazy world, anything could be. We'll never know the truth or make sense of what happened. I hope she returns to Rafe. They will mate. He will claim her. Their world will right itself just as ours did."

"It's strange."

Everything in the highlands was strange, sometimes more than strange, most of the time unbelievable. Magic happened in the highlands. Mystery was key. There were no rumors that weren't bounded in truth.

"Do you think I might see me in the future with Rafe?"

"You haven't been born yet."

"Does that mean no?"

~ * ~

Everything Roc told her about the ceremony, the rituals along with the traditions happened just as he told her. After his comment about the claws, he didn't mention the claiming again despite numerous attempts to cajole the information from his lips.

Lainie thought back to last night. Now, after the Clan Chattan ceremony, he held her naked body next to his while the witnesses left the church. She shivered while he stroked her back trying to sooth her. Even in his arms, she felt vulnerable, chilled to the bone. Remembered the heat of the earth twirling and spinning then the wind. The wind was cold then hot as the currents changed to fire. Finally, as she clung to Roc, felt his body pressed against her, water drenched her, rain spilled down upon her. During the time she saw him, them...together. He raced the heather clad hills of the highlands. She would always watch. He would come to her in his human then take her into his arms. They would fall to the ground, make love. Every time she saw him, there were subtle differences.

He held her. Minutes ticked by while she gained strength while her breath evened and her heart slowed. She sat on the floor of the church, held within his strong embrace. Lainie soaked up the power that was Roc. He was patient with her. Didn't ask about the time while she was in a different place. There would be private moments later to speak. Time for her to depict the scenes she witnessed. She understood how much he wanted to discover what she saw.

His hand beneath her chin, he lifted until she looked into the startling clarity of steel gray eyes. "We have to dress," he whispered, kissing her lightly on the tip of her nose after that her forehead. He closed her eyes with his kisses. After he finished on her lowered eyelids, he brushed a series of soft kisses across her lips. "When you are recovered, you must tell me what you saw. How you felt. I held you when you lacked the strength to stand. Felt the trembling of your body when emotions overtook you. Your knees gave out. I didn't allow you to fall." His voice was deep, husky smooth. "It is my responsibility to always protect you. To keep you from harm."

Breaths came in puffs of air, short, sweet. Lainie wished she could tell him everything. Had to wait for each second to gain the use of her words. "I saw you so many times. Your hair was always darker than it is now. Your eyes always the steel-blue that sometimes turns to pewter. Just as they are now. Every time you came to me, you would make love to me until I cried out with the wonder of it all."

Roc stroked her arms, cupped one breast with his hand. His thumb roamed over the tightening peak. She heated, the chill that took over her body earlier began to warm.

"What did you look like?" he asked as he one more time kissed her tenderly on her forehead. He rubbed his thumb over her lips. She met it with her tongue, touching, hearing his rumble of masculine pleasure. "Did you appear as you do now? As the woman who left here in the portal that brought you to me?"

"Much the same as I do now. Though one time the color of my hair was different, varying shades of bright red. Once my blond was nearly white. You are always a black panther. When you ran, you looked wild and free. Even in your human form you looked free. You don't have that appearance now."

The sigh he uttered left her feeling sad for a past they would never have again. "Not as free as we used to be. I'm not surprised you could see the difference." He pushed hair away from her face, touched the sensitive curve behind her ear. "We need to dress. If we stay as we are for much longer..." Roc reached for her underthings. Held them out to her. "Can you do this yourself? Do you need help? If we don't get to the feast, Mother and Father will come looking for us. They would want to know if you recovered. Don't want to spend much time in the church in our naked state."

"If I don't try to stand, I can dress myself. You will have to lace my corset."

"Are you certain?" His words sounded skeptical as did the look on his face. Then, "Would rather unlace it."

"Yes, just my corset."

"That is something else. Hawk tells me you shouldn't wear the corset. Will harm the babe."

"I understand. Don't know why though," Lainie told him.

In minutes they were both dressed. Roc stood slightly apart from her, looking at her as if this was the first time he saw her. As his wife, it was the first time. "All your clothing seems to be in order. The dress is beautiful. I'm glad my first sight of you was when you came to me on Father's arm."

"You are handsome in your kilt," she whispered smiling shyly at him. "Your knees are *verra bonny*," she spoke with a sultry Scottish burr that started creeping into her speech about three weeks ago.

Oh, his shoulders were so broad, his hips narrow. Lainie loved looking at him. Could never get her fill...and when he was naked...

His laughter barked from his throat. "I would never call my knees lovely. Now, your knees...I will see more of them tonight. Will kiss each one among other wonderful places that deserve my attention. Come." He held out his hand. "We've food to eat so we will be fortified for the long night ahead of us. I plan to keep you awake so I can pleasure you until you can't keep your eyes open."

Without permission, Roc swooped her into his arms, carrying her to the keep. Once he strode inside with her in his arms, they were led to the big table on the dais meant for the happy couple. On the way, they were met with celebratory cheers and good wishes for their future. Many a jest was made about the wedding night as well as the result of a *bairn* in nine months. Their *bairn* would come sooner than that.

After he set her down, the call for a kiss rose in the room. Roc pulled her to her feet. His hands on her waist, he tugged her toward him. Bashful, she looked down. Kissing in front of all these people left her wanting to hide.

"A first kiss for your husband with the *bonny* knees." Tenderly, he touched his mouth to hers. Brushed light kisses from one corner to the opposite one. Touched upon every part of her smile. When he finished with the first exploratory touches, he deepened the kiss sweeping his tongue along her lips then pushing deeper to enter into her. She opened for him, forgetting they were the main attraction. Her arms wound around his neck as she pulled him closer.

A sound broke from her. Fragmented from her throat. Splintered. He pulled away grinning. She was breathless from that first kiss, her blood surging furiously. What was it about his kisses that always inflamed her?

"That is the way I want my wife to respond. You please me."

When he pulled away, his thumb smoothed the bottom lip that was damp from the taste of him. His scent evocative and spicy, his taste so compelling she could barely think or breathe.

"Roc," she wobbled, her knees beginning to give way. "I can't stand any longer."

With instant meticulousness, he pulled out her chair. "Sit. I will take care of everything else."

Her attempt at sitting was awkward, though his hands steadied her. Wine was brought to their table. Food already was piled high in anticipation of the new couple. Roc poured her wine then filled a plate they would share with all the delicious foods they both enjoyed. "Hush," he interrupted her thoughts. "You can drink the wine tonight. It will help ease whatever jitters are left to you. Tomorrow will be a new day. Tomorrow, I will insist you stick to the regimen."

Lainie found she wasn't hungry. Her stomach seemed to still reel from the strain of the ceremony, the whirling of the room, all the elements conspiring within her. The flames. The wind. The icy water. With hesitation, she sipped her wine thinking about Hawk's words of warning. Hawk didn't know why she shouldn't have the wine. He just thought it was for the best. For some unknown reason so did she.

"Tonight, I don't want you to worry about anything. This evening is for both of us to enjoy. Drink your wine. When you feel like eating, the food will be here. This is our time."

Nodding her head, she agreed with him. This time Lainie drank deeply of the goblet filled with the sweet wine. She closed her eyes, leaning against him absorbing his strength along with his heat. Roc encircled her with his arms. She heard the strong beat of his heart, felt the warmth of his body slipping away the remaining chill. With no effort on his part, he heated her. Inflamed.

"I am exhausted. You were right about that. How long does it take to feel rejuvenated?" she pushed away from him, raising her face to stare at his handsome, strong features.

"Don't know. I think it is different for every woman."

He held a piece of cheese between his fingers. "Take a bite then another drink of your wine. All will be well soon."

He let his fingers linger on her lips when she opened her mouth to bite into the cheese. Traced her bottom lip. Roc kept what was left for himself. As minutes slipped by, she began to feel better. Ate more. Drank the wine until the goblet was refilled. Roc kept his arm around her, holding her secure against him.

"I am better," she told him breathless when she felt his hand on her thigh. Knew then he wasn't jesting when he told her what he would do beneath the wedding table. "W—what, what are you doing?"

Lainie didn't need to ask. She knew he was exploring her. It was part of what he told her he would do at the feast. Was what all the men did with their brides. Embarrassment flamed on her cheeks.

Cool air hit her leg. Beneath the table, her gown was around her waist. His hand smoothing across naked flesh. Her breath caught in the back of her throat when his hands settled on her belly. "Do you recall the part where I give my bride pleasure? Hush... No one will see. Don't give anything away with those expressive eyes of yours. You should close them." His warm breath fluttered across her cheek.

She nodded her head as he gently moved her legs apart so his hand would fit between them. Delicate and with ease he traced tender, sensitive flesh. Dark secrets jumped to life. She closed her eyes leaning into him, her head against his chest, relishing the feelings he orchestrated. The soft purr of pleasure seemed to delight him. Lainie wanted to touch him too.

"Is your sweet nectar raining down? I would find out. Touch all those tender parts we've discovered over the last few weeks."

Carefully, he bit her neck, licked while she twisted moving her cheek across his chest. At the same time his finger moved tenderly, intimately, sliding closer. He enticed with each small move. The mercuric enchantment divine.

"I—I didn't believe... oh..." Her lips parted as she buried her face into his chest.

When she lifted her chin for the kiss she wanted, needed, his lips gave them the attention she searched for. He continued his gentle assault on her body. She arched against him. One hand clung to the huge forearm that was mostly beneath her skirts. The other hand to the part of him that held her head while he kissed her, thrilled as well as excited her. Her sigh of pleasure was caught in his mouth. She met his tongue with hers, dueling, dancing rubbing across each other. Her breasts ached. She wished he could touch them. Wished she dared set her hand on his heavy arousal. She could. No one would see. Would that cause him to turn red? Lainie doubted that. Nothing sexual seemed to discomfit her husband.

"You should always believe what your husband tells you, love."

One finger then two entered her, found the same rhythm as his tongue. His thumb found then worked her most sensitive places. The secret places only he knew.

Desperate, she clung to him. He told her he would do this. Sweet enchantment swept through her touched her everywhere. Lainie was unraveling one small particle at a time. If she survived this, she would seduce him. Would make him yowl with the pleasure she meant to give him. He would never object.

"That's it, sweetheart. Let it come. Give into your needs."

Lainie whimpered sweetly accepting this plan of his. When she nearly cried out his name with the ecstasy, he ignited, he absorbed his name into his mouth. When she completely came apart, she collapsed against him. Her blood still beating furiously, her breaths ragged. She couldn't move.

"The first pleasure you will feel tonight, but not the last," he whispered, his breath washing across her.

With the tip of his tongue, he touched the sensitive place behind her ear. Bit gently. Teased even more with his tongue.

The beating of his heart against her cheek told her he was as aroused as she had been. She set her hand on the cloth above the hard evidence of his desire. He brought his hand to her face, touched her cheek.

"This is your pleasure, the nectar that greets me when I enter you. You rained on my fingers. You are so sultry, so velvet to my touch. The dark warmth of your body beckons to me more than the finest Bordeaux."

"You didn't...I would see to your pleasure. Free you. Touch you. Move my hand upon your length."

"Hush, there will be more than enough pleasure in an hour or so when I come to you."

He ran his hand along her back. The motion soothed, calmed as the caress always did. Her breath now filled her lungs. For a few more minutes she rested against him. Listened to the sounds his big body made when he breathed.

"Drink some wine," he told her. "I'll fill your glass."

She drank. Smoothed her bodice though he never touched her above the table. Her breasts ached for his attention. Lainie filled her lungs with slow deep breaths.

The room hummed with the chatter of the people of the clan. Myriads of colors flitted around the room, swirled with the light from the lanterns. The men wore their kilts even though the wearing of them was against English law. There tartans along with the velvet jackets appealed to her. Beneath the jackets the men wore white frilled shirts. The ruffles enhanced the sheer masculinity. The sporrans hanging around their slim hips and the knee-high socks heightened the picture. No Sassenach would be allowed in the room. Except for Ashton.

Roc's family sat at a nearby table. Ashton sat with Harris. He held her hand within his. Sometime in the last ten days he returned. He was Sassenach. The couple though they were still at odds with each other, were leaning toward each other, speaking in soft low tones as lovers would do. Given enough time coupled with patience on both their parts, they would figure this fledging relationship out. Yesterday, Harris told her that he was leaving for London within the week. Business. He'd wanted to be wed before he had to go. She firmly refused him. Harris was a stubborn little thing. She wished for all the traditions of a clan wedding. Didn't want to infringe on her brother's special wedding day.

Ah, they might have a long road to happiness. If the two stuck to this course, happiness might take quite some time. Her road to this point seemed relatively easy when compared to Harris and all she endured.

Roc held an apple slice to her lips, urging her to eat. He whispered close to her ear before delicately biting the tip. She shuddered from the heated sensation that coursed through her. Even though he chose not to be so outrageous, one hand remained beneath her skirt on her belly.

"The little shifter is content. He is enjoying the festivities from your womb. Do you think he understands what is happening when you delightfully climax," he told her his voice soft. "Are you quite recovered?"

"From what? The ceremony or the seduction?"

She blinked a few times watching him. Waiting.

He barked, laughter lighting his eyes. His right brow shot to the ceiling. "Both? I'd like to dance then cut the cake. The sooner we move on, the sooner I can make love to you. First, though, I've a need to dance you to a secluded spot where I can kiss you again."

His fingers touched her belly lightly then dipped into her navel.

"You want to keep my knees weak. I wouldn't think you needed secluded after what you just did."

To the tips of her toes, he shocked her. She didn't believe him when he told her he would do just what he did. Told her the seduction of the bride at the wedding feast was also tradition. All the men brought their women pleasure in front of the clan. He couldn't let his brother and cousins down.

"I like your knees weak. When they are, you must lean on me. Push your voluptuous curves that I enjoy against me." He stood holding out his hand for her. "Dance."

"You might have to hold me while we dance," she breathed, the sigh signaling contentment whisper thin. "I still feel *verra* week."

Roc did dance with her until he found a semi-private place where he could kiss her. His attention to her mouth was limited. Elliott tapped her on the shoulder, his grin wide to claim a dance. Next Hawk whirled her around the room to a lively tune played by the bagpipes. She was surprised when Ashton danced with her, telling her he planned to be part of this family as soon as possible. After all they shared, he couldn't pass up this opportunity for a dance with the new bride. Told her too that soon she would dance at his wedding.

Perhaps Ashton was too confident. Lainie didn't know if Harris would succumb to his masculine wiles. The process might be entertaining to some degree to watch. Though she never believed that Harris would enjoy the process.

She was given back to Roc, who led her to the cake. "You're not going to smear the cake on me."

She hoped her voice and tenor were strong enough to dissuade him. He grinned. She understood he would do as he pleased. If it pleased him to be outrageous, he would. So be it. Lainie knew she could be just as outrageous.

When his hand met hers to make the first cut, his grin told her all she needed to know. Taking the small piece with her fingers, she allowed him the bite then managed to smush it on his face. His eyes blazed with silver fire, something she expected. Lainie also understood he would retaliate.

"Is that how you wish to play this out? I was going to be nice," he asked while she was wiping the frosting from his face with her fingertip before giving the tip of her finger for him to lick.

She was pleased. The touch of his tongue on her ignited all the flames he stoked since they first entered the room.

With sure deft strokes, he cut another piece, allowing her to take the bite. Smoothly he rubbed the icing across her lips. To cheers and ribald sayings, he licked the icing from her mouth only to repeat the process. The devil, he tasted of the sweet confection.

"Enough!" It was Heather's voice she heard. "Time for the bride to prepare herself for her groom. First, the two of you need to clean up."

She handed them both damp rags. Roc gently cleaned her lips then his face while the women clamored behind Lainie as they led her from the great hall then up the steps.

When Lainie looked over her shoulder, Roc stood, flanked by his brother and father, watching. Hawk stood slightly behind. She sent him the best smile she could muster under the circumstances. Lainie wished he was by her side, walking with her.

"Don't worry," Heather told her, "my son will be along shortly."

Maisie and Aila walked with her as did Wynnie and Brenna. Harris wasn't allowed since she wasn't married. Anticipation hummed through her. It had been so long since they'd been intimate. Except for the few minutes of seduction at the feast they had not dared to share even a few stolen kisses.

They walked into the tower room. A fire flamed in the hearth. Light from the flames cast red-gold shadows around the room. Candles flickered in several locations. There was more food as well as more wine. Lainie sifted in a long deep breath that was scented with spices and freshly baked bread. Everything could be eaten with their fingers. She thought of the way he touched her when he fed her. Her body hummed with pleasure. Heat ignited. Flamed. She wished he was with her now. Not the women.

On the bed a negligée was set out. It was a soft peach color. Roc told her he would be able to see all of her when she wore the garment. A bath scented with gardenia steamed nearby.

"Oh my..." Before she knew what was happening, her wedding gown along with her undergarments were removed and neatly folded on a chair. Wrapping her arms around herself she shivered. She wasn't used to being naked in front of anyone except Roc.

Rafe? I posed nude for him. Who was he?

"Get in before you freeze to death," Heather ordered. "Wash quickly, we've a great deal to speak of before I can retrieve your husband. I hope he had better sense than I gave him credit for before the wedding. Hope he kept certain information about this night behind his teeth."

"Hawk wanted him to tell her everything," Maisie said. "Did he?"

In the bath she soaped herself, trying to do this with as much speed as possible. While she didn't mind being naked with Roc, this was embarrassing. "No, he wouldn't tell me about claiming if that's what you are asking. He did tell me about the Clan Chattan ceremony."

Also told me about the seduction in the great hall.

"Good," Heather breathed as if she was relieved by the information. "Neither are we. What I can tell you is that there will be a tiny amount of pain. Cameron will tell you what he deems sufficient."

"He will be tender with you," Aila said. "From what I've heard and known, all the men are as gentle as they can be. It's something that must be done."

"Now," Heather went on to say, "Roc will give you more details before it happens. Other than what has been said, we will leave you and Roc to decide what is best."

"You mean Roc will decide."

"Yes."

Once she was rinsed as well as perfumed, Heather held out a huge bath sheet. Lainie stepped from the bath. It was wrapped around her. "I purchased the negligée for you and Roc. I'm certain he will enjoy it as much if not more than you."

"Do you have any questions?" Heather stepped back as if to peruse her handiwork after Lainie put on the gown.

Shaking her head, "No, no questions." Her hands went to her

belly. No one said anything about her lacking innocence. Others, as Roc told her, were often seduced before the wedding, often carried a *bairn* of their own.

"Are you ready for your husband?"

"Yes."

Epilogue

Spring, two years later Roc and Lainie were at the home high in the highlands owned by the McKennas. The cabin that was used by the McKennas along with all the relatives. It was their first visit. Heather and Elliott, were taking care of their little shifter while they took a much-needed week all to themselves. They walked along a creek where they fished for their evening meal. Roc took her to all his favorite places. Showed her where he first shifted.

They spoke of their growing family. Hawk and Maisie now had two children. She was expecting another child. This time Roc didn't tell her. Even though she understood he would know, he didn't say anything. She liked that. Today, she would laugh with him. She would entice then wait to see if he could keep himself from informing her about the child growing inside her womb. He read her mind with alarming ease.

Roc stopped, pulling her into his arms, his lips finding hers. He wanted to taste her wild abandon that was always part of their love making. While the breeze hummed and the stream tumbled along the rocks, she tasted of spring rain as well as gardenias and sultry woman. Beneath his questing lips her mouth softened for him. He ran his hands along her arms, tugging, pulling at the fabric of her corsage until the fabric slipped down her arms. With tender loving care, he kissed each of the ten marks left from the night of their wedding.

"There are five here," he moved to her left shoulder, "There are five here." His lips left a path of moisture that glistened in the sunlight filtering through the oak tree they stood beneath. "Did it hurt too much? You didn't say anything that night. I was terrified."

"I forgot about the pain from the claiming because you cast an enchanting spell around me. I came unraveled in your arms splintering into a thousand tiny shards of flickering lights. You know, I did see Rafe and Dallas that time. I know you as much as told me that Dallas wasn't born. I saw them. Saw them together. Our line of shifters will go on. As you told me, fate stepped in to bring us together."

"So, my claws didn't hurt."

Roc wasn't at all certain why he pursued this. It was obvious to him; she didn't want to answer. He supposed he needed to be vindicated. The events he questioned had been a long time ago.

"I'd rather you kissed me again. Touched me. Made love to me. Don't want to remember that time."

"Tell me," he ordered as he tried to sooth the command with a softer voice.

"Yes, if you must know. Yes, but as I said not too much time passed before the pain vanished. Was replaced with the pleasure. I was also mesmerized by the site of you so many times while you ran free of restraint. You always returned to me."

He tugged again on the fabric of her gown. As the material lowered with slow finesse on his part, her breasts showed themselves. Pink tips so ripe for the taking. They were larger now. She no longer nursed their son, but she was increasing again. He bent his head to taste her, to savor, to flick his tongue across the tightening bud. He vacillated between her breasts, sucking, delicately biting, teasing with his fingers. In a million years he would never grow tired of the taste and texture of Lainie. She was his delight. He'd always known how he liked his women.

Her fingers wound into his hair, holding his head close to her breasts. Small dark sounds floated from her lips as her body twisted with need. Roc bundled her into his arms, striding to the blanket they set on the ground near the fishing poles.

Their clothes littered the moss-covered ground. In seconds he was deep inside her, loving her, feeling her pulse wildly against him. Her nails raked along his back to his buttocks. She arched and heaved as he kissed her again then again. When he needed to attend to her breasts, he brought his hands to fondle them. In his arms she whimpered. Small moans of her pleasure left her lips to be swallowed by his mouth.

Later, much later, she lay spent in his arms. Her nakedness

pressed against him; soft curves met hard muscles. She was so beautiful. He rose above her, touched her mouth with a fingertip. Languidly, her eyes opened. The smile she flashed him, sent his heart leaping. They'd been together for more than two years.

If she didn't love him yet, he could live with that. It was the not knowing that made him tremble at night while he held her.

"Are you hungry? Thirsty?"

Roc didn't want to dress. Didn't want clothes to come between them for the next week. Nonetheless, a slight breeze blew from the north. He sat up. Grabbed his clothes along with Lainie's.

When she sat, pushed away from the blanket, a pensive expression was on her face. "What is it? That sixth sense of yours?"

"Maybe, maybe not." He looked around the area. "As we are now, we're too vulnerable. Wouldn't want to take any chances. Let's dress and eat something. Talk, too..."

"Talk?" she asked. "What now? When you want to talk it always seems so serious. When you're like this, you frighten me."

"To me it is serious," his voice deepened. He had to clear his throat.

"All right. Whatever you want."

Once they were clothed, he poured her wine. Mrs. Jenkins, the housekeeper at the lodge, made sandwiches for them. While they ate, Roc kept checking the sky along with the fishing poles. They caught two before they made love. One more would be perfect. If not, they would have to make do with the two rainbow trout swimming in the bucket.

Lainie leaned against the boulder while she ate most of the food he gave her. She sipped casually on the wine.

"Do I need to guess what you wish to speak of or are you going to tell me?" She paused for a moment, smiling with her eyes. "I know." She shook her head seeming to change her mind. "Roc, I've meant to tell you something for a long time now. The time never seems right...and... I'm afraid."

"Afraid of me?"

"No! never afraid of you. Terrified you don't love me the way I love you."

Wine sputtered from his mouth. He coughed. Never would he have guessed she loved him, let alone say the words. Afraid to tell him because he didn't reciprocate. Didn't she understand that a man always loved his true mate. "You love me?" to him his voice sounded weak. "Say it again."

She turned away. "I'm sorry. I should have never said anything. Of course, you don't love me. Suppose it was too much to expect. I dropped in on you from somewhere you never heard of."

He wiped his mouth with a linen napkin before he pulled her into his arms. "That's exactly what I wanted to talk to you about. Don't you know woman? I love you to distraction. Have always loved you. Will always love you."

"You do?" She looked stunned then she smiled. Reaching up she pulled his head down for a hard deep kiss.

"Yes, you're my steadfast heart, always and forever into eternity. You, Lainie, are Roc's steadfast heart."

Lainie ran a fingertip along his chin then across his lips. "I love you so much. You are my heart. Will always be my steadfast heart."

The words were repeated over then over again by both.

Coming soon are the stories for Harris and Ashton as well as Rafe and Dallas. I'm looking forward to writing about their journeys. We shall see what transpires for the two couples.

Coming Soon

Harris' Reckless Heart

Scottish Highlands 1757

Music played. Harris Frasier's foot tapped in time to the lively tune of the bagpipes. She watched Ashton whirl her sister-in-law, Maisie around the dance floor. Hawk, Masie's husband leaned, one hip on a table watching the pair. The scowl on his forehead told Harris her brother was not pleased. What did he have to be worried about? Maisie was madly in love with her husband. It was the type of love Harris wished for herself. She wondered who Ash would dance with next. Another sister-in-law or someone from the village.

The wedding tonight was celebrating Roc's marriage to Lainie. Just like Kit's wife, Lainie came from another time. Lainie came from the future. Somehow in Roc's life...well...if Lainie had not returned they would be fated to never find their one true love. Harris swallowed the lump in her throat, turning away from the dancers. She could not bear to watch the scene. As the days ticked by in her life, she often wondered if she would find her mate. A year ago, she thought Ash would be that man. Now, she wasn't certain.

Harris wandered outside to the gardens needing to find a respite from the celebrations. Her head ached with all the questions swirling in the muddied depths. Since Ash returned, he'd acted standoffish, aloof. True, she would never let him get too close. She was afraid if she did allow him to kiss her, hold her as he'd done in the past, she wouldn't be able to think one coherent thought.

Not that she didn't want her brother and Lainie to be happy. She looked back to the hall. Light filtered out from the open doorway. Her mother along with the other women would be taking Lainie to the tower soon. The men would bring Roc after a signal that all was finished.

A long-drawn-out breath of air left her mouth as she turned to continue her walk down the path. In her case, she was trying to figure out what made her happy. Ashton told her that he wanted to marry her. Harris didn't know if she should believe him. The man was Sassenach. He was assigned to the highlands. All Sassenach despised the highlanders. Highlanders reciprocated the notion. Highlanders could not abide Sassenach. Her cousin, Crissy, wed a Sassenach. They were happy. At least it seemed that way when they came to visit.

She searched for her mate. Had to find the man. How the devil could Ashton Wolcott be her mate? She didn't feel the connection as she thought she should. There was no mind changing event that told her the man was hers into eternity. Stopping in front of a rose bush, Harris plucked a flower. Touched the soft velvet of the petals to her cheek. "So soft," she murmured thinking about all the things Ashton told her after he kissed her that first time. She found she wanted more from him. Acted the outrageous flirt to his arrogant confidence. Thought the world was hers to explore. So, she teased him, challenged when she should have backed off.

A little over a year ago, she made a huge mistake. She ran after Ash when he was leaving. Harris understood she should have let him ride away. That day he'd been angry. Harris didn't understand the reasons. He always kept his feelings about her bottled up inside him. Knowing he'd be gone for months, she had to see him one last time. So afraid he would never return, she...she made a fool of herself.

He told her he would give her a woman's pleasure. As usual the man never asked if that was what she wanted. He seduced her into believing what he wanted was what she wanted. That day while she watched the leaves above her flutter with the soft breeze blowing through the glen, she let him have his way. He made her promise she would not see another man. Told her she was his. Told her she must wait for his return.

The blasted man didn't think the vow went both ways. This was something she couldn't forgive. Harris wished for a partner who would not chase skirts. Who would be satisfied with the woman he married. After his return from England, they spoke. Ash wanted to know if she kept her promise to him. Of course, she did. She didn't want to allow any other man to touch her, kiss her.

When she asked him if he kept his vow, he stared at her, his brows furrowed. After that he said, "I didn't promise anything." His words were harsh. He turned from her, walking away for a few tense seconds. While she stared at his back, he stood stiff as if stunned by her question. After he turned, his face was blank.

Harris' heart hurt. She turned from him unable to accept the salient fact he was sleeping with other women. If she wasn't enough woman for him, she didn't want to have anything more to do with him. She didn't let him kiss her. That wasn't the only reason. Harris understood if she allowed him to get close to her, she would give him whatever he asked for. In doing so, she would betray herself.

Keeping her distance was imperative for her peace of mind. She sipped in a deep breath smelling the tantalizing aroma of the rose she held in her hand. In the castle brilliant lights cast shadows on the grounds. She held the rose to her breast wishing she dared trust Ash.

In the weeks following the incident at the cave that left her brother along with Lainie wounded, Ash did keep his distance. Harris tried to confide with Laine. Roc intervened threatening Ash with violence. Despite her deep-seated anger with the blasted man, she didn't wish for her brother to hurt him. Harris needed her fears assuaged so she could move on. Ash never explained himself.

Who was she kidding? Ash was capable of defending himself. He didn't need her intervention. Because of Ash's size, Roc didn't stand a chance in a fair fight against Ash. Harris supposed she should return to the wedding festivities. If she didn't, someone would come looking for her. Getting caught alone in the garden by Ash would be difficult to explain. Her brothers along with her cousins were protective. As was every encounter she had with the man. Alone or with company, he had this icy way of staring at her. The blue of his eyes filled with thoughts she would never understand. Harris didn't appreciate how he could say he wanted her then look at her without warmth.

Harris shivered. Wrapped her arms around herself.

She didn't wish to return to the McKenna keep. Didn't want to have Ash confront her. Dancing with him would put her in too close proximity for her to think straight. There were places he could take her so they would be alone. Harris didn't want that either. She couldn't be alone with him without coming out of the experience damaged in some way.

The last two weeks he tried to get her alone on numerous occasions. So far, she'd been successful by surrounding herself with friends as well as family. As the days passed, it was only a matter of when, not if, she would find herself in his arms again. She passed her tongue across her dry lips. Looking at the man made her heart beat faster, made her remember that shattering climax she felt in his arms over a year ago. That day, Ash didn't take her virginity. He stole her dignity. Her pride.

After that experience, she would never be the same. She was no longer innocent. He stole that from her too. Harris sank to her knees before sitting on the grass, staring at the star-studded sky above. Once, not so long ago she believed in fairytales, in dreams coming true.

Ash never told her why he was leaving. Something about being called home. Elaborating was not something Ash did when it came to himself. Now, he was back. That was the problem as well as the blessing. Harris wasn't certain which was the case. Night and day, he left her guessing as to his plans. A week ago, he told her that he would again have to leave soon. He couldn't stay here until she stopped acting like a petulant child. He didn't elaborate. Harris supposed he thought her childlike behavior was because she wouldn't obey all his mannish orders. For all she cared, the man could go to the devil.

The snort she emitted was far from ladylike. Running her hand along the soft grass rifled through her senses. Harris couldn't help what she felt. Ash didn't have the right to call her names. He didn't commit to her. Did ask her to marry him. Except that he did ask. Never told her he loved her.

Love was something she needed. Wanted. Desired.

Even prayed for.

Ash said he was going back to England. Told her she was coming with him. Harris had something to say about that notion. This was a choice about her life she would make. He would need to do something nice to compel her to return with him. Nice, as in marry her at the keep in front of her family along with her best friends. Next week would not be too soon.

When he told her that wasn't going to happen. She wanted to toss her wine in his face. His reasons for leaving were not compelling. She would continue to tell him no until he gave in to her wishes. In this one thing, Harris meant to have her way. It wasn't right or fair that he would order her life around him to suit him. He never asked. Wasn't this something that should involve a conversation?

He told her she was acting like a little girl, pouting because she didn't get her way. Harris didn't see this in the same light. She had a right to her feelings. It was only fair that he listen to her feelings. The devil, he was so closed off. Didn't he understand about discussing something?

A shadow passed across her. She looked up. *No!*

Harris jumped to her feet, her heart flying to her throat. The rose fell to the grass. Petals falling. "Who is it?" She didn't know why she asked. She knew who the man was.

"Only me," Ash said, his tone gentle. "You've nothing to be afraid of. Know I won't hurt you." He stepped toward her shortening the distance between them. He reached out to her before dropping his hands to his sides.

Ash stood too close. Harris caught the spicy tang that was his scent. Backing away she ran into a trellis. Felt a few thorns from the rosebush. If she moved forward, she would be far too close to him. "You were dancing."

In a masculine gesture, he lifted his massive shoulders. "Missed you. Was going to ask you for the next dance. Your mother told me she saw you wander outside. Decided I would follow. Hear the music?" Ash looked over his shoulder. "We could dance here."

"Mother gave me away?" Why? Harris didn't understand why her mother would send Ash to find her. Her mother knew she didn't want to be alone with this man who twisted her heart every which way.

"Because." Again, Ash lifted his broad shoulders in a lazy shrug. He stared at her, his gaze penetrating, uncovering parts of her she didn't want him to understand. "She wants us to talk. To figure out what we want. We both know we won't see eye-to-eye. So..." He paused while he gazed at her with his clear blue eyes. "So..." Ash dipped his shoulder to her waist.

Before she could counter his words with the truth. He spoke again. She was atop his shoulder. *What?* They would never agree on anything. His long strides were taking them from the keep. "What are you doing!" Before it was too late, she should scream. Her voice wouldn't work. She tried to wiggle off his shoulder.

"Taking you with me. Have to go. Waited for you as long as I could. Tried to do everything your way."

Perched on his shoulder, she tried to look up. Pushed on his hard back to see around him. "You can't! Where? You can't do this!" Her mother and father would have his head. Her brothers would tar and feather his big hide.

He jostled her so she wouldn't work her way off and fall to the ground. She didn't want to land head side down. "Put me down!" Harris understood the words were wasted on the uncompromising man. They were going out the big gate. Soon it would be too late to scream. The devil, no would hear over the bagpipes.

"No!"

"Ash," she paused while she tried to think of words that might sway him to tell her what was happening.

"I've both your mother's along with your father's permission. If you're worried about your brothers rescuing you, think again. They both know what will happen. Since that day at the cave, they've known all about me." There was an inevitable silence while she tried to digest what he said. "As well as their blessing."

Permission?

Blessing?

"What are you talking about?"

Ash stopped. Just as she was snatched off his shoulder, she tumbled to a seat in a carriage. She tried to rush past him, the need to escape overwhelming.

He stopped her. "Not so fast, love. You aren't going anywhere except with me." Ash stepped inside before sitting down across from her. He thumped on the ceiling. The coach picked up speed.

His last words were an outright lie. Harris understood she could try for the door. Try...he would stop her if that was what he wished. Ash never used brute force on her. She felt as if he did just now.

"Seems I am..." Harris retorted. She scowled at him even though she felt certain he wouldn't be able to see the expression of disdain she shot him. Tempted to stick out her tongue, she restrained herself.

"Imagine so."

Unable to do anything else, she leaned back, crossing her arms over her chest. Impatient for him to explain, she tapped her foot on the floor. "I'm waiting."

"As did I for several weeks. Now we're doing this my way. I'm going to London. You are traveling with me."

Harris felt his lopsided smile to the tips of her toes even though she couldn't see the smirk. He was grinning from ear to ear pleased with his accomplishment. She hated being small. Despised not having the strength to get her way.

"You're abducting me? Against my will? Isn't that against the law? If it's not, it should be. Should be a hanging offense." As soon as the words left her lips, she understood them for the truth. Ash couldn't get her to leave with him by his sweet-talking ways. He had to result to violence.

"For yours as well as my best interest. For our future."

"That's your opinion."

"Yes."

Harris knew his grin was growing. "I object." She told him. He wouldn't heed her two words. She found herself shaking her head at him. "Don't have clothes." Harris understood he wouldn't mind if she wore nothing.

"Your mother packed what you would need. They will bring or send the rest in the next week when there is more time."

She was pouting. Pouting all the way to the tips of her toes. Ash had an answer for everything. "As soon as we stop, I'm going to find a means—"

"You can try."

If necessary, she would shift. In her cat form, he wouldn't be able to keep up with her. At night they wouldn't be able to travel far. The distance wouldn't be so great she wouldn't be able to get home on her own. The pure confidence she heard in his voice made her angry. She could try. Of course, she would try. She didn't wish to go with him to England or anywhere else. Had told him numerous times she wouldn't.

"I will!" she blurted before she realized she should not have said anything. Why give him a reason to watch her.

"You can try."

The sheer fact he repeated himself set her on edge. The fact he discounted all her feelings set her teeth grating. She wasn't going to get over this transgression anytime soon. Somehow, she would set the record straight.

"Let's start over." This train of conversation wasn't getting her the information she wanted as well as needed. Though Harris felt certain her guesses would pretty much be right on the mark.

"Good idea. Where do you want to begin?" Ash stretched out his long legs that took up most of the space between the two seats.

"You are taking me to your home. Which one?"

"The country estate in Dover. We will stop in London first." He crossed his legs then his arms, his pose relaxed, negligent, all powerful.

"Was that so hard?" she asked her words coated with sugar. "I don't want to go. I'm telling you no."

"That's too bad."

"Why?"

"You're going to marry me," he said the words with no expression. "We will have a life together. Raise children."

"Don't I need to agree?" Harris didn't understand how his confidence seemed to overshadow her words. She was negative to his suggestion. He understood that fact. "So, you are going to force me. Don't see how you can do that. A preacher wouldn't marry us if I say no at the altar."

"Let's just say, I will change your mind." He sat up. Pushed his too long hair from his face.

"You can't." Well...he could. Harris didn't believe he would spout tender words of undying devotion or love. A few words of love would, indeed, change her mind toward him. *I love you, Harris would change everything.*

"You want me. Want that wonderful climax my fingers seduced

from you. Admit it, Harris. You are just being stubborn."

Seems he cut to the chase. Yes, what he claimed was true. She wasn't going to tell him so. "No, you're wrong. There was nothing special about that afternoon."

"Liar."

All he said was true. She wanted what he could give her. Nevertheless, she also needed what he couldn't give her. "I'm not going to settle."

At that juncture, Ash closed his eyes. By his silence he was telling her speaking with a child-woman as he often called her was a waste of good time. Harris stared out the window. She stared at Ash; at his chest, down his torso, to his feet then back. He was her dream of a man.

For several seconds as the coach rumbled down the road, she focused on his lips. They were firm, sensual. His jaw strong. His nose straight. Since he returned to Coronach, he kissed her a few times. Whenever possible she resisted the pull, he ignited her along with the way he commandeered her body. Harris didn't want to like the man.

The heat he ignited.

Dragons seemed to shoot fire into places she'd rather not think about. She fumbled with her skirts. Rubbed her hands down her arms. The night was growing chilly. She needed a coat or a blanket. His chest moved up then down with the easy breathing of sleep. His eye twitched. Was he asleep while she roamed his body with her eyes, wishing he didn't see other women when she should be the only one?

Honesty.

Integrity.

Sharing her man wasn't possible.

Her fingers feeling like icicles, Harris began her search for a blanket in earnest. There must be something. After looking beneath her seat, she turned her attention to the space beneath Ash. One knee was bent the other stretched out to the opposite side of the coach. She was kneeling on the floor, between his legs. Her face was at his crotch as her fingers searched the space. She gulped. Years had gone by since she saw her brothers naked. He would have... Her cheek almost touched...

Him there.

This whole unannounced ride was bad planning on his part. He swept her from the garden in the gown she wore at her brother's wedding without a thought for her comfort. If she didn't find something soon, she was going to freeze to death. She gave the space one last swipe with her hands. Bumped his thigh with her chin. Looked up.

The devil.

What she wasn't looking for was to see him wide awake, a smile contracting on his lips. Heat flooded her. Silence circled around her, threatening more mortification if she could come up with a satisfying reason for being here.

Where she was.

She wasn't.

Couldn't be between his long muscular legs, her chin almost on his...

"Looking for something?" The low husky timbre of his voice shocked her. There was humor to his tone. "I'll show you mine if you'll show me yours."

Harris didn't see anything humorous about this situation. Her chin rested a bit above his thigh. She swallowed down the lump of surprise. "You...you're awake."

"Never been asleep."

"Is this new position, kneeling at my feet, something I would be pleased with? Are you asking forgiveness or praying. You seemed to spend a great deal of time staring at my crotch. If you say the right words..." He cleared his throat. "Never mind."

Her face flamed more. How could he be so insincere? "Why would I do that? Stare at your...your...your...?"

"Crotch?" he added to her thoughts.

"No...well...don't mean..." She pushed back giving herself much needed distance.

"Why don't you tell me why you are on your knees staring at my crotch. Could be an interesting story. Would you tell the truth? Would you concoct an interesting tale?"

"I wasn't...staring there." If she could disappear without a trace, she would do so right this instant.

"What were you up to?" He sat up, catching her chin in his hand.

His thumb brushed across her bottom lip, once, twice.

The touch seared... She was shaking. Trembling. "I'm cold. Looking for a blanket." *Take that you over...you arrogant Sassenach.* "You ripped me from the festivities without a shawl or anything to cover myself."

I'm not staring at your male parts. You just wish.

I do wish.

She wondered if the shock on her face showed. How did he know what I was thinking?

Ash patted the seat beside him before stretching out his arm. "I can keep you warm. Come here."

He could do that. Heat her to an inferno. She wasn't about to give him that opportunity. Harris recalled how she burned when he touched her, stroked places on her body that sent a tempest boiling in her blood. She couldn't give in to her hunger. Wouldn't let him badger her into doing so.

"No."

"Ah...well...a man can hope."

Not too many seconds passed before his frock coat was settled around her shoulders. Even with the coat gone from his broad shoulders, he was covered in more clothing than she was. Harris pulled the lapels close around her. The coat smelled of Ash. The tangy spice he wore.

"Not going to give anything away about your feelings? Can't compromise even when your lips along with your fingers are blue. If you sat next to me, you would be much warmer." Ash settled back against the seat again. "We'll be at our first stop in a bit. You can warm up there. If you wish, I'll order a hot bath."

Harris found she was curious about his plans. If he expected her to sleep with him, he needed to readjust his thinking cap. As long as he kept his distance, she would be able to tell him no and no and after that another resounding no. Both of them knew if he closed that distance, if he kissed her once, she would be a liquid puddle at his big feet. So far, it didn't seem he meant to do any of those things.

"I'm fine now," Harris told Ash through her chattering teeth. She didn't know when the temperature dropped to frigid. "A warm bath would be nice as long as you give me privacy." Harris didn't know what he expected. How he planned to move forward. The man would have to understand her feelings about the abduction.

"If you think so, I won't bother to argue. If you get any colder, your shaking is going to turn over the carriage." Ash opened his arms again as if she would jump at the chance to have him warm her up. Harris turned her head away.

Pulling his coat closer she settled into the seat. The large coat held the promise of the man. She breathed in deep, enjoying the semi-closeness. This was as close as she meant to get to him. It didn't matter what he said or how he cajoled.

Harris had a plan. She would not be with him after he fell asleep. She was going to leave. Tonight.

~ * ~

Leaving Harris over a year ago was the hardest thing he'd ever done. Bloody eyes, he never wanted to leave the woman behind. She had a penchant for trouble. Acted with little to no thought. Had not intended to be gone for more than a year. For him, there'd been no choice. His father fell ill. The older brother that was supposed to inherit the title couldn't be bothered with anything except himself along with his newest lady-bird. Chandler was the family reprobate. He gambled. Drank too much. Spent a fortune on each new mistress. Thought the family's wealth was infinite.

When his father wrote begging him to return, he'd had no choice except to stop what he was doing and come home. Ash didn't waste any time selling his commission. As a younger son, it had been expected for him to serve his country. He spent five years in the Scottish Highlands. Those years...much of the time was used to protect the Clan Chattan. Some were reckless. Some a bit wild. As the years passed, they became more cautious. The posters asking for information about the shifters were numerous. Ash burned everyone he found.

In doing so he met Harris. She was young. Beautiful. So flirtatious he had a difficult time resisting her. Until he could not. When he left, she'd been seventeen and full of herself. Harris. He should have taken her with him.

Harris. His mate. She didn't know it. Had failed to recognize the signs or the potent surge of hunger between them. He'd known her in another life. Would know her in more to follow. She would learn. Ash never told her. He wanted her to figure it out for herself.

She was the spoiled younger sister of two doting brothers. Before he left, she taunted him with the name of another man. Told him if she felt like seeing him, she would. Those few words were his nightmare for over a year. If she saw this man, it would change nothing. She was still his mate. Ash was surprised when he returned to find her working at her oldest brother's office. Hawk told him she was good at what she did. Her stitches were neat as well as small.

At first Ash thought Hawk talked about needlepoint or sewing dresses. He couldn't figure out how she was good in his office. Hawk was a doctor. He didn't believe the Frasier women sewed their clothing. He was certain they went to the village modiste. Doubted if Harris ever sat down long enough to enjoy needlepoint. Ash was also surprised when he discovered Hawk was talking about stitching his patients. Her brother along with her cousin went into enough details he was left with no doubts she was useful at the office. When he realized what she did, he felt proud of her.

Well, his Harris was still full of herself, still spoiled thinking she could have her way in everything. She could have her way with him anytime she wished as long as he agreed. The woman was a fighter. She was courageous. At times, too brave. Willful. Spoiled. He kept coming back to the spoiled part of her character. She wasn't ready to become his wife though if he had his way that was going to happen in a month. The banns would be read as soon as they reached his home in Dover. Her parents would arrive in two to three weeks with the rest of her things. Convincing her this was right would be a formidable task. He smiled. That was what the three weeks were for.

Convincing.

Ash knew he had his work cut out for him. If he told her the truth about his sexual activities, she would believe he was lying. His silence cut deep. She wasn't going to forgive that moment when she took him by surprise. Bedeviled by her accusations, he'd not had words.

Bottom line, Harris needed to learn to trust him. She thought his silence about seeing other women convicted him of the crime. What she didn't understand was that he was too dumfounded by her question to answer. By the time she made her lack of trust in him clear, he decided silence was the best way to proceed. He was hurt by her indictment. Celibate now for the two years he'd known her. The time together the day he left, took all his restraint to keep from making love to her. She was right to deny him. Harris wasn't ready for sex then and he wasn't positive she was now either. He never wanted to risk leaving her with child. Despite her unwillingness, he had to take her with him. Had to bind her in marriage. He couldn't take the risk of her seeing or becoming attached to another man. She was so damn irresistible.

Ash remembered their first encounter. Even though he wore the red and white uniform of a hated English soldier, she flirted with him. Lowered her sooty lashes only to open them wide to show him the silver-blue of her gorgeous eyes. Tossed her hair over her shoulder then had the audacity to wink at him.

He was certain he lost his heart to her the first time she flashed him her signature smile. As if she was a siren, she beckoned to him. Called his name. His body jerked to attention every time he was with her. Ash knew from the first encounter with the pretty girl sashaying her hips as she walked in front of him, she was his mate. What he didn't know at the time was that she was also a shifter. As to this point in time, Ash didn't believe she knew he had the ability to shift. Her brothers knew. That very fact gave him the needed advantage if she tried to shift and run back home.

Their first kiss was in the alley between an inn and the local printer's shop. She teased him as they walked together. When they reached the alley, he pulled her into the sheltered privacy. His hands on either side of her face held her still. He captured her mouth, touched until she made this throaty beautiful sound in the back of her throat. It was all he could do to stop himself from taking everything she offered. He found out later the printing shop belonged to her middle brother, Cameron. Lainie was the only one who called him Roc, which was a short version of his middle name.

That kiss was memorable. He held the moments close to his heart. There would be more kisses. Thoughts of that first time still held him spellbound. Harris didn't know the first thing about kissing. She learned. It did not take long for her to flash her pretty smile then get what she asked for. Until that day in the glen, he only kissed her. On the day he left, he needed to show her all he could give her. Ash needed for her to remember how she felt when he loved her.

Roc was the brother getting married tonight. Ash closed his eyes, wondering what plans Harris had for escaping him. He understood she would try. Harris had not been given a choice to come with him. She was here unwilling. What must infuriate her was she was with him by her parent's permission.

That day, the first time he left Coronach, Harris ran after him. She'd told him she didn't wish to ride with him. Implied she didn't want to see him again. That surprised him. He had not expected to see her again until he could return to claim the woman who was supposed to be his wife. The gamble he was taking left him sweating as well as breathless. When he walked with her, kissed her, he was certain she didn't think of him as her mate. He was. There wasn't one doubt in his head.

Harris had not wanted to promise him to remain chaste. There was a boy she insinuated who could hold her attention. He was furious at the notion another man would kiss her. That she would allow that. When he seduced her that day in the sun dappled glade, he didn't take her innocence. He hoped to have that privilege either on his wedding night or when she committed to him. When he claimed her in the ceremony. As was their custom, he would claim her before the marriage ceremony. The sooner the better was his thoughts on the subject. In doing so she would see their pasts come alive. Then and only then she would understand his persistence.

Watching her with the top of her head close to his crotch, her silken hair brushing across his hands, his thoughts of celibacy where she was concerned vanished. She had no idea what she was doing to him. He clenched his teeth tight then breathed in deep once and once more to calm his raging body.

She might be the death of him before he could slip a ring on her slender finger. Harris had the most beautiful hands. The fingers were long, slender, soft... The nails well-manicured. When she clung to him, her hands sifting through his hair, it was all he could do to keep his deep groan of desire behind his teeth. Since his return, she stayed as far from him as possible. Ash understood what she needed.

Words of love.

When the time was right, he would say the words. Now, he needed for her to return that love. At every turn, she denied him. More importantly, he needed her to move away from his crotch.

Her body was womanly soft, pliant. She was passionate. Ash knew she wanted him. Could have made love to her, stripped her of all her clothing that day. He felt the same way she did. Leaving her pregnant to face the consequences alone would have been unconscionable. If he'd had courage that day, he would have taken her with him. Set her atop his horse then left. She would have gone with him. That day, she would have followed him with no coercion, no abduction necessary.

Harris would try to leave him tonight. They were so close to McKenna land it would be easy for her. What he didn't know was how. He thought on as many different possibilities as he could. His mind was a muddled mess. He kept coming back to the notion she would shift to get away. That was a dangerous strategy...for both of them.

If she tried that, she would find out he was also a shifter. While he never meant to keep that bit of information from her, it also was never prudent to divulge a secret to soon. She would need to be his before he wanted to enlighten her.

Harris was his.

The woman didn't know it yet. Maybe she did know. If she did realize, she wasn't accepting.

He smiled. Watching her was like devouring candy. Harris was so full of flavors; spicey, sweet, soft in the center, hard nowhere. She wanted to make all decisions. Needed to control all events. She would learn it would be bloody hard for her to command him. Her parents let her run around the village. Sometimes into the highlands. It was one of those times he first saw her. He was on patrol that day. In her cat form he saw her swimming. Thank the god above he rode ahead of the other soldiers. He was able to lead them away. When he returned to make certain she was alright, she was sunning herself.

Naked.

The sight remained etched in his head over the years.

After that, he kept an eye on her. When she flirted with him, he couldn't resist her. Two weeks passed before he was able to spend time with her. Her spontaneity delighted him. She was never boring.

When he looked up, Harris was staring at him, playing with a long strand of hair that fell from the elaborate chignon that had been created for the wedding. She was twirling the lock between her fingers before examining the ends. Ash didn't understand. She noticed him looking then dropped the hair.

"Oh!" She lowered her lashes.

Once that was the way she flirted with him. Ash wondered if she was after something. Thought to keep him on his toes. She could try to bargain with him. He understood she would like him to turn the carriage around.

"We're almost there."

"Where?" she asked her voice butter soft.

The woman did want her way. She was willing to do anything to get it. He wondered if she would go as far as making love with him. He could push that idea when they reached their rooms. The thought shot across his brain. "Believe you know where."

She scowled at him. "What inn?"

"The Witches Inn," he laughed at her new expression. "It is almost Halloween."

"There is no inn by that name this close to Carnoch. You're making things up."

"We are close. Close enough for you to try something. I'm warning you, Harris. If you try to run, I'll bring you back. You won't like what comes next. If you do manage to get home, your father will bring you to me. Suppose we might meet half way. That...would be an incredible waste of my time as well as your father's." Ash thought of running his fingertip along that vertical crease in the middle of her forehead. Smooth it out.

"Did I tell you I don't want to be here?" she asked her voice petulant with her annoyance. Doesn't that make a difference?"

If Harris intended to look sullen for the rest of the trip, that was her prerogative. While he did care, he didn't have a means to put an end to the grump in her voice.

"Yes, you told me. In this situation, no, what you wish for doesn't concern me."

The coach rolled to a stop. Ash jumped out to give her a hand down. She stumbled when she tried to dismount the carriage by herself. His hands caught her by her waist. She fell against him. He held for several seconds that didn't need counting for him to feel her precious curves against him. Harris was so right for him. Fit him. His nerves screeched, raced with anticipation.

Holding her elbow, he escorted her to the inn. Nodded to the man in the front. "Bobo."

Bobo tossed him the keys. "A bath along with a bottle of wine. Perhaps a small plate of cheeses." Ash turned to Harris. "Are you hungry?"

"I overate at the celebration feast." She was still in a pout.

"I'm famished." Ash would rather devour Harris than the cheese board that would be sent up to the rooms. Thought if he could get enough wine down her throat, she would fall asleep. Hoped when that happened, he could rest and not worry about her slipping out in the middle of the night. He resigned himself to a sleepless night.

"Should have stayed to partake of the meal rather than kidnapping me. If you'd done that you wouldn't be so hungry."

Bobo grinned. He too had been warned about the possibilities of tonight. Harris would take flight. How and when were the only questions. Ash bent down close to her ear. "You can try."

Harris stiffened.

"You won't get very far."

She still didn't speak.

"There are twenty miles you will have to run. Flee if you wish... Are you that afraid of me...of us? What we can have together if you allow us..." Ash left the sentence hanging in the air. "Let's get you that hot bath. Some wine inside your stomach to relax you."

"A hot bath would be nice." She slipped out of his frock coat, handing it to him. "Thank you."

"Yes, it would. The door will stay open. As long as I hear you splashing, I won't come into see if you are still in the room."

Wrenching her elbow from his grasp, she lifted her skirts then hurried up the stairs. Fascinated with her pert bottom, Ash watched the provocative display. Every now and then, he caught the view of a slender ankle.

"Fine...very fine... You did find a pretty one." Bobo said with a grin. "Think you can keep up with the *lass*? She's spirited. High-strung."

Ash nodded then followed in her wake to discover her standing at the top of the stairs studying the closed doors.

"Waited for me? That was full of thought."

He almost laughed at her when she grunted. Harris wouldn't know which room was theirs. Rooms, he amended. They would only use one door. The other one he had Bobo lock it from the outside as well as the inside. When she tried to run, she would have to go through his room. That fact gave him a needed edge. He slept light. His years in his majesty's service taught him to sleep with eyes as well as ears open.

The small bag her mother packed for the trip arrived. After that the hot water for the bath was brought inside. The bottle of wine along with the cheese board appeared next. He poured her a glass of wine. Brought it into the room he told her was hers for the evening.

"What's wrong?" Ash was looking at the well-known scowl. This time the expression was different. He realized as if she hit him in the gut, she couldn't get out of her gown by herself. When he walked in with the glasses, her arms were behind her back, her breasts taking center stage. In his line of sight, they were pushed out...so tempting. If he didn't know better, he would think they were begging for his attention.

"As if you didn't know."

"Not at first. Had to take a study of your body posture. Would you like help?" Ash was thinking the line of her spine would be a delight to trace. All the way down to the crack between her delicious backside.

"You..." Harris fumed her shoulders shaking. Her bottom lip quivered. "Alright. It's the only way. Don't touch!"

Of course, he would touch. A brush of his knuckles here then there. A bit of foreplay that wouldn't amount to anything except making her want him. He wouldn't be able to touch to see how wet those few caresses would make her. It was just as well. She wasn't ready for anything intimate between them. He wasn't a gambling man. Didn't wish to stake his future on one bit of bad judgement.

Ash studied her trying to decide if there was anything he could say that might diffuse some of her anger. "Would never dream of touching you, love. Last thing I want or need. You're too bloody prickly tonight. Have been since I returned. To think I believed you would be pleased to see me. Found how far from the truth my thoughts were."

With a loud splutter she turned her back to him, holding the corsage as if he'd unfastened everything holding her together and the gown was about to reveal all her luscious curves. He expected Harris to call him out on his lie. She didn't. That was another point of confusion for Ash. She ran hot then cold. The little woman confounded him. Never knew what to expect.

Ash proceeded as planned. He meant to tease a few emotions from her. Needed to tempt her passion. See if he could seduce her. The first caress brought a shiver to her slender shoulders coupled with a small gasp followed with a quiver. The response was encouraging.

"You promised you wouldn't touch me," she accused as the tip of his finger settled on one bone after that the one below then the one lower still. He slid his hand along the contour of her back. Her skin was silken, so soft.

"Never promised a bloody thing, love. Now let me see if I can get you out of the gown then perhaps into the bath, after that your nightgown. Don't want the water to grow cold."

Another touch and a shudder. The brush of his palm on her nape to move long hair from the fasteners. He let strands slide through his finger, teasing the insides. His gentle seduction went on. She held herself stiff. He understood she was fighting her feelings.

He stepped back, pleased with all he accomplished. Ash knew she lied. Understood by the soft sound, the little sighs of pleasure, she wanted him. "There, all finished. Don't spend too long in the bath. I'll be in the other room."

Ash sat. Sipped his wine. Heard her skirt swish across the floor when she turned. Listened to the sound of her clothing hitting on the rug by the bed. He wondered if she would leave all her clothing there to be picked up by someone else.

Water splashed onto the floor when her body filled the tub. His body hardened. His imagination spun. Blood roared to life. Those sounds could drive him mad. He reminded himself this might happen every night on their trip south. No, in the future, he would lock her in then go downstairs for a pint of ale coupled with a few laughs with the locals. He wasn't into torture.

After she rose from the bath, he heard everything. Knew when she slipped what would be a virginal night dress over her head. Pictured her sitting in front of the small fire combing her hair. Imagined how the hard tips of her breasts would press against the fabric inviting him to touch.

"Your turn," She stood in the doorway between the two rooms. The glass of wine he poured her in one hand. She sipped. Backlight from her room highlighted her slender form. Even covered by the thin white fabric he could see the outline of her entire body.

His gut clenched tight. He brought in a large breath of air. Nothing calmed the raging heat searing him. He was so aroused by this virginal apparition, he ached. Bloody eyes, how was he going to last through this trip south. It might be best if he returned her to her family before she reduced him to a pile of ashes. He could do things her way. Marry her here. To torment him, if he gave in to her wishes of marriage in Carnoch, she would still say no.

Ash just didn't have the time now to give her what she wanted. He would tell her as soon as she was willing to listen that in another year, they would return to Carnoch. At that time, if she wished to be married in the traditions of the Clan Chattan he wouldn't protest. While he'd been speaking with her parents, he'd told them he would bring her home. Going back on his word was not an option.

"More wine?" she asked while she walked into the room holding her glass out. Her smile flipped his failing restraint.

Ash tried not to look as he splashed the red liquid into her glass, filling it to the brim. Looking down he saw her bare toes. They were small. Exquisite. Hell, toes weren't exquisite. They were appendages. Most the time toes were ugly. His were. Her toes he wanted to...wanted to see how they tasted after her bath. He'd never stared at any other female's toes. Was this some new fetish that would suck him under? Drown him. Incapacitate his mind. He shook off the thoughts to concentrate on this next phase of the evening.

"Is the water still hot?"

"Tepid."

As hot as he was at this moment tepid would do fine. Frozen would be better. "I won't be long."

"Don't hurry on my account."

"The door is locked." Harris wasn't in any shape to run. Not in that nightgown which hid nothing at all. Her feet were bare. The thought of her running around the countryside in that attire left him sweating. He fetched in much needed air catching her scent as he did so. Lavender. He would end up bathing in her scent. That was not a bad notion. He needed to learn her scent, memorize it in case she did slip away. It would be easier to find her.

She tossed him that flirty all or nothing smile that always left him with his gut turning over. The plans she had would not come to fruition. Ash understood she was biding her time until he let down his guard enough for her to slip from the room. She would wait until he was sleeping. He didn't plan on doing that. Tonight was the most precarious.

In the adjoining chamber, he undressed then slipped into the tepid water that smelled of Harris. Ash groaned. Set his head on the lip of the tub long enough for him to bring his emotions under control. Washed then slipped on a clean pair of buckskins. He'd thought to put on a robe. Thought better of that when he realized he might have to make a hasty exit in the middle of the night. He needed to be ready for anything unexpected that might happen.

Once in the other room, he filled the wine glasses again. Ash was pleased. Harris drank deeply. She'd also eaten. He sat down next to her. She moved away as if his touch was abhorrent. How long would she play at this game of hers? He knew firsthand this wasn't the way she felt about him.

He sat back, stretching out his legs, trying to relax while at the same time tried to see into her pretty head. Wished he could get closer so he understood what she plotted. "Why, Harris? Why have you taken such an aversion to me? I can recall when you wanted me to kiss you. Touch you."

"I don't share." She stared at him over the lip of her glass. "Won't be part of a threesome."

Bloody eyes, where did she learn about something like that? He wasn't positive he wanted an answer. "You don't trust either. There is more. Tell me." Ash needed to get to the truth before she convinced herself they were all wrong for each other. "What if I told you, I was so flabbergasted by your question, I couldn't breathe, let alone think or spout an answer."

"You mean the one where I asked if you saw other women while you were away in London doing whatever was so important you had to leave."

"Yes."

"I don't believe you."

"Why don't you try honesty? What else has you so steaming mad at me, you turn your back on everything we can have? I've offered marriage numerous times. I know that is what you wish for too." Ash watched her features pale. Saw the shaking of the wine inside her glass. The red liquid caught the ever-changing light from the fire.

"I didn't see the man I told you about. Expected you to remain...didn't expect you to continue seeing women. Do you even now have a mistress you are keeping? Is there someone waiting for you when we reach Dover? I won't be a part of that. I cannot stand thinking of you making love to another woman. It's not right!"

Bloody everlasting hell! Ash thought of Lila. She lived in his Dover home. Had played mistress there for going on seven years. She meant nothing to him except as a responsibility. He rescued her from a bordello in Paris. She spoke little to know English. Harris would meet her. He would need to tell her about the woman. There would be another nail in his coffin.

Lila had never been his mistress. He never slept with her. Though she made her feelings clear. She wanted to be in his bed. Harris would never believe that fact.

"What if I told you I haven't taken a woman to my bed since the day I first saw you. That was three years ago when you were only fifteen." He sat down, crossing his legs studying her ever changing emotions coupled with the play of shadows across her face.

"I wouldn't believe you." She set the empty glass on the table.

"Is that all you have to say? Should go to bed. Imagine tomorrow will be a long day."

"Don't you want to know when that first time was?" Ash asked thinking she would be shocked when he told her. He wanted to see her eyes when he mentioned to her the small fact that he watched her sunning herself when she was naked.

"Should I wish to know?" Harris didn't get up to leave. Instead, she downed the last tiny drop of wine in her glass.

Good, her curiosity was growing. Her back wasn't as stiff as when they entered the room. "Only if you want. What I will tell you is that it wasn't that first day in Carnoch when your outrageous flirting caught the eye of every soldier in the vicinity. Were you flirting with me or the other men? Everyone wanted a piece of you including me."

Her eyes widened to huge pools of silver-gray. "If there was wine in my glass, I would toss it in your face. If you must know, it will make you more arrogant than before. I've never flirted with anyone except you. If those Sassenach thought I was flirting with them, they were wrong."

"Since I met you...saw you, I haven't taken anyone to my bed." He would say the words until she realized he spoke only the truth. How the hell long would that take? He wasn't about to beg.

~ * ~

Heather lay in Elliott's arms. She was thinking of all the things she should have done different. They didn't tell Harris about Ash's plans...or his request that the two should leave during the festivities. Since Harris was still a maiden, she would not be allowed to go with the married women to prepare the bride for the wedding night. They didn't tell her he was a shifter...on his request. There were too many secrets between the couple. They argued constantly. Except at night when she went to bed, Ash never left her side. He tried to soothe her temper. Their little girl was too stubborn. Spoiled too. Something about Ash spooked her. Before he returned, she meant to marry him. Talked of little else. Harris told them she loved him.

Ash told them he needed time alone with her. Time to ease the one major conflict that rose between them. He told her he felt as if he was banging his head against a brick wall. She was still too young but as things progressed, he needed to marry her as soon as possible. He expected to spend only a few days in Carnoch. Instead, he spent a few weeks.

"Did we do the right thing by our daughter? I worry so much. Ash is right. Harris is still young…idealistic." Heather asked as she smoothed her palm across Elliott's chest. "I just don't know what to think any longer."

She felt his shrug, against her cheeks. His big hand roamed her back. "We never heard a scream. Who knows she might go willing. Sometimes you over think. They will be fine. Believe the man loves her."

"I *ken* she loves him." Heather was still attempting to make sense of this relationship that fired hot then cold. At the moment, for Harris, it was frigid.

"You've noticed the way they stare at each other as if they are star-struck. They are meant to be together. We've seen that same look on our sons."

"She doesn't *ken* anything about the man. For the life of me, I don't *ken* why. He wants it that way." Heather lifted up so she could look at her husband. She touched his mouth with her fingertip.

"Our daughter was too young to marry a year ago. By the way she is acting, I'm still not certain she is old enough," Elliott said biting with gentleness Heather's finger. "I *ken* age wise she is old enough to be a wife." He paused, running the strands of Heather's long hair between his fingers, enjoying the sensation. "She is spoiled."

"Willful," Heather said with a snort.

"Used to getting her way in everything."

"Isn't that spoiled?" Heather trailed small biting kisses down his neck.

"That too."

Don't believe he's a man to allow our daughter the kind of freedom that would put her at risk," Elliott continued as he caught her hand descending lower threatening to end the conversation. They still had a few things to reassure each other about.

"There are no highlands in Dover."

"No Sassenach soldiers to catch her while she runs wild," Elliott agreed. "He was a Sassenach. Was... he told me he saw her first when she was swimming in our favorite loch then sunning herself."

"Imagine he saw her without a stitch of clothing."

"Imagine so...," Elliott said pulling his wife on top of him. He held her bottom, caressed. She felt him against her. Felt his need. He pulled her up so she could sit on him. He filled her.

"They will have a few rocky days ahead of them. Are we expecting her to come running home tonight? The first place they are staying in not far from here. Quite doable for a stubborn woman bent on having her way about everything."

"I would tell you yes except I've more confidence in the young man. He will thwart whatever wayward plans she has," Elliott said. Groaned when Heather moved up then down on him.

"If I know my daughter, she will shift then run."

"The man is stronger as well as faster than Harris. My guess is that he won't sleep until they are far enough away from here, she won't try anything stupid," Elliott said as he found tender spots that made her squirm. His hands cupped her breasts. Played with the hard buds he always adored.

She would never get her fill of this man she loved so much, was so lucky to find. Every day he filled her heart with joy. All she wanted for her daughter was to marry her mate and find the same type of man. Ash was that man.

"We will leave in two to three weeks unless we hear that the wedding has been cancelled or delayed. We will see her then. Will have the answer to all our questions," he nipped her shoulder.

"It won't be. I'm praying nothing will be cancelled. Ash will never let her return here even if there is not a wedding. Don't know how he will keep her against her will if she doesn't want to stay."

"With gentleness..."

Connal's Eternal Love
Sweet McKenna Book One

A few days shy of All Hallows' Eve Connal McKenna, Laird of Clan Chattan stands on the parapets of his castle. Bonfires line the hillsides while his clan prepares for the upcoming festivities. Drawn by the whispering of the wind, Connal McKenna feels a strange restlessness in his soul. Setting out to discover the wickedness that is calling to him, he discovers his mate. With gentle words and sensuous kisses, the auburn-eyed highlander conquers his mate, the beautiful, defiant Wynnie Adair who he comes upon during an evening ride. She must ultimately put her trust in the only man who can save her from the ruthless plans of her father and succumb to his gentle coaxing.

In Brady's Arms
Sweet McKenna Book Two

Forced to run from the only home she knows, beautiful, headstrong Lillian Townsends seeks shelter in the wild highlands where the McKenna clan live. Trying to avoid a betrothal contract signed by her stepfather to an aging lord, she is desperate to find a means to sidestep the inevitable, including a marriage to the oldest son of the laird. Lilly is enamored of the young lord who pursues her with unrelenting determination flashing his devilishly handsome charms. She is hard pressed to resist.

Besotted from the first moment Brady McKenna sees Lilly, he is determined to find a means to coax her into his arms and bed. With only the promise of carnal pleasure as his mistress, Brady relentlessly pursues the woman who has unwittingly forged a place in his heart. She is like no other woman, proud, defiant and enchanting. Despite his father's advice to stay away from her, he cannot. He boldly seeks her out and makes her his own.

Nobody but Walker
Sweet McKenna Book Three

The Highland Lass...

She was brought up, adored and loved by a doting mother and father ardently protected by her brothers. She was everything sweet and innocent until she was faced with betrayal and an unexpected and out of wedlock pregnancy. When she gave her love to a man who couldn't return her passion and commitment, she was left devastated and furious. Faced with the loss of her child if she didn't comply to his demands, Crissie McKenna followed him to Belfast then on to his country home to discover he was already married.

...The Irishman

Stunned to find out his one and only encounter with the woman he wanted to love forever created a child, Walker Endicott, Earl of Briarwood, claimed his child as his only heir. Walker threatened all her previously held values even while he thrilled her senses. From the moment he first saw her to the second she ran after him begging him to make love to her, his captivating masculinity held her fascinated. In his arms she would know tempestuous passion, bitter despair, and a soaring joy that would humble them both before the power of love.

Roby's Moonlit Night
Sweet McKenna Book Four

Once she'd been a pampered child with high expectations for her future blessed with love. Then she became an innocent pawn in a terrible game of greed and power. Now, with a noose around her neck, Pippa was to hang before she had the chance to unveil the men who drove her from her home, before she had the chance to live.

Roby McKenna was a man blessed with endless charm and wit.

While he searched for his eternal love across the Atlantic in a new land, he would have to come home to find her. His silver blue eyes could sparkle with amusement or harden to steel gray with displeasure. He had all the women a man could want or need. As he grew older, mistresses were not enough. A quirk of fate brought him to the gallows, a spark of destiny made him claim the condemned Pippa as his bride.

Made for Houston
Sweet McKenna Book Five

Leah Kennedy is as wary of people as she is strikingly beautiful. However, the shocking death of her father that forever changed her girlhood has left her terrified of the very love she desperately longs for. Only in the untamed splendor of the Scottish crags does she feel safe from the feelings she stirs in men and the cruel mockery of Selkirk's villagers.

Debonair, well-educated doctor Houston Stuart has turned his back on social privilege along with professional honors to set up a medical practice in the lowlands of Scotland. There, serving those who need him the most, he hopes to forget the bitter memories and disillusionment that disturb his days.

Coincidence brings the cultured doctor and this fey mountain girl together. Something as bizarre as destiny disrupts the obstacle of birth and breeding, stubborn pride and fear which has kept them apart...as each seeks to heal the other's wounds with a raw passion neither can deny and all the odds against them cannot defeat.

Say You Love Kit
Sweet McKenna Book Six

Fascinated...

When the woman stepped through the door of the pub, the sun

setting her fiery red hair glowing around her delicate features, Kit Stuart finds himself captivated by the sight. The moment he sees her he knows she will be his. Convincing the fire-haired lady of that fact isn't easy. After she calls out another man's name when he kisses her that night, he is instantly enraged as well as jealous. The road they travel is fraught with secrets that neither can tell. Trust is an elusive quality that neither can give.

Intrigued...

Forced to run for her life, desperate and afraid, Aila MacDuff willingly enters into the Kinnel Stones, a mysterious place where people disappear then appear magically in different times. At the first sight of Kit, she finds herself inexplicably drawn to him. She's been told to search for her mate and that she will know when she finds him. Aila doesn't know what this man's name is or what he looks like. Nonetheless, she is certain he will be similar to her mate from one hundred years earlier. Despite the fact she is falling in love with Kit, he can't be her mate. Her mate is a shifter. Kit is not.

It Had to be Riley
Sweet McKenna Book Seven

Her anger assured retaliation...

Shawna's only concern with the contemptable scoundrel she had been forced to wed was the return of her dowry. She had not seen her husband in three years, and now Riley Stuart furiously repudiated there had ever been a marriage. He even went as far as to tell his family he'd never seen her before this day.

... Her passion promised love

In the heather clad hills of the beautiful Scottish crags surrounding the small village so near to the Mckenna keep, the ferocity of her loathing yields to the intense hunger of unquenched longing. In the powerful arms of the dark and handsome husband she thought she reviled, Shawna shivers with the honeyed torment of awakened desire and powerlessly submits to the wild, enchanting ecstasy of burning passion. Together they abandon themselves to the exquisite pleasure of the love their hearts cannot escape.

The Magic of Hawk
Sweet McKenna Book Eight

With her extraordinary silver-mauve eyes, Maisie McRae struggles with the return of her lost love. She finds solace living with her half-sister and existing on dreams. After three long years the man she once dreamt of marrying asks her to make the same foolish mistake again. Holding herself aloof from the arrogant man, Maisie refuses to let his sweettalking words seduce her into his arms.

Smitten from the first instant Hawk Frasier sees Maisie, he is determined to find a means to entice her into becoming part of his life. A missing letter keeps the unlucky couple from realizing their dreams. Defeated by her rejection, Hawk searches for a way to ignore the woman. Unable to forget the way she feels in his arms, Hawk returns from the colonies, ready to try again. Despite the chance of a second rejection, he forges ahead. Boldly, he seeks her out and makes her his own.

www.ingramcontent.com/pod-product-compliance
Lightning Source LLC
Chambersburg PA
CBHW060353260626
47160CB00006B/2295